JAZZ1CAFÉ

VOLUME I: THE NEOSOUL STARR
(FEATURING SOULSHINE SESSIONS)

THERESA VERNELL

JAZZ1CAFÉ
VOLUME I: THE NEOSOUL STARR
(FEATURING SOULSHINE SESSIONS)

This is a work of fiction. All of the characters, names, incidents, organizations, and dialogue in this novel are either the products of the author's imagination or are used fictitiously.

iUniverse books may be ordered through booksellers or by contacting:

iUniverse
1663 Liberty Drive
Bloomington, IN 47403
www.iuniverse.com
1-800-Authors (1-800-288-4677)

ISBN: 978-1-4917-6216-5 (sc)
ISBN: 978-1-4917-6218-9 (hc)
ISBN: 978-1-4917-6217-2 (e)

Library of Congress Control Number: 2015904961

Print information available on the last page.

iUniverse rev. date: 05/08/2015

TABLE OF CONTENTS

Dedicated to my oldest son, my first LOVE...

CHRISTOPHER MARKEL KEEYS
July 25, 1984 – February 26, 2011

ANGELA JOHNSON "Hurts Like Hell" IT'S PERSONAL

Bismillah, In The Name Of GOD,

Do You Ever Think Of Me Up There?
While Sitting On Heavens Stairs
And If I Could Climb That High
I Would Be Right By Your Side
No Doubt I've Tried
I Know You're By GOD'S Side
I Know You Answered The Call...

ERYKAH BADU "Telephone" NEW AMERYKAH PART ONE (4TH WORLD WAR)

Bismillah, In The Name Of GOD

Now I Lay Me Down To Sleep
I Pray This Dream I Keep
And If I Die Before I Wake
My Last Breath Will Find The Path
That Leads Me Straight To You
And That Will Be My Last Prayer

Bismillah, In The Name of GOD.

-Peace Quadir

LISA CHAVOUS & THE PHILADELPHIA BLUES MESSENGERS
"Knocking on Heaven's Door"
BLUES ADDICTION (BOB DYLAN)

Rest In Peace My Friend Susan Hughes - Fatimah Ali (The Real Deal)
Wings to Heaven 01/23/2012

ACKNOWLEDGMENTS

Throughout this long and laborious process only my faith is what keeps me smiling. I acknowledge that wisdom is delivered and knowing is my strength and I thank GOD continuously for the sense I have to understand it is all part of the plan.

I must thank all the musical artists mentioned and playing @ www. jazz1cafe.com the Internet Radio Station. Without you this story would be without sound and beat-less. I'm truly a fan and highly admire the art of sound created.

AUTHOR'S NOTE

My whimsical musical mind always ticking to a rhyme, verse and lyrics. Always writing song lyrics and I can't wait for you to hear it. As far back as I can remember, I've had my ears glued to the speakers. Singing along, remembering every harmony. And like the old television game show *"Name That Tune"* from the first musical note, I can tell yes or no, if heard it before. Getting lost in the music and not care if I abuse it because every song is my cure. One song can bring back so many memories and the emotions of the beats are so deep, I become lost in another song woven into the parables of my imagination. The story of my life my fall upon some pages, but this is a fiction novel.

This is a musical work of fiction. Though the music artist and songs are real they are inserted to give you an idea of what the character is musical experiences, and also samples of the music played @ JAZZ1CAFÉ. However all events and characters in this story are solely the product of the author's imagination and any similarities between any characters and situations presented in this book to any individuals living or dead actual places and situations are purely coincidental.

INTERLUDE

TRACK 18: PEACE AND BLESSINGS (Outro)

RACHELLE FERRELL "Peace on Earth" RACHELLE FERRELL

"How can we heal the wounds of the world?
If we cannot heal our own?

Arriving early in the morning to the 'Munroe Funeral Home' on North Broad Street in Philadelphia. In the wee hours cars and people were scarce. All she could think is 'he is gone' and feeling like a black and white movie with no sound, STARR stood in the middle of Broad Street eyeing the building.

"And where does this peace on earth begin?
If not in the home?"

Eying the brick interior, STARR Wondered if she was at the right place, knowing she was. Goose bumps covered her body as she walked towards the doors. Thinking of him laid stretched out dead in a casket and ready to be viewed in a few hours, had her head pounding with the aftermath and trying to grasp reality.

DJ CAM "He is Gone" SOULSHINE
(KIDLOCO Remix)

Leave STARR alone, she don't care anymore. *"He's gone."* The drops of rain started falling heavier and she didn't have an umbrella. Wishing she had a joint and finding shelter on the porch of the funeral home. The winds picked up slapping her face wet. Even if she smoked 10 pounds of weed it wouldn't get her high enough, plus she had stopped smoking.

AVERY SUNSHINE "Blessin' Me" AVERY SUNSHINE

GOD woke her up and clothed her in her right mind. The LORD didn't let her sleep too late, STARR woke up on time. The LORD is blessing her right now, she had to believe. Through it all she had to believe the LORD is blessing her now, right then and now. Feeling so low that hell felt like it was above her. Puffing on wind she thought, *"To feel HIGH as HELL, Do you know how low you have to go? Damn!"* Her heart jumped when the lights on the first floor of the funeral home came on.

The wet chill of the morning didn't faze her numbed body and mind. Now, standing at the double mahogany doors with watery eyes and awareness of her now being wet and him dead, she wanted to run. A deep scared grunt came from her, as she rang the bell reading the gold plague on the door.

"Welcome to Munroe Funeral Home"

Forced to read the sign on the door over and over and over again. Until, a woman dressed in black answered the door with greetings. *"Welcome to Munroe Funeral Home."* STARR wanted to snarl, don't fucking greet me to see the dead. Have some damn sympathy. But, instead speaking in a suffocated whisper, *"I'm here to view. Please, I won't be long."*

Inside the funeral home there was another welcoming sign. This is not a place for welcoming signs, she thought.

Still trying to hold it together, she walked into the foyer wanting to turn the sign over, but immediately stopped. Her eyes focused on M&M's on the floor. The woman's eye traveled to what had startled her. Walking over to the candy on the floor the woman replied, *"Sorry it is just candy, no rodent droppings or whatever you thought it was. My husband Mr. Munroe's loves M&M's."* Keeping the smile on her face and throwing away the candy the woman extended her hand. *"How are you? I'm Mrs. Munroe."*

LEJUENE THOMPSON "This Too Will Pass" METAMOPHOSIS

This too will pass, STARR's pain won't last always. A tear dropped, STARR tried not to cry, eyeing her surroundings. She didn't want to be surprised by any unwanted family members, paparazzi, old friends or strangers. Almost instantly the clouds crashed and hard rain knocked on the windows and doors. It was eerie enough to make her want to run, but she was tired of running.

Noticing a dim lit room and all she could see was the end of a black casket. Mrs. Munroe stared at the dark rings around STARR'S swelled eyes and asked, *"Can I get you a cup of coffee."* Coffee was not what she needed and almost vomited from the faint scent of coffee on Mrs. Munroe's breath. STARR replied offended, *"No coffee! Please let me get it over with!"*

THE ROOTS 'A Peace of Light" HOW I GOT OVER
(Featuring AMBER COFFMAN, ANGEL DERADOORIAN, HALEY DEKLE)

Following the shocked Mrs. Munroe as she walked toward the dim room and turned up the lights. STARR with a praying spirit observed him lying stretched out in the ebony black casket and many flowers. She became more nervous than ever in her entire life. Her stomach twisting was proof of her emotional state. Forgetting that Mrs. Munro was beside her, STARR was startled when she spoke, *"My Husband did a wonderful job. He looks good doesn't he? He is at peace."* STARR looked at her bewildered and blurted, scarcely unaware of her own tone, *"He looks dead and is there peace in death?"*

S.O.U.L. "Praying Spirit" SOUL SEARCHING

Walking slowly up to the casket with a *'Praying Spirit'*, STARR wanted to stop, but it felt pushed. Standing at the foot of the casket, she thought his hand moved. Panicking and losing her mind or was she just that delirious? Looking closer, he almost looked like he was smiling, and she would remember every detail of his dead face. His lifeless body dressed in a charcoal gray pinstripe suit. She wondered if he could be dreaming. She reached out to touch him and stopped. She wondered if he could be dreaming. She reached out to touch him, stopping and reading his name, 'Ralph B. Urbany' on the gold plaque inside the casket and the date, March 1st... The same exact date, 1 year prior that she walked into the Coffee Shop.

SOUL TEMPO "Trust In God" TRUST IN GOD

WELCOME TO SOULSHINE SESSIONS
DJ CAM "Welcome to SoulShine" SOULSHINE
(Featuring INLOVE)

"Welcome! Welcome! Welcome to SOULSHINE SESSIONS!"

Welcome ladies and gentlemen, please allow me to introduce myself. My name is SoulShine and you're on time. I'm your iJ / internet jockey for this JAZZ1CAFÉ musical flight. Please fasten your headphones. We should be arriving promptly as soon as you log into www.Jazz1café.com or download the mobile APP: LIVE365 Radio

I'm your hostess with the most-est and yes I'm a music-holic! Music is my infatuation and obsession. I'm ready to get you grooving and moving, head bobbing and fingers snapping and hands clapping! Sharing a playlist of some of my favorite artist and hundreds of songs listed. So, you can read, listen and sing along. Plus thousands of song paying @www.jazz1cafe.com Promising pure satisfaction of ear candy to listen to and buy. The music never ends when you tune into *JAZZ1CAFÉ*.

PLAYLIST EXAMPLE:

ARTIST "Song Title" ALBUM
(Featured ARTIST)

Broadcasting 365 - 24 / 7 "It's all about the music..." Emails are still coming in with the same question, *"What is Neo-Soul?"* I'm here to break it down - giving it to you real talk – real rap. The music genre Neo-Soul is still very much an underground term used for artists and their emergence from the sounds that branched out of Philadelphia with artist such as The Roots with Erykah, Jill Scott, Musiq Soulchild, Floetry, Jaguar Wright, Bilal, Jeff Bradshaw, Vivian Green, Kindred the Family Soul, Zhane,

JazzyFatNastees, Ursula Rucker, Vivian Green, Carol Riddick, Aaries, Ayah, RES, DJ Jazzy Jeff, King Britt, Lady Alma and the list goes on.

Neo-Soul is the sound of musical liberation. Experimentation of soul, hip-hop, jazz, funk influences and whatever lies in between. You're hearing nothing new except for the artists who are introducing themselves to the music industry, THEIR WAY.

MONDO GROSSO "Star Suite I – New Star" MG4

Some artist treat *"Neo-Soul"* like a dirty word. Forget that. Ok, the genre is typically independent artist and some with many interludes, which I happen to like. But what stands out most about Neo-Soul artist is that each artist is a talented musician in their own right and do not rely on corporate sounds to accomplish mass sales. Instead they succeed from sheer originality and rawness of their musical talents. Don't worry I'll be back to break down the etymology of Neo-Soul.

CHOKLATE "Thank You" CHOKLATE

Just A Few Clicks Away from JAZZ1CAFÉ...

1. Download 'LIVE365 RADIO APP
2. Launch the LIVE365 RADIO APP
3. Type: JAZZ1CAFE (Click GO!)

BECOME A V.I.P. MEMBER!!! FREE 5 Day Trial Membership and No Credit Card Required!

Please become a V.I.P. Member and help support JAZZ1CAFÉ Internet Radio Station and the music artist. Portions of you subscription go towards the royalties for the songs played.

Enjoy zero commercial interruptions, no banners or ads, just you and the music. Listen on multiple devices, tablets & desktops. Go anywhere with the LIVE365 Mobile APP for. Listen in the comfort of your home on devices such as Sonos, Roko, WDTV, Grace digital wireless radio, Tangent, TIVO and more.

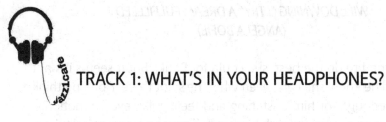

TRACK 1: WHAT'S IN YOUR HEADPHONES?

MINNIE RIPPERTON "Baby This Love" ADVENTURES IN PARADISE

The things STARR say and do may not come clear through, her words may not convey just what she's feeling. But she, hoped Rofiki recognizes what's right before his eyes. Oh, his heart should realize from where she's dealing. But all she could sing was, *"Bull – Shit ain't nothing, but chewed up grass..."* The lyrics that haunted her, as she hurried to meet Rofiki at their special coffee shop. Fearing Rofiki would be a no show, she sat at the first available window seat looking for him. He was her manager / Rastafarian boyfriend, who indeed was running late, as expected. *"Baby, I'm trying to show you that I love you."* She was panicking and at the end of her ropes and not a strand of mercy for him, but needed him. *"Babe I'm try to show you that I care."*

JILL SCOTT "Do You Remember" WHO IS JILL SCOTT?

Do Rofiki remember STARR? It was if, he didn't remember her anymore. Mind mixed up and remixed in a world of songs and lyrics thinking and waiting and wondering. Oh Rofiki, honey why he got to be so mean? Don't he remember her? They built sandcastles in North Philly. Don't he remember her? He said, he would splash her face with Nile water. She remembered when, he brought his first pair of sneaks. Oh they were phat! Mmm, Jordan's she thinks.

When they first met STARR was surprised to get that feeling, the kind that don't wash away with soap. Now STARR couldn't get a whiff of his scent in his absence. Luckily the coffee shop had wifi. STARR'S cellphone was off, but she could still log into JAZZ1CAFÉ internet radio station hosted by SOULSHINE SESSIONS playing the best in Smooth Jazz Vocals, Neo Soul, Nu-Soul, Nu – Jazz, Quite Storm, Inspirational, Spoken Word poetry, Hip - Hop and more.

WILL DOWNING "I TRY" A DREAM FULFILLLED
(ANGELA BOFIL)

STARR tried to do the best, she could for Rofiki. But it seems it's not enough and he know she care, even when he's not there. Don't he think she's good enough for him? Listening and feeling like every emotional, tear jerking song playing through her headphones and woman's intuition had STARR'S eyes wide open. She was seeing all the signs in Rofiki's bullshit.

Like when returning from a recent trip from New York, Rofiki slept with his cellphone under his pillow. Late night calls that had him whispering in the bathroom over running water. STARR knew there had to be another woman. The thoughts and his behaviors were dragging her down. Their relationship was dissolving, though he would never admit to any foul play. Even if she caught him.

The love of her life, her man, her manager Rofiki was supposed to be negotiating a recording contract for her with VHR -Vicious Heat Records. It would be normal for him to stay away on so called business for a day or two. Never would he take her on any journeys. But this excursion, he dropped out of sight for three weeks, leaving her heart broken and singing and feeling the blues.

The day after Rofiki disappeared, STARR'S cellphone was cut off for nonpayment. It took her 3 weeks to catch up with him calling from unknown numbers. They chatted briefly and he instructed her to meet him at the coffee shop on North Broad Street. How ironic? Ain't this some bullshit, the same exact place they met 10 years ago. The same place where her innocence was lost, again.

KINDRED THE FAMILY SOUL "Stars" SURRENDER TO LOVE

So many times STARR could have walked away, Rofiki didn't have to say a word to convince her to stay, because she knew it and he knew this thing was real. After 10 years of the bull-shit of Rofiki 101 the cleverest way to pull at her heart was to say, *"Catch up wid me where me meet STARR and see ef we can start ovah."* She was trying to calm down before Rofiki arrived. Yes, she was upset with him and he was well aware. Knowing he didn't care when on his grind.

After thinking about how bad she wanted and needed a recording contract, STARR would have to find forgiveness. They had been living together 10 years to long, until Rofiki announced his mother Haile sold the house and they had to move. Coincidently they had been arguing and there was serious talk about breaking up. STARR had even found another place to live. In the transitions Rofiki hyped the situation up assuring her with just word that everything would be *"al'ight"* once she signed a recording contract and them moving to New York, New York big city of dreams!

SADE *"Never As Good As The First Time"* PROMISE

Their relationship started out stargazing, but realistically things have not been good for a while. Catching the teardrops before they roll down her face. On her knees day and night with every breath praying for good news. She needed to hear some good news. Aware that many unsigned bands and artists record demos in order to obtain a recording contract. Demos are usually sent to record labels in hopes that the artist will be signed onto the label's roster and allowed to record a full-length album in a professional recording studio.

> *"Natural as the way they came to be*
> *Second time is not quite what it seemed*
> *It's never as good as the first time*
> *As the first time, the first time..."*

However, large record labels usually ignore unsolicited demos that are sent to them by mail. Artists generally must be more creative about getting their demos into the hands of the people who make decisions for the record company and Rofiki's slick mastermind was able to get STARR'S demos in the hands of Vicious Heat Records C.E.O. Big Tank.

Rumbling and grumbling, STARR'S belly moaned fighting past the hunger pains, and holding on to the $5 in her pocket. The waiter appeared and she could barely hear, his baritone voice over the loud music pumping through the headphones. *"Coffee?"* Startled she wondered, *"What did he call me?"* The waiter stood tall and straight like a towering spruce announcing, *"Today's special free cup of coffee."* Watching his hand pouring the mug of coffee, embarrassed her as she opened the menu skimming through for $1 items.

LIZZ FIELDS "When I See Love" BY DAY BY NIGHT

*"When I see love between two loves it make me want to love again
When I feel love between two loves lets me know I'll love again"*

Admiring a couple in love, just 2 seats in front of her with hopes to inhale loves virus. Watching them sip coffee, STARR sipped coffee. Maybe what they drink is the key to love. Despite the cold air their love affects her. The scent of the coffee was welcoming and caffeine and warmth her body longed. Feeling a wave of panic, STARR wondered if she was at the right place.

A bitter cold despair dwelt in the caves of her soul. Until noticing, Rofiki walking down the sidewalk towards the coffee shop. His profile was sharp and confident. The waiter returned and so did the citrus musk scent, powder blue shirt and big tanned hands. STARR couldn't even look at the waiter trying to serve, her more free coffee. Feeling sick and nervous replying, *"Give me a sec, no wait ah bring me a glass of water with no ice."*

Seeing Rofiki made STARR feel humiliated. Feeling so much shame, she dropped her lashes to hide the hurt as the waiter in the blue shirt walked away. Sliding down low in the chair STARR paid close attention to Rofiki strolling down the street. He had a hip – rhythmic D.J. cutting and scratching bounce to his walk.

Reminding people of all of Bob Marley's sons and told people his last name was Marley. His hip - hop - rap and styles was wild like Busta Rhymes and aggressive like DMX, or as political and intelligent as KRS 1, Tweib Kwelb, Mos Def, and Common. His stride was as cool as Morris Chestnut walking like he was feeling a good beat.

ATJAZZ "All That" LABFUNK

Wondering if her life would have been *'All That'* if she was the woman beside him pushing the baby carriage. A baby is what he wanted and a baby is what she had been trying to give him. She watched Rofiki allowing the woman to pass in front of him displaying his pearly white teeth – long dreads bouncing free - leading the baby carriage safely through the crowd on the side walk.

Wondered what if she would be *'All That'* if she was the woman walking behind him dressed in corporate attire? Who was probably heading back to her office with a belly full of lunch? Yes, a degree or a corporate career could have secured a different future. And she wouldn't be sitting there with a grumbling stomach.

Crossing the street along with Rofiki, STARR watched a female cop bouncing, her big ass past, him and his smile of approval. Did she need a bigger ass to get his attention? Yes, she knew the answer was of course. But if she asked Rofiki to buy a roll of toilet paper, he would have complained. Rofiki couldn't afford a woman with a bigger ass.

THE FLOACIST "What R U Looking 4?" FLOETIC SOUL

An ego the size of a King, Rofiki used to be someone, who had to be loved, he used to be someone who had to be heard, he used to be someone who had to be wanted, he used to be someone who had to be flaunted...

When Rofiki was gone STARR'S life was filled with peace. Now wondering if she had been a cop would she have felt safer? Yes, she would have a license to carry and would probably use it on Rofiki. She knew the charm and effect he had on women. But, she had to admit, he was looking good and everything he had on was designer and brand spanking new. Checking Rofiki out, he was so fine and fly wearing a new black shearling leather jacket, a white Ralph Lauren Polo sweater, as cold as it was his jacket wide open to flash labels, designer jeans for sure, new black Timberlands boots and new Gucci sunglasses.

KYMANI MARLEY "I'm Back" RADIO

It's the music that moves in a mystery, Rofiki has been running around, yes it's been a while since he been up in the place. Been a while since he been up in STARR'S face, reloaded again and street living and it ain't for change. *"Rofiki's the name and meh going to hit it until meh black out, meh back!"*

Even Rofiki's long locks had a new bounce and shine. STARR was now feeling the shame of her old black wool Pea Coat and thrift store scarves.

She caught glimpse of happiness, something was pleasing him. She could tell in his stride that he was sleeping well. Not like her on an air mattress on the floor. His long dreads bounced around his face in a familiar royal vibe beat she once wrote lyrics to.

LIZ WRIGHT "Speak Your Heart" THE ORCHARD

Wanting to speak her heart, STARR knew what Rofiki wanted to say, she could see the words behind his eyes. By the time he showed her what he was hiding it wouldn't be a surprise. He was now on the phone whispering? Talking with his face turned away. He said that love don't come easy for him. What makes him think she wasn't afraid? Either he let her back in or let her go. Just waiting for him to open up his mouth and say it, baby.

"Speak your heart, speak your heart"

Really, STARR didn't know what to say to Rofiki, yet she had plenty to say, but how dare him show up looking so good. The only thing that seemed familiar was his scent of coconut oil he used in his hair. Removing his sunglasses they made eye contact and his smile vanished. Just as Rofiki sat the waiter returned with a glass of water with no ice.

The waiter's manicured hand placed the glass in front of STARR, she immediately pushed it over to Rofiki. He didn't like ice in anything, not even in his water. He pushed the glass aside and spoke sternly to the waiter, *"Somethin' in meh wata."* waiting for him to break out into laughter and wave the recording contract in her face. Instead he said nothing observing his surroundings.

N'Dambi "Broke My Heart" LITTLE LOST GIRLS BLUES

Broke STARR'S heart and tore it all apart. Broken hearted and trying to read Rofiki's blank expression and wanting to hurt him too. Watching his blood shot chestnut brown eyes darting around the coffee shop, she knew he was high. It was just like Rofiki to always check out and size- up every man in the place, to be sure no one was gritting on him, or hating, or ready to step.

Most of the times Rofiki tried playing the discreet role in public, As if he was a celebrity, due to his fashions and wild long locks, he always stood out and always mistaken for a rapper or reggae singer. A bit uptight he was still inspecting the coffee shop. STARR picked up the cup of hot cocoa and made loud sips to break the silence. Finally she couldn't take it any longer. Her voice broke the stillness almost singing a Marvin Gaye song asking, *"What's going on?"*

Brushing his long black dread locks off his honey gold face, Rofiki pulled his hair back. Securing his locks with a thick black rubber band that he wore around his wrist, he spoke in his rough – hard hitting Jamaican accent of patois mixed with the Queen's English twisted into Ebonics. Making sure everyone knew he was a Rastafarian. *"Jah- Rasta – Fari! Whad up wid yuh STARR? Yuh Good? Meh deh call yuh from chewsday. Meh tire was flat. Check this out! In dis music business – Dey only cares 'bout records yu selling – Sexy sells. Yu haf ta do some- ting' with yu looks."*

MAYSA "What about Our love" MAYSA

"What about our love?
Will we be together?
What about our love?
Will it last forever?

What about our love?" So many questions were flying through STARR'S head. Rofiki had her waiting, sitting all alone. Did he still love her? Were the feelings gone? All that was left were broken dreams and promises and she wasn't feeling it, no, what's going on?

Needing to know, will it last forever? Not wanting to give up. Wanting to know where she went wrong. Needing peace of mind. Feeling insecure and assuming folks walking past the window and inside could read the imaginary neon lights on her forehead that flashed, 'Fool!' She held her head low as she prayed for the anxiety to stop wanting to be her best friend. Feeling like a fool and listening to the same bull-shit they argued about before Rofiki left for New York.

Unbelievable, STARR couldn't believe he had gone and left her for three – weeks. Just to return and say that her appearance is not what the music industry wanted to see on stage. Standing 5'5 and 140 pounds remembering being heavier when they met, she shed the fat quick due to stress and the vegetarian diet she had been on since they met.

INCOGNITO "Where Do We Go From Here" POSITIVITY

Without Rofiki, baby there's no love in STARR'S life, no. Her head's been spinning. These small cuts like a knife. Oh, Rofiki. Without Rofiki baby, STARR'S lonely heart can't find a way. Her whole world's falling apart when he go running away. Without Rofiki there is no love in STARR'S Life. Feeling the insults in his words that she wasn't sexy sent disturbing quakes to her self-esteem.

The music industry doesn't care if you can carry the powerful vocal range of 7 Octaves. Though it has been a long time since, she wanted to sing that high. Rofiki also suggested that she lose more weight and perm her hair and get a long weave. Maybe blond colored hair streaks for flare.

Bewildered she wondered if he remembered the first day, he twisted her hair. What happened to, *"Meh loved meh locks meh grow."* STARR had long dark locks like Rofiki. Did he forget the long nights of sitting between each other's thighs, puffing weed and twisting each other's hair? Playing old school hip hop loud and free-styling to beats and instrumentals. Where did all that go?

Though STARR was pleased on how she was handling Rofiki. Because repeatedly, every day she recited a prepared speech cursing him the fugh out! Nauseas and feeling woozy with throbbing temples, emotionally all together messed up. Paying attention to every word, every action, every remark and every pose.

SY SMITH "Broke My Heart" PSYKOLSOUL

Breaking STARR'S heart and tearing it all apart and making her cry telling her lies. Rofiki's voice was alarming and a bit higher than normal. Something was bothering him other than her, and she felt it. She sat listening to him continue to break her down.

Making reference to her clothes saying the Bohemian gypsy gear is what all broke - poor Indie - artists were wearing. *'Yeh mon wear de pum – pum dress!"* She listened to him and his *'Yeh mon'* expressions and wanted to scream, 'I am not a man or mon' but sat listening.

Suggesting that she wear tight dresses with splits that expose hips – thighs and legs, like she was a jerk chicken dinner. Suggesting making her body t'werk and work, shake, wear makeup, eye shadows, glittery eyeliner and luscious lipsticks. Lips are what everyone focuses on when she sings. Add lipstick and work the crowd by moving more seductively. Also saying, she had to make her music reach out to all and stop making reference to GOD in her lyrics, because she was not a gospel singer.

INCOGNITO "Don't Be A Fool" WHO NEEDS LOVE

Don't be a fool, STARR couldn't put the blame on no one else. She gave Rofiki all that she had and there's nothing more. Oh no, there's nothing left to give. Don't be a fool to herself and she can't put the blame on no one else. Bewildered Rofiki questioned STARR, "Yuh no see it? Meh try da 'elp ya wit da problem." Trying to peace it all together, STARR placed her elbows on the table to hold the coffee cup study. Taking deep breaths until she was strong enough to raise her head.

When STARR thought Rofiki was finished, she placed the mug on the table wanting to scream. She pressed both hands over her eyes as they burned with weariness, shit was getting crazy. She removed her hands from her eyes wondering how? How did she let herself get this messed up? He had broken through her fragile control. Trying to keep a calm pose as she eyed his new designer fashions, she bit the inside of her jaws softly. Taking a look at what's left of the man that she once knew. Oh, she's got nothing left to give him.

NUSPIRIT HELSINKI "Trying" SAINT GERMAIN DES PR É S CAFÉ III

The waiter was ready to take their order. STARR was trying to order a slice of the sweet smelling pound cake she had been eyeing, but didn't get a chance. Rofiki handed the menus back to the waiter zipping up his jacket as if he was cold and barked, "Na meh good - turn up da heat!"

The big gold customized jewelry imbedded with diamonds always stood out making Rofiki feel important. But, he had a new gold piece the shape of a lion's head on a coin, she didn't say anything when she seen him quickly tucking it away in his shirt like he forgot he had it on and didn't want her to see.

VIVIAN GREEN "Caught Up" BEAUTIFUL

Caught up, STARR was already used to Rofiki. Caught up, who wants to start again? Caught up accepting in the end. Caught up, maybe she'll get a ring. Caught up 'cause he pacified her. Watching Rofiki zipping up his new leather Jacket fast. Hiding the gold lion medallion around his neck that resembled the lions head ring that he never takes off, for reasons that STARR now knew.

Uneasy by how Rofiki was looking at her and talking to her, STARR'S mind was a crazy mixture of hope and fear. She heard all the under tones in his voice. She was just about to interrupt until. he mentioned the meeting with Vicious Heat Records. Before STARR could interject and ask questions the waiter reappeared asking her directly, *"Have you decided what you would like to order?"* Rofiki snapped, *"Na mon meh just bring da coffee!"*

4HERO 'Star Chasers" TWO PAGES

STARR is finding herself doing the same thing and walking the same old life. Looking back on yesterday and dreaming the same dreams. Wishing away the time. Then she answer her feelings and looked deep inside. So caught up, hmm mmm. Chasing Rofiki trying to make this old thing new. Caught up trying to make this earth thing groove.

The waiter didn't run from the aggravation of Rofiki's voice and he didn't offer him the free hot coffee. Instead he poured STARR another cup. Annoyed and needing caffeine Rofiki said to the waiter, *"Bring meh large cup of regular coffee extra suga' to go. None of dat cow cream shit."*

Paying attention to Rofiki instantly dropping his Jamaican patois accent, STARR seethed with anger and humiliation. She was used to this, but today it was an eye opener. Inside something was pushing STARR to get up and just run until she was out of breath and out of sight. But where could she go that Rofiki couldn't find her.

CONYA DOSS "Coffee" POEM ABOUT MS. DOSS

Like a fresh cup of coffee stringing STARR along, she knew, she had to keep on – keep on. Sulking and not wanting to become some made up fake Barbie doll singing what others tell STARR to sing. Her voice didn't work that way. It came with a spiritual flow that had to do its own thing. Make its own pitch, recite its own dialogue, a free spirit that only worked with freedom, not pressure.

Now Rofiki is preaching for her to get on stage, sing, shake dat azz and make dat money. He said he wasn't running around burning music and hustling the music at open mic's or gigs and out of the back of the car, chasing money from CD's sold on consignment at Ma & Pa record stores. He wanted more, and wanted STARR to want more. Unable to pretending for anyone and would rather be independent then trapped in a no win record deal. she became increasingly uneasy under his scrutiny. Everything he said made her feel uglier, despite all the compliments and greetings, winks and smiles she got on her way to the coffee shop.

JAZMINE SULLIVAN "Need U Bad" FEARLESS

"Hey, baby! What you ah deal wit?
We come true a lot. A tings you know?
So what happened to you?
Me make one little mistake
You want done us"

If, STARR had Rofiki back in her world, she would prove that she could be a better gyal. *"Oh, oh, oh!"* If Rofiki let her back in STARR would sure enough never, never let him go again." When STARR first met Rofiki, she had bone straight perm hair and a long fake pony tail. He was the one that convinced her to lock her hair. He was also strict with her vegetarian diet. He also picked out the beautiful materials she would wrap around her head and body. She never dressed hoochie, so dressing like that was out the question. But there's nothing she won't do to get back with her boo saying, "Oh, oh, oh, oh.

"Hey, baby..." Compliments used to come from Rofiki admiring her thickness - naturalness and that she didn't need to wear cosmetics. Now, he was sitting in front of her contradicting himself. What really made her fume was the statement he made about her not being a gospel singer. There was no way she would change her lyrics or remove any form of GOD from her mouth.

LES NUBIANS "One Step Forward" ONE STEP FORWARD

"One step forward - 2 steps backward
One step forward - 3 steps backward
One step forward - 4 steps backward
One step forward..."

One step forward, 2 steps backwards... One step forward, 3 steps backwards... One step forward, 4 steps backwards...The waiter returned with Rofiki's cup of coffee in a tall Styrofoam takeout cup. Rofiki sensed STARR was ready to jump ship and leave him for good, especially after him acting like Terry McMillan's 'Disappearing Acts.' So he knew he had to smooth things out and bring the conversation to a softer tempo.

Though STARR had the heart to move out, it was actually part of his plan. However to ease her pain and to buy more time, he said what she had been waiting to hear, *"I got da deal worked out."* She raised her eyes to find him watching her. Making straight eye to eye contact he smirked, *"Meh tell yu meh gonna take care of ya and we getting ready to do this Shit - Big ups! Meh heading back to Nu Yok fast try'n to work sum - ting fast why they offering. Sign here!"*

FIVE POINT PLAN "Sign Your Name" RARE

Wondering if she should sign, her name across the dotted line. Now is the place and time. Giving it all away and not looking back. Here is STARR'S chance, her lucky day. Nothing is for free, she had to pay to play.

It was time to set her trains up on its tracks and no looking back. She had to keep on moving and no back tracking, she had to keep on grooving. Like most musicians that wanted a record deal, STARR knew nothing about the ominous pages of single-spaced recording contracts. Yet, she had no other choice but to trust Rofiki.

As an independent artist Rofiki argued that she would not make it, but as a major label artist she could live the bling – bling life. Rofiki wanted more from STARR not just winning radio or poetry contest or open mic's or karaoke contest. He would say, *"Folks na pay if dey see yu fa free."* She on the other hand enjoyed the free spirit of open mics where she would meet new singers, spoken word poets and plenty of musicians.

Gifted with a lyrical memory and the rhythms of her words, Rofiki thought STARR was to theater - radical and told her to tone it down. He told her that she looked like a singing stage – play and he definitely didn't like when she interacted with men while on stage.

JULIE DEXTER & KHARI SIMMONS "Fooled By A Smile" MOON BOSSA

The ink pen was in STARR's hand and smiles were exchanged. Words, when said with tenderness become any less. Broken promises taking their toll. Temptations and lies could leave her ambitions standing still and all her dreams left behind. She needed to make up her mind while there was still time. Fooled by a smile and lies that would leave her again, cold as ice with a pain too hard to hide.

Mentally battling with the decision to sign the recording contract that would be a legal binding agreement between them, twirling the pen and quickly trying to read. Jovial and smiling wide Rofiki pushed the papers towards STARR to sign the management agreement. She was hesitating but isn't this what she wanted. She began to read the agreement naming him manager and co/writer.

Already out of her mind, STARR signed. Grinning, Rofiki showed a full display of his gold grill with diamonds, which she thought was now corny. He knew she loved him. She was his good luck charm. Tucking the contract under his arm and ready to run and fumbling in his pockets saying, "Yu a smart gyal STARR. Gotta learn da patients of fame. U t'ink meh wanna live at meh - mom's forever. Meh just wants t'ings to be right for US! But for now yu got your own spot, 'cause dat's whad yu want. Meh just giving yu whad yu want. Now let meh get back to the N.Y. Let's get dis money."

SWEET BACK "You Will Rise" SWEETBACK
(Featuring AMEL LARRIEUX)

STARR got a story that must be heard, about a little girl who wished she was a bird. She was unhappy living in her ghetto cage. But it gave her hope when her sweet Auntie would say, "Baby, you will rise. Rise because the limit is the skies. Don't let nobody fill your head with their lies. Nobody! Never compromise! Milk and honey is waiting for you on the other side. Yeah!"

Becoming upset, STARR let the mug hit the table hard, as she crossed her arms and leaned back in the chair. Exasperated she mumbled, *"What am I supposed to do until you return?" Continue to sleep on an air mattress in a cold room? And eat what?"* Rofiki spat, *"Meh 'elp yu wit dat problem. Yu pay dem $100 a week right?"*

Adding it up in her head, STARR had been there 3 weeks and still owed $200, since she only paid the first week. She was checking out how Rofiki flipped the argument calling it her place. She could see the words behind his eyes that he didn't say. Taking heed to him saying she was responsible for the rent. Not to mention the weeks she sat cramping and bleeding from another miscarriage, restless, cold and hungry awaiting him to rescue her.

AYO *"Down On My Knees"* JOYFUL

If they were not in public STARR would have dropped down on her knees and begged Rofiki not to leave her, again. She was sick of the nonsense, he continued to feed her. Did Rofiki really think another woman could love him more than her? Did he really, really think so? Did he really think, she can gave him more than her? She won't, because STARR loved him, unconditionally. She gave Rofiki even more than, she had to give and willing for him to die, because he was more precious to her, than her own life.

"Down on my knees, I'm begging you
Please, please don't leave me."

Dropping her head shamefully with regrets for being there waiting for him and signing the papers. She mumbled, *"Bull-shit – Ain't nothing but chewed up grass."* She sat pitifully listening as he talked over her seeming to enjoy her struggle to capture composer.

Looking at his *'Gucci'* watch it was about that time. Eyeing his new watch he said, *"Meh late wid linking up wid A&R peeps. Talk to dem crazy dirty people, the Jenki's yu rent from and tell dem give us a couple of days and meh need a key too if meh paying rent."* A ring of rope seemingly raced through her when he said us, as in them.

Then instantly it began to feel backwards and that was the bullshit, he did to her. She didn't feel like she had any other choice except to do it his way. But doing it his way was causing her pain. Aware that A&R was responsible for artist development, she would have felt better if she was part of that meeting. She couldn't really protest. But it wasn't just about the meetings, the contract and their personal belongings in storage. She asked him thickly, *"What's up with us? And you could at least ask about the..."*

KIM HILL "Right Now" RIGHT NOW

No, STARR waited forever and she want her shit, *"Right Now!"* Trying to get far away from the drama rising to his feet as if propelled by an explosive force, Rofiki avoided her questions placing a $100 bill on the table and topping it off with a $1 bill. In rhythmic arrogance he spat, *"Yu know meh, Rofiki, 101 about chasing dat green! Tip $1 to yu bald head blue eyed boy, looking like Vin Diesel and Howie Mandel. Yu be al'ight take a cab to da crib and chill meh be back. We rap about da rent later."*

Vibrating, Rofiki's cellphone was blowing up and he could no longer ignore the vibes. He stood up, slide on his sunglasses and straightened out his gear letting free his long dark locks.

The sound of STARR'S heart breaking didn't faze him anymore. The king of the games he played. Things were getting out of control and she felt like, he was trying to dump her in the same place they met. She reached out to grab Rofiki's hand.

A wretchedness of mind STARR never known before colored her face fiercely. She choked back tears knowing Rofiki wanted to leave fast. Raised her voice for attention, *"You don't care anything about me. It is always about you."* He pulled away from her reach and stood holding the Styrofoam cup of coffee. He hastily muttered, *"Yu act like every - ting meh do is bad. Meh not da Taliban. Meh just a Rasta man, yu got some issues too. Jah na sleep and neither is Rofiki!"* In a quick breathe, she spat words that would insult and sting him verbally, *"U fuckin' Bumboclaat!"*

2000 BLACK "Dealt A Bad Hand" A NEXT SET OF ROCKERS

Always feeling like she is being dealt a bad hand. Try putting yourself in STARR's shoes. No one can feel what she feel or fear. When you've witness what she seen or felt. That's why she stands in her shoes strong and Rofiki hated being called anything similar to blood-clot, bumbo-cloth, pussy-clot, etc.

Thankfully, STARR wasn't in Jamaica because the word 'Bumboclaat' is actually a very vulgar swear word and can get arrested for using it in Jamaica around police officers as well as dismissed from a class or formal business place. Her eyes darkened with hate watching him carelessly walk away. She shouted loud enough sure he heard, but he kept on walking.

It was apparent he didn't care about her or the baby. She reached for her empty cocoa mug wanting to hit him before he got away. Because if he had asked about his seed that she carried for 3 months, he would have learned, she had another miscarriage. It happened the day after he left for New York. The same day her cellphone was cut off, yet his stayed on. She had perfect aim targeting the back of his head. Just as she swung back and ready to release the mug a big strong tanned hands grabbed her arm and the mug.

It was blowing her mind, STARR don't know why she keep fucking with Rofiki. She could hardly wait to be through with him. Hardly wait, still she keep on fucking with him. He don't celebrate her. Oh, but she keep fucking with him. The bells on the door hammer loud against the door commencing the slam of Rofiki's dramatic, yet smooth exit.

N'DAMBI "I Can Hardly Wait" PINK ELEPHANT

The waiter's baritone voice replied, *"Let him go! You'll be okay, I'll get you another cup of coffee."* She was too humiliated to do anything else but to let Rofiki go. Woman's intuition told her that Rofiki wasn't being totally honest. She couldn't believe what was happening. She felt abandon and lost. Fatigue settled in pockets under her eyes remembering the many nights worrying. Burden about him being in the streets selling weed to accommodate his ghetto fabulous life styles and now he had a new ride.

"STARR could hardly wait to be through with Rofiki.
Hardly wait, but still she keep fucking with him"

The waiter returned almost instantly with a new cup of coffee then walked away. Still embarrassed, STARR was glad the coffee shop was empty. It still didn't alleviate the tension and the pressure that was so deep in her muscles feeling her body cramping. She had to relax, breathe, understand, regroup, and remember where she was literally, and what the hell was going on? She knew Rofiki was selfish and materialistic, but she never thought he would behave this selfishly. Leaving STARR to hustle for the glamorous life with the "Bling – Bling" seen on most of the people in the music industry. He would always daydream talking aloud about owning a 15 bedroom mansion in Miami or California with a pools, hot tubs and tennis court, maids and a personal limousine driver.

Talking so much trash, Rofiki was saying so much to clean up, amusing STARR with lies talks about having three sons and two big dogs. He would tell her that his sons would look like him. He would charm her by saying they would have a daughter, a little princess that would be beautiful and dark chocolate like STARR. She loved the idea of having a family and desperately wanted one, but miscarried every time.

"Bull-Shit ain't nothing but chewed up grass." Rofiki was now gone and she was still sitting there confused. But if he had stayed long enough. She would have told him about the gigs, she had lined up with BearLove. She was planning to share her surprise performance, updating Rofiki on what has been going on since his disappearance act. But after all his insults and the money on the table it was obvious he didn't care.

RHONDA THOMAS "Breathe New Life" BREATHE NEW LIFE

The wind was blowing to bring new life in STARR. She always knew the clouds would part and the winds would only blow to bring new life to her. After spending hours, days and the last few weeks thinking, singing, thinking, writing about how to get their situation right. She wanted him to be proud of her for setting up paying gigs. She was being one of the independent women that he beamed about. She wanted to say "fuck it" and cry. But what good would it do, Rofiki couldn't hear or see her, he was gone.

Arms crossed and STARR'S cheeks sucked in and teeth biting down hard on the inside of her jaws. She felt lost needing peace and wanted to go home. "Damn where was home?" She looked like an angry fish gazing out the window. She stared at the empty parking space where he was parked.

There was no kiss hello and there was no kiss good - bye. They stopped kissing on the lips a long time ago, but he would normally greet her with a peck or two on the cheeks. If he would have kissed her, he would have noticed instantly that she no longer had a tongue ring. She wondered if he even noticed or just didn't care to notice. She prayed, *"GOD please grant me the strength I need to continue."* She became startled by her own thoughts and loud whispers forgetting the time, she was now late.

AYAH "He Don't Want It" 4:15

What STARR was doing for Rofiki, wasn't enough for him, no! If he didn't want her, he doesn't want it? He showed and told her enough times before, but she is stubborn and thinks things will change. She'll be okay, that is her Word!

"And if he don't want it, he don't want it..."

Feeling utterly miserable, STARR quickly began gathering her belongings. Thinking about how BearLove taught her how to make more sounds with her mouth and tongue without the ring. Now she was tongue popping and making all kind of beat box sounds. Remembering BearLove words, "Be on time!" Looking at the clock, she was late and mad she decided to meet up with Rofiki. Just as a tear slide down her cheek, out of the blue the waiter reappeared with his warm baritone voice, *"Do you mind if I sit with you?"*

This time STARR'S hand reached for his big hand that was holding a tissue and then looking straight into his sky-high-blue eyes. A small gasp escaped and she quickly closed her mouth afraid she might break down and cry. Confused she watched him sit down and noticed he had a slice of pound cake for her. She was actually trembling now.

The waiter was concerned and bending his slightly forward he said, *"I just want to make sure you're okay. Please enjoy a slice of my famous sour cream pound cake with cream cheese icing, I baked it myself."* Swallowing the sob that rose in her throat, STARR looked at the thick moist slice of pound cake that could feed 2 or more. She couldn't refuse the scent that haunted her belly since she walked in the door. With her mind on Rofiki, she ate the cake.

DEBORAH BOND "Don't Waste Your Time" DAY AFTER

In love, STARR was there once and not feeling it anymore. All the things folks say, she said them before. Once in a while she had to open her eyes. It was time that she realized. She knows, she thinks he loves her but shouldn't waste her time. He don't treat her like he supposed to forgetting her love was divine. So, why she want to hold on to him like no other man would treat her right. She wasn't going to waste her time.

GOAPELE "Salvation" EVEN CLOSER

Searching for her salvation, oh yeah she was tired of dragging on and on, on and on. Day by day, feeling the pain of her world resting on her brain feeling the hurt of a broken child. STARR is searching, STARR is praying, she is looking. Knocked out of her thoughts watching the waiter place a small black book on the table, she assumed it was a Bible. Wondering if the waiter came to save her? She eyed the black book not wanting to reject the Bible. But, wasn't this what she was just praying for? She reached for the book appreciative and asking, *"Thanks are you some kind of preacher?"* Wondering if he felt the sadness that owned her? Because he sure seen the hunger in her belly and the cake tasted like heaven.

CAROL RIDDICK "Brown Eye Girl" MOMENTS LIKE THIS

Most people may know who they are and some people may not know who they want to be, STARR always knew she wanted to sing. Most people don't know the strength they have inside and they lose themselves from the things they see, but not STARR. Her wide coffee brown eyes was observing it all and when they gazed into his electric blues eyes, did he see her poor soul? Yet again, STARR looked at the black book. But, she didn't reach for it. Thinking back to the many church services, she had sat through growing up. As much as she thought, talked, and sung about GOD, she could barely remember one Bible verse. Her earth brown eyes to his cornflower blue eyes looking directly into his blue hues for a few seconds, before turning away.

Suddenly, STARR became inquisitive to the sapphire of his eyes but asked, *"Are you a preacher or something?"* He responded with a rhetorical question. *"Would you like to call me a preacher or something?"* Now STARR was observing the coffee shop the way Rofiki had been scoping it out. She was happy to find it now empty. The waiter answered projecting his strong voice, *"I'm just a man that looks for salvation from the pains in this world and thought you may need some comforting."*

After taking another bite of cake STARR responded, *"Hmmm this is so good.* She sung out lyrics from an old jumping rope song, *"You could be a doctor, a lawyer or a soul power chief?"* Proudly he laughed out humorously, *"I could be a soul power chief!"* She began laughing amused with his humor. Surprisingly STARR said, *"You're a Bluesy washing away the blues with this wonderful pound cake."* He blushed, *"Well actually my nick name is Bluesy. Well, my mother only calls me that."*

Sharing nick names she said, *"My mother only calls me Coffee."* She sat back and waited for his response not believing she told him the endearing and painful nick name that identified her skin tone. She also mentioned her mother, which she never did. She was surprised when he extended his hand smiling an approval, *"You're Beautiful and the perfect name. Nice to meet you Coffee."*

AMEL LARRIEUX *"Your Eyes"* BRAVE BIRD

Letting go of the embrace of a very intimate hand shake, STARR noticed his hands were strong, smooth and warm. His neon eyes greeted her mahogany eyes and whispered softly, slowly, a secret only for her (she didn't blink). His periwinkle eyes took their sweet time silently penetrating sending waves straight through her, just for her. His indigo eyes, the sleepy kind. So still and warm, she had to dive so deep, deeply to where his meet hers. His azure eyes, round and sweet blueberry fruit if they were, she have a piece and they would fill her sweetly. Sleepy steel eyes, will they meet again? Did her pecan eyes make him feel like she was feeling?

Also, he didn't say his real name or did he? But, he did call STARR beautiful. Was he flirting? Was she flirting back? Guilt hit her and dropped off as she looked at the $101 Rofiki left on the table. Feeling like a world of tamed soft winds rushed through to rescue her.

It was unbelievable there was laughter in STARR'S voice, when just minutes ago, she was at the verge of exploding in tears running to the top of the Ben Franklin Bridge, ready to jump. Now sitting across from her was a man smiling with the bluest eyes that held the powers of a soul power chief. Actually enjoying the company she wasn't ready to be left alone and it didn't look like he was ready to get up. She followed his lapis lazuli eyes as if hypnotized, she had to shake her head, and not wanting to confuse or involve him.

LAURYN HILL "Lost One" MISEDUCATION OF LAURYN HILL

Still trying to get over what just happened and what was happening. It's funny how money changes a situation. Miscommunication leads to complication STARR'S emancipation didn't fit Rofiki's equation. She was on the humble, him wanting to play her like she was young and dumb. Knowing there is not a game new under the sun, everything he did has already been done.

"You might win some but he just lost one"

Knowing all the tricks from Rofiki carrying bricks to his life resembling his father Kingston. Her ting done made his kingdom want to run. Now understand STARR is nonviolent. But if anyone tests her, she has been this way since creation. A groupie calls and Rofiki falls for temptation. Now he wants to ball over separation. Garnish her image in his conversations. Who he going to scrimmage like he is the champion.

"Rofiki might win some but he just lost one"

Thankful with sincerity, STARR looked into his turquoise blue eyes, as if she had nothing to lose and nothing she wanted to gain. *"Look I don't know who U R? Or what can be gained from all this? But I have so much shit going on in my life and I guess it is obvious that I'm in need of some kind of spiritual guidance or therapy."*

Hearing the sorrow in her own voice alarmed her. They were interrupted by the bells jingling and the coffee shop door opening. STARR'S shoulders tensed thinking it was Rofiki coming back to rescue her and to apologizing and love her. She was fooled again noticing the time and the young college guy that came in apologizing for being late for work, because of classes at Temple University.

ADRIANNA EVANS "Calling Me" EL CAMINO

"I can hear you calling me..." Running later too, she had a show @ JAZZ1CAFÉ with BearLove and his new music project / group, THE NEO SOUL STARR. She had hoped that Rofiki would drive her, but he was gone in the winds of highway I-95 on his way back to New York. She was going to be late. Her face showed a sign of panic. She stood up apologizing, *"I'm sorry but, I have to go. I'm late for work."*

Without hesitating Bluesy stood up asking, *"Which way do you have to go? Let me take you."* He pushed the black book and $101 on the table towards her. STARR didn't ask any questions putting the black book and money in her bag wanting to get far away from the memories of Rofiki, and followed Bluesy out the door, who might have just won one.

TRACK 2: JAZZ1CAFÉ

MONDAY MIRCHIRU "Philosophy Road" ROUTES

Just when STARR thought she knew it all. What did she know? Life throws her a loop and she falls. Now where do she go? Looking to the heavens to call to be saved before she go too low. She could only hear the rain fall and knew she had to keep on going. Off the beat and on the path of Philosophy Road. Where she will find the truth in life and leave it all. Every day she go along Philosophy Road. Naked as the air she breathes it humbles her soul. She tries to make sense of it all a world so full of distance.

JAZZ1CAFÉ was STARR'S official first paying gig. She couldn't believe she was able to hook up with BearLove and be part of his new projects and group 'THE NEOSOUL STARR.' She had been rehearsing every day and night with the band and everything was feeling just right. They didn't have any original material recorded but was working on it in the studio. In the meantime they reprised and remixed some of their favorite songs and created a show. Excited and upset at the same time she had to try to get her mind together, remember the lyrics and the address to JAZZ1CAFÉ.

ROBERT GLASPER EXPERIMENT "Let It Ride" BLACK RADIO 2 (Featuring NORAH JONES)

STARR'S never been a gambler, she stay on the same side, in all. So she know she's alright. But all that's forgotten when, she looking into his blue eyes. Probably out on a limb. Only out from inside, love. He show her what it feels like. She is not guaranteed anything, so their love is on the line. But she let it ride.

"I let it ride, I let it ride, I let it ride"

Holding it all together STARR willed her mind, body and soul to at least try to feel better. Being driven swiftly and safely in the winds of the busy city streets, STARR eyed a gold round medal of Saint Christopher hanging from the rearview mirror. The medal depicted the saint crossing turbulent waters with the child, Jesus on his shoulders and a staff in his hand. Out of curiosity, she touched it reading the scripture on the back. 'I am a Catholic In Case Of an Accident Call A Priest.' Bluesy broke the silence explaining, *"Saint Christopher is the patron saint of travel. My parents gave it to me for blessings in my travels."* Wanting to know more about STARR, he smiled wide asked, *"Can I call you Coffee?"*

Welcoming the new friendship STARR replied, *"If I can call you Bluesy?"* Curious making polite conversation she asked, *"So how long you've been a waiter?"* Chuckling, Bluesy replied while keeping his eyes on the road, *"I am the waiter and manager and owner of the coffee shop."*

Thankful and impressed STARR expressed her gratitude, *"Thank you again, and may you be blessed for taking your time out to help."* Bluesy grinned explaining, *"GOD already has blessed me, but I don't mind a few more blessings. I just moved back to Philadelphia. I was in the Marine's for 6 years, but spent the last few years in Iraq. I just bought the coffee shop last month. I haven't changed the name. I'm getting ready to start all the new renovations."*

INDIA ARIE "Thank You" SONGVERSATION

After being embarrassed for assuming, STARR thanked Bluesy for being one of the few sacrificing and risking his own to save a life know that we all are praying. She couldn't stop thanking him. *"Thank you for everything and that sour cream pound cake I could eat every day. I thank you!"* Touching her hand, he kindly spoke, *"I thank GOD for this nice drive with a beautiful woman. Reminding me that GOD is in charge of our day."* She agreed, *"Amen!"*

Realizing Bluesy was flirting and preaching again STARR said, *"I knew you were a preacher!"* They laughed seeing the humor in it all. Checking out his smile, she noticed the dimples in his cheeks. She felt his honest aura and knew if it wasn't for him, she would have blew this gig and her future.

SLEEP WALKER "Wind" NEUJAZZ (Various Artist)
(Featuring Yukimi Nagano)

There was something in Bluesy that blew through STARR, the words of mystical winds. She could inhale the feeling, something about him soothed her. She smirked feeling better knowing more information about him, but the thoughts of Rofiki was creeping back up causing anxiety to feel like two heavy boots pressing between her breasts.

PHUTURISTIX "Give It A Miss Lads" FEEL IT OUT

Pulling up to JAZZ1CAFÉ, they noticed the huge crowd of people lining up and waiting to get in and security giving some of the special guest on the list a hard time, joking around. STARR felt a wave of nervousness, happy she made it on time. She began looking in the mirror trying to be sure there were no tear stains on her face.

Trying to assure STARR, Bluesy complimented her beauty and told her to wait while he opened the car door for her. But, she didn't have a clue to what he was doing and was half way out the car when he reached her.

A degree of warmth and concern was in STARR'S voice when she asked, *"So, Bluesy did you have dinner yet?"* He shook his head no. she said, *"Well let me treat you to dinner."* He replied, *"I would love that beautiful but would rather wait until you can join me. I don't want to upset your boss and get his prettiest waitress fired."*

To be sure STARR was alright Bluesy asked, *"I hope you will be okay getting back home? Do you live far from here?"* Hearing Bluesy's compliments and assuming she's a waitress. She straightened herself with dignity and feeling awkward for not knowing his real name. But looking into his marine blue eyes that beamed bright with hope and beautifully matched his blue shirt, she felt safe. Then taking Bluesy's hand they walked into JAZZ1CAFÉ noticing the colorful stylish attire of the people.

2000 BLACK "So Right" A NEXT SET OF ROCKERS

So right, something in the vibe that makes it soul. So good, something in the vibe that makes it nice. It was something that made STARR glow enough to cause a smile like some kisses down her back, and that brings some finger snapping. How elevating and joy is the only feeling that love is real. The taste is so delicious and precious and how it feels good. STARR had to take a second look and then she questioned is this dream just for one day, just hoping everything was true? Following behind STARR, Bluesy bopped his head to the music digging the lyrics.

BLUE SIX "Music and Wine" BEAUTIFUL TOMORROW

Approving his inspections of JAZZ1CAFÉ. The delicious plates of Tapas and appetizers aroma were making him hungry. Bluesy said, *"There are a lot of folks here. This place is packed. We may even run into some super stars."* She enjoyed his enthusiasm leading him to a small table by the stage teasing, *"Come on hurry up and I will take you to see a STARR spelled with 2 R's!"* He humored her showing his music knowledge, *"Oh like in the group ATLANITC STARR?"*

Giving Bluesy a devilish grin and a happily nodding, "Yes, STARR as in ATLANTIC STARR. She didn't mention that is where her name came from. But for assuming she was a waitress, she waved to the maître d' that she was seating her guest. Bluesy felt his heart skip a beat and being swept of his feet. Like touching a four-leaf clover and feeling so right.

ERYKAH BADU "4 Leaf Clover" BADUIZM
(ATLANTIC STARR)

"Touch a four leaf clover - Maybe you'll get over
Try and luck might - Come your way"

"Bootzilla, baby!" Touch a four leaf clover, Maybe they'll get over. Try and luck might come his way. Here is Bluesy on a cloud. If STARR want him take the chance cry, love, out loud. As he drift through the sky shooting cupid's loving arrow. She just might try, so don't miss him. Take his time and aim. 'Cause he's only got one chance. Bluesy think he better touch, touch a four leaf clover. Maybe he'll get over.

NICCI GILBERT "Rhythm And Blues" GROWN FOLKS MUSIC

"Rhythm And Blues..." The stage was set up and waiting for action and STARR was feeling so right and had to hurry saying, *"Okay Bluesy let's see*

how much Soul Power you have tonight! (They both laughed) If you have to go don't worry, I'll get a ride." Bluesy quickly replied, *"Hey this seems like a cool spot. I can hang out a little after I eat. It looks like there is a band about to play, so I will enjoy the entertainment. I will wait no strings attached. But, hey just remember no throwing mugs on duty."*

Knowing Bluesy was only teasing, though STARR was still mad that she didn't get a chance to crack Rofiki upside his head. She grinned, *"I'll behave, but will be a couple of hours and you might get bored waiting for me."* She gave him a wave good – bye, as she disappeared behind doors that he watched trays of food come from.

4HERO "Holding It Down" Featuring LADY ALMA

Moving her body, now STOP! Moving her mind because in this place and time, STARR was there to hold it down. Clocks ticking she was late, woo. The seconds turned into minutes, she was ready to hold it down. Rushing into the ladies room, she changed into a fresh pair of black leggings and a sexy pair of very high heeled black boots. She wore a sexy black crochet top that was very unique looking. She undid her scarves, letting her locks fall down her back. She added a little lip gloss and black eyeliner. She wasn't big on cosmetics but thinking about what Rofiki's comments, she added gold eye shadow to her dark eye lids and rubbed a little of the gold dust across her lips. Needing a little bit of fresh air, she noticed the back exit door ajar. She step outside catching the dish washer and bus boy smoking a joint, they gladly passed and she puffed with pleasure.

AQUANOTE "One Wish" THE PEARL

"One Wish" and one last puff, STARR noticed the beauty of the night and seen a shooting star. She closed her eyes tight and made one wish. Wishing she had a way to prove love exist. *"Please show me the way to his heart and make my wish come true."* Heading back inside, STARR to find the drummer BearLove, he was the reason why she was even there. If she had one wish, BearLove was making it come true. If she had not run into him on her way out of Temple University Hospital after being discharged from having the miscarriage, she knew she wouldn't be there.

ERIC DARIUS "What's Her Name" RETRO FORWARD
(Featuring ERIC DAWKINS)

They were on the elevator together and as noticeable as BearLove was with his big afro with the black fist afro-pic in his hair, she didn't recognize him. As she was getting off he asked, *"Yo are you the sistah 'STARR' that performed that joint by 'Phyllis Hyman' a few months ago at the Black Lily over at the 5spot?"* She recognized his voice and noticed it was BearLove from the Hip-Hop group 'THE ORGANICS.' She was super-surprised that he remembered her.

FLOETRY "Now You're Gone" FLOETIC

Now Rofiki was gone. Why did STARR'S mind and body believe that he would never leave them? Who would steal him when she still feel him? Now Rofiki was gone and she was trying to physic her self-esteem. She swallowed still feeling like Rofiki's new black boots pressing against her jugular. But when she opened her mouth she could feel her freedom releasing in songs.

BearLove was there visiting a friend, and assumed STARR was doing the same. He informed her of the music project he was working on with other musician and looking for a lead female vocalist. He asked her did she want to be down, she responded, *"Alright."* They road home together in a cab and he dropped, her off first. The next day she was at his house and in his home recording studio for rehearsal. Yet, still in pain and bleeding from the miscarriage and reason at the hospital. Knowing now, she would have bleed and starved to death waiting on Rofiki. Now tonight at JAZZ1CAFÉ it wasn't about Rofiki orchestrating her show and it will be the best night she'll ever have.

JOHN LEDGEND "Tonight" THINK LIKE A MAN (Soundtrack)
(Featuring LUDICRIS)

Tonight ain't this what Bluesy came for? Yes, he wished he could come more? What was he playing for? Ah, he should have kissed – yes missed her, but they just met. What's wrong? Let him fix that, twist that. Bobbing his head and singing along to the lyrics. Alright, okay there was no harm in having a little fun. Fond of the way STARR called him, "*BLUESY!*"

If only STARR knew, she had just rescued Bluesy, by needing him, and he wanted these feelings to stay. Browsing the menu and the restaurant looking for her to appear in a waitress uniform or was she a bartender, he wondered. He never asked her age, but assumed she was older from her conversation, though she looked young.

> *"Baby, tonight, you need that, tonight, believe that*
> *Tonight I'll be the best you ever had."*

Trying to relax Bluesy's Marine instincts kicked in remembering the incident at the coffee shop. The establishment was being surveillance like a trained scout sniper, infantrymen skilled to gain intelligence on the enemy and the terrain. Seeing people sipping alcohol beverages, he assumed she had to be over 21.

Still twisting and turning towards the bar and the kitchen, still trying to look for Cocoa. Giving up and assuming maybe she was working in the kitchen, maybe she cooked his wonderful meal. His attention was pulled back to the stage as he listened ready to hear some good music. The host of the evening walked on stage introducing herself, but it seemed many people already knew her from the radio station.

DJ CAM "SoulShine" SOULSHINE
(Starring INLOVE)

"Welcome to SoulShine – Welcome to SoulShine – Welcome to SoulShine"

Sashaying across the stage to the microphone it was show time. "*S-O-U-L! SHINE!* Welcoming and thanking everyone for being there and for tuning into JAZZ1CAFE and supporting the station and artist, by becoming V.I.P. Members. Then instructing the crowd to pull out their mobile devices and cellphones since most already had them in their hands on Facebook or Tweeting or taking selfies for Instagram while eating. Next everyone who didn't already have the APP Download the LIVE365 AP, Launch APP and enter station name: JAZZ1CAFE. Then immediately wasting no time and getting right into the show giving everyone one what they came there for.

"Coming to the stage a group that packed the house tonight. Their sound is Neo- Soul, Nu-Jazz, Smooth Jazz, and always Hip-Hop flavored! Let's put our hands together and welcome to the stage Philadelphia's own 'THE NEOSOUL STARR!'"

The band came on stage and before playing a single note, before even sitting down at the keyboards Ronald Glasshouse's known as Ronny G. Kindly asked for the stage lights to be dimmed. *"We like it kind of sexy,"* he insisted. The vibe and atmosphere were all-important to the experience. The lights go down and the room grows to a hush. Then he began to play a smooth jazzy intro. The shadowy figures of the band are playing along creating the smooth jazzy music.

ROBERT GLASPER EXPERIMENT "Baby Tonight" BLACK RADIO2

The food arrived just as the band began to play. Bluesy's was enjoying the smooth soulful sounds looking for Coffee and wondering, her real name. His attention was still on stage and the crowed was clapping, cheering and there was even whistling as the show was starting. Next came the STARR, he been waiting to see with 2-R' came pranced across the stage to the beat and swaying to the music. Mind blown Bluesy thought, *"OMG!"*

Impressed Bluesy was fascinated enjoying the show. Blown away, he had no idea. He could have never predicted this as he watched STARR jamming across the stage. He literally almost choked on his food, instantly recovering enveloped by her sugary purrs of welcoming lyrics, he put his fork down. He was now laughing inside for assuming she was a waitress, so they were even. He felt like a groupie lost in her enchantment and not wanting a cure for the spell.

YAHZARAH "Strike Up The Band" THE BALLADS OF PURPLE ST. JAMES

Hey, what's a hero without its theme music? Somebody strike up the band, STARR is here. The music raced through her head, merely split seconds before she walked on stage. Action! The band was in full intro and the crowd clapping. STARR'S heart was pounding after listening to SoulShine introduce the band and her stepping on stage on time and on point.

The music was jazzy, soulful blended with the heavy bass inviting the drums, inviting her to sing more. She was center stage bouncing her hips with a seductive wiggle. The crowed clapped excitingly as the show began. STARR controlled the microphone and singing with liberation and perfect pitch. Yes, she was a JILL SCOTT fan, but sorry she had to own it and sang "Let It Be."

JILL SCOTT "Let It Be" THE REAL THING WORDS AND SOUNDS VOL. 3

"If it's hip-hop, if it's bebop, reggaeton, of the metronome

Feeling the recharged by the music and pointing at Bluesy who was grinning, STARR was into funky jam. Her powerful voice delivered appreciation in attempt to give the crowd their money's worth. From calling fans on stage to jumping to the floor and singing to the audience, she was determined to get everyone into the mix. The neo -funky grooves of the songs had heads bobbing and hands clapping and waving back to her. She put everything into her performance knowing from the first note, she had to have the audience's attention and participation.

"If it's classical, country mood, rhythm and blues, gospel"

The stage was STARR's zone, she wasn't shy, she forgot to be quiet, and she forgot to be lonely. STARR pointed at people in the audience. Pulling in listeners on the first note. It was like sweet innocent love filled with pleading passion thanking each and E-V-E-R-Y-O-N-E. The band's vibe was the hippest and the funkiest. Heads were bobbing and wobbling to the soulful flow of musical energy. The steel strings of the bass vibrated the room and in Bluesy's eyes STARR was shining.

"Whatever it is, whatever it is, let it"

The audience loved STARR, but noticing one person in the audience that wasn't feeling her. It was Mina, BearLove's fiancée. STARR kept it going not caring as she embraced her second wind of energy. She felt Bluesy was probably shocked to see her on stage. Since he assumed, she was a waitress. But, that would teach them both not to assume.

DJ JAZZY JEFF & AYAH *"Tables Turn"* BACK FOR MORE

"Now y'all gotta baby and it's hard for you to leave. It's easier to make believe. That's when the tables turn." Since the moment STARR met BearLove, her burdens seem to be lifting. She wanted to enjoy every moment of it before Rofiki returned to take it away. She didn't feel like all her problems had disappeared. But she was feeling better than the day before.

The hero of the day she wanted to thank. She would have never made it to the gig on time. No work (gig) meant no rent, and no food. She had been hungry for a couple of days, and that was nothing Rofiki was worried about. She dismissed it from her mind as she got heavy into her groove singing the hook to the song. She asked the audience to sing along. Her lively voice verbalized her love for music, as well as her vocal strength. Closing her eyes and went into that place where no one can touch her when she song.

AMEL LARRIEUX *"For Real"* BRAVEBIRD

"I can feel, I can see
I can tell, you are for real"

Sauntering to the center of the stage, STARR sat down on a stool. She crossed her legs and inclined her head in compliance to the music. The way her body was positioned, her stance emphasized the force of her thighs and the fullness of her hips. Stylishly embracing the microphone she sang and scatted to the seductive Neo - Soul groove. Showing her good vocal vibrato techniques and sounding fantastic.

Introducing the band members, STARR knew they needed no introductions. Everyone was wonder who she was. She was the new voice and face on the scene. STARR sang out, *"I can tell, you are for real! Please put your hands together for the jazziest fingers, smoothest piano players on the black and white keys! Ronny Glasshouse on Piano!"*

Born and raised to play the piano Ronald Glasshouse is a P.K. (preacher's kid) His father was a pastor and his mother the choir director of a Pentecostal Church. Needless to say he broke their GOD -fearing hearts leaving home to join a funk band. R.G. Showing off his 10 talented fingers, rolling them up and down the black and white piano keys. Inspired by Herbie Hancock and Robbie Williams, funk and soul was his passion. The theory of funk music is built on the notion of improv and adding his own improvisation into the mix is was what his fingers did best.

ERYKAH BADU "Orange Moon" MAMA'S GUN

"I'm an orange moon reflecting the light of the sun"

"Please put your hands together for the soulful – grooviest bass player Joe-Daddy! Play for me Daddy!" Pro Funk- R&B - Soul Bassist know as Joe-Daddy was now showing off his multiple string talents. On acoustic guitar and bass carrying the crazy – groovy – bass – lines, showing of at times playing both bass & guitar at the same time.

"Then he said to me how good it is
How good it is, how good it is"

The bands chemistry was sweeping through the audience and hands were clapping and fingers were snapping. Joe played the upright bass, electric bass, guitar, fiddle, harp, banjo, and the Violin. He loved playing any instrument that produced sounds by vibrating nylon or steel strings. Whether it's Hip Hop, R&B, Jazz and Blues, Jo -Daddy can bring it! Playing a solo riff right into the next song.

FLOETRY "Say Yes" FLOETIC

"I'm about to let you know you make me so, so, so, so, so, so, so, so"

The crowd went crazy and each band member was caught up in one each other's groove and the explosion of their musical combinations was heard by all that could hear. And for the deaf impaired the vibration was felt all the way out to the sidewalk and street.

"You make me so, so, so, so, so, so, so, so"

There were people who just happen to be walking past, now glued to the windows looking in captured by the sounds. Listening to BearLove hitting the drums, STARR introduced him. *"Please put your hands together for the funkiest drummer you all know its true - BearLove!"*

The audience was now fixed on the musical connection of STARR and BearLove beating on his black onyx 'Pearl' drums. His drums were his babies, he barely let anyone help him carry them or set them up. So, they knew not to touch the Pearls. BearLove went into his funky drum solo looking like he was losing his mind.

Head wobbling like it would fall of his neck, BearLove's black Cazal eye glasses stuck to his face, despite the sweat, and his trade mark black afro-pick with the fist never fell out of his afro. His hands squeezing on to the drum sticks for dear life. Everybody was up on their feet whistling and clapping. STARR felt it and wanted to keep it flowing. It had come to that part of the night, they were on their last song and the music was about to stop. Life off stage will resume.

THE ROOTS "You Got Me" THINGS FALL APART
(Featuring ERYKAH BADU)

"If you were worried 'bout where
I been or who I saw or
What club I went to with my homies
Baby don't worry, you know that you got me"

The crowd wanted more, so they gave their audience more. M.J. began playing the sympathizer and the rest of the band following his cords. She knew now that this was no coincidence, he had her back, and he didn't even know her. She nodded to the funky beat and blew Bluesy a kiss. It was unbelievable the surprise siphoned the blood from his face. He only saw this kind of stuff in movies.

A beautiful woman that could have any man she wanted and she chose to blow him a kiss. He felt like running up to the stage. If only he had a bouquet roses. He felt the heat in the room adding to his nervousness as he thought, don't sweat, stop shaking, be cool, just smile, close your mouth, it's all a dream.

ZHANÉ "This Song Is For You" SATURDAY NIGHT

*"This song is for you
I dedicate all to you
Nothing more is true
Than my love for you"*

"What you say? What you say that you and I fall in love any day." JAZZ1CAFÉ was full of folks swaying and clapping, STARR could see the clear – cut lines of Bluesy's profile. Making contact with him, she noticed him smiling and clapping. She pointed at him and sang, *"This song is for you Bluesy - I dedicate all to you - Nothing more is true - Than my thanks for you!"*

All the band members covered their shocked looks as they wondered, who's Bluesy? Never would she blow a kiss or dedicated a song to Rofiki, he already thought every song was about him. Not tonight. Her Lips parted in a dazzling display of straight white teeth. Bluesy was caught up in the moment and the dream every man in the audience had of her. But it was much more than that with her, because it didn't begin with her on stage.

ALISON CROCKETT "Love Is Stronger Than Pride" BARE (SADE)

*"I won't pretend that I intend to stop living
I won't pretend I'm good at forgiving
But I can't hate you though I have tried"*

"Mmmm," When Bluesy first seen STARR sitting alone in the coffee shop, he was drawn to her. Then the guy she was waiting for came through the doors. Not planning on picking up women who came into the coffee shop. In fact he was through with women! With such a rocky past with relationships, he was done with soul searching. And it had been a very long time since he found a woman attractive. He thought his heart was a poor lost soul and now all this.

LIZZ FIELDS "Simply put" BY DAY BY NIGHT

"Simply put – I love you – I love you simply, I do"

On fire and in the magic of music, STARR was swaying her hips while singing. Becoming conscious that her performance was a lot better when Rofiki wasn't around. Relaxed and able to sing songs without worrying if Rofiki thought they were about him. He thought every song contained subliminal messages about him or them.

The crowd gave her a standing ovation. Bluesy included was standing, clapping, and whistling. He actually did this the whole show. STARR bowed and stepped back up to the microphone, *"We thank you all. But we got to go."*

The groove of the band switching up the beat and began playing 'Herman Kelly's *"Let's dance to the drummer's beat."* They switched up the beat real quick with a snippet of 'Rock Master Scott & The Dynamic Three, 'The roof- the roof -the roof is on fire.' The crowd sang back, *"We don't need no water let the mother... Burn - Burn mother... Burn."*

STARR kept up with the pace of the drummer "BearLove" who was very – very energetic and dramatic giving up a rhythmic double – trouble-funky beat, with his head bobbing up – down, and all around. His black fist afro pick stuck in the back of his afro, stayed in place. Showing why 'BearLove' is known as 'The King of Philly Style Beats.' BearLove stood up holing up his hand and two fingers flashing into the peace and never missing a beat drumming with one hand. He spoke into the microphone, *"Peace Quadir!"*

JILL SCOTT "Running Away" HIDDEN BEACH PRESENTS
THE VAULT VOL. 1

*"I put my heart on the back burner. Didn't wanna
face my own misery... I was running"*

Back on the microphone reintroducing the group was SOULSHINE SESSIONS cheering with the crowd, *"Come on give it up – Keep clapping for the voice that has touched us all- after tonight you won't forget this STARR of Philadelphia's own THE NEOSOUL STARR!"*

Exiting the stage STARR the crowd cheered for more it had been an incredible show. After being paid and assuring BearLove she didn't need a ride home, she noticed Mina was glad to hear they didn't have to drop her off. She went over to Bluesy's table swinging her oversize handbag over her shoulders. Bluesy looked around for the waitress to pay his bill. STARR said, *"Come on I took care of the bill."* She noticed, he did leave a nice tip for the waitress.

As they were leaving the club, Bluesy noticed they got a lot of stares. He knew that every man had to be wondering how he got the privilege to be with her. Exchanging a subtle look of amusement Bluesy opened the car door complimenting her, *"Yes you are a STARR with 2 R's. You know you're incredible. You are HOT!"*

Smiling STARR said, *"Yes, named at birth STARR with 2 R's. I'm just blessed to have a talent that can feed me. Because I have no idea - how I would have survived tonight without it."* Bluesy said, *"I love your name STARR and I'm sure you have many survival skills. Singing is just one of your spiritual gifts you choose to use."* STARR thought, if he only knew.

MIKE PHILLIPS "Heart Beat of The City" UNCOMMON DENOMINATOR

Feeling the heartbeat of the city and directing Bluesy to West Philly refusing to call it home, STARR sat in the passenger seat, her thin fingers tensed in her lap from holding the microphone tight. Thinking about getting out a block before at the gas station next to the Philadelphia Zoo, but she was exhausted, cold and hungry and ready to close up from the world. She didn't see what harm it would be if he knew where she lived. Parking the car he noticed, she held her stomach a few time.

Questioning, *"Will you be okay?"* She opened the car door not giving him time to get out and open it for her. *"I'm just a little hungry, I suppose. Don't worry I will eat a bowl of oodles of noodles or something."* Bluesy felt bad, he should have thought to ask her if she wanted something to eat when they were at the restaurant. He jumped out the car to walk her to the door. He asked, *"Why didn't you eat at the restaurant, I would have loved to buy you dinner."* STARR smiled, *"Don't sweat it. I get one free dinner. I wanted to feed you tonight. Plus I am a vegetarian and picky."*

TRIBALJAZZ "Blues For Bali" TRIBALJAZZ

Now in the late night still feeling the jazzy blues, Bluesy was really feeling bad that STARR didn't eat. She said a quick *"Thanks"* and closed the door. Watching her close the door and go inside the house, he exhaled a sigh of contentment. He stood there for a sec, just as she assumed he would.

On the drive home he passed a few restaurants and began feeling bad that he had not thought to ask if, she was hungry before taking her home. He came upon an Indian Restaurant and pulled into the parking lot. He went inside and browsed the menu. He had no idea what to order for a vegetarian other than vegetables.

Taking a chance ordering vegetable samosa, mock fish tikka with Basmati rice and vegetables. He also picked up a bottle of apple – raspberry cider, he wasn't sure if she drank wine, so he played it safe with the non- alcoholic beverage. He returned to her door 45 minutes later with everything in a big brown shopping bag. He couldn't let her eat a bowl of noodles after the performance she gave.

ME'SHELL N' DEGEOCELLO "Outside Your Door (Talk To Me)" PLANTATION LULLABIES

Here Bluesy was waiting. Just waiting and anticipating if he should knock on the door. He could sit there for hours thinking of the wonderful evening then came the rain showers. For just another glance, another chance to talk to STARR. She would probably think he was crazy for coming back. He prayed she wasn't a dream and when he wakes up, she would be talking to him.

Now standing outside STARR'S ringing the broken doorbell then knocking hard, then hearing the loud, slow moving thumps coming down steps. Ms. Freda, Mr. Jenki's wife came to the door dressed in her yellow terry cloth robe and a head full of pink sponge rollers, covered by a red handkerchief head scarf and a cast iron frying pan in one hand.

MICHAEL FRANKS "Mr. Blue" THE ART OF TEA

"We lived we laughed we cried and they will never die..." Now thinking of STARR and since she closed the door and disappeared, he changed

his name to Mr. Blue." A welcome blush crept into Ms. Freda's cheeks as she pointed Bluesy to the third floor commenting, "*Delivery man this late at night? It sure smells like ya got some good grub. That Gyal needs to eat - looks like she falling off to nothing.*" Almost hesitating, he followed the woman who simultaneously looked like Madea A.K.A. Tyler Perry and Big Momma A.K.A Martin Lawrence. Stepping over cats and trash he didn't want to disturb STARR unexpectedly. He knocked on the door at the top of the narrow stairway that led to the third floor.

Freshly showered STARR pulled her sweater tightly around her damp body. She opened the door and Frisky the cat ran inside. She was expecting it to be Mr. Jenki looking for his rent money. Bluesy couldn't hold back now handing her the big brown paper bag explaining, "*I brought you dinner.*" Looking embarrassed holding an empty bowl of oodles of noodles she said, "*You didn't have to do this.*" He softly replied, "*Yes, I did. I apologize for coming unexpectedly, but I did have to do this.*"

Noticing a shadow in the hallway, she was hesitant, but invited him in. Not wanting to continue the conversation where it could be over heard. Plus she couldn't take the stench in the hallway of Ms. Freda's cats litter boxes. STARR cleverly decorated the 3rd floor studio apartment with her shabby chic thrift store finds. She apologized for not having a chair to offer him to sit down on. She patted the side of the air mattress that was covered with a red bedspread with shades of orange and gold pillows. Frisky jumped on the bed.

GEORG LEVIN "Can't Hold Back" CAN'T HOLD BACK

Can't hold back, his love, no. Bluesy was hoping STARR was digging his flow. Can't go on without her and don't know what he should do. Maybe this is new to STARR and could cause suspicion. That is why Bluesy wanted her to get down and listen. She might think his way is too much for love sake, but if she opened her eyes, she would see he wasn't a fake.

Bluesy's heart had no room for a sad man. He knew for sure this ache would never end. He hoped, she didn't think he has already gone too far. Hoping it don't break his heart. He can't hold back and don't know what he is going to do. Hoping STARR was digging his flow. Can't go on without her and don't know what he should do.

SNARKY PUPPY "Free Your Dreams" FAMILY DINNER Vol. 1 (Featuring CHANTAE CANN)

STARR was ready to live this thing called life and taking it one day at a time. Embracing her future, learning from her past. She's counting all her blessings. OH! OH! OH! Embarrassed and fussing at the cat, STARR picked her up, "*No - No bed!*" Bluesy asked, "*Is that your cat?*" She quickly answered, "*No, all 4 cats and litter boxes belong to the Jenki's. Frisky is the only female and the other cats knock her around sometimes, so she runs to me for shelter.*" She felt momentary panic wondering why he came back.

Holding Frisky she began to rattle on about the cat before locking her in the bathroom, "*She is calico cat and that is not a breed of cat, it is a color pattern. To be called "calico", three colors must be present are black, white and orange. Variations of these colors include gray, cream and ginger.*" Bluesy chuckled, "*You know a lot about the cat that isn't yours, and what about the one that tried to paw box me at the front door?*"

There was something special between them going on. She could hear the piano softly playing and the violins plucking her heart strings longing to see the thing they had in common. Noticing Bluesy was getting closer STARR was also watching him playing with frisky and even picked her up. Rofiki would have never touched the cat.

SNARKY PUPPY "Something" FAMILY DINNER Vol. 1 (Featuring LALAH HATHAWAY)

"*Ooh, ooh, ooh, it's something. Bluesy and STARR have something. You better believe it.*" Nervously, STARR talked about the cats explaining, "*The cat at the front door is Tyson, because Big G is too fat to attack and rarely out in the hallway, and I doubt if it was Midnight, because all he does is sleep. Midnight is the oldest cat a 14 years old black Bombay cat, slightly long body and when stretching looks like a panther with copper eyes. But, he is friendly.*" Bluesy joked, "*You sure they're not your cats?*" She laughed, "*Trust me I would never have this many cats. I know about them because, I looked it up on the internet –I love the internet!*"

Knowing that she was rambling on about cats, she got quiet. Against the wall were stacks of milk crates with a board over top of them. Gold material with silver stars covered the make - shift counter, so you couldn't see the milk crates or the board and on top was a microwave oven and a wicker basket that held paper plates and plastic utensils.

In the other corner of the room was a small folding table used for incense and books. In fact, she was burning incense and had a few boxes of baking soda opened to cover up the smell of cats, but mainly to cover up the weed scent. And she was hoping the scent of the ½ of blunt, she just smoked was covered up by the citrus air freshener sprayed.

YAMAMA'NYM "Mr. Incredible" 2:00 AM

Mr. Incredible, Mr. Invincible why don't you use STARR like she thought you would. And she was Ms. Amazing, Ms. driving Bluesy crazy she was remarkable in a sweet way... Looking at his cellphone that was ringing, Bluesy noticed it was 2 AM when turning the phone off to avoid it from ringing again.

Noticed her living conditions, but wasn't judging her by it. He also noticed the sweet smell of her place verses the hallway. Pulling the food out the bag, she was still worried he could smell the scent of marijuana. Her high went unrecognized, but not her embarrassment as she waved her hands around explaining. *"As you can see I don't have much here. I'm in a temporary situation."*

Not wanting to bring herself to say Rofiki's name she said, *"I was living with the guy you seen me with at the coffee shop. We lived together before I moved here. Don't worry he doesn't have a key. As you noticed we are not getting along right now. Not only did I allow him to manage my business, but my life."* Still waving her hand around she said, *"This here bull-shit is all I have after years this is my place, 'Fool's Paradise.'*

RUFUS "Fool's Paradise" RUFUS FEATURING CHAKA KHAN

"It's just a fool's paradise, was it very nice?
Fool's paradise, ooh it's just a fool's paradise
Was it very nice?"

After Bluesy put his mobile phone down, STARR picked it up and he didn't object. But he did ask her what she was doing playfully touching her. She giggled because he already downloaded the APP on his phone for JAZZ1CAFÉ and was already logged into the radio station.

Pulling out the earphones and turning up the volume, STARR smiled to the sound of music. Now they were both listening to the internet radio station. Music is just what she needed to help heal the silence. Not wanting to tell Bluesy, she couldn't play the station without wifi, because her service was disconnected. Music was now playing in the background and the glow of the candles set the tones for a romantic evening.

Still calling her place 'Fool's Paradise' he welcomed her hand that was waving around into his hand. Bluesy wanted her to have a peace of mind saying, "*You don't have to explain yourself to me. We all have gone through personal recessions and have lost a lot of personal things. I don't see anything but a stunning woman that will live a good life. You're a special person and very blessed to only have lost things and not self. I'm sure your family is proud of you.*"

Smiling STARR had to believe things were going to get better. She had been through so much in her life and knew that shame was a harmful emotion. Just earlier that day she really had thought about ending it all. Jumping off the Ben Franklin Bridge wasn't her original plan to exit the world. She had taken plenty of pills, only to wake up. Now here she was sitting with a total stranger that had saved her, and now he telling her, he was proud of her.

BONEY JAMES "Dedication" SHINE

Seeing STARR'S head drop and not sure if he had said the right thing. Bluesy said, "*Well, let me be proud of you and your performance tonight and thanks for the dedication.*" Life was feeling very strange. Bluesy slid closer and pulled her into a friendly embrace. Her hair tickled his face. He closed his eyes and inhaled the lemon grass oil in her locks. He opened his eyes and knew that he had entered the danger zone. He vowed not to let another woman tread into his heart. She pulled slowly away and brushed the long locks off her face. He watched her wipe the tears from her eyes.

STARR pulled it together quick squirting hand sanitizer in their hands and enjoying the fresh aroma. The embarrassment made her feel like slowing it down. Stress had her head pounding for the last few weeks. Now it was dissolving with his touch. She moved away afraid she was sending the wrong message.

Opening the bag of food, STARR picked up a deep fried triangle pastry and smelled it. She smirked, *"Well at least it smells better than Ms. Freda's cats."* Bluesy laughed at her and said, *"Take a bite it is called a Samosa. It is pastry dough filled with spicy potatoes and green peas."* STARR bit it and smiled loving the new food.

When she was finished eating the Samosa, Bluesy fed her forks full of the fish tikka as he explained what it was, *"This is mock fish tikka. Tofu marinated in herbs and spices, cooked in tandoori Indian seasonings, accompanied with basmati rice and steamed vegetables."* STARR laughed trying not to let food spill out of her mouth. She managed to say, *"I feel like I am on the food network being feed by one of those exotic chiefs."* He agreed, *"Yes you are being feed by the brown paper bag Chief Bluesy."*

ALISON CROCKET "How Deep is your Love" BARE

How deep is your love? Is his love like a river wondering in and out of his heart? Is his love like a star that lights the way out of the dark? How deep is his love? Bluesy wanted to know. Falling into her beauty watching her eyes light up to the new flavors and enjoying the food. Bluesy reached into his jacket pocket and pulled out a bag of M&M's with peanuts. *"I've already had dinner thanks to you. This is my snack and I'll save you some."* Star couldn't respond with her mouthful, she shook her head up and down.

Watching Bluesy pour the entire bag in his hand and pick out the brown ones and putting them back in the bag. Then he ate one color at a time. She laughed at his silliness. It seemed like forever since STARR ate food that good. She was tired of her problems and didn't want to talk about her asking, *"So, what is your real name?"*

Jokingly, Bluesy guffawed and pulled out his driver's license and showed her. She giggled and said, *"I will stick to calling you Bluesy."* Jokingly he snatched his license back explaining, *"It means 'carried' in Hebrew and the name of one of the twelve minor prophets of the Old Testament, the author of one of the oldest prophetic books.* She joked, *"Go ahead and preach."* He chuckled, *"But I like it when you call me Bluesy."*

JULIE DEXTER "Ketch A Vibe" DEXTOROUS

Running out of ideas looking for inspiration wondering if it appeared STARR needed consultation. She just wanted to feel and ketch a vibe while the feelings were alive, she didn't want to lose it! Letting lyrics flow like deep waters rippling with emotions like an ocean not undermining the feelings, because it's what she believes and love is what she is guilty of.

Yes, STARR found her inspiration and Bluesy had reached the same destination. Feeling the magic of the night, she knew the moment Bluesy left haunting thoughts were waiting to attack her. He reached out and gave her a hug. Feeling his tight embrace made her feel a sense of security. When their eye's met a sense of urgency drove them to kiss.

Obeying the lyrics STARR didn't want to lose it! It was a natural high of seduction moving them slow, yet fast. She was feeling like old rhymes ready to be remixed, *"don't want to lose it."* Bluesy's hands clung around her hips throbbing to feel her flesh, as his hands slid under her shirt feeling her warm inviting flesh. His juicy warm lips sent wild chills to her lips that parted and kissed him feverishly.

The enchanted feeling was like her high - notes, he felt it too. All she could do was breath to his tempo of shuddering moans. It was a natural feeling and his sweet long thickness of warm flesh was hard and on fire pulsating against her thighs. Ketch a vibe while the feelings alive, don't want to lose it! Don't let it pass by.

IMPROP2 "Is it cool?" DEFINITION OF LOVE

It's been a long time since Bluesy had someone to kiss good night. A long time since he had a woman to treat him right, a soul mate to call his own. He wanted STARR to take his hand and understand. In a bass filled voice seductively he asked, *"Is it cool if I said, I want to spend the night?"* He wanted to be with her and keep her warm all through the night. All she had to do is take his hand and he would gladly be her man. STARR slid her hand over the bulge of his warm belly, and lingered.

They looked at each other wordless. Bluesy smirked, STARR grinned. Liking the way his solid belly vibrated when he finally let out a sexy chuckle. He pulled her closer for a soft wet kiss. She shuddered when both his hands simultaneously grabbed both of her nipples. His powerful kisses caused some of her love to come down and moist her panties as they kissed wildly into the next song.

KEM "Love Calls" KEMISTRY

There is nowhere to hide when love calls your name. When they thought they knew all about love it was calling and not far. When love calls your name there is nowhere to hide. Love calls, love is calling their names. Thinking about the way STARR was making him feel. The sweetness of her touch and the softness of her voice. Bluesy thanked her for calling him into her life, her love, into her arms.

The flickering of the candles gave light to her smooth nipples, perked and alert for more attention. He slid her sweater off her body and admiring her full hips, her full curves and her black ass. He slid his hands over the smooth round butt. Her fingers crawled up his shirt unbuttoning three at a time and his pants too.

DAVE MCMURRAY "Love Calls" I KNOW ABOUT LOVE

Love was calling and just as Bluesy was about to make his move and let go of his long thickness throbbing between his legs, he realized he didn't have a condom. STARR broke their embrace and felt his disappointment, because she was disappointed too. He wanted her like a fat boy wanted cake, but just not this way either. She was special and he had to show her, but he wanted her bad. He felt her kisses of hesitation.

URSULA RUCKER "Black Erotica" MA AT MAMA

Embracing bare it began, STARR went slowly with dis' so Bluesy didn't miss this quick glimpse inside her Black Erotica. Knotty dreads cascade over thighs, crying and crying for Jesus. Should she really be calling him in moment of sin? Wait, not yet it was the longest minute in cunnilingus history. Showering each other with wet kisses and tangling in the sheets of multi colored floral patterns.

The foreplay and his tongue tricks felt like a marathon full of pleasures that had her very aroused. The inspirations of their kisses were long and accompanied by tranquil moans. His hand, his lips never left her lips, his hands slid around to her firm round ass and held her tight against his

49

thickness that was pulsating between his legs. He didn't want to inhale without her taste in his breath. Their hearts beat to the bass of the music.

It was a natural high of seduction, she felt the churning in the pit of her stomach, knowing that was her first experience of butterflies. Bluesy couldn't lie, he wanted to make love to her. He had to find control, but it was nowhere to be found pleased with the fullness of her breast and ass.

ZO! "Make Love To Me" SUNSTORM (Featuring MONICA BLAIRE)

Yes, STARR wanted Bluesy to stay and make love to her with intention and purpose. Show her, he knew how to get down-down-down-low down... Not stopping going hard and giving it all they've got. STARR moaned, *"I think I see the stars."*

Sweat and the heat from their passion rippled under Bluesy's skin as the lust of sexual desire flushed through his mumbling, *"Yes, I see them too."* STARR moaned in sync to his breathing. She wanted a taste of this feeling that was soaking her wet. Wanting more of this flavor of passion, the new scent, the new feelings and new taste.

The new feeling of teeth biting her neck for the first time she would discover a passion mark. His tongue circling her earlobes confused her as his will power slipped away. His raw sensuousness carried her to greater heights. Skin to skin they were as one.

Waves of pleasure throbbed through her breathing in deep soul-drenching drafts and her body began to vibrate with liquid fire. Passion pounded the blood through his heart, chest, and head freeing in her a bursting sensation. *"That was beautiful babe."* He seemed to satisfy her in a way she never thought could be. When the lights were off, he fulfilled her fantasies. When the lights were off he completed her. With the lights off she did him so sweetly. He gave her everything when the lights were off and she appreciated his love.

LINA "Morning Star (Interlude)" MORNING STAR

"You amaze me," STARR loudly moaned afterwards. Sunrays were trying to come through the dark sheet covered window. West Philly was up and moving. The sound of garbage trucks and trash men talking loud awoke them. Bluesy wrapped his arms tight around STARR, alerting her

that he was awake. The closeness of his chest against her back felt warm sexual and secure.

Locked in the bathroom Frisky purrs were getting louder. Bluesy's nearness made her senses spin. Nude he whispered, *"I better get going or I will be late for work and that means I would have to fire myself."* Playfully he gathered his clothes, feeling a sudden sadness that their night had ended.

Wrapped in a blanket STARR watched him dress. She eyed his t-shirt on the floor and he tossed it to her. Admiring her shy behaviors, he observed her trying to put it on without dropping the blanket. Once she had the t-shirt on she climbed out the bed and grabbed her long sweater to walk him downstairs. Before she could open the door, Bluesy stopped her and kissed her letting her know she had a friend.

DJ KHAMIN BROWN "Funkopolitan – Full Attention"
DIRECTIONS IN GROOVE VOL. 2 UNTIED FLOW

"If you want it, you got it
If you need it, you got it"

Immediately when, STARR opened the door the funk hit them. Ashamed of the odor from trash and junk the Jenki's hoarded, she tried her best to ignore it wanting to call them, *"The Junkies!"* The first one out the door was Frisky, and as soon as they hit the second floor landing Mr. Jenki opened his door. The fat cat named Gio - short for gigolo, now gracefully just called Big G. Wobbled out the door. He was overweight and too lazy to chase mice. He would rather stretch out and have his belly rubbed and wait for his cans of tuna and chicken wing bones for treats and whatever else the Jenki's would feed him. Ms. Freda bragged that the cat could eat a whole hotdog in under a minute. Big G was not the average cat in many ways.

The average America Curl weight for adult male cats range from 7 to 11 lb. Big G the gigolo weighed 25 lbs. weighing slightly more than the average 2-year-old boy, he waddled down the hall towards Frisky and Midnight the black cat that was sleeping.

NAJEE "Dis N Dat" THE SMOOTH SIDE OF SOUL

'*Dis N Dat*' and swearing that Big G could be in the Guinness Book of world records for biggest cat. Big G might be viewed as special since he was the only cat the Jenki's allowed inside their apartment. Mainly because he was the only cat they had as a kitten. But the moment Ms. Freda left the house Mr. Jenki would put the overweight and loud purring cat right out in the hallway with the rest of the cats.

After a wonderful night, only to be greeted by the hilarious Mr. Jenki. Talking '*Dis N Dat*.' Reminding STARR of both David Mann from 'Meet the Browns' and Lavan Davis A.K.A. Curtis Payne from "House of Payne' television shows. Only Mr. Jenki was louder, imagine that. He stood in his doorway giving Big G a slight boost with his foot, pushing the obese ass cat into the hallway. At the same time Mr. Jenki was eating bacon, his big eyes bulged bigger rambling in his South Carolina accent. "*Well, butter my butt and call me a biscuit. Hey delivery man! Yall's up early! I'm heading to the bank this morning. So if you can pay the rent before I go, I's appreciate it.*"

JAZZANOVA "Another New Day" IN BETWEEN

Self-conscious STARR stopped suddenly and smiled in exasperation. Wishing Mr. Jenki could have waited until, Bluesy was gone before asking for the rent money. She replied, "*Sure Mr. Jenki give me a few minutes.*" Mr. Jenki closed the door chewing and still talking, "*Let the dollar circulate, not perpetrate! Okays, don't pee down my back and tell me it's raining.*" she gave Bluesy a quick look to see if he had the same puzzled expression, and he did. After Mr. Jenki closed the door STARR removed the baby gate that kept the cat Tyson from coming up to fight with the other cats.

Walking down the steps STARR wish she could avoid Tyson a 4 year old mackerel tabby cat that was hissing and waiting at the bottom of the steps. Tyson's distinctive jet black and silver stripes, dots, and swirling patterns formed an 'M' mark on his forehead. The series of fur patterns of vertical stripes on his side resembled the mackerel fish. He was beautiful, but vicious. Named after the boxer Mike Tyson, due to his huskiness and paw boxing abilities that made all the other cats stay away, he was the bully. His back was arched and ready to attack anyone coming or going.

J. SPENCER "Till I Found you" CHIMERA

Stepping around the angry cat that Bluesy remembered from the night before and avoided the litter box that had been turned over, STARR opened the front. Just as she did, Mr. Jenki could be heard yelling, *"And don't let Tyson the hell out!"* Feeling her humiliation Bluesy replied in a low voice, *"Goodbye."* He reached out to kiss her, she paused rejecting the kiss, but hugged him hard. She shut the door still smelling the faint citrus scent of his cologne on the t-shirt.

TRACK 3: CO-STARRING

ZAP MAMA "RAFIKI" ZAP MAMA
(Featuring THE ROOTS)

"Nilipata Rofiki! Na penda Rofiki! Na bakie..." Singing along smiling at his self-proclaimed theme song. While rolling down the highway in his 525i BMW on 20 inch rims and trying not to be noticeable with dark tinted windows. The FM / AM radio stations never played the shit he wanted to hear, plus it was out of range. He

Cellphone on charger and LIVE365 mobile APP launched, Rofiki was tuned into JAZZ1CAFE internet radio and digging it. Shaking his dreads free from the Philadelphia drama, heading to the new, New York drama. Rofiki didn't give a mutha-fugh, he was feeling good and safe with the registration and identification of his friend Jamal. They looked alike but one had dreads, the other a nappy head locked up. As long as Rofiki sent his homeboy money, he used Jamal's information to get him out of jams. Plus if he was stopped he knew what to do, he pull out an asthma inhaler pump and faked the funk.

"Sit down here and tell me a story
When you're with friends no need to hurry
No more rush - No more haste -No more"

Now on cruise control 65mph down the Pennsylvania Turn Pike to the New Jersey Turnpike heading to Lincoln Tunnel Straight into New York City. After the toll booths he pulled out a blunt wrapper filled with green mixture of dried shredded flowers, leaves of the hemp plant Cannabis sativa. Lighting the blunt and puffing while turning up the Afropean vocals of one of his favorite songs enjoying his Bose speakers, Rofiki choked out puffs of smoke, *"Meh no more!"*

Without a doubt Rofiki's blood type is THC at the highest levels. Puffing on a phat blunt rolled with 'Sour Diesel' lime green Cannabis he was now famous for always having. In fact he was so exclusive with his shit that he no longer fughed with regular marijuana. No more petty hustling nicks and dime bags in North Philly. New York was big time and bigger money. Having the connections that would last him a life time if he played his cards right.

MESHELL N'DEGEOCELLO "Forget My Name" COMET, COME TO ME

"*Blood-clot,*' the words of STARR echoed. Rofiki was thinking, she could forget his name if she loved him. That was one name he never forgives. One thing Rofiki knew for sure was that names held power. Kingston his father's name still held power in the boroughs of New York. Giving Rofiki access to many of the best suppliers of 'Green Crack.' Grade A+ Top Shelf and LOUD smelling Sour Diesel, Grand Daddy Purple, Lemon drop, Purple Kush.

No more nicks or dimes, he was big time selling Kush for hundreds by the ounce and now making bigger moves selling by the pound. A pocket full of money and feeling just fine banking on new business deals that would have Vicious Heat Records writing him checks too big to cash. Thankfully Big Tank was a cash flowing man always paying in cash to avoid the tax man.

Nothing problematic for Rofiki, cruising down the highway rubbing his full belly of red snapper, rice and peas, cabbage and plantain. Sipping on ginger-beer, he felt a ting of remorse for not taking STARR out to dinner. But he left her money to take care of that problem. Inhaling long draws of smoke into his lungs and feeling the music playing as he sang along, "*Here we are - Here we are. Yeah! This one right here is for the people.*"

NAS & DAMIAN MARLEY "Patience" DISTANT RELATIVES

Puffing and puffing and rapping to the music, "*Some of the smartest dummies can't read the language of Egyptian mummies. An' a fly go a moon and can't find food for the starving tummies. Pay no mind to the youth's 'cause it's not like the future depends on it. But save the animals in the zoo. Cause the chimpanzee dem a make big money.*"

Puffing clouds of smoke on cruise control Rofiki blew out the window as he drove from Philadelphia to New York bobbing his head to the music. He knew he should have stayed at least one night in Philly with STARR to be sure t'ings were okay. But from the looks of her in the coffee shop, she looked like she could hang in there a few more days without him. Plus she wanted her own life and he was teaching her a lesson.

Needing time and more time to do ROFIKI, so he could get his shit together. He didn't forget about his seed that was growing healthy in her belly. Judging by the looks, she still wasn't showing. He figured he had time to get back to Philly and make t'ings right. But he was on the green mission of fully getting paid. Talented indeed Rofiki thought STARR was but missing that aggressiveness to step out and do whatever it took to be international. Kandi Gyal on the other hand was going to get him where he needed to be.

ZIGGY MARLEY "True To Myself" DRAGONFLY

"Life has come a long way since yesterday, I say. And it's not the same old thing over again, I say." Nodding his head and singing along to the music, Rofiki drummed his fingers on the steering wheel. *"Got to be true to myself - Got to be true to myself."* It was time for a new flavor of Puerto Rican – African American swirl. Thinking of Kandi always made his dick hard, along with thinking about how much money he was going to make managing her. Thoughts of Kandi's 36 DD's and tongue tricks caused him to put his hand on his dick and laugh out loud. Smiling and still puffing and hungry for her blood like a vampire awaiting the night to fall, he was heading back to New York to attack.

Puff... Puff... Turning the music up and nodding his head and listing to the lyrics. Life was feeling crazy running around STARR and Haile the two women that where a part of his Philly world. In his New York world he was getting what he needed a new Gyal. He was falling in deep, feeling something like love. The new Gyal was so fine any man would drink her bath water and she was worth the gamble.

SIZZLA "Smoke Marijuana" THE OVERSTANDING

Yea (herbalist) smoke all day. Let music keep on play. Sometimes the t'ings Rofiki need in life may be difficult. Not all the time it's gonna be easy. A so it go, *"Smoke the marijuana and get high. Stay above the wicked and fly. He's feeling so very good about himself..."*

Getting high, Rofiki puffed and puffed all the way. The 2 hour drive from Philadelphia back to New York he suppressed, regressed and puffed until his cellphone displayed a text message from the infamous Ms. Kandice Perez A.K.A Kandi Gyal. She was dominant and he had to admit it turned him on sometimes, but he had to get a tighter grip and put Kandi Gyal in check and down with 'Rofiki 101.'

ALICIA KEYS "101" GIRL ON FIRE

The sound of a heart breaking don't faze Rofiki anymore the king of the game that he's playing, he played it a hundred times before. But then there is Kandi Gyal and there is no use in pretending, Oh Kandi Gyal will be 101.

KANDI GYAL: *"Don't be late!"*
ROFIKI: *"Yo mon, Rofiki 101- Patience!"*

Circling the block a few times looking for a parking spot. Rofiki smiled knowing he had Kandi wrapped around his fingers and awaiting his return to New York, along with the signed papers from STARR in his pocket. Feeling like he was on top of the world and in charge. While thinking he should have maybe given STARR a little more money, at least enough to turn her phone on. He knew his own guilt was making him a mean mutha - fugha towards her.

FREEWAY "Flipside" PHIALDELPHIA FREEWAY
(Featuring PEEDI CRAKK)

Rofiki got the hood on smash! Trying to get to his 'Flipside,' but still thinking of STARR and irritated by her lack of knowledge, her naïve ways and how, he could tell her dumb-ass anything and get away with it. He needed more of a challenge. But then thinking of how STARR would have been blowing his phone up calling none stop, he was cool with her phone off. He felt it was time she became a big gyal and stopped waiting for him to make all the moves. Then he thought of the baby and knew he should have at least turned her phone on. *"Na she be al'ight,"* he mumbled.

REEL PEOPLE "Can't Stop" SECOND GUESS

"Can't stop the way he feel..." Circling the block again, Rofiki reminisced about the night Kandice walked up on him @ JAZZ1CAFÉ re-introducing herself. The shit was crazy, because STARR was right there. It was like a blessing dropping out the sky giving him a chance for that change he wanted in life. That was a few months ago, also the night STARR won the radio contest and performed at JAZZ1CAFÉ.

After finding a parking spot and walking toward yet another coffee shop. Rofiki was checking out his surroundings as usual, eyeing a gyal walking towards him that reminded him of STARR. It was haunting. They had the same coffee brown skin, slim face and full crimson lips, and the same long length of locks. But she didn't have STARR'S walk and he would bet she couldn't sing like STARR. He fought back the flash backs of his afternoon meeting with STARR and all the demons in his mind. Trying to stay focused on Kandi Gyal and remembering to stay true to the mission(s) of 'Rofiki 101.'

RAHEEM DEVAUGHN "Love Drug" LOVE BEHIND THE MELODY

Kandi Gyal got Rofiki hooked, he got her sprung. Now add that up and she's his love drug. She's what he need and he's her pusher man. Like a 'Love Drug' costing Rofiki 2 cups x $7 coffee, money he didn't plan on spending on coffee. Kandi Gyal was late. He had to pump the breaks on Kandi's upscale coffee cafes, restaurants, bottles of Moet, Boutique shopping. He reached in his pockets clinching a few $100 bills mumbling, *"Meh at me limits."*

Close to sealing the deal with Vicious Heat Records. That is when Kandi Gyal would be putting the money right back in his pockets. She was a good advisement and she had the image VHRecords wanted, but STARR had the vocals and songs VHRecords wanted to hear.

Reasoning with himself, Rofiki looked at Kandi Gyal an asset especially after confirming that she recorded her demo in an accredited studio and her X - manager was her X- boyfriend's cousin (or some shit like that). Rofiki cleared all that up by showing up with her at VHR as her new manager.

Now waiting on his investment and scrolling through the cellphone, he watched taxis drive bye. He was in the middle of texting Kandi Gyal when noticing the black suede high heels stepping out of a taxi. His heart did a leap between beats and his dick did a twitch watching, his new money walking in the doors. Feeling like a lucky man that won all 5' 10" of the lean flesh that was prancing towards him.

KELIS "Ah Shit" KELIS WAS HERE

"Hicky-Hicky-Hicky - Aww shit!
I can make a whole song talk shit!"

Ah shit, Kandice Perez came frolicking in the doors with a hip-hop Bossa nova, samba and jazzy bounce. Looking fierce Kandi Gyal brushed her long wavy Spanish black hair from around her face and putting the black 'Jimmy Choo' sunglasses on top of her head. Rofiki and everyone else in the dimly lit coffee shop watched, her big ass hips bounce inside the doors and towards him.

TREMENDO "Intro" VIDALOGIA

A New York fashionista Kandi was always ready for the camera and new fans. Counting every footstep Rofiki watched as she entered the coffee shop like she was walking the runway. Cavorting to her own sexy bubbly beat.

1 – 2 – Kandi Gyal was stepping in designer Christian Louboutin's Daffodil 160 black suede pumps with *a feminine* red bottom.

3 - 4 - Rofiki's eye's traveled up her firm attractive legs wearing sexy black fishnet stockings. Not missing a beat he watched as she began to seductively unbutton the Maximilian mink chocolate cardigan exposing her sheer ivory lace low cut shirt, Sandro Phenix Anthracite leather black ass squeezing mini skirt.

5 – 6 – large platinum and diamond hoop earrings and matching bracelets 7 – hot pink painted fingernails – 8 - Louis Vuitton bag securely tucked under her arm – 9 bouncing 36 DD perky tits with no bra, and cleavage was in his face.

SUNLIGHTSQUARE *"As The Beat Goes On"* URBAN LATIN SOUL

10 - Of course Rofiki stood up to greet and grab that solid big ass that the last boyfriend brought and received an embracing kiss. *"As the beat goes on,"* Kandice is moving on and looking like a glamour- shopaholic, Kandi Gyal swayed her newly salon styled hair from side to side with arms full of shopping bags. Her long newly extended lengths of hair weave was longer then superstar Cher's hair. Her face was painted in bronzing blush and gold glittery eye shadow.

The scent of an expensive exotic perfume trailed and was now right under Rofiki's nose when he greeted Kandi Gyal with a kiss saying, *"Siéntese."* She sat down in the booth next to him as instructed. He liked feeling bilingual speaking the little bit of Spanish he learned from the Dominicans at the corner stores of North Philly, actually Kandi Gyal rarely spoke Spanish, so he liked to test her too. He knew all eyes were on her. Because she looked, acted and walked like she was the shit!

MINT CONDITION *"Bossalude"* 7...

Like a sweet treat Kandi Gyal reminded him of banana pudding. He once thought of STARR as an entrée. Now looking at Kandi, he knew that every man looked forward to dessert. He knew his gear was too casual to be sitting across from her, who was in every word a fly girl living in a material world. *"New York, New York big city of dreams,"* She was singing ready to party, he was ready for bed. But, he came back to step up his game and now Kandi Gyal was sitting right across from him. Her invitations of lust were hard to resist.

Cocky, Rofiki knew he wasn't a typical dude. Aware of his uniqueness and his original Rasta- swagger was enticing. Charming Kandi Gyal with a big smile and nice warm wet kiss, he used a napkin to wipe off the sparkling pink lipstick left on his lips from the kiss.

Pushing her body close enough to Rofiki to feel his hard on. He sat smiling feeling like a winner chicken, even though he didn't eat meat. He was thinking that it is always about the dick with these kinds of Gyals. His conceited thoughts were interrupted. *"What time does Big Tank's party start? I don't want to be late."* He smirked wanting to tell her to shut da fugh up because he was not in the mood for all the questions.

Putting down her bags for love, Kandi Gyal knew what Rofiki was thinking. She's on his mind and she's right, she's right, He's right. He's running so fast, he just might take flight, Hope he's not tired, tonight, tonight! No need for telepathy, he knew what Kandi Gyal was thinking, sex was on her mind and he was right, right, right. The waitress appeared grinning at Rofiki offering to pour him another cup of coffee and he suggested a cup for Kandi. She exploded, *"No Coffee!"*

COMMON *"Come Close"* ELECTRIC CIRCUS
(Featuring MARY J. BLIGE)

It's just like a fly love song, what? Are they living in a dream world? Are her eyes still green gyal? He knew she was sick and tired of arguing, but she can't keep it bottled in. Jealousy, she got to swallow it. He was going to do the best he could, because he is the best when with her. *"Come close to me babe' let ya luv hold me. Me, know dis' world is cra-z-z-zy. Wad' dis' without ya?"*

Instantly, Rofiki had flashbacks of his afternoon with STARR. Before he could respond Kandi screeched, *"Are you crazy? I don't want coffee stains on my teeth?"* He responded, *"Da coffee drinkers like me brush dey teeth."* She waved his response away as she picked up a menu complaining about being hungry, but needing to watch her waistline. She showed her pearly white veneers pretending she wasn't pissed off that he went to Philadelphia without her. But, she couldn't help but ask, *"So what was so important in Philly that I couldn't go with you?"* He heard the sarcasm but was too tired to check her.

After spending 10 minutes extolling how wonderful and sexy Rofiki was Kandi popped the question *"Are you seeing someone else?"* He hated these kind of chick questions. She knew the answer, since he explained 'Rofiki 101' over the last several weeks. He still knew he had to handle this potentially delicate situation and avoid a scene in the restaurant and since they were in a public place, he wanted to avoid any public humiliating scenes. *"Yo mon wad wid ya now chill out – me here. Cool professional relationship in public. Better for business, just keep it good company and enjoy the life."* She slid slightly away as if feeling a ping of rejection.

Then Kandi Gyal went on to say how she didn't care if he was broke or ugly - blah - blah - blah, but if he was seeing another woman, she would just walk away. He sipped his coffee listening to her bull-shit because she ain't never deal with a broke mutha - fuka. He pulled her closer to assure her that she wasn't going anywhere, plus other men were checking her out.

DWELE *"Wants"* W.ANTS W.ORLD W.OMEN (W.W.W.)

Wants, everybody have an alter ego, Rofiki wished he actually had Gucci sneaks to go with the Gucci bags. Yeah, he was a Rastaman but he can want it, right? Truly, he can rock diamonds if he wants to and Kandi Gyal can get naked if she wants to because it was what wants. Wanting her to be caught up, he wanted her on him. The first W- is for W.ant her to be on it, W.ant her to be horny.

Now, Rofiki wasn't thinking about STARR, who was always his main punaani until he got twisted up in Kandi Gyal's world and as far as other woman they have always been just for sport. He was a real *'gyalis'*, a real player. Skilled at seducing women, normally by tricking them into thinking they are the love of his life, when in reality, only sexual favors are desired. He managed relationships with multiple women, normally with each woman being oblivious of the other women in his life. However, Kandi Gyal seemed worthy of being his main *"pum – pum tun up,"* good pussy.

Talking about threats of walk away if he cheated, she had to believe that she had some leverage, something that he couldn't get from another gyal. She was her own proof that he could pull bitches, she came to him. But he also knew he was dealing with an extra big inflated ego, larger than his. Rofiki figured if he continued to fugh Kandi good and often, and throw her a couple of dollars, she would tolerate anything. Gyals can't help themselves as their brains want attention and approval by being freaked. Rofiki 101 was in full effect and she would do as he say, not as she want and class was in session.

STEVE SPACEK *"Dollar"* DILLANTHOLOGY 1

"Let your dollar circulate – Let yours circulate..." Fronting, Rofiki dropped enough names in the music business and introduced her to a few people,

and that had her wide open and feeling the fame. He boosted about knowing Biggie Smalls before Puffy. He still had cassette tapes of Jay Z's from back in '96. When bragging he would compare Kandi to the beauties of Beyoncé Giselle Knowles-Carter and the gorgeous and ass bigger than Jennifer Lopez and the seductiveness of a porn star and her curves and swerve could be compared to rapper / actor Ice T's wife Coco, and just like them Kandi Gyal would be a superstar!

At first glance people questioned her ethnicity, but when she opens her mouth and all the slang and rawness rolls off her tongue letting people know her mother was Puerto Rican and her father was African American, but died when she was a toddler.

AMY WINEHOUSE "Just Friends" BACK TO BLACK

When will we get the time to be just friends? It's never safe for us not even in the evening, Yes, â€~Cos Kandi Gyal has been drinking. When will they get the time to be just friends? From the start Rofiki stressed, he just wanted to lay low and chill and keep it friendly. Now, Kandi Gyal was begging him to move in. He knew that he was treating her different than STARR, well because she was different. She had a Rasta jumping through hoops trying to keep up with her and the lifestyle.

Investigating, Rofiki did his homework and learned Kandice Perez sucked off more pro ball players than video vixen 'Super Head' Karrine Steffans, who is now a famous author of the controversial book that tells it all including names of her victims. He knew Kandi's 1st recording sessions had been paid for by a New York NBA player. He also knew that Kandi was no longer dealing with him after, his wife found out, and he was traded to the 76-Sixers. He also knew that Kandi's apartment had been leased by an ex-boyfriend, who is an NFL player sitting the bench for the Giants.

BREAK REFORM "And I" REFOMATION

Rumor is Mr. NFL got her the apartment because Kandi was pregnant. She was so excited and bragged about it to everyone. She had a miscarriage and that blew the child support, she was already counting and he dumped her. Leaving Kandi with a high rent to pay or move out. Rofiki knew the deal and knew time was ticking because the rent was due. That was why she was trying to roll him up into her spot. He had been chilling with her for the past few weeks, but he wasn't trying to make any permitted moves. She did give him a key before he left for Philly, but he gave it back being cocky. He didn't want to be in any trap, but he could get the key back.

The cool and the hustle of this rude boy knew this diva never had a man with rude boy swaggerific and stylish. Full of Rasta influences and Jamaican folk tales remixed and Americanized with a hip hop sex appeal. Rofiki also knew Kandi was the kind of gyal that needed a man always there. All women were like this he assumed. But Kandi was also a new breed for him too. She was over the top and needed to be the center always purring, *"I'm in love with you."*

THE AVILA BROTHERS "Mix It" THE MOOD: SOUNDSATIONAL

Mix it or remix it. One thing for sure like the lyrics of RUN DMC, "She talked too much and she never shut up." Rofiki didn't bother to answer Kandi Gyal's questions, because she didn't wait for an answer before asking another question. He was tired and really needed to get some sleep. Kandi's salad came to the table and he was glad hoping she would eat and be quiet, so he could think. Reminding Kandi Gyal every time she tried to order a bottle of Moet champagne about her calorie count and to cut expense of feeding her, Rofiki put her on a strict diet of salads and lemon water. She objected until he reminded that videos will make her beautiful body look 20lbs heavier. Next he would have to find ways to cut her shopping habits. He almost wanted to tell her to find another pro-ball player boyfriend to finance them.

SUNLIGHTSQUARE "Faya" URBAN LATIN SOUL

"Faya" Can't help the way he feel the new gyal on the scene was *"Faya!"* Kandi Gyal wasn't a woman of simplicity like STARR. Rofiki knew that he would have to spend lots of cheddar to keep *"Faya"* Kandi's nose wide open. Watching her eat the salad in a posed straight prissy position, shoulders thrown back napkin spread across her thick lap.

Hair down her back and bangs swept to the side, Kandi Gyal crossed her legs giving her hips a twist. He didn't missing anything she did as he also made observations around the place. He paid attention to everything, even the minor details as he noticed everyone noticing them a good looking couple. He tied his wild locks back and eyeing the two bulky brawny dudes at the bar. He could tell she didn't know these dudes, but they were eyeing them.

Keeping on his sunglasses on to hide his beet red eyes observing and listening to Kandi Gyal all excited about Big Tanks birthday bash. Kandi kept her elbows off the table and dabbed her mouth after each bite, and it was starting to fugh wid his nerves. The socialite, booshy, snobbery acting princess was bothering him. He knew he was just tripping and needed some sleep and more weed. But he had to play the games and escort her to the party and deliver her as promised to make the business deal go down.

When Rofiki asked Big Tank what he wanted for his birthday, Big Tank replied, *"Kandi Gyal!"* Rofiki knew he wasn't kidding and knew he wasn't there to battle no man over pussy. But he didn't think Big Tank had the swagger to keep Kandi satisfied, but he did have more cheddar, he had millions.

LES NUBIANS "War In Babylone" ECHOS (Featuring QUEEN GODIS)

"War in Babylone..." Now eyeing the two dudes standing at the bar looking back at Rofiki. The tallest was big and black as ever wearing a black Kangol hat and Cazal glasses, black leather jacket looking like a hip-hop thug. What made Rofiki suspicious was the dude kept his hands in his pockets, like he was holding on to something.

The other big dude was Hispanic and wearing a black Adidas jogging suit (he could tell by the 3 white lines that ran down the sides of the pants), white Adidas sneaks and also a black leather jacket. Rofiki watched him light a cigarette and the other dude complained. Rofiki played this game where he would match people up to famous people.

Comparing the looks of these dudes to rappers Biggie Smalls and Big Pun, 2 intimidating looking nigga's. Watching them joke around, he wondered if these blood- clots were checking him or the black rose tattoos on Kandi's thigh. He was tired of the show and ready to go.

KYMANI MARLEY *"Fell In Love"* THE JOURNEY

Kandi Gyal fell in love with a Rastaman and when Rofiki is gone, she sits alone trying to understand. Telling herself this could not be. But now she found herself in love with Rofiki. She promised herself in life, she would never fall in love with his type, because she heard they were nothing but vagabonds in peace. She said she would never stoop to his level it would be like dancing with the devil. She fell in love with a Rastaman and when Rofiki is gone, she sits alone trying to understand.

After Kandi Gyal played in her food twirling the fork in the salad like it was pasta, she went to the bathroom before leaving. Rofiki chilled in the seat trying to get his head together, trying to figure out his next move. Sucking in all the caffeine he could. The two big dudes were now paying their tabs and leaving. The waiter walked them to the door holding it open waving good-bye. Now was the time for him to make a move. He had to wait for Kandi Gyal to come out the ladies room.

SLAKAH THE BEATCHILD *"Ain't Nothing Like Hip Hop"* SOUL MOVEMENT VOL. 1

Waiting outside the 'Ladies Room' Rofiki noticed the two dudes reentering. Like they were in a rush walking straight towards the directions he had been sitting. Unnoticed he hurried into the one stall men's room. He locked the bathroom door in full panic trying to figure shit out. He knew these dudes looked suspicious and he should have left out the side door. But that meant leaving Kandi behind and he was no punk.

Double checking his leather jacket pockets the 'Black Book' was missing. He was now tripping he had it in his jacket when he was in Philly. His brain raced for a plan that would get him out safely. He listened for any commotions going on, but everything sound normal. Sweat forming on his brows for 5 minutes. Ear against the door listening to normalcy felt like an hour standing still and waiting to be attacked. He knew this is why he couldn't join the military, though being on defense was his strong point.

SUNLIGHTSQUARE "Gengere" URBAN LATIN SOUL

Battling the war within and opening the bathroom door slow expecting someone to be waiting for him on the other side. Rofiki peeked around the corner expecting them to be holding Kandi hostage. But she was standing there talking to the skinny waiter cleaning off the table. In a panic he was at the table going crazy looking for the 'Black Book.' *"Yo mon ya see meh black book?"* Nonchalantly Kandi was still chatting about reality televisions shows with the waiter. His heart jumped out of his chest confused.

Paranoid Rofiki snatched Kandi up ready to go search his car. Outside the coffee café he made sure the big dudes were not in sight. This didn't feel right so he questioned, *"Ya see dem dudes from earlier come back in?"* With a puzzled looked Kandi questioned, *"What dudes?"*

XANTONÉ BLACQ "Samba De Lagos" THE HEAVENS AND BEYOND

It was almost midnight when they stopped by Kandi's loft apartment so he could drop off more of his shit and they could change their clothes, though he pretty much decided to only change into another white shirt and throw on his Gucci Loafers. He put his bags in the closet observing to make sure the pounds of cannabis was still sitting in the position he left it in earlier that day. Everything was cool so he put his stuff away being sure it would be easy to grab in case, he needed to break out. But, now the only escaping he was interested in was laying his head on a soft pillow than a party. But they weren't going to just any party. They were going to the 40th birthday bash at a private pent house for Hip Hop and R & B's biggest music producers Big Tank.

KELIS "Circus" KELIS WAS HERE

"Come join our circus where we all wear masks
Lie to our fans and expect it to last
Could it be that the trick is on us?
Masquerading like we are the ones"

Can you blame Kandi Gyal? Of course it always starts out as fun. She played in Rofiki's long beautiful dreadlocks, knowing this game their playing must be won – sorry. Rofiki enjoying the attention and all along thinking of the 'Circus' he had to go through to get checks – cheddar – dough – green – cash - died presidents in his pockets. There was no real money yet, but a lot of fringe benefits like the party awaited them. Unsurprisingly Kandi asked, *"Do you want to take a nap before heading out?"*

FUNKILINIUM *"Like I Never Left You"* FUNKILINIUM

Stepped into Kandi Gyal's head again and she will find Rofiki in her bed again. He knew he'd been up and down her so many times like he never left her. 'Cause gyal he got cha, girl he gotcha, bitch he gotcha! Grinning like a Cheshire cat, Rofiki was ready to go to his own 'Wonder-Land' knowing this was the cue to fuck Kandy Gyal. He tried to smash her out the night before, but she was a white liver, a nymphomaniac He kept a close eye on her and studying her every move, creating new paths for her to follow. He calculated her routine and introduced her to his. He had no strength to fugh her and then go to the party. He needed his head straight for business. Rolling up blunts for the party, he bragged about being a young buck and smoking bud with Tupac Shakur.

Pleased and feeling like he made the right choice. He never told Kandi he was coming to live, but he knew he could do what he wanted. As long as he had her thinking she was the *"Bomb Diggity!"* And he knew that sex and money was the only thing that made this kind of woman feel secure, because being alone is not an option. She was a woman that always had a man some way or another in her life. She still had men calling, but he already started shutting that shit down. He was slowly wrapping her around his fingers. Kandi was a booty shaker that would shake and sell millions of records.

RADIO CITIZENS *"The Night Part 1"* BERLIN SERENGETI

It was a big gamble to take with Kandi and Rofiki was glad that it looked like it was paying off. He would take care of STARR later. Handling Kandi Gyal was actually a challenge he was enjoying. With STARR'S talents he knew, he would always be able to eat, but he needed more than food. He wanted the house, the car and the bank account that allowed him vacations to Jamaica. He was tired of day dreaming about his mothers' stories of the tranquil blue waters. He wanted to see them with his own eyes. Kick his feet in white sands and puff on a big spliff. VHRecords were putting out artist that stayed on the charts. Rofiki's was gambling and playing 21 Black Jack and dealt 2 aces, and without a doubt he was splitting them. STARR was an Ace and Kandi was the other Ace, just waiting to hit 21 Black Jack with both.

NOTORIOUS B.I.G. "Party and Bullshit" NOTORIOUS SOUNDTRACK

"And Party and Bullshit and Party and Bullshit
And Party and Bullshit and Party and Bullshit
And Party and Bullshit and Party and Bullshit!"

BIG TANKS 40th BIRTHDAY BASH was a private penthouse party in upper Manhattan. It was like something out of the movies. The doormen stood aside while security had a list and asked for names to all the familiar and unfamiliar faces. That was just to get in the first door of the building.

BEYONCÉ "Freakum Dress"

"Hold up, bring the beat back
Stop! I ain't ready yet
Wait! Let me fix my hair, yes, yes"

Nervous and observing her appearance in the mirrors she passed, Kandi Gyal conceited mind approved singing along, *"Yes ma'am, yes ma'am my dress past the test, yes!* All eyes were on her as they entered the first floor and had to have their pictures taken for security reasons to combat or gain justice for any problems that may occur while visiting. Once their pictures were taken they were directed into an elevator that took them up into the penthouse known as #1.

The elevator opened into the foyer area that was rather large with walls full of gold records and plaques. There were two floors that you can venture around in for a change of scenery and music. Rofiki heard that the penthouse was on sale for a few million$ since Big Tank and Lil' Pam were getting married and moving together. Rofiki had to admit the place was tight, just mind blowing.

Recognizing a cool young Indian dude name Rahjee Shabazz, he is Big Tanks assistant. Rofiki's new and best customer of course he was now Big Tank's supplier too. Shabazz was waving them towards him eyeing Kandi's big round juicy ass squeezed tight in a metallic gold Beyoncé freakum dress that was shorter than a tennis dress. Only she didn't wear bloomers underneath, ready to shake her thong, thong, thong, thong.

BUBBA SPARXX "Ms. New Booty" THE CHARM
(Featuring YING YANG TWINS)

*"Booty, booty, booty, booty, rockin' everywhere
Rockin' everywhere, rockin' everywhere"*

The party was in full swing with hands in the air and booty shaking. Rofiki found Ms. New Booty, Kandi Gyal better ge*t it together and bring it back to him.* Rofiki asked Shabazz about the birthday man of the hour. Shabazz informed them that Big Tank was upstairs and would make his appearance soon. Rofiki looked at his watch and noticed it was way after 2AM.

Observing the party in full swing it didn't look like anyone was missing the birthday boy. Recognizing many of the video vixens in attendance. Rofiki's head was spinning admiring the 'A-List' of beautiful woman that got an invitation just for being fine. Everyone in the place was dressed to the nines, there literally was no limit to how dressed up you could get. Now Rofiki was glad he wore a pair of slacks and not jeans. Shit he should have got dressed to the max.

USHER "She Came To give It To You" SHE CAME TO GIVE IT TO YOU
(Featuring NICKI MINAJ & PHARELL WILLAMS)

"If you knew what I knew, she'll be yours tonight"

Folks already knew not to wear anything sagging, no sportswear and no cameras or any phones. For women it appeared that the code was to wear as little as possible. Rofiki tried to capture with his photogenic memory. This was just what he wanted and he knew with Kandi Gyal, he could get it, if he got this close.

RHIANNA *"Birthday Cake"* TALK THAT TALK

*It's not even my birthday
But he want to lick the icing off
I know you want it in the worst way
Can't wait to blow my candles out"*

All up in the mix with some of the most prestigious people in the music business Rofiki was admiring it. Eying Kandi Gyal prancing around in Dolce & Gabbana pumps and globs of makeup! Kandi looked skanky sexy. He let her do her thing if it was going to make him rich. He wanted that cake, cake, cake, cake, cake, cake, cake...

Meeting producers had Rofiki hype and remembering strolling into the VHR meeting with Kandi Gyal on his arms, introducing her as one of his artist. Though Kandi Gyal could sing, still she wasn't as lyrically skilled as STARR'S voice. What Rofiki found out later was that the producer Big Tank had privately monitored the meeting.

A day later Rofiki received a call from the millionaire C.E.O. of Vicious Heat Records 'Big Tank' inviting them to the party and joking about Kandi Gyal being his birthday present. Rofiki knew he wasn't joking even though Big Tank was engaged to one of Hip Hop's sexiest female rappers Lil' Pam.

BLACK STAR "K.O.S. (Determination)"
MOS DEF and TALIB KWELI are BLACK STAR
(Featuring VINIA MOJICA)

"Determination is knowledge itself..." The things Rofiki say and do may not come clear through, he's words may not convey what he's feeling. In post 9/11 New York City was still mourning, but you couldn't tell on this night. Smiles were brightened white and veneers were glowing. Rofiki knew those smiles cost over $20,000.00 because he priced it out for STARR. He was happy that Kandi had already had some sucker before him to buy her Anna Nicole smile.

Cling – Cling could be heard as champagne glasses rung with Moet and greetings. The old school hip – hop artists among the new school rap artists, and R&B singers intermingled with video vixens amongst the crowd. Waving his hands in the air and rapping along knowing every lyric and feeling like he was in the right place to network and find out who was who.

VISIONEERS "Apache (Battle Dub)" HIPOLOGY

Hype to be among the elite party guest, Rofiki's spirits ran high when he recognized all the celebrities, music artist, rapper, DJ's and music he was raised on with RUN DMC and R.I.P. Jam Master Jay Grand Master Flash and the furious five, Sugar Hill Gang. The bass rattled the speakers as the DJ on turn tables 1 and 2 played music that commenced folks to dance and bob their head. Everyone was feeling the mix of classic old school hip – hop blended with the new. Rofiki walked around nodding his head at the old heads up in the party, feeling like a young buck, but cool feeling music.

Trying to handle the many request for cannabis smuggled inside, Rofiki slapped Kandi Gyal on the ass and saying, *"Mingle and jingle. Go meet nu friend's meh B –back."* She was glad he was no longer breathing in her face and took the opportunity to mingle. Just as she stepped away Shabazz, Big Tank's assistant appeared telling Kandi Gyal, Big Tank wanted to talk to her privately. Without Rofiki, she was escorted into a private office. Shabazz opened the door and practically pushed her inside the darkened room, closing the door behind.

JSOUL "Frequency (Remix)" BLACK SINATRA

A body hotter than the sun, trust Big Tank, he know just what Kandi Gyal needs. He was impeccably dressed to kill influences were primarily influenced by the 1983 remake version of the movie 'SCARFACE' that became popular in Hip - Hop. Gang-inspired wardrobe was in favor of classic gangster fashions such as bowler hats, double-breasted suits, silk shirts, and (gators) alligator-skin shoes.

JAY-Z & KANYE WEST "Nig*as In Paris" WATCH THE THRONE

It was his birthday and selfishly Big Tank was thinking he should have stayed in Paris. He needed to get his mind right, and off the shit that had him stressing. Watching his throne, New York City which he thought he owned. There was enough money in his bank account to open his own bank, Big Tanks Bank. He was thinking about it. He thought he could buy whatever, well he can.

"I ball so hard mutha-fugha's wanna fine me
But first nig*as gotta find me"

A *'Baller'* the shots caller, Big Tank was at the top of his game and fully established in numerous social circles, his status in society has earned him his possession of 'Stardom.' He was living large with girls, money and always looking for a new honey, though he was engaged to the Queen B.

What's 50 grand to a mutha-fugha like me,
Can you please remind me?"

Always in tailor-made attire, sharp as a needle Big Tank's fashions was set off with a stunning pair of eggplant deep purple Louis Vuitton sunglasses. Positioned front and center of a 30 foot, floor to ceiling windows overlooking the Hudson River with his massive back towards Kandi Gyal when she entered the room. Prior to summoning for Kandi Gyal, Big Tank had been watching the party guest on his home security monitors in his office.

TANK *"Dance With Me"* STRONGER

"I'm all into you
I'm try 'na find my way
The right things to do
The right things to say"

Watching Kandi Gyal's every move, watching her hips sway and jiggle, between star gazing out the windows. Big Tank danced up behind her and getting a good grind, as they still could hear the music and bass pumping, though he turned the monitors off just before Kandi entered the room, but was still recording his party that was awaiting his début. He had been drinking champagne – alone - waiting for Lil' Pam who called to inform that she wouldn't be attending due to their fighting.

Tensed, Kandi Gyal entered the room with Rofiki's words echoing to keep it strictly business. Meeting Big Tank personally was the moment she had been waiting for since she walked into the party. A little nervous Kandi entered the room and there was no need for introductions.

Anxiously Kandi Girl greeted the honey brown large frame of about 300 lbs. or more, standing about 6'9 with a silky smooth bald head shinning, and full jet black 'Grizzly Adams' beard. He wasn't what Kandi would call fat, but he had a nice round pillow in the middle area. *"Happy Birthday Big Tank!"* Big Tank replied, *"I see you know how to start the party."* She took this moment to personally sing, *"Happy Birthday to You..."*

BIGGIE SMALLS "Juicy" BEST OF BIGGIE SMALLS (MTUME)

"It was all a dream, Big Tank used to read Word Up magazine..." Clapping his hands and loving Kandi Gyal's sassy happy birthday song. Big Tank's husky voice's bellowed, *"My birthday present has arrived!"* She blushed ready to let him unwrap the present, but knew such behaviors shouldn't be exerted, well not now.

Wearing a Chinchilla mink jacket that was as smooth as butter, Kandice held on to Big Tank tight enjoying the soft mink tickle her face giving him a birthday hug. Feeling small standing next to the giant of all ballers. She felt his wide hands glide across the curves of her ass. She side stepped away not wanting to linger in case he got the wrong idea.

"Birthdays was the worst days, now we sip
champagne when we thirst-ay"

Never seen or photographed publicly without his trademark dark shades, because of Big Tank's blind left eye. There was always paparazzi trying to attack and grab his glasses for the money $hot. Then there was lawsuits after lawsuits, always someone wanna fine him, but they got to find him, Oh and he ain't hiding.

CONYA DOSS "So Fly" POEM ABOUT MS. DOSS

"You're so fly, I can't deny you got my eye..." Regardless she was ready to give him her left eye to feel his style and deep conversations, Big Tank was so – so – so – so damn fashionable and fly. Kandi Gyal was astounded because he was the biggest dollar $ign she had ever been this close to.

Getting to the point Kandi Gyal asked, *"What's up? You wanted to speak to me privately."* He didn't speak, but waved his hand for her to join him by the window and enjoy the view of the twinkling lights of New York, New York. Penthouse high, 40 floors above the city with panoramic views of the most noticeable land marks like the Hudson River and Statue of Liberty.

"It was about 2 O'clock in the morning and I been checking you out for a moment." Flabbergasted, nerves and curious about the mystery of Big Tank's eye. She had to compliment his stylish designer sunglasses, *"I love the fly shades you're sporting!"* Big Tank grinned, *"Here you want to try them on? I just picked them up last week in the UK for £2,500 – twenty –five hundred pounds, Euros that equal to five thousand American dollars. I spend 50 grand a year on custom designer sunglasses."*

RICK ROSS "Magnificent" DEEPER THAN RAP
(Featuring JOHN LEGEND)

The magnificent with the sensational style down to all of his automobiles with no miles and ready for a new change. Big Tank was charming and had a swag like no other. He was checking her out no doubt. Examining Kandi trying the designer sunglasses (no prescription) he said, *"Damn now look at you – looking all good and shit. Keep them happy birthday to you - Kandi Gyal."* Jokingly Kandice replied, *"I Love early birthday presents. I bet I would get more than 100% UV protection with you around."* She was in shock, not just because he was giving her the Louie sunglasses, but because of his left eye.

"Oh, I, I can show you
Show you better than I can tell you"

The trade mark that got him the nick name Big Tank. Kandi read articles in magazines such as Ebony and Essence, Jet, Sister2Sister, The Source, Vibe and XXL magazine. The 40 year old Hip – Hop millionaire music Mongol was blind in his left eye due to a childhood accident. He was playing around big old water tanks. The incident left him blind and scarred in his left eye. It was like an eel's eye, scary and sexy simultaneously. He was aggressive, but smooth with his moves.

ELLA VARNER "Refill" PERFECTLY IMPERFECT

Refilling the glasses of champagne they were standing face to face. Kandice was, *"Feeling like the girl at the bar who's been there too long, she can't stand up!"* Big Tank's wasn't thinking about his main chick Lil' Pam looking at his new Kandi Gyal. Moving closer still rocking the designer sunglasses Kandi Gyal took an obvious whiff of his cologne and seductively purred like a cat that just smelled catnip, "Meow *you smell tasty birthday boy."* Feeling like Snoop Dogg, Big Tank was laid back with his mind on his money and his money on his mind.

Bragging Big Tank barked, *"You can't get this cologne in the states. I got this shit in Paris. It is a custom blend costing me a grand ($1,000) an ounce. My essence is a special blend - You feel me? No other man can smell like me!"* Though Big Tank was a little intoxicated, he wasn't slow thinking, only a sucker would leave a woman like Kandi Gyal unattended with Big Tank around scoping and watching, because she was mind blowing!

SNOOP DOGG "Beautiful" PAID THA COST TO BE DA BO$$ (Featuring FERRELL)

"Beautiful, I just want you to know
You're my favorite girl
Oh yeah, there's something about you"

After having many different types of women imaginable, Big Tank often came across one he just had to have. It was a man thing. He said, *"Give me your number in case we get mixed up in the party."* Kandi was a step ahead holding her cellphone in her hand ready to dial. He gave her his number and she let his phone ring once, now he had her number. Then he asked, *"Are you here with your man, friend, manager? Which one is his? Or is he all 3? What's up with yall?"*

The special cologne fusions of anise, lime, cardamom, Haitian Vetiver, patchouli, and white musk were capturing. Kandi noticed he was one of those big spenders – big ballers that liked rattling off price tags. She would call his bluff and keep the expensive sunglasses.

Listening to his last question thinking he wanted to talk about Rofiki. She thought about Rofiki preaching to keep business - business. She answered, *"I'm here with my manager."* Quickly Big Tank replied, *"Cool then we can hook up later. Wanna catch my attention, babe, throw up a dollar sign and make a deposit in Big Tanks bank. Yo, kick the party off with me and take a hit - a little sniff."* As he was talking and pulling out rolled up hundred dollar bills and a tray of white powder. Kandi's eyes lit up gamed and needing a little spark to wake her up.

GROOVE THEORY "10 Minute High" GROOVE THEORY

*"Just for a little while she's floating through the sky
What's she gonna do when she no longer can fly?"*

After mingling and networking, Rofiki got curious and began looking around the lavish upscale penthouse suite and admiring the walls filled with gold record plaques and awards that had everyone in awe. He noticed Kandi Gyal being escorted to the top floor that was blocked off to party guest, but was able to sneak past security talking to a video vixen, and went hunting. When looking around Rofiki found one of the four bathrooms finally empty. He dashed in and take a quick piss.

Zipping his pants up, he heard someone directly behind him lightly giggle. After washing his hands he walked over to the closet door. He wasn't a punk, so he opened it. Interestingly sitting on the floor of the empty closet was a pretty white chic, or was it a boy? Looking split image to pop star Jordan Beaver. Looking so much like the pop star it actually confused Rofiki. The wanna-be look-a-like was sitting in the closet smoking and looking through the keyhole watching people piss.

There had been a weed scandal with the pop star, which emerged after photos of the singer holding what appears to be a blunt were published by TMZ. Beaver's fans, believed the damning photos of the pop star smoking weed was a conspiracy, and blamed it on a look- alike. Fans claimed because the photos don't show Beaver's tattoos in TMZ's photos it's not him. But Rofiki didn't need to see photo's he could see with his own eyes the smoke rings and tattoos.

Before Rofiki could freak out Beaver ran out. He would have hollered, but didn't want to alarm anyone that he was there too. He looked out in the hall and there was no one there. He could still hear the music pumping loud and the DJ was holding down the wheels of steel mixing in another fly song. He wanted to sing along with the music, but quietly went back to check out the closet.

2 CHAINZ "Birthday Song" BASED ON A T.R.U. STORY
(Featuring KANYE WEST)

"It's my birthday and if I die bury me inside that Louie store - inside the Gucci store..." The closet was like a maze, but carefully with his cellphone light, Rofiki carefully tip- toe-toed across all the alligator, crocodile, snakeskin, leather, cowhide and many other shelves of rainbow colored shoes in Big Tanks 3,000+ shoe assortment seen on MTV Cribs television show. It took half of the national television segment to profile Big Tank's estimated $1 million shoe collection. The shoe connoisseur claims no one ever knew about all of these pricey shoes he hidden in a secret room.

The penthouse was a decent size, but Rofiki completely oblivious to how 1,200 pairs of sneakers autographed by most of the NBA. Such as Dr. J, Jordan, Magic, Iverson, and customized LeBron James sneakers could be hidden in any New York City apartment?

Stepping through shoes and sneakers, following the sound that lead to another door. Voices and Behind the sound of laughter he could hear Big Tank rapping, *"It's my birthday and if I die bury me inside that Louie store - inside the Gucci store..."* Now, Rofiki was peeping through the keyhole to another room. Damn it was Kandi and Big Tank. Rofiki watched how quickly Big Tank pulled out rolled up $100 bills and dipped it in powder and how Kandi sniffed and purred out their business agreement, *"Rofiki is my acting manager for now, but I'm looking for someone stronger in da game, someone like you papi chulo."*

Yeah, Big Tank will be Kandi Gyals *"papi chulo"* meaning the hottest guy or pimp playa. She knew what time it was, every tick on the clock was about him and he was now ready to party and not interested in talking business. He rapped along to the music like he wrote the song, *"It's my birthday and the bad chick contest and you're in first place. I'll show up with a check to your work place. But I don't want no beef! I thought you were under contract?"* She continued her purring and lying, *"I have not signed anything yet."*

The bass of the music muffled out the noise as Rofiki watched through the keyhole Big Tank and Kandi sniffing cocaine. They were interrupted by Shabazz knocking to let Big Tanks know Lil' Pam was about to enter the building." Rofiki couldn't believe that money hungry dirty bitch sniffed coke. Pulling his head out of the clouds of disbelief, Rofiki was cursing

Kandi under his breath. He couldn't believe what she said? Did she have his lost black book also? He still couldn't get over she was a coke head. Well, actually he was tripping on what she said. He had been naive to Kandi in many ways. Luckily the bathroom was empty and he was able to get back to the party.

Tonight was a test for Kandi and she failed. Rofiki couldn't believe she was trying to cut his throat before the ink dried. STARR would have never disrespect him like that. His conscious was nagging him to get back to Philadelphia to make sure STARR was cool. He assumed STARR who was probably home listening to Jill Scott records crying over him and head hanging over a trash can vomiting from early pregnancy symptoms. He would fix the problems when he returned.

THE BRAND NEW HEAVIES "We Won't Stop"
THE BRAND NEW HEAVIES REMIXES

The bull-shit just wouldn't stop happening. STARR wouldn't stop. Kandi Gyal wouldn't stop. Looks like the birthday boy, Big Tank won't stop, and there was no fucking way Rofiki would stop. We won't stop. Putting thoughts of Philly on ice and concentrating on what he saw and overheard in the closet. Rofiki knew he had to come up with a quick plan. He had Kandi's slick big ass in eye sight.

When Rofiki caught up with Kandi, she was holding a glass of Moet Chandon high in the air toasting with Big Tank. The room full of people that had waited for hours for him to make an appearance at his own birthday party. Rofiki let his glass click amongst those around him toasting. Out loud Kandi Gyal giggled, *"Oh there is my manager."*

Flabbergasted after overhearing Kandi Gyal trying to replace him, Rofiki played it cool like nothing ever happened, for now. Watching and listening to her introducing him, as her manager. He knew she was trying to run a good game. His mind was going a mile a minute trying to figure out his next move. Now he had to keep his eyes on Big Tank too.

LIL' KIM "Lighters Up" THE NAKED TRUTH

"Now put your lighters up, New York!" There was a nice crowd of people, and everyone seemed to be enjoying the night. Throughout the night Rofiki reminded her about the signing bonus meeting, and the band

he put together. She smiled at the idea of being on stage with her own band and money to go shopping again. *"Put your lighters up, D.C. Keep putting your lighters up!"*

"Philadelphia, put your lighters up!" Exchanging a quick glance with Big Tank that was arm to arm with Lil' Pam who was sporting a 10 carat diamond engagement ring with her lighter up in the air flickering. Now everyone was flicking their (Bics) lighters in the air.

"Detroit put your lighters up!" Not a fan of all the lighters flicking near her newly weaved hair, Kandi Gyal swinging her hair away from the flames. She didn't want a Michael Jackson episode and her hair catches on fire. Flashing a bogus smile at Lil' Pam, she walked off arm and arm with Rofiki. *"Chi-town, keep putting them lighters up!"*

"Atlanta put your lighters up!" The Penthouse's ultimate feature was its large windows and panoramic view of the Upper East Side of Manhattan. It felt like you were literally dancing under the stars. While working the room, Rofiki met Marty Gibbs of 'Rebel Hill Entertainment' and chatted about Kandi Gyal. Everyone seemed interested. *"Tampa, keep putting them lighters up!"* Playing his role, Rofiki was handling business and Kandi Gyal loved it. Women eyed Rofiki, like men eyed Kandi. Rofiki was still testing her, as he noticed Big Tank peeping and Kandi trying to stay in view. *"Yup, she was a money hungry bitch! No 'ting more."*

MARY J. BLIGE "I Can Love You" SHARE MY WORLD (Featuring LIL KIM)

"I can love you, I can love you
I can love you, I can love you
I can love you better than she can"

It began to crystallize for Rofiki while overlooking Manhattan's skyline. Despite the cities absent Twin Towers, his attention was captured by the cities lights thinking of ways to keep Kandi in check. Kandi Gyal walked up on him disturbing his thoughts asking, *"What is out there that got you so mesmerized?"* Rofiki thought that was the dumbest thing she could have said out of her mouth. After her watched her lip singing to Big Tank, "I can love you better than she can."

Fuming undercover and thinking of what was overheard and witnessed. If Kandi wanted play games he was ready to give it to her. His cellphone rang, *"Big – Ups Smokey! Nigga what? Nigga who? Nigga you, ya man meh knows who dis is! Na meh in N.Y. Oh, Really? Performing where?"* Kandi's eyes lit up. Rofiki realized she was ear-hustling on his call. He continued, *"Ya meh da manager handling. Let's talk in da new day."*

Ending the phone call giving Kandi a faux grin, but fuming. He took a sip of champagne and winked at her, *"I'll be right back."* He turned to walk away from her. His head was pounding after hearing that STARR had a show and it was one of her best performances. How could this be? He just left her just hours ago, looking hopeless and lost like she was ready to jump off the Ben Franklin Bridge. Now he hears she performed to a full house and a standing ovation? And performing with BearLove? What was going on?

FAITH EVANS "Just Burnin' (Burning up Remix) FAITHFULLY (Featuring P. DIDDY AND FREEWAY)

On fire, blazing and going crazy trying to figure out what the phone call was about, Kandi Gyal walked towards Rofiki grabbing his arm to stop him from walking away. Thrilled she squeaked, *"Was that R & B legendary producer Smokey B from Cali? Was that phone call about me?"* Rofiki loved playing this game with her. Instead of telling her that was his home boy Smokey from North Philly. He played the game. He said, *"Meh can't talk about dis at VHR event. So keep it quiets Smokey may have a bigger offer on the table. He in Philadelphia and meh might need to catch up before he take off, he wants to see our contract."*

Animatedly Kandi Gyal squirmed looking over and noticed Big Tank eyeing her with his arm around his fiancé Lil' Pam looking plastic surgery and Botox happy. Thinking for sure now that Rofiki would be her manager, she knew would sign the contract and let Rofiki work his magic. So far he was doing wonders and as far as Big Tank, Kandi Gyal knew he could afford her and she was keeping the LV sunglasses.

CHINGY "Pulling Me Back" HOODSTAR (Featuring TYRESE)

Always something kept pulling Rofiki and STARR back together. Now, Kandi Gyal was sticking close by Rofiki the rest of the night like he was the nigga with the figures, she looped her arm around his. Everyone had a mission and money was on everyone's mind. Reminding Kandi that he was there to work, not play, Rofiki said, *"Let's call it a night. Meh have to drive back to Philly and meet up with Smokey in the new day. But first we have to deal with our contract in retrospect to some funds."* He was talking shit, but he need Kandi to sign the contract too and get back to Philly to see whad up with STARR.

TRACK 4: THE CITY OF SISTERLY LOVE (Double Play)

ZHANÉ "My Word is Bond" SATURDAY NIGHT

STARR said it once, won't say it again. Rofiki's got to learn and understand. She's not that child that he once knew, she's not the fool he could lie to. From this day on he's gonna learn her word is bond, her word is bond.

ZHANÉ "Love Me Today" PROUNOUNCED JAH – NAY

Love STARR today and hate her tomorrow. Put all of those feelings aside. Why should they lay in all of this sorrow? True feelings cannot hide, STARR was just about over Rofiki. She really thought that they were finally through. But there was something there (*something there*) that just would not break. And she kept wondering what more would it take?

MUSIQ SOULCHILD "Ms. Philadelphia" LUVANMUSIQ

STARR lived in Philadelphia on the west side, the city of Philadelphia, not just the city of 'Brotherly Love,' It is also the city of 'Sisterly Love. Some of the most innovative artist talents have been produced in Philly. The Philadelphia scene is old school to the heart. It is where you can make a name and build your fame. However, this is a tricky place and you will learn the rules by trials and errors, but it may be necessary.

AMEL LAURRIEUX "Get Up" INFINITE POSSIBILITIES

"I know you're down, when you gonna get up
I see you down, when you gonna get up"

Getting up out of bed to answer the phone call from BearLove barring bad news. She hung up and then turning on JAZZ1CAFÉ Internet Radio on her new cellphone. Sitting on the wide ledge of the drafty window, she listened to the music again hoping one day her name and songs will be played, but after the phone call from BearLove it looked like their dreams were up in smoke.

AMEL LAURRIEUX "For Real" BRAVE BIRD

"I can hear, I can feel, I can see
I can tell you're for real"

Pondering the wild shit that was going on in her life included the phone call from BearLove about canceled shows @ Jazz1Café due to an electrical fire. She watched cars, trucks, buses and folks walking along Girard Avenue, but no Rofiki. Wondering how she was going to continue to pay the rent, while tapping to a beat with an ink-pen on the note book. Thinking about the canceled shows and the after party with Bluesy, along with her heart breaking situation with Rofiki, she wanted to evaporate into thin air. She had a strong feeling that Rofiki might show up and explain what was going on in New York. Then she would be able to tell him about losing another baby.

FLOETRY "Butterflies" FLOACISM LIVE
(Michael Jackson)

STARR just wanna touch and kiss and she wish that she could be with him tonight, because Bluesy give STARR butterflies inside, inside... Mind trapped in the songs, STARR put the head-phones on turning up and drowned in music listening and wondering if being with Bluesy was out of revenge or need or love or all three.

Thoughtfuls of Bluesy brought on the new feelings of butterflies fluttering in the pit of her stomach. Trying to shake it all off she began to roll her last bit of weed in 'Top' paper and puffed out the window. Swearing off men and wanting to scream, *"I hate men!"*

FLOETRY "Say Yes" FLO'OLOGY

"All you gotta do is say yes
Don't deny what you feel let me undress you baby
Open up your mind and just rest"

"You make me so, so, so, so, so..." Still singing along to the music hours later, STARR sat in the window and bobbing her head to the music with the headphones turned up to the max. Watching, and hawking and spying on folks like she was F.B.I. seeing all that was going on in the streets. Inhaling and holding, swearing she wouldn't forgive Rofiki this time. Remembering the first puff with him and hearing for the first time his emotional feelings for her. *"Jah, meh like yu much! Just know meh might act crazy, but meh never hurt yu. You're mine STARR!"* Of course now she realizes their whole relationship was just a big puff of smoke. In denial, delusions and making decisions she was in very much need of self-love.

JAGUAR WRIGHT "Self Love" DENIALS, DELUSIONS & DECISIONS

Listening caught up in a web of deception. From this shit STARR done learned new lessons. So what should she do, keep on playing? She play on, playa. Standing on the cold floor, STARR jumped back after feeling something small and round under her foot. She bent down and picked up a brown M&M. She tossed it in the trash talking to it, *"Fugh you too."* She turned out the bathroom light, blew out the candles and bundled up in her blankets trying desperately to stay warm and fall asleep thinking, *"Self-love, self-preservation - Self-love, self-preservation - Self-love, self-preservation."*

Bluesy drove to STARR'S place looking up at her window to confirm he was at the right house, and noticed the third floor window was dark. He contemplated knocking on the door, blowing his horn or leaving her a note. Thinking the worse, he thought maybe her boyfriend, the guy from the coffee shop returned. Though recollecting the night before aroused and angered him getting back in his truck and driving away.

JAGUAR WRIGHT "Same Sh*t Different Day (part 1)"
DENIALS, DELUSIONS & DECISIONS

"Same shit different day, things change but what about me"

Hearing a car door slam, STARR hesitated before getting out the bed stepping on the same brown M&M and fussing. She caught the tail lights of a pickup truck. She wasn't sure if it was Bluesy's silver F10 Ford truck because it was now at a distance.

VIVIAN GREEN "Emotional Roller Coaster" A LOVE STORY

"I'm on an emotional roller coaster
Loving you ain't nothing healthy"

Flopping back on the air mattress, STARR swore she would have to stop allowing herself to be used over, and over again. She had been with Rofiki ever since, she escaped from her haunted past. All her life she had been vulnerable and a victim to someone else's needs on an emotional roller coaster.

VIVIAN GREEN "Free As A Bird" GREEN ROOM

"This is the real me and I just gotta be free as a bird in the sky"

Waking up to another day with tear stained pillows over her face, STARR was feeling used, feeling abused, feeling like she was the Twin Towers. Yes, both 'Twin Towers' falling! The first plane hitting and knocking her to her knees making her missing her mother – $hantey Money - she could feel every window being blown out. The pain of Rofiki and the miscarried babies felt like the second – plane that hit. Feeling the headache medication settling in, she forgot just how many pills she took. Not caring about Rofiki's warnings of capsules laced with potassium cyanide and people dying. Maybe she wanted to expire popping another pill.

LIZZ FIELDS "What We're Left With" PLEASUREVILLE

What happens when hard times move in and nothings as it was, not like it used to be. Heart aches and pain in STARR'S life they seem to rein. Because nothing is like it was, not like it used to be. She is wondering when will it end and what do she have left?

LIZZ FIELDS "I Gotta Go" BY DAY BY NIGHT

Might have been good for Rofiki but it was hell for STARR. She gotta go. Now at the end of her rope and can't cope no more. She gotta go, his ruthless ways will take him as far as his grave. If he had time would he change his direction and lift his foot off the hearts of the people you pained, she gotta go.

The cloudy day wasn't helping STARR feel any better, she needed motivation to wanna be spontaneous. She rolled over wondering if she should get on her knees and pray. She laid there wondering if her life is pre-planned, why pray." She answered her own questions in her head, knowing she is given free will like everyone else to make choices and needed to be praying!" Managing to sit up, STARR immediately regretted her surroundings and got down on her knees. Her prayers were interrupted by hearing Mr. Jenki yelling and cussing about something. She put her headphones back on and turned up the music playing @ JAZZ1CAFÉ.

URSULA RUCKERS Release" SILVER AND LEAD

"Release your heart, my heart release, release
Your heart, my heart release"

Releasing her heart, so here STARR stand at the crossroads of her life. Do she choose plata or plomo? Silver or lead? Zipping up her hooded-jacket and heading out the door to the store to buy a blunt and hopefully find a dime bag of some good weed. Buying weed was something new for STARR. Due to Rofiki's 101, she could only smoke what he gave her. It felt like a blessing getting it for free, but the curse was who she had to smoke with. She thought that now that she had to buy it she would smoke less. It was the complete opposite, she was smoking more.

URSULA RUCKERS "I Million Ways To Burn" SUPA SISTA

"Burn from passion or displeasure - Burn, slow burn
One million ways to burn choose one
Choose one"

Slowly rolling and licking and lighting. Puffing and observed her living situation. Everything was thrift store or trash treasures, but it was hers. And always clean and in order without Rofiki and his bags of clothes and many pairs of timberland boots, Jordan's sneakers kicked off where ever.

Rofiki was very messy and she was very organized and knew exactly where everything was.

There was nothing to treasure all she owned was jeans, leggings and t-shirts, a pair of sneakers and a pair of boots and plenty of scarves. She could actually get up with her eyes closed and find everything, now that he wasn't around. In a rage of tears she began pulling on her favorite Bob Marley T-shit that she wearing. Both of her hands twisting and pulling until she could feel the fabric ripping off her body. She clawed at it as if it was Rofiki's face.

RES "For Who You Are" BLACK GIRLS ROCK

Rofiki was once STARR'S lover. Used to be one of her best friends. Someone she really loved to talk to. When her day was coming to its end but people come and then they go. She know they had to grow apart. She wish he would have told me before. But she never knew things would get so hard. Since it wasn't meant to be and she'll always love him for who he is.

> *"See I don't blame you for running*
> *Never seen a darker place*
> *I never seen the dark places you've been"*

There was no more toilet seats being left up, no more caps off the tooth paste, dirty clothes under the bed, no tobacco leaves or ashes on the floor and yes there is more, but she would rather not think about it. Feeling the needed to toss a few things on the floor to exhort her anger, STARR restrained. But nothing felt dirtier than her body. Attached to a long brown extension cord was a mini space heater that warmed the room. STARR picked up the heater and guided the cord to follow her into the bathroom. Warming the bathroom and tossing the ripped Bob Marley t-shirt in the trash then sitting on the toilet. She relit and puffed and puffed lost in day dreams until she burnt her fingertips.

RES "Golden Boys" HOW I DO

> *"Now would they love you if they knew all the things that we know?*
> *Golden boy life ain't a video"*

The past few weeks without Rofiki had STARR going crazy with many nights of tears and anxiety attacks. She wanted to believe he was taking care of business. The time apart was painful at first feeling like rejection. But the quiet days and nights were becoming welcoming and a little confusing – misusing her feelings. She needed a break from all the fussing, cussing and fighting. But without it things were starting to feel strange and unfamiliar. Thinking back to the coffee shop, she noticed Rofiki was still healing from the fresh scratches put on his chin from their last fight. She was glad he didn't mention it.

Time apart was what she had wished for many nights and now it was here, she was going insane. Or was she? She knew shit wasn't making any sense. She knew prayers were being answered when she hooked up with BearLove. After being offered the lead vocalist for his new project 'THE NEOSOULS' instantly they became the 'THE NEOSOUL STARR.'

Practicing with a new group of musical friends, another blessing and the feeling on stage with them was explosive. It was interesting when BearLove explained, *"I've been trying to track you down for months. I actually came up with the name 'THE NEOSOULS' because of you. It is fate that we meet again and 'The NEOSOULS STARR' was born."* Every time she thinks about it, she breaks out in goose bumps.

JAZZYFATNASTEES "All Up In My face" TORTOISE AND THE HARE

Judas, you seem so jealous. Cautiously friendly, he think he's still trying to be friendly. Thinking STARR don't see (Rofiki's crazy). He think she's dumb but she see everything. Every time he around it's always the same. Looking tough but something tells her he's running a game. Trying to be what he see till he can't see himself. In the end makes him look the fool.

> *"I don't know where you're from or who you are*
> *You're getting all up in my face"*

Sitting on the toilet, STARR reminiscing about the first time meeting BearLove. She was mad at Rofiki about some bull-shit he did, she hopped on the 48- Septa bus and toke it to 2nd & Market Street. Downtown Philadelphia always amused her though she rarely could afford to do any shopping or anything without Rofiki. But that night she got on the bus and went over to the Black Lily @ The 5-Spot for open mic night and remembering the night her name being called to the stage by the host RYVA, *"The Black Lily Music stage Philly's Neo Soul Artist give it up for our home girl – Philly's own STARR!"*

JAZZYFATNASTEES *"Breakthrough"* ONCE & FUTURE

How can STARR break through? The closer she get the further away from Rofiki. Why was he pulling away from her? She only want to comfort him and heal all his pain, take it all away. Thinking about the 'Black Lily' woman music series was a weekly fixture in Philadelphia called 'The 5-Spot.'

Founded by Mercedes Martinez and Tracey Moore of the group the JAZZYFATNASTEES,' Black Lily helped launch the careers of many Neo – Soul artists. When the series closed down in 2005, a significant gap was left in Philadelphia's music scene. The movements values politically conscious art and underground art, and dedicated to education, diversity and collaboration through art, culture and entertainment.

JAZMINE SULLIVAN *"Lions, Tigers and Bears"* FEARLESS

STARR'S not scared of lions and tigers and bears, no she's not. But she's scared of loving him. She's not scared to perform at a sold out affair. That's right, but she's scared of loving him. Oh how she also loved the 'Black Lily' a coalition of women committed to supporting women artists. Spot lighting their work on stage and providing opportunities for networking and training, after most open mic night are primarily males dominating the microphones.

Though men were not excluded, Black Lily values women's voices of organic funk, soul, and rare grooves with smooth female vocals that seek to educate the general public about the importance of women's art showcasing cutting-edge-raw- articulate women artists of all races and nationalities and genres, Neo-Soul, Hip-Hop, R&B, Rock and Spoken Word Poetry.

JAZMINE SULLIVAN "Excuse Me" LOVE ME BACK

Oh, Excuse STARR if she's sounding crazy but Bluesy's been the one she's been hoping and waiting for. She have searched all around but there's nobody else in the world who love her like he do. She ain't never had another man that give her what he give to her.

PATTI LABELLE "If Only You Knew" I'M IN LOVE AGAIN

STARR must have rehearsed her lines a thousand times, until she had them memorized. But when she get up the nerve to tell him, the words just never seem to come out right

"If only you knew - How much I do - Do love you
If only you knew - How much I do - Do need you"

That was the night STARR performed and had the crowd in tears and blowing' them away! She hurried out the door right after noticing one of Rofiki's homeboy's. Smokey was pointing at her and holding up his phone. Which meant Rofiki was on the other end. Just like Cinderella, she ran out the door before anyone could congratulate her. The party continued to proceed without her.

The second times was when she won the radio contest and got to perform with the house – band with special guest drummer BearLove at JAZZ1CAFÉ. That was also the night Rofiki was there orchestrating taking everyone's info as he posed as her manager, and no connections were made due to Rofiki's ignorance. Moving forward and out of the tight bonds of Rofiki, she was free, happy, and with a band and grateful to have BearLove, as a new friend.

PATTI LABELLE "You Are My Friend" PATTI LABELLE

"You are my friend, I never knew it 'til then
My friend, my friend"

BearLove, a friend that she was really digging and couldn't help but be get caught up in his charisma - smooth beats, his proper speech, his Philly swag and slang, his good hearted nature of providing advice that was motivating. She was already a fan of his. Turning up the music high as a kite and still sitting on the toilet STARR came out of her day dreams of the Black Lily.

PHYLISS HYMAN "You Just Don't Know" LIVING ALL ALONE

"You just don't know what it feel like to be lonely, STARR felt like she was dying." Sucking and puffing hard, killing the joint puffing until it burned STARR'S finger tips then flushed the burning roach, she was high as a kite. Shivering remembering her nice warm pink robe and other belongings packed away in storage. She put on her sweater and growled, *"Fugh Rofiki, I'm going to get my shit out of storage soon as I find out how."*

PHYLISS HYMAN "Living In Confusion" PRIME OF MY LIFE

"Seems like I'm always going through changes
Living in confusion, confusion, confusion"

Flopping down on the air mattress, she noticed it needed more air, as usual. Moving the air mattress to add air, she found Bluesy's driver's license. She couldn't understand how it got there. She was sure she seen him put it back in his wallet after showing his real name.

JILL SCOTT "Slowly Surely" WHO IS JILL SCOTT?

Slowly, surely, she'll walk away from that old desperate and tainted love. Caught up in a maze of love, the crazy, crazy love. Thought it was good, thought it was real. Thought it was, but it wasn't love. STARR just don't know where she should go? Slowly surely, she'll walk away.

JILL SCOTT "So Gone" THE LIGHT OF THE SUN

"I try to keep it intact, but I'm here in this bed
I need to listen, listen"

STARR got that ocean of soul. Baby she's super thick and Bluesy's the man of steel with skills call him Super Dick. He got that technique that keeps you cumin' back to back. A Kama Sutra pro. Kitchen table down to the floor, ass in the air while she biting that pillow (*That's what a diamond chip dick do*).

DJ JAZZY JEFF & AYAH "Forgive me Love" BACK FOR MORE

Messed up, STARR know she was wrong. She didn't know which way to go. So, she fessed up, her consciousness is torn. See she can't get beyond! How Rofiki gave up, he gave up too soon. But now she knew which way to go. It was Rofiki's way, it was now Bluesy's way. Rofiki made the choice easy for her. Though knew with Bluesy she still had to slow it down.

AYAH "Slow It Down" 4:15

"*Ah, ah, ah, ah - Ah, ah, ah, ah.*" Is this normal? What is crazy? Is this strange? Is it real? See no one can tell STARR nothing if she is standing by her will. All she really gotta to do is take her time don't rush her fears. She will find what's deep inside and maybe they can make a deal if he will. She don't even know him, baby. Right now she ain't going now where. Taking her time and it's alright, baby. Slow it down.

Looking at Bluesy's identification made STARR's heart feel like a construction site with all the hammering, she tried to slow it down. "*Ah, ah, ah, ah - Ah, ah, ah, ah.*" He didn't do anything that she didn't allow. She remembered his touch being oddly soft and caressing, a sense that was powerful. On stage seeing him smiling and clapping for her was lively and rousing and she couldn't get him off her mind.

THE FLOACIST PRESENTS "Just Breathe" FLOETIC SOUL

If, STARR was feeling low it is best to expose any thoughts of doubt. She gotta air out. Awake, she greetings another day with the choices that she make. Decide what she will leave what she will take. Like, what was said, versus what she think? Sometimes her own assumptions are the ways that make her sink.

"*Breathe, you gotta let it go, let it go, so you can grow!*
You gotta let it go, let it go, just Breathe"

THE FLOACIST *"Speechless"* PRESENTS FLOETRY RE: BIRTH

No words, no term can describe Bluesy. If beauty could be measured, what would the gage be? Would it start with him and end with STARR? Would it last till eternity or die at an age? Like the story in a book, revealed with a turning page. No words can describe what her eyes caress, and for the first time in STARR'S life she's speechless.

MARSHA AMBROSIUS *"Cupid (Shot Me Straight Through My Heart)"* *FRIENDS & LOVERS*

"Cupid shot me straight through my heart"

Quickly her disappointment turned into concern. Maybe, just maybe something happened to him? The citrus of his cologne was still on her pillows or was that in her mind. Her heart took a perilous leap and she was on her feet. Without hesitation she dressed and headed to the coffee shop. She was sure, he would have at least returned for his driver license. Unless maybe, just maybe something did happen to him.

Walking through the doors of the coffee shop unnoticed as Bluesy was helping a customer at the counter. He looked up and was pleasantly surprised to see STARR. She misread his expression. She thought his eyes were wondering why she was there. She held out his license and said, *"I thought you might need this."* He reached his hand for the identification and held on to her hand. His touch reminded her that she liked his touch. STARR pulled away bumping into a customer.

MARSHA AMBROSIUS *"Your Hands"* *LATE NIGHTS & EARLY MORNINGS*

"Ooh, baby, baby, baby, baby." In Bluesy's hands *"oh, oh."* His hands hold the small of STARR'S back apologizing. She managed a faux smile and a swift exit out the door. Bluesy was right behind her calling out and catching up to her. *"Wait STARR what's wrong?"* She wasn't really sure what was wrong. Tired of being used she said, *"If you wanted a one- night stand you could have been straight up.*

STARR gathered, her strength as Bluesy words began to flow began explaining, *"STARR I would never do that to you. We must have had a misunderstanding. I waited for you all day yesterday to come by the shop.*

After I closed up, I went looking for you. I wasn't sure if you were performing, so I went by the club that is now boarded up. Then about 11:00 last night I came by your house to see if you were home, but your lights were out. I'm glad you came by today I was worried about you." He left out the part about assuming she was back with her old boyfriend.

JOSEPHINE SINCERE "Shame" WILDFLOWER
(EVELYN CHAMPAGE KING)

"Wrapped in your arms is where I want to be
Wrapped in your arms that's my high-igh-igh
Shame"

Shame and whole body burning, STARR remembered the approximate time she went to bed and the truck she saw driving away. She felt awkward and couldn't blame him for thinking she had too many physiological insecurities and past issues. Apologizing, *"I'm sorry. I am having a horrible week. The truth is I'm going through a mental battle right now. A battle that has me fighting against me. I'm sorry if I just caused a scene in the coffee shop. You seem like a really nice guy and I don't meet people like you often. So, I assumed you were a part of that world that wants to hurt me."*

JOSEPHINE SINCERE "Still Feels Good" WILDFLOWER

"It still feels good to hear you say
You Love me, you love me, yeah-yeah-yeah..."

Reaching out to hold STARR'S hand, Bluesy guiding her back inside saying, *"Let's go inside and enjoy a cup of coffee and a slice of cream cheese pound cake together."* He gave her a quick wink and led her inside. He had been praying all day mumbling under his breath, *"Dear GOD please send her back to me."* Now sitting at a different table, but STARR couldn't help notice the couple that was sitting at the table where Rofiki broke her heart and Bluesy began healing it. She and Bluesy were laughing and joking when his parents walked in the door.

Even with the loud bells on the door Bluesy hadn't noticed them until they walked up to the table. He didn't break his smile introducing his parents to STARR. She noticed that his mother shot her a twisted smile.

His father grinned blandly, *"Nice to meet you."* It's a shame what she have to go through now with his parents.

EVELYN CHAMPAGNE KING "Love Come Down" GET LOOSE

"Love come down
All the way down"

"No sleep last night, been dreaming of Bluesy..." Bluesy excused himself to show his parents around the shop. It was their first time seeing it open for business. Before buying the coffee shop, his parents expressed that they thought he was crazy for buying a business in North Philadelphia with all the violence and robberies going on. They thought showing no interest would change his mind. So it was truly a surprise that they came by that afternoon. His parent's loud mutters were heard, *"What are those things in her hair? It makes her look wicked and evil."* She had one encounter with them and that was enough.

Walking his parents to the door and after hugging his father and kissing his mother on the cheeks, she heard his mother reminding him, *"Don't be late for dinner. I'm making your favorites Italian wedding soup and baked ziti, capisci?"* Before they could say anymore he was walking them out the door responding *"Capisci, I understand."* After his parents left, he apologized. She joked about him having loving concerned parents, and left out their ignorance. He knew they had been rude and downright embarrassing.

EVELYN CHAMPAGNE KING "Don't Know If It's Right" SMOOTH TALK

"I don't know if it's right
To let you make love to me tonight"

The smile on Bluesy's face was as intimate as a kiss and made STARR want to ignore his parent's comments. The coffee shop became busy and Bluesy left her sitting alone, but she just can't help the way that she feel, *"she just can't help the way that she feel."* Never feeling alone watching Bluesy and bobbing her head to the music playing. He was a V.I.P. member of JAZZ1CAFÉ listening to the station 24/7 commercial free all day in the coffe shop. Every song reminded him of STARR.

BAHAMADIA *"Spontaneity"* KOLLAGE

*"Mad explosive spontaneity - Mad explosive spontaneity
Mad explosive spontaneity - Mad explosive spontaneity..."*

STARR doesn't know if she should give her love to Bluesy; he just might be no good. The cake once again was good, she ate the sour cream pound cake and nursed a cup of 'English Breakfast' tea while. Looking across the room at the table just a couple of days ago, she sat with Rofiki, she thought of Bluesy's parents comments along with Rofiki telling her to change her hair and perm it. It was the most hypocritical thing she ever heard. Again she had to shake her head free from the thoughts of Rofiki, as Bluesy sat back down with her. Pulling back her locks she asked, *"So what do you think about my locks? Do you think they're dreadful?"*

Without any hesitation Bluesy answered her question. Not only did he answer the question, he told her things about locks that she never knew. He began to explain, *"I don't like the term dread – locks, never did. And Rastafarians were not the first to wear locks. There is archaeological evidence proving that people were wearing locks way before towns were erected, way before the alphabet was created, and even before taxes were established. Mummified corpses with locks have been found in Egypt, South America and Central Asia. And today many holy men and women in India wear locked hair known as 'Jatta.'*

BAHAMADIA *"Confess"* (Non-Album Release)
(THE ROOTS Remix)

Word to life boo, STARR was checking Bluesy out. Looking sweet enough to chew with them saint eyes like that brew. Her mission, is getting into him like a religion, her woman's intuition tells her cupid's arrow's hitting. She's *"Sending My Love"* like ZHANÉ...

Bluesy continued to explain as STARR listened, *"Wearing locks don't make you Rastafarian. Praying 5x's a day don't make you a terrorist, and being a politician doesn't mean you're honest. Though I am Caucasian, I couldn't wait able to vote for OBAMA an African American president, even if he had locks. I'm no hair fashionista. If wearing locks are a symbolic jester of your rejection of contemporary fashion or your acceptance to your own natural style, then why not. It's your hair. Look at me I'm bald (giggles)."*

CAROL RIDDICK *"You Better Not Hurt Me"* MOMENTS LIKE THIS

*"You better not hurt me – You better not dessert me
You better not mistreat me, cause I love you deeply"*

The coffee shop was like a melting pot of one nation. Everyone was polite and STARR realized that she never really interacted with many different types of folks, due to being under Rofiki's scrutiny, jealousy and authority. At the coffee shop she was now meeting and being greeted by Caucasians, Hispanics and other nationalities.

CAROL RIDDICK *"Fairytale"* LOVE PHASES

A girl afraid of the world, STARR was afraid of the sun and the dark. Something was changing and she felt the need to fly letting down her hair. The coffee shop began to get busy again. Bluesy picked up STARR'S empty cup and said, *"More tea for the beautiful woman with lovely Jatta's!"* Enjoying Bluesy's attention lost in the fairytale, she forgot to be afraid of the world.

SOULSHINE SESSIONS: NEO – SOUL 101

INCOGNITO "Everybody Loves The Sunshine" BEES+THINGS+FLOWERS

WELCOME TO SOULSHINE! Thank you for tuning into JAZZ1CAFÉ! I'm here to play the sounds and break it all down simply Neo-Soul 101. The organic feel of the music is a stark contrast to the bubblegum pop that had been infiltrating the charts.

Though some artists, however, sought to distance themselves from the term, maintaining that it was merely a way to box them for marketability. In today's times, the tag 'Neo-Soul' is needed more than ever. Some of R&B'S most popular artists are opting for the 'Euro sound,' leaving the more soul-rooted singers struggling for position in the underground.

There is a unanimous outcry from music artists and lovers alike for a return of soul music to mainstream radio, and neo-soul is the answer we're looking for.

MONDO GROSSO "Star Suite II – Fading Star" MG4

What is Neo – Soul? Is it Hip-Hop, Jazz, R&B, Funk, what is this underground groove? Is it new or just a new era of sound? Remember when they thought Hip – Hop wouldn't last? Now what they rapping about, Neo – Soul?

As unsatisfactory as the term may be to some artist, 'Neo Soul' is still an effective label to define the mix of chic newness that distinguished the artist described. Neo Soul artists highlight a mix of styles, a musical style that obtains its influence from more jazz styles and often called bohemian musicians seeking a soul revival. Setting themselves apart from the more contemporary sounds of their mainstream R&B counterparts with their organic soulful sounds with the use of live instrumentation.

ETYMOLOGY OF NEOSOUL

Neo Soul is a term coined by music industry entrepreneur Kedar Massenburg during the late 1990s to market and describe a style of music that emerged from Soul and contemporary R&B. A marketing music genre following the commercial breakthroughs of artists such as, Erykah Badu. Through the production work of The Roots' drummer and producer Questlove, neo soul became popular in the late 1990s with also the successes of Lauryn Hill, D'Angelo, Zhané, Maxwell, Eric Benét, Raphael Saadiq, Les Nubians and many others.

ERYKAH BADU "Certainly (Flipped It)" BADUIZUM

Neo Soul is notable by a less conventional sound than its contemporary R&B counterpart, with incorporated elements ranging from Jazz, Funk, and Hip Hop to Pop, Fusion, and African music. While some artists have ignored the label, others have received the designation with controversy, viewing that it can be seen as manufactured by music audiences and imply that soul music had ended at some point in time.

In a 2002 interview for Billboard, Kedar Massenburg expressed his view on the backlash and intentions of marketing the Neo Soul term, stating: *"People don't like the term, because they don't want this music to be looked at as a genre. Because, when you classify music, it becomes a fad, which tends to go away. But soul music is soul music."*

Just A Few Clicks Away from JAZZ1CAFÉ...

1. Download 'LIVE365 RADIO APP

2. Launch the LIVE365 RADIO APP
3. Type: JAZZ1CAFE (Click GO!)

BECOME A V.I.P. MEMBER!!! FREE 5 Day Trial Membership and No Credit Card Required!

Please become a V.I.P. Member and help support JAZZ1CAFÉ Internet Radio Station and the music artist. Portions of you subscription go towards the royalties for the songs played.

Enjoy zero commercial interruptions, no banners or ads, just you and the music. Listen on multiple devices, tablets & desktops. Go anywhere with the LIVE365 Mobile APP for. Listen in the comfort of your home on devices such as Sonos, Roko, WDTV, Grace digital wireless radio, Tangent, TIVO and more.

TRACK 5: TURNTABLES OF OUR SOULS

Feeling free in the rain STARR headed from West Philly to the Germantown section of Philadelphia over to BearLove's for rehearsal. Getting off the crowded Septa bus and opening her umbrella trying to avoid the lightning and raindrops. She was feeling wonderful like Gene Kelly's 1952 classic *'Singing in the Rain."* Turning the headphones up and blending her tear drops with the rain drops, she sang along to the music coming out of her head phones. Pulling her emotions together, she realized the rain was feeling like sunshine compared to the storms she weathered.

DEZZIE "Let It Rain"
DYING DAILY... A JOURNEY THROUGH SPIRITUAL GROWTH

STARR wanted to be like Job and go through anything for him. She wanted to be like Mary, give birth to the only begotten. She wanted to be like Rahab and save the land in spite of race and sin. She wanted to be like Noah saving people 2 by 2. So let it rain. Let the rain fall down on her. *"Thank GOD,"* She said out loud. For the peace she prayed for. She was no longer a prisoner of Rofiki 101 the man -made hell where everything had become dreadful and she had heavy wet locks on her head as a reminder. Avoiding the cracks on the sidewalk remembering the old saying, step on a crack, you'll break your mother's back.

Evading the cracks on the side walk, because she didn't want to break Shantey's back, where ever she was. Then she thought of Rofiki's mother Haile, the polite motherly friendly phone calls from Jamaica that tried to warn her – school her – inform her – educate her that she had to be her own woman not controlled.

OLI SILK "Ahead of the weather" ALL WE WANT

The relationship between Rofiki's mother Haile and STARR has ended with both of them out of touch without Rofiki. STARR missed Haile's gracious voice and words of wisdom that a mother would give to a daughter. Warning that Rofiki was just as controlling as his father Kingston. Often Rofiki would remind STARR he could never marry her, because she too had fughed up paperwork and no proper identification. A hypocrite and talking all that bull-shit because his friends' identification that was in prison.

Witnessing his loyalty to his friends, and their loyalty to him. His mother, Haile returned to her home in Kingston, Jamaica after years of missing family. When Rofiki and STARR showed up to the empty North Philly house with a for sale sign, he learned his mother returned to Jamaica. After Haile learned of his father Kingston's death, she didn't sell the house due to Rofiki refusing to leave and not wanting to return back to Jamaica before getting his own paper work straight.

Never personally meeting Haile, but STARR seen plenty of pictures of her youth and beautiful facial structures. Cheek bones delicately carved, her mouth full, her thick dark hair hung in long locks in graceful twists past her hips, and always a wide smile. Although they never had a face-to-face they had formed a good long distance phone relationship, and often exchanged things through the mail.

INCOGNITO "Heavy Rain Sometime" TALE FROM THE BEACH

"It may rain sometime it can't be all sunshine
May even snow a little because the heart is brittle"

However, they didn't lived in Haile's house for free and when the rent was late, STARR would be the first to hear about it. Rofiki would avoid his mothers' calls. Then when he did send Haile money, he would complained about paying rent, taxes, cable, water and electric. Never mentioning most being illegally hooked ups. Then brag he owned his house and there was no white man that could throw him out. Many times he would take his anger out - curse her out for him even being in North Philadelphia like it was her fault.

JAMIROQUAI *"Virtual Insanity"* TRAVELING WITHOUT MOVING

Oh this world has got to change. 'Cause STARR just, she just can't keep going on in this virtual, virtual insanity. That she's living in, that we're living in. 'Virtual Insanity' is what is… Checking the time and date on her cellphone, she realized it had been 2 months since she last seen Rofiki. He didn't have her new number and she deleted him from her phone though she still had it memorized. She didn't want to hear his voice, his lies, or his games.

On her journey between lyrics, again she thanked GOD for the strength and new directions and for a new place to lay her head, new foods, new languages and music, she was beginning to feel her new soul. Though she couldn't understand why she was letting thoughts of Rofiki haunt her. She prayed for this freedom and now she couldn't be scared of it. Now she was seeing the truth about Love. It could easily turn to hate. And now she constantly wanted to hate him.

Crossing the street dodging pass cars and still avoiding cracks she thought maybe Rofiki got into a car accident, or had an asthma attack, or both. Maybe Rofiki was in the hospital? Noticing a very passionate couple holding hands, she had second thoughts. Maybe Rofiki is with another woman holding hands? She had feared he left her for another chick. She had seriously at one point thought about calling Jerry Greko from the television show 'Cheaters.' But she knew whatever they had on video Rofiki would turn into 'SHAGGY' singing, *"It wasn't me!"*

VISIONEERS *"Run For Cover"* DIRTY OLD HIP HOP

One of the houses she walked pass reminded her of the time, she caught Rofiki coming out of some Jamaican chic's house at 4 AM. It was the night he started a fight with her so she didn't want to go to the party.

The truth was she really didn't want to go to the party, but he would make a fight out of everything just to manipulate. She knew what happened at those parties. The bitter after taste on Guinness Stout mixed with ganja on his breath making him feel more masculine. Jamaican women and the few American women would be in the middle of the floor, winding their hips, asses and grinding there twats in dude's faces.

PROPHET BENJAMIN "Throw Wine" THROW WINE

STARR wasn't going nowhere tonight, ah should have follow her mind. It would become a contest of bodies to bodies sweaty and grinding. Chicks with their faces up against the wall with their ass poked out for humping pleasures. The woman throw wine on Rofiki. So, STARR ah throw wine. That make everyone sing, *"She throw wine, ah throw wine!"* The moment STARR decided to wiggle her ass and the fellows are singing and looking, Rofiki would grip her up ready to fight dudes like he was, his favorite Philadelphia boxer 'Bernard Hopkins' and ready to knock nigga's out. He was skillfully ready to throw right and left jabs. His would always publicly humiliate her screaming, "Rastafari meh *gyal is meh gyal na fa show*!"

DREADLOCK TALES "She Has A Soul Of Fire" SYNCHRONICITY

Then get her home and hate her for being there and stopping his show, then want to fuck. Remembering that party and walking 15 blocks in the wee hours of the night to a dark house and no music. She heard whispers inside as she peeped through an open window with broken mini blinds. Rofiki sitting on a sofa and some thick light-skinned bitch – blonde short chic-wig – Booty shorts and high heels only - blowing him.

Flash backs of throwing a brick through the window and Rofiki chasing to keep up and pleading. *"Meh luv only STARR! Yu na see meh! Dat was meh bwoy. Meh in da basement slamming dominoes. It wasn't meh!"* Of course his lines all night were in chorus again with Shaggy. Rofiki would never just come right out and say I love you. He waited until he was caught and used it as a get out of jail monopoly card.

BREAK REFORM "Fractures" FRACTURES

Thinking of the fractures of the past. Rofiki said he loved STARR, and now he doesn't. Saying he wanted her, but then he won't. Readjusting this situation, because she wasn't his prime consideration. Peek-a-boo, he wasn't expecting her. Here it is she takes him back. Doing her best to understand, trying her best to get through the fractures. A smiled ruffled STARR'S mouth, she wasn't living that fractured life anymore. Now the rain was getting heavy and she hurried running past the memories of

Rofiki and getting to BearLove's. Snapping out of the day dreams she rang BearLove's doorbell.

Since the JAZZ1CAFÉ was closed due to the fire they were now working on new music. They were lining up new gigs Friday & Saturday nights for the next couple of months, meaning that would be more than enough to pay the rent at the zoo, her new name for home. Since she lived footsteps away from the Philadelphia Zoo.

JAZZTRONIK "Spur" ZOOLOGY

'BLACK BEAST STUDIOS & RECORDS' housed in the private setting of his large basement. BearLove lived in a big 100 + year old historical single family stone house on Germantown Avenue in the Germantown section of Philadelphia. In the basement of his home was his gold mine. All he worked for was invested in his future and his dreams 'Black Beast Studios and Records.'

The multi - million dollar recording studio occupied the basement of his home in the 'hood' nicked named 'Brick Yard.' Brick Yard had a bad reputation for nigga's always getting robbed or shot. But BearLove had been there all his life and everybody knew who he was and where he was and didn't mess with him. Comfortable and secured in his hood never feeling like he was missing anything. Since growing up he was never allowed to play outside. His mother, Khadijah, kept him out of trouble and in school and after-school music lessons at the Settlement School of Music the Germantown branch. Not far from his home on Germantown Avenue.

From years of the neighborhood deteriorating and new business popping up on Germantown Avenue many people just assume it's a rumor that BearLove still lives there, since they never see him, because of his vampire schedule. In the wee hours of the night fancy cars would pull up and many well-known recording artists would come through to lay tracks.

A very modest man of simplicity was BearLove's fashion. A new pair of jeans and a new white-T shirt, and 2 pairs of draws (boxers & Briefs) was his gear most of the time, unless it was cold and he wore a black-hoodie, and now always in memory of Trayvon Martin. He never was a big profiler, flaunting his money.

ROY HARDGROVE "Interlude" THE RH FACTOR HARDGROVE

The studio basement ran the whole length of the house. It was if the interior design recording studio pimps came and pimped out the basement with warm cool colors throughout. There was an amazing collection of new and vintage outboard gear, as well as new and vintage microphones collection including models from Neumann, Sennheiser, Royer, Shure, AKG, Blue, Audio Technica, and more.

All secured by alarm system and a heavy iron gate with a clear sign that read 'Beware of Dog' was to keep the robust and powerful Rottweiler named 'Negro' from tearing up the world that tried to enter invited or uninvited. The dog's cleverness, endurance and willingness to protect made him as suitable as a police dog, therapy dog and devoted companion to BearLove only. He was large in size and his coat was black with rust to mahogany markings. An inherent protector, Negro was self-confident and responded quietly with a wait-and-see attitude.

Not a fan of dogs BearLove's fiancée, Mina barely wanted to feed Negro and would never let their sons play with the dog or say the dog's name they called him dog, d-o-g. But for sure Negro was a guard dog to BearLove's empire. The funny thing is that STARR never knew that the rule was to call BearLove when out front, so he could put Negro away. From day one she had been coming into the gate and petting and rubbing Negro's belly and ringing the bell.

ALI SHAHEED MUHAMMAD "Lord Can I have This Mercy" SHAHEEDULLAH AND STEREOTYPES

Smiling easily BEARLOVE greeted "As-salaamu 'alaykum" (Peace be unto you). STARR smiled comfortably back also greeting, "Wa'aleichem Ashalom" (and upon you be peace). Glad BearLove was home alone and checking him out sporting his vintage Allen Iverson #3 – 76er's basketball jersey and sweats. Looking like he was ready for a Philadelphia 76er's basketball game. STARR and Negro both entered the house happy to be out of the rain. Immediately kicking off her shoes.

Before entering the house, Bearlove stopped STARR in the doorway, and handed her a towel to dry off saying, *"Please let me teach you something today. Upon entering the house, any house, my house, your house, any store, any building, before coming in say, 'Bismillah.' It is an Arabic phrase meaning, 'In the Name of GOD.' Upon entering the house it is good to recite to remind and be bless with good intentions, leaving all the fitna outside. You know bad feelings and conflicts. It is a good way to remember to keep your mind right."*

A sense of strength came to her and her despair lessened listening to BearLove continuing to explain, *"The Prophet (S) recited in Arabic,* "Alahumma inni assaluka kheryil mawlij wakheryil makh'ridge, Bismillah walijna, wa Bismillah kharajna, wa alalah rabana tawakalna." *Breaking it down from Arabic to English he translated, "O Allah! I ask you for good both when entering and when going out. In the name of GOD we have entered, and in the name of GOD we have gone out, and in our Lord we count..."*

Always moved by the spiritual side of BearLove it showed a very caring and aware side of him. After drying off and discovering Mina and the boys were not home that give them a chance to puff before the rest of the band showed up. They were in the studio puffing and chilling and listening to instrumental tracks. Negro wanted to go back outside in the rain and could be heard barking at a motorcycle that passed by the house. BearLove knew all of Negro's barks. He even knew the bark that alerted that Mina and the boys were home that was more like a heavy whining growl.

THE ROOTS (Black's Reconstruction) "75 Bars" RISING DOWN

Black Beats Studio was divided into many rooms of equipment for a commercial facility set to create high-quality music recordings in the A tracking room with a 96 input SSL Duality Console, plus a stone drum room to record the 'Pearl Drums' in all their glorious ambience and to overdub the cymbals in a more controlled space. Beating on the white - opal 'Pearl Drums.'

Interested in everything and every word BearLove elucidated as STARR obtained mentally notes. *"For that killer kick I mic the kick drum with a Senheiser 421, but only after throwing a sandbag in the drum to weigh it down. Letting the sandbag touch the head that the beater hits, just enough to dampen out any obnoxious overtones, but not the good, the natural sounding ones. The mic should be placed about half way in the drum and pointing at the beater. If I bring the mic in from the right side of the drum and angle it at the beater I will be avoiding leakage from the snare drum which is a good thing to do. I always keep the mic pointed at my shin bone on my leg that controls the hi-hat and in line with the beater."*

It was all foreign as STARR continued listening to him explain the mic-tech science of BearLove. There were kick drums, snare drums, Tom – Toms, Cymbals and too many drum sticks to count. Equipment racks, large tape machines and tall shelves filled with vinyl records. A set of 1961 'Leedy' drums that sat on display like in a museum. BearLove clearing up and letting it be known, *"They still play and in pretty good shape. These drums were my Pops, he was a drummer. They are made of mahogany and I just put on a brand-new snare head and the clear head on the floor tom gives it a bigger, badder, boomier high volumes sound."*

THE REBIRTH *"Everybody Say Yeah"* THIS JOURNEY IN

Feeling what she is supposed to feel, STARR was saying *"Yeah!"* Paying close attention to the new information STARR was learning and once again admiring the intelligence of BearLove and still singing, *"Say yeah!"* There also was a vocal booth ready for any group or solo artist. A large mixing room featured a SSL XL – 9080K console and large overdub booth. BearLove explained, *"The overdub is a technique used by to add a supplementary recorded sound to a previously recorded performance. For example, when the bass guitarist Joe Daddy is temporarily unavailable, the recording can be made and the bass track added later, and editing features an SSL Matrix console and SSL X-Logic outboard gear. Among the most widely used computer programs including Avid Technologies Inc. Pro Tools HD, Steingerg Media technology cubase, and Apple Inc. Garage Band."*

THE ROOTS *"The Pow Wow"* RISING DOWN

The rain was falling harder and members of the group Joe Daddy the bass player, Ronny Glasshouse the piano player and DJ Jazzy X and Dark Mind were on a conference called explaining why they were canceling because of the weather or something else concerning the music they already did for QUADIR and money and their time.

The name sound familiar, STARR sat quietly wondering if it was the same QUADIR. She listened to the conversations because it was on speaker phone. They both heard the caller ID beep and Mina's name flashed, BearLove ignored it. After the buzz-kill explosive conversation there was nothing else to do but get their heads right. They relit and puffed until they got cottonmouth - dry mouth and thirstiness common after getting high. After drinking up all the bottled water and having the munchies they ordered take-out and waited for the deliveryman.

Teasing BearLove's about his cheese steak obsession. However, STARR'S cheesesteak crave ended the day, she met Rofiki, who is also vegetarian, like Mina. Really wanting a Greek salad but feeling rebellious and greedy, she also ordered a cheese steak wanting to taste the fried chopped red beef, smothered in white American cheese, fried onions, hot banana peppers, dill pickles and ketchup on a toasted Kaiser roll.

It was hilarious STARR joked, *"Mina will kill u if she finds out your eating meat."* BearLove quickly replied," *Well she won't find out because she is staying the night at her mother's tonight."* He didn't say much more, but the frown on his face showed they were having relationship problems. Bearlove reminded STARR that he don't eat pork, but Halal meat is prayed over and it's all good.

URSULA RUCKER "Untitled Flow" SILVER AND LEAD (Featuring KING BRITT)

To support SOULSHINE SESSIONS they stayed tuned in faithfully as V.I.P. Listeners of JAZZ1CAFÉ when not working on their own music. How could they not support the station? The loved the smooth flow of commercial free, Smooth – Jazz, Nu Jazz, Neo Soul, and R&B, Spoken Word Poetry, International sounds, conscious Hip-Hop and more.

"What's in your headphones?" Sharing the mobile phone and tablet APP with everyone. BearLove was on his cellphone and other mobile devices sharing it on all his social media sites. STARR only did text she knew nothing about social media due to Rofiki's 101 restrictions. She was thinking about opening a Facebook account, but decided not to give Rofiki a chance to eye-hustle her pictures, her where-about and locations tagged or comments on her comments.

FRANK MCCOMB "More Than Friends" The Truth Vol. 2

Becoming aware of the closeness in their friendship, BearLove was like a new beat to her literally every day and she was like a new song to him. She let her back relax and her eyes close for long seconds, as they listened to Jazz1Café Radio. Lost in their high and contemplations, She wondered what her life would be like if she was Mina? Pretty biracial with long hair and nice full figure and 2 beautiful sons. STARR didn't think that BearLove would even think about cheating on Mina. Looking like she could be Rozonda 'Chilli' Thomas of the R&B group T.L.C. or Kimora Lee Simon's sister with all the Baby Phat bags to promote it.

The vibe and chemistry and laughter enjoyed in each other's company could not be discounted. Feeling like they knew each other forever. They liked the same foods, like the same colors on the gray scale varying from black to white. They were also compatible on the 'Kinsey scale, also called the Heterosexual–Homosexual Rating Scale. It uses a scale from 0, meaning exclusively heterosexual, to 6, meaning exclusively homosexual. They both were zeros with votes of gay rights. What really brought them together was the music, so it was inevitable for musicholics like them not to talk about music.

After the heated phone conversation with the other band members BearLove began explaining his plans with his new record label 'BLACK BEAST STUDIO and RECORDS' for independent artist that inspire keeping the blue notes and the black chords alive in good music.

ERYKAH BADU "Telephone" NEW AMERYKAH PT. ONE WORLD WAR (SOULSHINE SESSIONS Remix)

"Telephone... It's Quadir, he wants to give you directions home. Said it won't be too long the day is gone its 1:16 A.M. Just fly away to heaven brother make a place for me brother. Save a place for me brother. Fly away to heaven brother put in a word for me. Telephone, Hmmmmmm. Telephone... Its Quadir, he wants to give you directions home said it won't be too long."

'THE NEOSOUL STARR' will be the first group on the new label, though BearLove had intended on his young boy, his hood-brotha, his dear 26 year old friend 'QUADIR' being his first Nu-Hip-Hop Artist, until his untimely death, he was murdered on the same day as Trayvon Martin February 26th, but the year before 2011, In Philadelphia. It was still too painful for BearLove to talk about it. Though he did everything he could to bring awareness to the gun violence in Philadelphia ending all his shows with a shout out, *"PEACE QUADIR!"*

Wanting Justice for the crimes of senseless gun battles on the streets of Philadelphia leaving a new mother sonless every day and him feeling like he lost a blood –brother, they were tight like that. Tapping on the drums getting into the groove and trying to get their minds in tuned, BearLove signaled for her to just get on the mic and freestyle. Off the top of her head and just let it flow. Feeling the melody the lyrics just flowed no pen or paper needed!

The spirit of QUADIR could be felt and the LOVE was unspeakable, but sung-able. Now to feel this happy and at peace after so many years of her own grief and then being inspired by a spirit she never met, but knew she would have loved too, she loved his music and all the stories BearLove shared. She sang a song that would be titled: PEACE QUADIR. Into the music she sung repeatedly. *"Mmmmm, mmmmmmm, mmmmmm, mmmmm, mmmmmm, mmmmmm."*

QUESTLOVE *"Good Bye Isaac"* QUESTLOVE
(SOULSHINE SESSIONS Remix)

"Peace Quadir – Peace Quadir – Peace Quadir
I Love You
Bismillah – Bismillah
Peace Quadir – Peace Quadir – Peace Quadir
We Love You
Bismillah – Bismillah"

After that emotional musical collaboration BearLove began breaking down the subject Major Labels vs. Indie Labels and changing the subject and trying to alter his mourning thoughts and back to business. Explaining why he became his own producer and music label. When he was signed to a major label that limited him to the label only and upon meeting and discovering a lot of musicians, vocal groups, solo artist, back - up singers that were locked in contracts and unable to work or record with other artist, and may have felt black listed once they were released.

Most artist feel like they are put on a shelf and abandon to rot, while still owing the record labels money for financial advances, video shoots and shit like that. Breaking down the pros and cons of being an independent artist, he explained that he didn't want to sign anyone to a contract that would jam them up keeping them prisoner and he didn't want any hostages. Wanting to be free to work with the artist and promoters he wanted. Wanting to play at the kinds of venues he wanted to play in. Be in more control of time spent on the road, when and how often he played.

Most importantly BearLove wanted STARR to be a part of it all and breaking it all down. She was all ears and wishing, she had paper to take notes. She had to pee, but the conversation and his brain power and knowledge was like a buffet of new information she wanted to learn about in the music business. His intelligence and wisdom and new words tasted too good to get up and go to the bathroom.

ANGELA JOHNSON "Hurts Like Hell" IT'S PERSONAL (SOULSHINE SESSIONS Remix)

Quadir now have a home in the sky, wasn't ready to say good-bye. But you answered your call. A hole left in my heart that won't heal. Much time has passed, but still think about him every day-ay. Some say-ay it will fade away-ay. The pain of losing him. But it hurts like hell that Chris' not here today. Can't pretend in life nothing hasn't changed. Longing to hear his sweet voice in our ears. Just a chance to hold him in our arms again! SoulShine will be free-ee-ee-ee.

REAL PEOPLE "High" SEVEN WAYS TO WONDER

Lately STARR had been calling BearLove and reminding him, she had the time, she would be there. He takes her h-high. Seasons change but never no fear, she'll be there in time. Like flowers that need the sunshine and rain to flourish over again. He takes her h-high. She was so high feeling like the stars of the night this was her moment, she has been waiting for.

Blazed and relaxed in the cannabis h-high she wanted to spread her wings and fly. BearLove enjoyed having STARR'S full attention. He check the time, they were cool. Not wanting to lose her attention he continued to educate, *"An independent label is a record label that is not affiliated in any way with a major label and uses independent distributors to get their releases into stores. Common perception of a 'Record Label' is the major record labels in Los Angeles or New York which include Sony, Universal, Arista, Capitol Records, and VHR - Vicious Heats Records are major corporations with hundreds of millions of dollars behind them, allowing them to properly fund all of the world's biggest artists. In the eyes of an emerging artist, a 'record deal' is the big picture and it has always been envisioned as a contract with one of these major players."*

REEL PEOPLE "Can't Stop" SECOND GUESS

Can't stop the way he feel, every time BearLove look into STARR'S eyes he's falling. Admiring everything about STARR especially the fact that she was paying attention. Plus the weed was so good it gave him the raps causing him to talk too much.

Exposing the music-geek, BearLove gladly continued breaking it down, "*STARR with the introduction of online social networks and the death of popular radio and digital music retail stores such as iTunes, Rhapsody and Amazon, independent artist have been able to market their music. Along with the fact that every major release in the past few years has leaked to the internet weeks before the release day. The ideologies of the past are no longer relevant. Major label companies are now in a transition period and are struggling to come up with the end-all-be-all solution to all of their problems."*

Black Beast Records is an 'Indie Label' making it feasible for artist to produced (fund) and operates their own music. Typically, major labels operate their own distribution and publishing companies. 'Black Beast' can produce the kind of large scale business that the major labels can with contractual relationships for their distribution and publishing services that major labels have to offer. The interesting thing about indie labels could consist of a guy with a computer and drum kit and a single mic in his basement and that is just how BearLove started.

JILL SCOTT "Dear Mr. & Mrs. Record Industry" THE VAULT VOL. 1

Listening to BearLove, STARR thought of what she would say if had to write a letter to the record industry. "*Dear Mr. / Mrs. Record Industry, I've only one place to be and I ain't looking for nothing not due to me. I'm just asking for what's necessary. Every song is a moment in time. Every line a reason a rhyme. Every voice is a choice. Every melody...*" All ears listening and mentally downloading and absorbing everything like a sponge, STARR'S heart rate increased when he mentioned VHRecords. BearLove was very intelligent and it was turning her on. She listened to him continue to rattle on, *"My momma always said this and then my home-boy comedian Kevin Heart quoted it in the movie Soul Plane, 'If you want me to kiss your ass then you have to put it in my contract.'*

Pausing for a puff and air and to admire STARR, BearLove continued saying, *"I hope this information was useful for you. Knowing some basics about the realities of recording contracts before you get involved with them can save you a lot of grief down the road. Remember, record company lawyers have a reason for every clause in their contracts and so should you. Since we are on the subject about signing contracts, I have to talk to you about that because we have just been recording having fun trusting each other, but we have to protect our music. I must also ask have you ever signed a contract, since you mentioned that dude Rofiki was your manager."*

STATELESS "Falling into" ART OF NO STATE

Falling into... Not missing a word BearLove said, STARR dropped her head in shame. Giving details about the demo CD and further explaining how Rofiki found a dude with a recording studio in a funky smelly bedroom, which consisted of an old model Mac laptop computer on an ironing board, speakers hooked up to a surround sound system and a long microphone cord that lead into a closet to singing in, but they had to wait for him to remove his clothing and bags of dirty clothes, before they could record.

Finally STARR explained the agreement, she signed with Rofiki to execute business deals with Vicious Heat Records, but she had not heard from him, so she didn't know what was up, since no contact. She then told of the day in the coffee shop and same night of their JAZZ1CAFÉ gig. She signed the management agreement, but never mentioning that was also the day she met Bluesy. She was more shameful telling him, she didn't have a copy of the signed paperwork.

QUESTLOVE "The Lesson Part 1" (INSTRUMENTAL)

BearLove asked, *"You have a copy of demo CD? I wish I knew what was going on with that paper work. So you want me to get in touch with your boy and see if I can get things straight before we release our shit. Cool. Settled I'll handle it. But it was only a contract to manage you right?"*

Wanting to know more about her, he asked, *"So where are you from? Tell me something I don't know about STARR?"* "Nor - Nor..." She stuttered and didn't know what to say it. She also didn't want to say Norristown or North Philly. She didn't want to claim West Philly and none of these places did anything to her, she had fond memories of all she just didn't want to remember.

Changing the subject and teasing BearLove about his autographed picture and having all of JILL SCOTT albums. He joked, *"You don't want me to play any Jilly from Philly, and she brings the freak out of me!"* STARR chuckled, *"We don't want the freak out plus I think you and SOULSHINE play enough Jilly from Philly!"* Laughing at her jokes, he sensed that she might like the big teddy bear.

ERIC ROBERSON "Obstacles" THE VAULT VOL 1.5

So many obstacles were getting in the way. That keep interrupting what BearLove truly wanted to say. Even if Rofiki wasn't on STARR'S mind, stepping to her that way just seems so out of line. So should, he swallow this frustration and hope that this temptation will subside or should he just try? The delivery man pulled up and BearLove hurried to get the food.

Finally, STARR got a chance to pee and wash her hands. Listening to Negro's obnoxious barking and the rumbling clouds warning of more rain and the storm was not over. Soon as the door closed the dog stopped barking and BearLove was back with the food.

Watching, BearLove dancing around and holding on to his sagging jeans and as usual, he wore 2 pair of underwear. She asked, *"What's the method to your madness of wearing 2 pair of underwear, 1 brief, and 1 boxer."* He didn't seem to mind the question. He washed his hands prayed over their food and then bit into ketchup packets and squirted them all over his large cheese while answering. He even stood up to model his trade mark. Speaking as if he was bragging, *"Always gotta have 2 pairs of draws on. I've been doing this all my life. My pants sag but my big ass won't show."*

DEBORAH BOND "Nothing Matters" MADAM PALINDROME

It's strange how people think they understand 'because this feeling is universal in every way. It's alright, because BearLove and STARR knew that they drive each other wild, baby! They're making music babe! After rubbing their full bellies they puffed and talked and still jamming to JAZZ1CAFÉ RADIO admiring each other. Teasing BearLove about all the drum machines and cymbals and drum sticks that he had collected as part of his memorabilia's. He had pictures on his walls of him and everyone she could think of. Her favorite picture was the one of him with Michael Jackson, and the one of BearLove and his mother, Khadijah Love.

> *"Nothing matters when you're feel it baby*
> *So sit back, relax, and enjoy this funky carpet ride"*

Giving STARR a tour of the house he inherited from his mother Khadijah, who inherited from her mother (Momma Love), his grandmother who gave him the nickname BearLove. He gave her a tour of the living room pointing out the 'Yamaha' ebony black upright piano. He explained it was grandmother who taught him how to read music.

Continuing the tour and leading STARR upstairs. The walls going up the steps were filled with pictures of BearLove from birth all the way through high school. There was a picture of him with the group 'THE ORGANICS' posing with his mother Khadijah before she died. They stopped to look at the picture as he explained his mother never met Mina or his boys, and pointing out his baby picture, his mother's favorite.

AALIYAH *"If Your Girl Only Knew"* ONE IN A MILLION

> *"If his girl only knew"*

What Bearlove saying, what he saying, what he saying, huh? Listening to him mention Mina's name made STARR feel a little uncomfortable since Mina wasn't home and going up stairs to their sleeping quarters. She felt Mina probably didn't want her in their house at all. BearLove enlightened that it was *"His house"* the house he grew up in and wasn't ready to leave, because of the memories. Recollections of a house full of love with his grandmother Momma Love's cooking, and his mother Khadijah's Islamic teachings, walking him rain or shine to school and always there to pick him up.

PHONTE "Not Here Anymore" CHARITY STARTS AT HOME

"Love don't live here anymore"

The house BearLove got his first set of drums. Furthermore he mentioned that Mina didn't want to fully move in wanting her own house. Spends a lot of time at her mother's claims the loud music and traffic of musicians was too much for her. Mina wants to buy a house in the suburbs, move out to Montgomery County and out of Philadelphia. Bear said, *"I understand, but this is my life too and how I pay the bills."*

"Love don't live here anymore"

Pay close attention, STARR eyed the colorful crayon drawn framed on the yellow walls, knowing instantly it was his sons' bedroom. She quickly glanced at a framed professional photo of BearLove, Mina and their two son's Nikko and Milan. Their sons were beautiful boys reminding her of little Tiger Woods when she see them. They looked identical though they were not twins. She always felt goose bumps watching them run into the arms of their father missing him too. She assumed the desire came from not knowing her father, or ever having a father figure.

KEM "A Mother's Love" INTAMCY: ALBUM III

Walking past the gallery of pictures in the hallways of his mother and grandmother, STARR knew that BearLove missed them dearly. *"In a mother's love, you are free to dream, because she sees what you can be..."* STARR wished she knew where her mother was. Walking past the master bedroom that was once Mama Love's and then Khadijah's, BearLove mentioned it was now Mina's room. Able to quickly peek into the pink bedroom with a queen size bed decorated with different shades of pink pillows, before he quickly led her down the hall. She was wishing she had a queen size bed with lots of pillows.

Opening another door to a blue bedroom, BearLove explained it was his room. He didn't have to say anymore, she understood checking out the vinyl record collections that lined the walls like a library. *"Wow you have more records then a record store! Who still has a record player?"* They laughed as she noticed the king size bed unmade and a couple of pair of his boxers on the floor. She pretended not noticing him kicking them under the bed.

GROOVE THEORY "Good 2 Me" GROOVE THEORY

"Are you gonna be, are you gonna be
Are you gonna be
Are you gonna be, are you gonna be
Are you gonna be good to me"

"Baby, we're so fly together," STARR and BearLove could touch the clouds if they go, she wanna know will he catch her when she come down. Limit is the sky if he can look her in the eye and without any doubt, say he'll never lie... There were walls of shelves floor to ceiling high and crates full of vinyl records a mile deep.

GEORGIA ANNE MUDROW "Break You Down" EARLY

"Don't let them make you forget who you are. Don't let them break you down..." Checking out his turn tables she asked a two part question, *"Do you DJ too? How many albums do you have?"* Again she, *"WOWED!"* at learning he had over 150, 000.00 albums and CD's in his collection and many autographed. He explained how his mother would take him to *'The Sound of Germantown'* or *'The Sound of Market Street'* record stores in Philadelphia. Buying new music every Saturday afternoon, right after watching 'Soul Train.'

Record stores always fascinated STARR remembering where Shantey Money brought her first record *'The Sound of Norristown.'* The first album STARR pulled out was 'LAFAYETTE AFRO ROCK BAND.' BearLove began explaining, *"The group 'Lafayette Afro Rock Band' was a French funk rock band formed in Long Island, New York in early1970's. Though almost unknown here in the United States, they are celebrated as one of the standout funk bands and admired for their use of break beats. The master of these beats drummer Ernest (Donnie) Donable, may he rest in peace, is my hero."*

LAFAYETTE AFRO ROCK BAND *"Darkest Light' MALIK*

Turning up the music BearLove explained it was a classic rare vinyl in his collection, and the track he was about to play was a very popular cut sampled by many well-known recording artist. She was about to hear it 100% raw, uncut, uncooked, unadulterated funk and she immediately wanted to hear it.

Lyric to lyric on the first note of the opening bars were very familiar to STARR as she giggled, *"That's my nigga – even if he didn't get any bigger! Hova - JAY Z and my favorite song from the year 2006 Show Me What You Got!"* Delighted BearLove applauded and explained how Hip -Hop was started just rapping over old soul records so why are people surprised that it is the bases of Hip - Hop And that's why I love good hip hop beats and samples like these and the message that those artists put in it.

Public Enemy "Show "Em Whatcha Got" (1988)
Queen Latifah "Latifah's Law" (1989)
Detroit Boxx & Step 2 Wisdom "Faith & Knowledge" (1990)
Kid Capri Apollo (1991)
Wreckx-N-Effect (featuring Teddy Riley)"Rump Shaker" (1992)
Heavy D & the Boyz "SlowDown" (1992 or 1996)
Cutty Ranks "Hustle Hustle" (1993)
Ice Cube "Friday" (1995)
FREESTYLERS "Freestyle Noize" (1998)
Deep Inc. "Tee Time" (2005)
JAY-Z "Show Me What You Got" (2006)
SKC and DIS "Salvation" (2007)
Influx UK "Show 'Em What You Got" (2008)
Riva Starr "Black Mama" (2010)

Every album BearLove mentioned he had in his collection. STARR added to his list of songs sampled as if his list wasn't long enough she mentions, *"Oh and the movie 'Shaft in Africa' starring Richard Roundtree."* He clapped his hands like she just won a prize. She picked up a CD that had a homemade - demo appearance with a very familiar male face on the cover.

JOHN LEGEND "She Don't Have to Know" GET LIFTED

Oh stealing moments just to be with STARR. Though it's wrong it's hard to tell the truth, oh no Mina don't have to know, she don't have to know. The black and white printed photo of the guy on the cover looked just liked JOHN LEGEND, but it was labeled and autographed by JOHN STEPHENS. STARR pointed it out swearing, "*Word up this dude JOHN STEPHENS looks just like JOHN LEGEND."*

Taking the CD carefully out of her hands BearLove's voice was filled with caution and laughter, "*Okay be careful shorty this is one of a kind. It was JOHN'S first CD when he was an independent artist doing his thing all over the Philadelphia area and before he became LEGEND.* Since then the singer-songwriter and actor has won Grammy Awards and he received the special Starlight and songwriters' hall of fame.

JOHN STEPHENS "Sun Comes Up" JOHN STEPHENS (JOHN LEGEND)

Looking for the sun to come up they peered out the window at the rain. BearLove knew STARR thought if she let him in he would break her heart. Tonight they're going to lose track of time. Body and spirit will intertwine and she'll stay there the rest of the night and babe when the sun comes up, he'll gonna be holding her. Wait a minute BearLove is not through. He intended to spend more than one night with STARR. A love affair that never ends like the old song said, "*Let's do it again!"*

All STARR had to do was go with BearLove, she knew she could stay and wake up in the morning to a brand new day. After reading and letting go of the John Stephen / John Legend CD, STARR laughed at BearLove pretending to dusting off her finger prints, then laughing he handed it back to her. Then she noticed the Phyllis Hyman signed album that was in a glass case on the wall. STARR was very – very – impressed eyes glued to the PRIME OF MY LIFE album, and reading the autographed message scribbled across her breast.

Singing along and both knowing every lyric to PHYLLIS HYMAN songs. BearLove explained how when he was a young buck his mother first took him to see the silky voiced, R&B and jazz-influenced vocalist. In concert at the Valley Forge Music Fair and the Philadelphia Spectrum. His mother Khadijah always had a hook up and they were able to meet the goddess of female songstress Phyllis Hyman. Meeting her in person and getting that album signed was a very special day for him.

PHYLISS HYMAN *"Living All Alone"* LIVING ALL ALONE

There used to be time in STARR'S life when Rofiki and she were lovers and they shared a place together, just them two. She thought about how they planned to get married. Thinking about how she used to know him well. Now she can't stand this living all alone. Now, she love what's in her life and she is finding it's a mellow world. Living all alone was painful and STARR understood the passion and love in the song. She began explaining more details about the alleged suicide of her idol, more then what BearLove knew.

On the afternoon of June 30, 1995. It was also said PHYLISS HYMAN suffered from bipolar disease. Allegedly she took her life because, her record company, Arista, had promised her she would be the next DIANA ROSS', however dropping her when they signed WHITNEY HOUSTON to the label.

PHYLISS HYMAN was scheduled to perform at the Apollo Theater in Harlem New York with the WHISPHERS in a series of shows at the Apollo Theatre. Rumors abound that she told a friend one night that this would be her last show. When she failed to appear at the Apollo Theatre, she was found in her Manhattan apartment unconscious, overdosed with suicide note found near her and several vials of pills were found. The suicide note read in part, "I'm tired. I'm tired. Those of you that I love know who you are. May GOD bless you..."

PHYLISS HYMAN *"Prime Of My Life"* PRIME OF MY LIFE

In the prime of STARR'S life and there's nothing that she can't do, she can't lose in the prime of her life. Growing stronger every day and moving mountains standing in her way. BearLove was surprised STARR knew so much and to hear her talk this much BearLove said, "*I knew you were special that night we met at the Black Lily and you sung "Meet Me On The Moon" By PHYLISS HYMAN from the 'Prime of my Life' CD, but how you know all that?*" STARR replied, "*I told you I was a fan that's why you blew me away the first time I heard you sing like her and how did you learn how to whistle like a bird too."*

One corner of STARR'S mouth was pulled into a slight frown, embarrassed. She didn't want to admit that she thought about exiting the world the same way, but had no courage and no desire to leave. Sitting back and listening to the wonderful sounds of music and smoking some serious killa, STARR started to choke.

Bringing comfort BearLove patted STARR on the back. Patting to a slow tempo down her spine, causing goose bumps. She had not planned to get this close to BEARLOVE, because #1 he had a girlfriend and groupies. Then BearLove asked, *"How come you never ask me anything questions about the group, 'THE ORGANICS?"*

It wasn't because STARR didn't care about asking BearLove why the group decided to take a break and work on their solo projects, it was self-explanatory. Plus anything she wanted to know she could Google BearLove. She was going to stick to her plan. Minding her own business and not wanting her personal feelings to interfere with paying the rent and she didn't want to mess that up. STARR wanted to keep it music only!

TALIB KWELI "I Try" THE BEAUITFUL STRUGGLE (Featuring MARY J. BLIGE)

Without a doubt, BearLove tried that's all he can do. Try, he knows he tried and will try and try again, yeah. In life he tried and got searched on the plane, because of his Arabic first name. *"I try, I try, I try, and you know I try."* Admitting to herself, STARR felt something deep for him admiring his charming sense of humor, his well-kept high afro with always a black afro-pic and handsome brown plump face.

Nonchalantly STARR consoled BearLove with the reminder replying, *'When we met up, you told me that 'The Organics' decided to take a break and work on solo projects, it was self-explanatory. I'm not TMZ all up in your Kool – Aid trying to know the flavor. But what I do now is that 'The Organics' '' first major-label album, 'Do U Need More' forsaking usual hip-hop protocol, the album was produced without any samples or previously recorded material."*

In the word of 'DJ Kool' BearLove said, *"Let me clear my throat..."* Impressed with knowing she was up on 'The Organics' and considered them her favorite and bobbing her head to the music BearLove re-lit and passed it. She noticed he had music, stereos and speakers all over the house, so he could listen wherever and whenever. STARR loved music just as much. She was glad that the love-seat in his bedroom was in front of a window and the window was facing the front of the house, so they could see everything. Bear explained that folks could also see them too, so the lights were low.

Given that they were talking about Hip-Hop BearLove asked, *"Since we're talking Hip Hop and arguably the biggest rivalry in hip hop history was Bad Boy vs. Death Row. Who do you pick The Notorious B.I.G. or 2Pac?"* STARR didn't have to think long or hard she quickly answered, *"Why do I have to choose? I love them both. But I admit I am a BIGGIE fan."* But she added, *"I really do think 2PAC is still living."* Laughing BearLove replied, *"In fact I talk to my man 2PAC this morning. He called saying his secret has finally been exposed and he was still alive and doing well with 3 kids. 1PAC, 2PAC Jr., and 3PAC."* To change the subject of the death, he played an old school hip - hop Philly jam asking STARR if she knew how to rap.

LADY B "To The Beat Y'all"

Nice and high STARR was still in the flow, *"To the beat y'all – check it out – Jack and Jill went up the hill – to have a little fun – but stupid Jill forgot the pill – and now they have a son!"* BearLove, Jumped up high-pitched, *"YO STOP UR killin' me! You know all my shit. I see you're true hip hop blood!"*

Now, STARR was schooling BearLove as she explained. *"The first example of a female rapper recording as a solo artist came in 1980, when the Philadelphia-based LADY B recorded her single 'To the Beat Y'all' for Sugar Hill Records. After that she ultimately made her mark as a radio DJ here in Philly as you already know. Nonetheless, she is a historically important figure and I am Hip-Hop 4 Life.*

Applauding and clapping his hands BearLove said, *"For those who have followed the history of Hip – Hop and Rap music as long as I, I have never met a chick that knew just as much hip hop as me. Historically, rap has been a very male-dominated idiom – full of testosterone. Nonetheless, female rappers have made some important and valuable contributions to hip-hop, which would have been a lot poorer without Queen Latifah, Salt-N-Pepa, MC Lyte or, Philly's own Eve.*

Joy bubbled in STARR'S laugher and shone in her eyes. She was very interested in hearing more as BearLove continued, *"My list runs long of female hip hop artist of the almost forgotten cult MCs like Nefertiti, Isis, Bo$$, Harmony, and Sha-Key on down to the likes of Sista Soulja, Monie Love, Da Brat, Foxy Brown, Lil' Kim, MC Lyte and Bahamdia. I can't forget Debbie Harry A.K.A. Blondie on the song Rapture."*

QUESTLOVE "Represent" INSTRUMENTAL

STARR was intrigued wanting more and BearLove gave her more, *"The female rappers who have succeeded in their fields and made a brand have had a reputation for being assertive, take-charge women. The early old school female rappers such as Queen Latifah, Eve, Yo- Yo, and shout outs to Sister Souljah and her sociopolitical militantly style. And then you have the sexually explicit Lil' Kim's debut solo album, Hard Core. Kim has never been the least bit shy about having X-rated lyrics and now Nicki Manaji is making heads spin."*

A part of STARR reveled in BearLove's open admiration of her. He leaped up and started digging deeper through, his crates of vinyl records. As he exhaled a long sigh of contentment searched and enlightening, *"But this here Female MC was and still is my favorites of all time and if you know this artist – I just might have to marry you! This record I wished I had autographed. Hold on let me see where I put it– I just had it because I was sampling this beat for one of our songs. Okay, guess who this is since you are Hip Hop 4 Life?"*

Satisfaction pursed BearLove's mouth chuckling with happy memories he said, *"This song I'm about to play ran thru Philly from Da Bottom, Hilltop, Cobbs Creek, The Plateau, North Philly, G-Town (Brickyard), West Oak Lane, Mt. Airy, everyone was on it."* He began naming clubs, *"Hotel Philadelphia, Club Library, Wagner's Ballroom, After Midnight, Impulse, 2nd Stories, La Ferry, Club La Zorro, Kim Graves, Jarretts, Circus City, High Rollers, and M&M Club! We traveled the 'hoods to the best house parties and macked the flyest honeys – old school memories but this is the best pure flow rap ever laid on vinyl."*

M.C. $HANTEY MONEY "Bull Shit" M.C. $HANTEY MONEY
J. DILLA (JAY DEE) "Bullshit" (Instrumental)

"I came tonight to rock the Party... Party... Party...
I came tonight to rock the Party... Party... Party...

Now wave your hands in the air...
Wave them like you just don't care!

I'm $hantey Money
Ain't a damn thing funny
Don't try to play me - Pay me!

Bullshit ain't nothing but chewed up grass
Ask me how I know? Cause you showed me your ass!

It was like listening to the soundtrack of her life. Sentimental lyrics every time STARR heard them. From the first beat she started choking and the heavy lashes that shadowed her cheeks flew up. BearLove patted her back until she swatted his hand away. He seen the shocked look on her face not understanding as if she seen a ghost. Frozen as if suspended in midair listening to every lyric of her mother's voice remembering every beat, every syllable, every noun, every verb and BearLove was reciting the lyrics, *"Bullshit ain't nothing but chewed up grass..."* Feeling like a champ BearLove cheered as he mixed in a new song, *"I win you don't know this cut."*

QUESTLOVE, HERBIE HANCOK, LIONEL LOUEKE and PINO PALLADINO
"Power Refinement"
BONNAROO

Appearing startled, STARR'S voice was fragile and shaking, *"That's M.C. $hantey Money."* BearLove jumped up yelling, *"What U know about $hantey Money? Will you marry me!"* STARR sat down holding her head and holding back the tears, until she busted out crying. Bear stopped the music rushing to her dropping crocodile tears. He was confused because he was only joking about marrying. He comforted while asking, *"STARR what's up? What's the matter?"* Still unable to lift her head mumbling, *"I've* *been singing that song my whole life – Rewriting the lyrics my whole life, remixing the lyrics and humming every beat like a lullaby every night since* $hantey Money, *my mom disappeared!"*

After crying it out and confided in BearLove about her past and sharing TRACK 8: STARR OF A STORY, she felt relieved, but scared that another person will turn her past against her to hurt or threaten her. She left out no details about her search for $hantey Money. BearLove said, *"I'm here to help and we can find her, through your music and her music together."* She asked, *"Can I use $HANTEY MONEY'S music, doesn't the record company own it?"*

THE ROOTS *"Good Music"* ORGANIX

Compassionate, endearing and assuring BearLove's voice had an infinitely compassionate tone saying, *"This moment has brought goose bumps, a feeling like we were meant to do this. I already have the track sampled and ready to rock and you already have the lyrics. Shit you're the lyrics. You got the powerful funky vocals it takes to carry that song and the message! You have that magic STARR and I'm just blessed if you let me be a part of it. Just let the lawyers and I handle the Bull - Shit. But, if you want me to explain what I know about 'copyrights' I can try to sum it up for you."*

Shaking her head agreeing, STARR was ready to be educated on copyrights. BearLove went on giving details, *"Technically speaking, the minute we put your music into a tangible form like a recording, the music is copyrighted. However, to really protect you, I will register with the copyright office. This will protect you in the event that someone, somewhere, steals one of your songs and claims it as their own.*

Pausing to pick up the unlit blunt, BearLove re-lit and puffed before continuing to explain. *"Registering a copyright is not difficult and whether we want to copyright just a single song (for possible digital distribution) or an entire CD of collected works, the process is the same. You just fill out 'Form SR', which we can get from the U.S. Copyright Office, and submit it with two copies of your CD and fees to the Library of Congress at the address on the form. Once we do that, every song on the CD you submitted is protected. Yes, it really is that easy."*

ROY HARGROVE "Bullshit" THE RH FACTOR- HARD GROOVE
(Featuring D'ANGELO)

"I say, I want, I want to tell you, ever told you the story about a man
I've been wanting, I've been longing to tell a story, oh gal
I'm ain't worried, I won't worry, don't worry about a thing"

"No way bullshit," Now back down stairs in the recording studio puffing on some mean green, STARR finished crying over her past and faced with the opportunity to do something that could possibly help find her mother. Mixed in emotional highs and the musical chemistry and the help of marijuana neither of them had any idea what time it was and that they had been together for 12 hours – half the day and they were growing even closer.

Mesmerized in STARR'S natural beauty since the day he seen her. Now his attraction was stronger. He got goose bumps just hearing her voice and when she sang it drove his inner emotions wild. He listened to her voice over and over after every session, unable to get enough of her. Her complexion was like a slice of chocolate cake with fudge icing. If there was a chocolate ice cream in her flavor, he would have a freezer full and would be eating forever.

Looking into her big wide and sparkling bright eyes, BearLove felt his heart actually racing with intimidation. STARR'S mouth was wide and full of pearly white teeth and lips plump and full naturally shaded red amber. Watching STARR'S head sway from side to side and her long jet black locks swaying to the funky beat, he cheered, *"I see you feeling it! This is going to be the Bull-Shit everyone will be singing!"* Bear was tapping his drum sticks on a drum machine and STARR cheered him on laughing at him acting like a cool fool. When the song ended he threw the drum sticks aside and pulled her close to him.

THE FOREIGN EXCHANGE "All The Kisses"
DEAR FRIENDS: AN EVENING WITH THE FOREIGN EXCHANGE

Depending on who you ask BearLove was a little bit crazy, for loving STARR. Depending on who you ask, she should leave and go start anew, he already had a woman. Cause on a day like today she will get all the kisses that he have for her. If he had his way, she would stay for all the kisses that he had for her. Depending on who you asked, she was his prisoner and he is the fool. Depending on who you asked they should never rendezvous...

Catching STARR off guard, because she looked like she wanted to reject, but if she did, he still wasn't going to let go. He couldn't resist, he kissed her. As soon as their lips touched, she pulled away immediately, because outside Negro began barking. Immediately BearLove knew that heavy whining growl meant Mina was home and trying to enter the house with Negro blocking the doorway.

RICH MEDINA "Music" CONNECTING THE DOTS

Immediately BearLove turned the music down and ran upstairs to put the dog in his crate, which Negro hated, so now he was barking frantically. Over the loud barks STARR could hear BearLove greeting his sons. She stayed downstairs in the studio still confused about the kiss, and not sure if she should hide. Looking at the time it was after midnight. Over the cheers of the boys greeting their father, she could hear Mina chasing the boys up the steps and into their bedrooms and shortly after that came the arguing from Mina's pink bedroom.

MINA: *What is this on the floor? A receipt for 2 Cheese Steak, 2 French fries and a Greek salad, when the fugh you starting eating Greek salads? And you're eating cheese steaks again?*

BEAR: *"Chill keep it down. We can rap later when I'm finished working."*

MINA: *"I called you and you texted me you weren't home. The receipt delivery time proves that you were here. U fughing bitches and buying Greek salads, texting me bull - shit, while your fat ass is eating cheese steaks?"*

BEAR: (chuckling sarcastically) *"Bull – Shit ain't nothing but chewed up grass."*

MINA: *"Bull Shit is what? FUGH U BEAR! I'm out trying plan a wedding and take care of our sons and you're still fughing with music. I'm tired of this you - we're supposed to be taking a break to get married, not working!"*

BEARLOVE: *What's up? I'm working and never said I would stop.*

That was STARR'S queue to go hearing bedroom doors slamming and the aftershocks caused a picture on the wall to fall. Then Negro started barking uncontrollably trying to scratch his way out. STARR tipped toed up the steps and slid on her shoes hearing all the arguing coming from upstairs.

NORMAN BROWN "Rain" CELEBRATION

On STARR'S way out the door, she noticed it was BearLove's baby picture that fell off the wall. She started to pick it up and hang it back up then noticed the boys standing at the top of the steps outside their parent's bedroom looking down the steps at her. She left out the front door closing it quietly. She was embarrassed and ready to get home as fast as she could. Thinking of how she just exposed her past life to BearLove and the bull-shit she literally just escaped at his house, and the kiss. Knowing that if Mina ever finds out there would problems, and more problems she didn't want.

A lot of things were going through her head especially the argument she overheard between BearLove and Mina getting married. She was caught off guard when BearLove kissed her, but she had the feeling that it was coming and then she let it come. She was confused and had thought about the possibilities, and pondered what if? *"What if there was no Mina? What if Rofiki came back? What if there was no Bluesy?"* Because truly those were the folks that had her questioning going any further. But the more she knew about BearLove the more she found herself admiring him and naturally emotions have come. But, what he is getting married?

Nevertheless she didn't want to continue to make a disaster out of with her life. She didn't want to be the cause of another woman's pain. She also didn't want BearLove and Mina's problems to become her problems. Their argument reminded her of all the nights she and Rofiki fought. Wishing she could erase him forever from her memory. She would never forgive or forget how Rofiki dis' and dismissed her stepping off without a care.

TEENA MARIE "Black Rain" LA DONA

What did Mina say? Do BearLove love STARR as much as he acted like he did? Alone now going home and knowing the marrow bone, a rolling stone, and her body's wounded on weed and coffee grounds tears of a clown love hand me downs, reverbs and nouns. Because she can't stand the rain falling on the inside of her window pane.

"Black Rain - Black Rain - Black Rain - Black Rain!"

Sweet black rain STARR been ordained. Taken from her again only plain rain remains her heart is stained baptized by flames. BearLove gave her pain sweet black rain. When STARR arrived home soaked and wet. As soon as she opened the front door TYSON greeted her with an arched back and puffed tail. He hissed and spit because it was his way of saying his sleep was disturbed. If she ever seen a cat who looks like this on the street, she wouldn't go near it. But, she had gotten accustom to Tyson's behaviors, since feeding him.

Ever since the embarrassment of Bluesy's first visit she took the liberty of cleaning up after the cats, sweeping the hallways and staircases. She couldn't believe how trifling the Jenki's could be hoarding piles of trash bags in the hallways, so she started taking out their trash too, after hearing their excuses of both having bad backs, hips and knees.

DJ JAZZY JEFF & AYAH "Hold On" BACK FOR MORE

Holding on STARR had to remove the baby gate that kept Tyson down stairs to get to the second floor. She noticed Frisky running her paws under the Jenki's door trying to get Big G's attention and Big G's husky loud purrs could be heard on the other side. The Jenki's had missed another trash day. She was sure they noticed the difference in the cleanliness and the aroma. She also began buying cat food to quite the cats at night, so she could sleep at night.

Immediately Ms. Freda's opened her door and came into the hallway talking super-fast, *"Hey night owl you had a delivery and a visitor. After the delivery an hour later your dreadlock boyfriend came knocking down the door. My knees hurt too bad to go back down to answer the door. Plus I haven't seen him around since the white guy so I don't know what is what.*

I'm not prejudice don't care if they are green or blue. But if they're sharing a bed then they gotta pay rent too, and speaking of rent do you have your rent money?"

Reaching in her wet pocket and giving Ms. Freda $100 saying, *"Now we're even for the month, I gave Mr. Jenki $100 already."* Ms. Freda handed STARR a white piece of paper folded in half saying, *"Good night sleep tight."* After dealing with Ms. Freda the vampire that never sleeps, STARR hurried up to her apartment with the paper in her hand and ready to put on Jill Scott and roll a tree and listened to the symphony of cars zooming up and down Girard Avenue.

STATELESS *"Falling Into"* THE ART OF NO STATE (SWELL SESSION BOY WONDER Remix)

Maybe expecting to find maybe some flowers delivered, but it was a queen size bed and pillow top mattress and plenty of pillows. The air mattress was deflated and pushed in a corner. She cried with joy stretching across the new bed. Yes, she did wish for a bed when she seen Mina's beautiful pink bedroom. And just like always Bluesy is there making wishes come true.

(CREDIT CARD BILL)

(1) Queen Size Platform Bed frame, Pillow-Top Mattress	$999.00
(4) Goose down Pillows	$100.00
(1) Queen Size Egyptian 1600 Tread Count Cotton Sheets	$299.00

It was now 2 AM and after charging her cellphone that had been dead most of the day and getting through the emotions of being happy and confused, she immediately called Bluesy letting him know how grateful she was for the new bed, her new bed, a new bed for new sleep, new thoughts. Covered in pure white 16000 thread count Egyptian cotton sheets new sheets. STARR was confused when his phone went straight to voice mail and his message box was full and she couldn't leave a message.

DEBORAH BOND "Sweet Lullabies" DAY AFTER

Now alone while lying there the constant thoughts of Bluesy was running through STARR'S head. She felt like a baby being rocked to sleep. Overwhelmed with happiness that Bluesy was a caring man. Looking over the receipt with Bluesy's home address. STARR now knew why Ms. Freda was demanding the rent money, because she thought STARR had money. Reading the receipt she couldn't believe the amount of money Bluesy charged on his credit card for the bed.

THE FUNKYLOWE LIVES "Float Through The Stars" CHILL OUT IN PARIS 5 (Introduces Kings Of Lounge)

Lately STARR began to believe that all the things she read and the things she dread about the weed plants and the seeds. Floating through the stars, wondering why she feels older. She fell asleep. Sleeping beauty will toss and turn no more with the innovative technology, like energy-foam & ventilated air –cool to keep her sleeping pretty through the night by increasing airflow over the entire surface of the mattress and providing superior support straight to the edge. That is what the receipt read. Plus the exclusive Titanium support system adds an additional support for her lumbar area. Enjoying the comfortable mattress that will give her proper posture and made in the USA.

TRACK 6: SPEAKERS BOOMING THE FUNK

CHAKA KHAN "Jamaica Funk" (TOM BROWN)

"Jamaica Funk - That's what it is - Let it get into you"

Driving in style down the highway I–95 South heading to Philadelphia from New York. with speakers booming, Rofiki cruised reclined in his new road bling. A diamond white HUMMER H3 customized lifted and loaded on 32" Asantis rims. Custom-made pimped out ride Xzibit styled personally for big Tank's cameo appearances in Lil' Pam's video that was canceled. Rofiki over heard him talking about getting rid of the Hummer and struck up a deal. It became part of the business deal, he worked out with VHRecords as Kandi Gyal's manager and also the fringe benefits of her having a big phat Kandi apple ass.

Navigating the fresh new road armor weighing over 8,400 lbs. A killer on the road and Rofiki' brand-new, wow! The super-sized gas guzzler was never friendly to his pockets. Driving with an unlit blunt in one hand and the other on the steering wheel of his new 'White-Gyal.' Yes, he named it, named her. The new ride 'White- Gyal' gave him character, self-worth, self-image, self-esteem, his ego was pumped and ready to flaunt. Every corner he turned the big body vehicle would anger pedestrians, cyclists and other drivers flipping up their middle fingers, not in favor of the over-sized vehicle that took up double parking spaces on the city streets.

Driving along the highway on the 2 hour drive from New York to Philadelphia, he could usually do in half the time. But, not in 'White-Gyal' that would surely catch the attention of anyone it passed. Making sure his police detector was in check and music Rasta loud and proud. Cruising with the Bluetooth from his iPhone linked to the new sound system and speakers booming the funk! Rofiki chuckled listening to JAZZ1CAFÉ awaiting to hear something by the group THE NEOSOUL STARR. Rofiki had to admit, he was loving the music.

Puffing all the way and feeling secure with the customized smoke exhaust fans and air freshener spray. So high and fully alert of his mission to Philly, he had an eye on the road and the other eye on the road behind him, just in case he was being followed. Shaking his long wild locks free and scratching his head, he cruised along the dark highway with his head pounding from the aftermath of STARR, Kandi, and all of the other crisis in his life that were fughing with da' head.

URBAN MYSTIC "Where Were You" GHETTO REVELATIONS

Where was Rofiki when she first heard 'Biggie' or 'Pac' and he knew, he was blessed with the best of Hip-Hop? And now he had to wonder about where was Kandi Gyal? Well, he knew who she was with. Since witnessing her behaviors at Big Tanks party and learning her twist is cocaine. He felt if he didn't pimp her to fame, some other nigga would. Shouting out his thoughts, *"She gotta a Rasta twisted mistaken meh for da sucker."* Before leaving New York he already knew Big Tank was pickings up Kandi Gyal and taking her to the casting for his new reality television show, #1 Video Vixen.

It was time for her to see what it felt like being thrown in a tank of fine ass women just as vicious as piranha and sharks. So, he left Kandi to fend for herself and then she would appreciate him when he returned. Though he wasn't invited, Rofiki felt he didn't have to be there at Big Tanks New Jersey mansion where the casting was taking place. He already owned the chick, since he got her that far and he had the contract to prove it.

ZIGGY MARLEY "True To Myself" DRAGONFLY

Life has come a long way since yesterday. Rofiki say, and it's not the same old thing over again, he say. *"Got to be true to myself,* Now on his way back to Philadelphia to put STARR on trial because word on the street was that she was running around town, performing at JAZZ1CAFÉ with the boy from 'The Organics' that big mutha' fugha – the drummer dude, while she is carrying his seed. After all he did for her she was trying to play him like this. Along with all the crazy shit going on with his mother Haile continuously calling daily from Jamaica.

Reminding him to pray and to check on the house in North Philly and demanding he pays the property taxes. Rofiki wasn't trying to pay no bills, especially not living in North Philly. He didn't pay for electric, water or cable. Poochie the neighborhood hook- up- man took care of everything. Food wasn't a problem for him in the hood, he kept a full belly because there was always someone selling their food stamps off their access card for weed all day - every day. Flicking his Bic, he lit his blunt, taking long drags with his money in his pocket and money on his mind. Screaming, *"Fugh dat shit. Meh do meh wid meh money!"*

LES NUBIANS "El Son Reggae" ONE STEP FORWARD

*"Jdeale, Jdeale un peu de weed de temps en temps
Mais soigner les mes me parat plus important..."*

Yeah, Rofiki's mother Haile always said, his appetite was as big as his father Kingston, and it was true. Puffing and driving the dark highway and mentally summoning up the spirit of Kingston with every smoke ring. Reminiscing about the time, he attempted to walk from New York to Philly and all the cars that passed him and didn't stop. Just as he was in thought, he noticed a dude walking along the highway, just walking, because it is illegal to hitchhike. Rofiki learned that the hard way.

*"Jdeale, Jdeale a bit of weed from time to time
But treat me most important..."*

Revolting straight up, alarmed he was now passing the dude that didn't look up, dressed in a dark hoodie, who kept walking and didn't try to stop a car cruising by. It was like Rofiki was already looking for someone to be walking along needing a ride. He had been waiting for the time to 'Pay it back and Pay it forward.' But, this person didn't try to hitch a ride. They didn't even turn to look towards the halogen lights, minding their own business the person just kept it moving.

Minding his own business Rofiki re - lit his blunt, because he was going to give them a ride. If only they stuck out their thumb or something. But fugh it he wasn't trying to get side track off his own mission. He sprayed air freshener, turned up the music and kept it moving. Stirring up recollections Rofiki turned up the music and thoughts drifted back again to the day he attempted to walk to Philly. That was the day Kingston was killed and the morning after Rofiki met STARR. Vividly, he could remember as if it were him back there on the road walking.

STEPHEN MARLEY (Acoustic) "Fed Up" MIND CONTROL

"Aye," STARR said how could Rofiki treat her this way? What they had was more than words could say. She's fed up said their relationship is over and remembering when his mother Haile was fed up and left him to be raised by his father Kingston. Life in Jamaica Queens, New York being the only child with both of his knowledgeable Jamaican born parents was powerful for him and when his mother moved it broke hearts.

The recollections of the paradise island nestled among the turquoise salt waters almost smack in the center of the Caribbean Sea and the distant land of Cuba, all the stories came from his parent's teachings. Telling him all about Islands Montego Bay, Ocho Rios, Negril, Port Antonio, runaway Bay and of course Kingston, Jamaica. His Jamaican proverbs and stories of the Blue Mountains that boasts the world's best coffee and his hard accent of 'Patois' all came from the education of his parents.

CHERINE ANDERSON "Angel" ONE LOVE – DANCE HALL QUEEN

"One love, one song, one heart
One love, one song, one heart"

FLASH BACKS... An Angel, Rofiki bobbed his head to the music thinking of his *"Angel,"* his mother Haile was a beautiful youthful humble woman with stunning features making her look young enough to be Rofiki's younger sister. She would tell Rofiki stories about her past and once well-known as the 'Dance Hall Queen.' Competing mysteriously in costumes in dance contest and winning cash-prizes, but now a very religious woman.

The big man Kingston, Rofiki's father was the spitting image of Bob Marley. But he did not portray himself to be anyone but himself – Kingston. Respected as the big man with big powers and always knew how to link up with the connections needed to survive. Kingston was 10 years older than Haile. His mother tried to keep Rofiki in check, but he was head strong and willed.

MESHELL N'DEGEOCELLO *"Friends"* COMET, COME TO ME (WHODINI)

Friends, how many of us have them? 'ROFIKI' means 'Friend' in Swahili. Most people nicked named him. Those in New York called Rofiki *"Philly"* and the folks in Philadelphia called him *"New York."* When he was young and they first arrived in America from Jamaica, *"Rofiki means friend is Swahili."* That was all he remembered Haile drilling the new name into his head, trying to make him forget his real name left back somewhere in the white sands of Jamaica. And out of the years he could remember, he had no clear memories of his birth place, Kingston Jamaica.

But, Rofiki do remember being 6 years old and them having to cut their locks off and become bald-heads. His mother wore her head tied-up for years until her hair grew back only for them too relock their hair. Pledging to never want to feel bald or lose their locks again for anyone. But he couldn't remember if he could walk. He remembered the cruise ship they stowed away on and then that was it.

BAFANG: A child who doesn't learn to how walk until 2 – 7 years old

10 Years later his mother Haile, left his father Kingston, he heard rumors of his father having other women and children, but he still couldn't believe his mother left. Haile moved to Philadelphia when he was 16 years old. Well, actually she went to visit her cousin for the weekend and never came back. Kingston never forgave Haile for leaving them.

Though shortly after Haile left, Kingston's Dominican girlfriend Mara, moved in. There were long periods when they didn't speak due to Rofiki's ignorance, high pitched voice and vulgarity. Most of the arguments were about Rofiki sitting around the weed spots and blowing his brains out with smoke and not going to school, not working, and not wanting to move to Philadelphia, so she could help him apply for U. S. citizenship.

BORN JAMERICAN *"Gotta Get Mine"* YARDCORE

"Mama she used to say, don't live by your knife
Mama she used to say, gotta get out the ghetto
Mama she used to say, morning comes and goes"

Mama didn't know, Rofiki gotta get his. He did not - not – not want to live in Philly, but he did visit his mother on holidays and summers. He would catch a Greyhound bus to Philadelphia to eat her delicious home cooked Jamaican dishes. Deep inside he knew his mother had to leave when she did. Rofiki's mother told him something about his father changing his name to Kingston the day they arrived to the states.

Legally Kingston's true identity couldn't be known to anywhere. The reason was a family secret that Rofiki still didn't know and the reason his identification was screwed up. There had been other shit that his mother told him about his childhood. Something about him being a "*Bafang*" and how Kingston would refuse to take him any place, until Rofiki learned how to walk.

To this day Rofiki still didn't know the age he walked. Puffing he felt like marijuana was his head healing medicine. Thinking of times when he didn't walk fucked with him for some reason. Thinking of his D.N.A His mind drifted back to STARR wondering if their baby would be a Bafang too. "*Na FUGH dat,*" He growled out loud puffing out the window to the sky and shaking his long locks and thoughts back to Jamaica Queens.

DJ CAM "Only Your Friends" FILLET OF SOUL

Yes, of course Rofiki loved his mother. He was just mad for her not being there to save him from a few extra ass kicks Kingston gave him into manhood. But, since his mother escaped Kingston and Jamaica Queens, she earned a degree in nursing and became a legal U. S. citizen, before returning to Jamaica. Thinking of his mother made his belly miss mornings that came with cornmeal porridge and then he shook his thoughts free thinking of her fussing about money.

From the poor and oppressed shantytowns of Kingston Jamaica to the boroughs of Jamaica Queens New York, Kingston was a true Rastafarian man with wisdom and well respected as the Ganja man, along with his love for reggae music and powerful liberating voice.

A medium framed man, but Kingston was gigantic and heavy with knowledge. Rofiki was the spitting image, but heavier in weight, he was the son of the lion. Folks loved and feared Kingston, who was a gangster in his own rights and highly protected. His father was a man of integrity and always quoting Bob Marley, "*Facts an' facts, an' t'ings an' t'ings, dem's all a lotta fuckin' bullshit. Hear meh! Dere is no truth but de one truth, an' that is the truth of Jah Rastafari."*

BEAT PHARMACY *"Slow Down"* CONSTANT PRESSURE

Slowing down and just nodded his head to the beat, Rofiki was feeling the constant pressure and thoughts the philosophy Kingston was full of and his knowledge made him king and just like Kingston, Rofiki wore bongo dreadlocks and showed off his wisdom through his hip – hop, rap lyrics and his love too for Reggae music.

Growing up Rofiki spent much time with Kingston reasoning with the elders in the weed spots and learning about JAH, Haile Selassie, Marcus Garvey and a good man named Jesus who's greatest lesson taught was love. Rofiki really loved hearing and talking about Peter Tosh, Joe Higgs and always talking and listening to Bob Marley religiously.

CHERINE ANDERSON *"Kingston State Of Mind"* THE INTRODUCTION

"Oooh, oooh, oooh well in come di t'ing call 'Kingston State a Mind,' Rofiki say so. Tell Rofiki who a-go teach the children what's right. In a Kingston state of mind, the ruler his father, Kingston had always talked strong about their birth place the island of Jamaica, white beaches stretches of palm-fringed sand and crystal clear tranquil blue waters. Told him stories on how it's true that marijuana is everywhere in Jamaica and even smoked right outside immigration at the airport.

Describing Jamaica like there was no better place on earth, but they never returned. Not even to visit family. Jamaica was in Rofiki's blood and like Kingston they both stood strong on being Jamaican citizens to the day Jah calls his lion's home.

KYMANI MARLEY *"Dear Dad"* THE JOURNEY

"Dear GOD, Meh have a letter here from meh to dad and meh wanna yu to know it might be a little sad..." Kingston educated Rofiki that his grandfather and great – grand father, Rofiki's great – great grandfather, we're all true Rastafarians. Rofiki was the 5th generation Rastafarian. Let the world tell the story, the Rasta movement began in the 1930's. The closest Rofiki got to his roots was through Reggae music and Jamaica

Queens or the JCAL (Jamaican Center for Arts & Learning), were Rofiki hung outside of most of the week with his friends checking for gyals.

Rumor was Kingston was a 'marijuana grower,' when he came to New York there was no more driving hundreds of pounds of cannabis from Arizona border. The east coast dealers had a new connect. His Mexican / Cuban suppliers in Arizona were now coming to Kingston. That was the rumor mixed with a bit of the truth. Kingston switched up the game since the arrival of seeds from Dutch companies and the introduction of hybrid indicas. He used to harvest all over Jamaica Queens.

SKALP "Funkin' For Jamaica" FROM MY HEAD TO YOUR FEET (Featuring SISTA PAT)

"This feeling's funk that's what it is
Let it get into you - Jamaica funk that's what it is"

"Rastafari 'til' meh die," Shaking his head Rofiki turned the music down roaring and talking out loud as if he was agreeing with himself, and talking to Kingston. Thinking about what happened to Kingston? There were many things STARR knew about his past that he would never tell Kandi Gyal the story about Kingston's death.

It was about 3 years after Haile left and Rofiki came into the house after celebrating with friends and feeling a bit elaborated from Hennessey and ganja high, hearing 2 fire crackers exploding in the kitchen. He ran into the kitchen knowing it wasn't a fire cracker, but gunshots of a 32 caliber. He found Kingston lying on the kitchen floor bleeding from a gunshot wound to the chest.

DREADLOCK TALES" She Has A Heart Of Fire" SYNCHRONCITY

Mara was standing over Kingston shaking with the gun in her hand yelling, "Accidente- Accidente!" Kingston's struggling to catch his breath and at the same time he was pointing towards the closet. Mara was hysterical covered in blood shouting at Rofiki, "Accidente help me save him!" Neighbors heard the gun shots and banging at the door. Rofiki knew Kingston was dying for some weird reason, he was prepared to spring into action remembering Kingston drilling and preparing him to escape from Babylon."

Kingston looked at Rofiki and closed his eyes. Rofiki's heart began to pound remembering the adrenaline that rushed through him scared of getting twisted up in Babylon (the cops), due to them not being legal citizens and all the marijuana in the house and all the horror stories of deportation, Rofiki did as Kingston drilled him. Rofiki grabbed the oversized duffle bag with pounds of ganja his father kept in the safe place. He assumed it was about 25lbs wrapped in a special black plastic wrap to totally conceal the odor. Rofiki grabbed Kingston's U.S.A. Army Jacket worn from his Kingston Jamaica journey.

BOB MARLEY "One Love"
THE VERY BEST OF BOB MARLEY & THE WAILERS

"One Heart! Let's get together and feel all right."

Remembering another Bob Marley quote Kingston used to say, *"Life is one big road with lots of signs. So when you riding through the ruts, don't complicate your mind. Flee from hate, mischief and jealousy. Don't bury your thoughts, put your vision to reality. Wake up and live!"*

Those words were in the spot light of his decision making. Now the words were hitting home and he had to hurry on. He barely visited or talked to his mother since he discovered his penis. He would rather be in Jamaica Queens sexing young girls, instead of being stuck in the house in North Philadelphia. Haile would be scared to let him out the house with all the shooting that went on in the hoods. He would be in the house all day and night looking through picture boxes and flipping cable channels. While eating brown stewed King fish, rice and peas, plantain and drinking plenty of homemade ginger-beer.

JULIAN MARLEY "All I Know" AWAKE

All Rofiki knew was if, he keep on taking water from the well it will all dry up, and he'll end up having nothing for himself. When Rofiki got the chance to roam the streets besides the mayhem there was always, gyals and music. Speakers booming in windows and cars riding down the block blasting the sounds he could relate too. He ran around on foot on errands all around North Philly to the corner stores, looking for coconut milk and ripe plantains while taking in the new sites. The crowded playgrounds and basketball games with players better than the NBA. The new chicks and admirers of his dreads. His locks was his swag and he would never be a bald-head again. *"Buyaka - Big ups to the young dread,"* they would shout!

Drifting back to the thoughts of the sounds of police sirens and red lights swirling outside the window and Kingston lying on the kitchen floor, it was no movie. It was as real as having to run down the basement and squeeze through the hidden small trap hole that led into the building next door.

FOREIGN EXCHANGE *"Leave It All Behind"* LEAVE IT ALL BEHIND (Instrumental)

News spread fast after the gun shots. Everyone in the neighborhood was outside looking at the police and ambulance trying to enter his house and never noticed him. Rofiki knew about the floor board and the hidden stash, the money was gone, but the 'Black Book' was there. Walking fast down the street with his hoodie on his head and brushing off the white wall plaster. Friends, personal belongings and memories, Rofiki was leaving it all behind, but he knew Kingston 101, *"Don't forget ur history nor your destiny."*

ERYKAH BADU *"On & On"* BADUIZM

"Oh on and on and on and on
My cipher keeps movin' like a rollin' stone"

Born under water with three dollars and six dimes. Oh what a day, what a day, what a day. Remembering the day and lyrics when Rofiki had to go on and on and on and on. When he tried to walk from Queens, New York to Philadelphia, Pennsylvania. The day KINGSTON 101 became ROFIKI 101. Surviving on wisdom, a Rastafarians true strength, intelligence and trust JAH will always feed you, cloth you, protect you. Leaving everything, his clothes (all his gear), his music, pictures, his sneaker collection, his whole life he had been taught to be ready for this moment.

BOB MARLEY "Rastaman Chant" A REBEL'S DREAM
(Featuring Busta Rhymes)

"I say fly away home to Zion - Fly away home
One bright morning when my work is over - Man will fly away home"

Flying away, Rofiki hurried to the NYC Transit Jamaica Center – Parsons / Archer Station and board the E train and the 36 minute subway ride felt like 36 hours. Rofiki arrived at 42nd Street port Authority bus terminal with pounds of marijuana wrapped in a special black paper and plastic to conceal the smell and $3.60 in his pockets. He needed to get rid of the weed so he could have some cash. He thought of making a few phone calls and that was when he realized, he lost his cellphone.

RADIO CITIZENS "Everything" BERLIN SERENGETI

"Solution's got to find a way
Yes or no, nothing ever dies
Everything that's true will survive
It's just change of form, day to day"

Rofiki need to find a solution, find a way. He was fughed up, hungry, no phone and tired as shit with a duffle bag full of weed. Heavy as bricks strapped around his neck, Rofiki had to keep moving. Clinging onto $3 and 6 dimes in New York City, he would be lucky to buy a bottle of water. He decided not to make any phone calls not trusting his memory or the N.Y.C. pay-phones that robbed everyone. Standing on the corner watching buses, cars, taxi's and people coming and going.

The traffic lights changed from Red – Green – Yellow, and back to Red, as he wondered what to do. Standing at the corner he noticed Babylon everywhere. There was no big flash of lightning and no angels appeared, just a traffic sign flashing 'WALK.' He felt like he was trapped in a science fiction flick starring: Rofiki from the area code 1-1-4-3-2!

Beep - Beep! Beep - Beep! BOOM! The sound of 2 taxi cabs banging into each other knocked Rofiki back to earth. That accident he still believes saved him. He hurried away from the incident that caused a traffic jam. Walking to Philadelphia from New York didn't seem crazy to Rofiki. He had nothing to lose, feeling like he was already lost everything.

He had no Kingston, no money, no clothes, no job and that was enough to make him continue his journey. He began to jog until he broke out full speed running, but the load was too heavy feeling like a small child on his back the whole way.

BUJU BANTON "Not An Easy Road" TIL' SHILOH

It was not an easy road as Rofiki prayed, "*Lord, help meh sustain these blows from the minute of birth... Oh, my GOD, cast away this curse...*" A few tears rolled off his cheeks as Kingston's words echoed, "*Be not mad at Jah.*" Shuffling the duffle bag from shoulder to shoulder, holding on tight as he passed by a few dudes sleeping on the side of a building trying to catch heat from a greasy restaurant vents. He hopped around bold rats bigger than cats, heading towards the Lincoln Tunnel.

The winds felt like ice water hitting his face as he thought about Kingston lying on the kitchen floor. Shaking his head all his locks flew wild, he couldn't seem to wake up from the Sci–Fi movie he was trapped in. He knew it was real, because he could still feel that it was real. Just as he thought about jumping in traffic to prove it, instead he stuck his thumb out and a car stopped.

The driver was a white guy about 30ish, Rofiki needed a ride and thanked JAH! The dude immediately rolled down the window with greetings. "*Hi my name is Greggy - well, Greg - but call me Greggy.*" Rofiki covered the shock of the flamboyant squeal in the man's voice. Rofiki said in a dry voice, "*Tanks G. fa da ride.*" There was no way he would ever call any man Greggy. He knew this guy was flaming gay, a battybwoy. He could remember G. Reaching over to pat his leg. "*Awe you can talk to me, I don't bite.*"

SOULSTICE "Illusion" ILLUSION

Shut off to the world outside in order to look in Rofiki caught up in a battle. All his life he felt confusion black and white the colors of his illusion. Swiftly Rofiki's swung his fist and hit the battybwoy's arm away. Greggy squealed like a pig, humorous, yet alarming. "*My gawd U R so – so – sensitive no problem.*" Rambling on Greggy didn't stop there he kept talking, "*Okay I'm gay - but I wasn't trying to be gay with you. Slow your role U R not my flavor, I only like gay men, not straight boys! Plus even if you*" *thought about robbing me, I am broke. I was just trying to save you from the humiliation of trying to hitch or walking 1.5 miles under the Hudson River. "Walking the Lincoln Tunnel is prohibited!"*

There was no chose and Rofiki was thankful he didn't get put out. He listened to the driver talking none stop as if Rofiki didn't just punched his arm, *"I found out the hard way trying to walk the Lincoln Tunnel. Because once, oh my gwad my old boyfriend literally and physically kicked me out in the streets, because he wasn't ready to come out of the closet. Seriously he kicked me in my ass in front of his apartment building, even in front of his doorman, talk about humiliation. Oh I was horrified! Anyway, I had to walk from Manhattan to my parents in Newark. Fortunately some Rasta - dude seen me hitching and gave me a ride. And he had the best weed; by any chance you have any? So, I was just paying forward and back the favor. Anyone ever tell you – you look like a young Bob Marley and all of his sons. It's crazy dude how much you look like a Marley. Are you a Marley?"*

JAMIROQUAI "Too Young To Die" EMERGENCY OF PLANT EARTH

Too young to die, Rofiki don't want no war, no, no, no, no. He seen others die, he seen his father die. What's the motive? In that madness, oh, he wish he knew… Riding along on the passenger side Rofiki didn't feel like they were not moving and still listening to Greggy rattling on talking fast and surely asking about marijuana. Rofiki replied, *"Na mi clean."* He did think maybe selling some, but the guy did say he was broke. Silently and cool biting his bottom lip to keep from punch this guy in the face.

Thoughts were interrupted when Greggy pulled over to the side of the road. He was about to go crazy. Feeling trapped and thinking, dis cha-cha fag is gonna try to rape and kill mi. Greggy spoke up clearing his throat. *"This is my exit - Newark. I can't take you any further. Here is all the money I have $3, you look like you could use it."*

Hesitant Rofiki wanted to reject the money, but his stomach knew better. He got out of the car fast before the nightmare got worst and the gay - white alien changed its mind and decided to eat him alive. *"Don't say Greggy never did anything for ya azz!"* Greggy shouted out the window driving off burning rubber. Looking at the $3 in his hand he thought, "Dang it looks like $3 is all anyone has these days."

In the pitch black of night Rofiki remembers walking and walking holding all his crazy thoughts in his head. He wanted to stop and drop with the weight of the heavy load. Some superficial force seemed to be giving him strength and pushing him further. Thumb out he walked as cars passed as if they didn't notice him. Weary spiritually he wasn't feeling good, though he repeatedly asked, *"Jah please help meh get to Philly. That is all meh ask."*

The muscles in his legs and all 33 of the vertebras along his spine, his inner thighs and hips were burning. It was getting harder for him to walk, especially when he had to step up on an incline. He walked over to a tree on the side of the road and pulled a branch off. He thought of what Kingston would say, *"Like meh African ancestors before mi. Meh thank da tree for da gift to meh."* The 5 foot branch was perfect. It was very straight, light and sturdy. He used it as a staff and it kept his body from aching, as he continued to walk.

ZIGGY MARLEY "Personal Revolution"

Rofiki needed, he needed a revolution. Heartbreak is so hard to take and he lay down in the bed that he made. Who can save Rofiki? Revolution! As Rofiki started walking again, he noticed from the corner of his eye red lights flashing from behind. It was a New Jersey State Police car. The Trooper asked, *"How you doing? You're not in any trouble or anything, but I do have to let you know that you can't hitchhike in Jersey. Have you been hitchhiking?"* Rofiki was hoping the trooper had more important things to do than to bother a man walking.

Speaking clear English, Rofiki turned off his broken Patwa accent. Sounding sad and looking for sympathy he said, *"No officer, I'm just walking home, my father just passed away, I lost my bus ticket and trying to make it home to my mother."* The Trooper said, *"Sorry for your lost. But you can't walk on the highway. Where are you heading?"*

PEEDI CRAKK "Rum-Pum" P. CRAKK FOR PREZ
(Host Big Mike)

A rude-boy and in Philadelphia it could be Rofiki's worst day, and nigga's be on his dick like it's his birthday, and it be nothing but his word play! Philadelphia was 100 + miles away and it could take 2 – 3 days. Rofiki was shaking his head free from the lyrics mumbling, *"South."* He knew it would be unwise to say he was walking to Philadelphia, Pennsylvania were he'll make the whole block haul ass.

The Trooper's face grew compassionate listening to Rofiki explaining and losing his accent, *"I don't want to call and tell her the bad news over the phone. I just need to get to my mother the best way I can. I lost my bus ticket, so I'm walking."* Sympathetic the Trooper offered to give him a ride into Edison so that he could get off of the highway clearing up, *"From there you can try to make a phone call to maybe a friend. Or you can walk on roads other than the highway, it's legal to do that."* Rofiki had no plans on getting in a police car with his duffle bag heavy with marijuana. But in the pitch black of the night the boogey-man could be out, he had no choice.

BEANIE SIGEL *"Hustlas, Haze And Highways"* THE SOLUTION

Rofiki was ready to skate through the city of Philly and shine brighter than a new penny from the 'Franklin Mint' and pop more than his collar... The Trooper had Rofiki stand against the side rail as he lightly patted him down. *"I'm sorry for the inconvenience, but this is still part of my job."* Rofiki almost peed after the trooper patted him down and then went for his duffle bag. A call came in over the radio and the trooper just handed him his heavy duffle bag looking him in the eye. Quickly, Rofiki thought of an excuse due to the weight and said, *"It's my college books – I still have to study."* The Trooper seen the army jacket sticking out the bag and handed him the bag, *"Come on get in the back I can drop you off on my way in."*

Opening the back door to allow Rofiki out the squad car the Trooper gave him a long speech, *"I told you it's illegal to walk on the highways in this state. The law related to hitchhiking in New Jersey says begging for rides is prohibited, but based on the state's definitions, the law states that no person shall stand on the highway for the purpose of soliciting a ride. Standing at a spot not considered part of the highway to hitchhike could be considered technically legal, although all of the property surrounding the highway, shoulder, and the on-ramp is legally defined as the highway. Though 'hitchhiking is illegal' if for some reason you end up back on the highway. It is supposed to get colder and rain and you're not dressed for it. There are call boxes on the interstate and they call directly to the police station. If you can't take the cold, call and someone will come and get you and take you to a shelter. But remember you're not supposed to be on the highway."*

SLAKAH THE BEAT CHILD "Delete" BEAT TAPE VOL 4

Unbuttoning the top pocket of his uniform, the State Trooper reached in and handed Rofiki $3. With sympathy in his voice he said, *"Here I was going to use this for coffee and donuts. I think you can have better use for it."* Watching the State Trooper drive away and clutching the money, Rofiki had $3 more dollars and knew he would figure out how to get back on the highway without Babylon harassing him, as he walked back to the ramp back to the highway.

Completely exhausted as the sun was beginning to rise on the horizon he walked the highway, he wondered what passing drivers thought about him, as they drove by. He didn't think he looked crazy or homeless. His clothes were a little ruffled from his journey and his Timberland boots were practically new, but heavy and now scuffed up. His dreads were pulled back and his black hoodie was over his head. Rofiki didn't think he looked like the average homeless guy. Then again, the truth was he did look liked the average homeless guy.

DREADLOCK TALES "Follow The Sun" SYNCHRONICITY

The pain had been so bad he had to go over to another tree and again pulling at a branches thanking the tree for its gift. Since, he had to throw away the last walking stick, before getting into the police car. He realized that it probably took years for that tree to grow that branch. All those years for that tree to grow that branch, so that he could come along and use it to ease his pain. He wondered if the entire purpose of that branch from its inception was to comfort him. Maybe this is true or maybe he was a bit vain. After all wasn't the universe about him, a small microcosm in the midst of it all.

Bearing in mind the second time Babylon and swirling red lights pulled up on him. He dropped his second walking stick knowing what to say. *"No officer, I'm not hitchhiking. I'm just trying to get home".* Again telling his story of his father dying and trying to get to his mother's house.

The Troopers kindness gave him a ride to a truck stop. 10 minutes later the State Trooper was dropping Rofiki off at large truck stop in New

Brunswick, New Jersey. There had to be 50 trucks parked in the parking lot. Thinking like Rofiki, the Trooper didn't pull into the stop. He dropped Rofiki off away from where the trucks were parked and gassing up, so that nobody could see him getting out of the police car.

This way the truckers wouldn't get freaked and think he was a criminal. Rofiki shook the Troopers hand and was actually looking for $3 to be put in his hand. Getting out the police car with his heavy ass duffle bag full of weed thinking that the ride was worth more than $3.

ANDRE LOUIS *"Sadness"* A STATE OF MIND

The truck stop was filled with trucks, and cars. Rofiki decided not to ask anyone in a car for a ride, since he had no luck with them on the road. He had to walk around to several truckers for a ride. One truck driver brushed him off fast, *"Nope!"* Another trucker who seemed pleasant because, he was smiling said, *"I am sorry can't help you buddy."*

Another Trucker was going south but his company did not permit riders. He could hear and feel his stomach growling. He walked into the service area to rest and think wisely about how to spend his money, though he already stole a few candy bars and already ate them in the bathroom. Feeling that he would actually have to walk 50+ more miles to Philadelphia.

That's when he noticed a short Hispanic dude walking back and forth from the service station to his black Yukon truck. Rofiki wondered why the dude was walking in circles like he lost something. All the other drivers just came inside to pay for their gas or food then leave. But this guy seemed to be lost from the look on his face. Walking back inside and sat at a table across from Rofiki.

TRIBALJAZZ *"Riders On The Storm"* TRIBALJAZZ
(Featuring Jim)

Deciding to try his luck Rofiki asked, *"I was wondering if you're going south? I sure could use a ride."* The man said, *"Si puedo ir yo. Me need help."* Rofiki introduced himself and learned the man's name was Pablo. Rofiki asked, *"What seems to be your problem since you have a car?"* Pablo was going to Philadelphia to make a delivery.

Unfortunate, Pablo seemed to be running into a stream of bad luck himself. He lost his wallet and needed gas money. He couldn't call his boss, because if he did, he would be fired. He had been walking in and around asking for help, but no one wanted to get involved. Rofiki pulled out his $9.60 and the rest was on luck. They paid for $9.60 worth of gas and the attendant walked away busy and filled up the tank accidently.

The windows were tinted very dark. Rofiki figured that was for the safety of the supplies that had to be delivered. He remembered a weird smell and figured there was garbage that had to be thrown away. He dealt with the smell if it meant him getting a ride. Rofiki buckled his seatbelt secured the duffle bag between his legs praying, *"Jah meh hope dude not crazy,"* But Pablo asked him, *"Yo pray no loco. Me don't want un muerto - amigos in back."* Rofiki wondered if he heard him right. Did he say something about murder in the back?

Ignoring the crazy remarks Rofiki interrupted, *"What you say in Spanish about murder?"* Pablo reached in a bag of chips nonchalantly telling Rofiki he work as a delivery man delivering dead body's out of state to different funeral homes. And that the man in back had to be delivered to a funeral home on Broad Street in Philadelphia.

THE PHARCYDE "Runnin'" LABCABINCALIFORNIA

"Can't keep runnin' away." Still on 95 heading south now that Rofiki is older, stress weighs on his shoulders heavy as boulders. But he told dem 'till the day that he die, he still will be a soldier and that's all he told dem and that's all he showed dem and all this calamity is ripping away his sanity. Can it be he's a hood-celebrity who's on the brink of insanity? Nobody wishing to be in his positions. 'Cuz in his position it ain't never easy to do any type of maintaining cuz all this gaming and faming from entertaining is hella straining to the brain and he can't keep runnin'.

Running and running, and running far away from what was in the back seat. Before turning around and looking, sweat rolled down Rofiki's brow. He remembered the long black plastic body bag that was on a flat gurney, just inches away from the back of the car seat. It scared some piss out of him. Pablo did laugh that a dead man was no harm. Also, explaining that his urgency to get to the funeral home because the body was not embalmed and that was the smell.

Leaping forward pressing his chest into the dash board trying to get as much distance from the dead body. *"Siéntese,"* Pablo giggled. Rofiki understood some Spanish from the Dominican woman that killed his father. How could Kingston's dead body be in the back of the station wagon? With every mile his heart beat quickened. They hit ditches and bumps and the body bag wiggled and wobbled. Pablo pulled a 6 – inch joint rolled in corn husk and handed it to Rofiki *"La hierba – Marijuana lit it up!"* Rofiki wanted to accept and reject.

VISIONEERS "Runnin'" DIRTY OLD HIP HOP

"Can't keep runnin' away." Though he smoked religiously with Kingston and bonded and made peace, though his father had his rules about Rofiki smoking from anyone else. *"No trust no 1! Yu puff mold? Yu puff dust? Yu not know!"* Kingston had a nose for every type of marijuana there was. Kingston blows would be worst then Babylon if Rofiki smoked anyone else's weed, or got into any troubles anywhere.

"Can't keep runnin' away." Puffing with Pablo on the corn husk was a sure sign that Kingston was with them also in spirit. Kingston had taught Rofiki how to roll with corn husk and also how to use the dry skins of onions as spliff wraps. Just when Rofiki thought things couldn't get crazier, Pablo reached under the car seat. Rofiki thought it was a gun and swung and hit Pablo in the mouth.

"Can't keep runnin' away." Luckily for Pablo he was out of reach for a solid fist to mouth connection. The car swerved and the body in the back rolled side to side. Pablo straightened the driving wheel yelling, *"Amigo chill out! Don't kill us! Siéntese mi got tequila!"* Pablo held the bottle up to show.

"Can't keep runnin' away." Rofiki felt like he was going crazy! *"Na meh not here for trouble. Meh thought yu was grabbing for gun or something."* Pablo replied, *"Stop smoking amigo – yo goin' loco!"* Puffing and Puffing, Pablo kept puffing, while Rofiki kept feeling the aches and pains from all the miles he walked with bricks on his back. Pablo was a short framed man about 5' 5 with a head full of wild untamed curls. *"My delivery is on South Broad Street in Philadelphia."* Pablo tried explaining that he couldn't take Rofiki any further. He was already behind schedule and had another body to pick up in Delaware.

THE ROOTS "Streets of Philly" THE BEST OF THE ROOTS
(Featuring J. PERIOD & BLACK THOUGHT)

When Rofiki is steady being forced to grind, especially when he been down for so much time, getting up don't really ever cross his mind. As the drove to Broad Street and from there he could walk to his mother's house. The drive to Philadelphia took the normal driving time, but it seemed longer with the dead body in the back of the car. As Rofiki puffed with Pablo, he thought he was understood the significance of their meeting. Pablo drove across the Walt Whitman Bridge, as Rofiki looked out the window at the Veteran's Stadium.

Not smiling like Rofiki usually would looking over at the Vet Stadium, home of the Philadelphia Eagles. Behind the Stadium he knew was the Spectrum Center where the 76' Sixers Played. Seeking words of gratitude for getting him and Kingston to Philadelphia, Pablo opened his mouth asking, *"Amigo so you come to see ya mommy. Mi bet ya ma hermoso (beautiful), mi nunca (never) with black woman. Tell ya mama mi..."*

ZIGGY MARLEY "Shalom Salaam" DRAGONFLY

Lost was Rofiki in my memories of my forefathers' legacy. *"I am one of yu, yu are one of me. Why don't we set the people free?"* How Rofiki grieved to see fulfillment of prophecy, but his fist was balling up ready to fight. He held off noticing they stopped in front of the 'Munroe Funeral Home.' Getting out the car Rofiki thought, *"Well Kingston meh guess this is where meh leave you, for now."* Pablo interrupted his thoughts. *"Amigo help!"*

"Shalom salaam, shalom salaam, shalom
Shalom salaam, shalom salaam, shalom salaam, yeah"

Not wanting to touch a dead man, but this wasn't just any dead man it was Kingston. Trying not to laugh at Rofiki trying to hold only the plastic at the foot end of the body-bag. Pablo said, *"One day amigo –someone carry you, so be careful with Mr. Gonzales."* Rofiki stopped in his tracks. *"Who is Mr. Gonzales? Meh thought dis' man was meh father, Kingston."* Pablo was puzzled. *"You loco? Mr. Jose Gonzales your padre?"* Rofiki said, *"Meh out!"* Pablo's face was in shock, Rofiki dropped his end of the body bag. *"Meh not helping no taco man insulting meh moms."* Rofiki trotted fast down Broad Street hauling, his heavy bag.

"Shalom salaam, shalom salaam, shalom
Shalom salaam, shalom salaam, shalom salaam, yeah"

Ducking out of site, Rofiki was too close to his destination for any problems to evolve. He walked until he was on the other side of broad street cutting through city hall. Now on the North side of Broad Street he walked pass more murals of paintings on the hall, until he couldn't walk anymore. He was broke, but he went into a coffee spot to rest and that is when he seen STARR sitting alone looking lost sipping hot cocoa.

STEPHAN MARLEY "Jah Army"
(Featuring DAMIAN MARLEY & BUJU BANTON)

"We are soldiers in Jah army..."

BACK TO THE PRESENT... Well, Rofiki had a religion, when he made his decision. He took a vow to spread Jah light, never loosing focus to mission... Pulling his head back to the future Rofiki was singing and driving down the same highway that gave him nightmares. He turned up the music in white –gyal to the highest volume pumping trying to forget the past. Yet, he could never forget that pain. It haunts him and he feels it every time he drove up and down Hwy I -95.

That was making Rofiki feel even worst for the dude he passed by. The gas gauge was once again low, in need of gas. Rofiki headed to the next exit for gas. Pulling into the gas station Rofiki's conscious kept pulling him miles back to the dude walking the Highway. He tried shaking it off, but it was personal, he always was in need to be of some good deed.

Drowning in the music and pushing the past back to the past, he worried about his present mission to Philadelphia. The Hummers gas tank was empty, and dude he passed walking was miles away on the highway. Recalling the oversize clothes and black hoodie that completely covered the face. He couldn't tell if it was a black dude or a white dude. Rofiki's conscious was bothering him, feeling he should have offered a ride. He consoled his guilt like always with promising to stop for the next person, when he wasn't on an assignment with little time to handle.

REACH "Jamaica Funk (Funkin Fo Jamaica)" (TOM BROWNE)

*"Jamaica Funk that's what it is
Got to get into groove can you feel it?"*

"Babe got to get into you!" Pumping gas Rofiki was singing along bobbing his head sipping on a tall cup of coffee chucking at the thoughts of perhaps picking up a serial killer and never executing his own tactics. Rofiki really wished he was sipping on a tall glass of Hennessey. As he was having those thoughts a newspaper truck pull up and out of the passenger seat was the dude that was walking on the highway. The newspaperman dropped off newspapers and said a few words to the dude in the black hoodie, before driving off. The dude still with the hoodie pulled over his head, hands in pocket hurried inside the service station.

"You know I never have enough..."

The dude was much smaller than Rofiki thought he was, but the same oversize clothes. Observing the wiggle and bounce to his walk. Immediately Rofiki thought the dude might be gay and a little flimsy. He jumped in the hummer ready to turn the key and go, but he was still curious and reasoning with wanting to grab a bag of chips or something, he walked in the store heading directly for a bag of plantain chips and was at the register paying, when he noticed there was no one else in the store except him and the clerk.

The flimsy dude in oversize clothes disappeared. Rofiki knew it was foolish to be checking the bathroom, but he did anyway. Baffled the men's room was empty. Hurrying out of the men's room they bumped into each other as she was coming out of the ladies' bathroom.

JAH CURE "Run Come Love Me" GHETTO LIFE
(Featuring Jah Mason)

"Run come love me tonight and let JAH loving share (watch yah nuh)." The hoodie was off exposing her pretty red high cheek bones, she looked biracial, but he could tell she was a sistah. Her gorgeous dark hair was pulled back, looking like she just came from the gym dressed in oversize

sweats. She was one of the prettiest woman he ever seen with her exotic features with lips that any man would kiss, her wide hazel eyes looked straight past him. But, not without him noticing that one of her eyes was blackened. She didn't even say excuse me, she kept walking.

Once back outside in the cold she put the hoodie on and kept walking. He was just two steps behind her pulling up to offering her a ride. Letting down the window and turning down the music, he pulled up on her asking, *"Yo shorty yo al'aight? Yo need a ride?"* Stopping in her track checking out the Hummer H3.5 and eyeing the rims before asking, *"So where is he?"* Rofiki was confused and didn't understand replying, *"Yo shorty meh confused. Meh not part of your situation. Meh just wanted to offer ya a ride."* He knew she was reluctant, but she did just get out of a newspaper truck.

Rejecting a ride in his cool whip, he knew she must have been crazy. But, she changed her mind and accepted the ride making it clear that's all she wanted and thankful he was going to Philadelphia too. Hoodie covering her head and face she sat quite as Rofiki bobbed his head to the music. Turning down the music and breaking their silence, Rofiki made his introduction.

JAY Z "Public Service Announcement (Interlude)" THE BLACK ALBUM

In his Jay Z voice allow Rofiki to introduce himself, *"My name is Fiki, OH! R-to-the O-F."* He used to move snowflakes by the O-Z. Back then you can call him CEO of the R-O-C, Rofiki! Fresh out the frying pan into the fire. As Rofiki was thinking this ain't a movie dog, oh shit.

Angelica interrupted Rofiki's public announcement, *"Now before you finish, let me just say, you'll never be able to say that this sistah lied to Rofiki!"* Checking out his swag' yo, he talked like a baller. Rofiki was who, he was before she got there. Only God can judge him, either love him, or leave him alone.

TOM BROWNE "Funkin' For Jamaica" (WALTER JUNE Remix)

Now back to the regularly scheduled program shuffling around a little before telling Rofiki her name *"Angelica"* emphasizing on *'Lica.'* Expressing amusement Rofiki chuckled feeling that she had the perfect name. *"So Angel-Lica do they call you Angel?"* She was quick responding, *"My name is*

Angelica and what is so funny with the name Rafiki a Disney character." He could tell somebody must have pissed her off, realizing he had a spicy - hot scotch bonnet habanera pepper on his hands.

Amusing her with some of his bullshit he protested, *"Na mi no character from The Lion King. Meh educate ya and give ya some Rofiki 101. Since you seem to refer to meh as a character. Rafiki spelled R-A-F-I-K-I is a mandrill with the tail of a baboon and lives in a baobab tree in the pride lands and performing shamanistic services for the lions of Pride Rock. Rafiki is never without his rod used for ritual purpose. The character Rafiki means friend in Swahili."*

Realizing he still had her attention and needing someone to talk to Rofiki spelled, *"R-O-F-I-K-I is a Rastafarian man and Mandingo and lives in the Philadelphia lands. Never without meh rod, also used for ritual purposes (holding up the unlit blunt). Rofiki 101 is the son of the lion, and now the lion. Let Rofiki be a friend and get you home safely."*

METHOD MAN "Let's Ride" 4:21... THE DAY AFTER
(Featuring GINUWINE)

There go the apple of Rofiki's eyes, his black butterfly. Trying to pass him by like she do them other guys. She probably had a bumpy last ride with her ex and don't try to fugh with Rofiki's knowledge or his pimp game. He was always on point when his name was being questioned or offended. He was glad to see Angelica intrigued.

LUPE FIASCO 'I Gotcha" FOOD & LIQUOR

"You know Rofiki gotcha, right?" Rofiki, Rastaman. Angelica know he have her right, right, right, right, right, right, right, right. They call him Fiki, he'll be her new day. She'll wanna smell like him, he'll be her bouquet. No doubt, Rofiki could tell there was something heavy on Angelica's mind, heavy enough to have such a beautiful woman walking the side of the road looking like a homeless person. He relit his blunt not worried about offending, because it was his ride. Puff – Puff – and when he went to pass she rejected saying, *"I'm cool – you do you – I'm thankful for the ride."*

Theresa Vernell

TOM BROWNE - new Jamaica funk (Newfunkswing Remix)

20 miles to PHILADELPHIA. Everybody and past memories were now pushed to the back of Rofiki's mind. Driving down I – 95 with Angelica's pretty ass in the passenger seat, stressed, literally overdressed, he learned why. She was engaged to some major league baseball player, she didn't mention his name. She mentioned that she was escaping after he tried to beat her ass, a cop happened to witness the public dispute and locked up Mr. Major League, to sober him up. Rofiki was curious why she was dressed in oversized gym clothes. She explained that Mr. Major League ripped her dressed off of her. One of the female cops happened to have some gym clothes in the squad car and the sneakers too. She said she had just given up and wanted to go home, before the police released him.

What really got Rofiki's attention was when offered money for gas, if he could do her a favor. Ready to help out, he declined the money. He drove to the waterfront condominiums and spa. Coincidently it was the same building next to the Sugar House Casino that Kandi Gyal had bragged about living on the 21st floor with one of those NBA suckers she used to fugh. He had also heard that Michael Vic, Jazzy Jeff, and a lot of other high rollers were up in there. So of course Rofiki agreed to take her to the condo to pick up money and clothes, and then drive her to a girlfriend's house.

OUTKAST "Prototype" SPEAKERBOXXX / THE LOVE BELOW

Shaking his head and dreads, Rofiki was trying to catch his second wind and hoping that Angelica was the one. If not, she was the prototype. They met today for a reason as he sung, *"Meh think meh in love again, stank you (yes, stank) very much."*

VIVIAN GREEN "Keep Going" A LOVE STORY

*"So I got to keep on going on
And I can't stop for nothing
So I got to keep going on and on and on"*

Rolling up to the entrance Angelica tightened the hood on her head and quickly grabbed the Versace sunglass off the dashboard that

160

belonged to Kandi Gyal. The sunglasses Kandi Gyal got from Big Tank the night of his birthday party. Now Rofiki was admiring Angelica rocking them to cover her black eye, she owned them now.

The guard at the front gate inspected Rofiki and the Hummer, while waving okay to Angelica as the gate lifted for them to enter. When they got to the front door valet parking was there to greet them. Rofiki was leery about valet parking, because he had the car lit up and had all his shit in it. Angelica explained it was proper procedure for them to valet all cars. He wanted to dispute, but that meant sitting in the car waiting. Still wearing the sunglasses Angelica was at the front desk picking up an extra set of keys and had to electronically sign her name. Then they dashed into the elevator and Rofiki watched her push the button for the 18th floor.

JAGUAR WRIGHT "Free" DIVORCING NEO 2 MARRY SOUL

"Free" Angelica was acting like she wanted to be free. The condo was exquisite When Angelica opened the door to the grand foyer Rofiki instantly noticed the exotic mahogany hardwood floors throughout the living room into the dining and straight into the kitchen. There were three full bedrooms and all elegant. The panoramic views of the Delaware River, Ben Franklin Bridge and the city skyline was breathtaking. While checking it all out, he watched Angelica stilled dressed in the oversize sweats scurry in and out of all three bedrooms with stuffed Louis Vuitton luggage. He could hear her wrestling in and out of closets and drawers. He hollered out, *"U cool?"* She yelled back, *"I'm good make yourself at home literally, there is Hennessey under the island and champagne in the refrigerator, but don't eat the sushi it is old."*

TOWA TEI "Funkin' For Jamaica" (SHINICHI OSAWA Remix)

"If ya feel it - Let it get into you
Jamaica funk that's what it is - Let it get into you"

Entering the stunning designer kitchen he opened the Subzero refrigerator observing the only contents of 5 bottle of Moet champagne and a plate of old sushi. Still looking for the cognac he checked out the built-in coffee center and a huge granite island that seats eight and in a cabinet underneath he found a big ass bottle of Hennessey. He could hear Angelica calling for him. The master bathroom suite was fascinating with heated marble floor and intimate Jacuzzi, he continued following her voice, and found her standing inside a giant walk in closet pointing at a jewelry box of men's watches she was offering, *"Choose whatever you like. I brought them all and they were never worn. Mr. Major League claims he can afford to buy his own time."*

There was a little hesitations, Rofiki started to step away from the jewelry box of watches, agreeing with Mr. Major League, until he seen the Rolex men's president 18kt yellow gold, with a 3.5 carat diamond bezel. He picked it up and she closed the jewelry box saying, *"Enjoy!"* It was like giving him a stick of gum, she could care less. She explained she was going to take a shower and change her clothes before leaving, if he had the time. Oh, he had the time he thought as he looked at his new Rolex.

LYFE JENNINGS *"Statistics"* I STILL BELIEVE

"Pay attention Rofiki gonna teach how to expose the 90% and show you what to do to keep the other 10%..." Rofiki 101, *"Never get caught chilling in another man's crib."* He observed more of the condo as he listened to the shower water, as he imagined Angelica nude, and her dress being ripped off her for all the right reasons. There was something unique and different about her. Not his normal type of woman, he assumed she has been educated due to her pose, her conceited manners and looking around the condo showed her lifestyle was no fast food menu. He noticed there were plenty of pictures of Angelica posed alone or with a few female friends or sisters? He noticed a picture of her college graduation and knew he had peg her right.

Picking up the picture of Angelica dressed in a tutu and realized she must be a ballet dancer. He looked around and noticed a dance book on the table with her picture on the cover. Then he seen a picture frame turned over on the table. He picked up the picture frame and couldn't fughing believe he was looking at Mr. Major League and knew just who he was.

There are not many brothers playing professional baseball and this brother was on top of his game. In fact Rofiki was a fan. Now he wasn't sure what to do as he laughed and shook his dreads free, still sipping Mr. Major Leagues Hennessey. Interrupting Rofiki's 101 and statistics thoughts as he was placing the frame back just the way he found it, Angelica entered the room in a white bath robe and wet long hair pulled back into a ponytail. Black eye fully exposed looking at Rofiki as if he could be her perfect revenge. She walked towards him seductively.

It was weird only because of the moment. She didn't explain anything to him, knowing he must have looked at pictures. Turning on some music to drown down the sounds of their voices Rofiki wasn't surprised when she turned on JAZZ1CAFÉ (everyone should be tuned in and listening). Walking Rofiki out on the balcony where the spectacular views of the city skyline caught him breathless and nauseous.

MARAR HRUBY "Is This Love" FROM HER EYES
(BOB MARLEY)

"Is this love - is this love - is this love - is this love that I'm feelin'?"

Acrophobia is the fear of heights and Rofiki knew it was his kryptonite, having a Rasta cornered on the balcony 18 feet up would be a sure defeat, because 18 floors were too far to fly, no matter how high and good the pussy or weed. Shit the whole atmosphere was making him think of the twin towers and people jumping to their deaths. She was standing fearless with her back against the clear glass railing as if relaxed and lighting a cigarette.

Watching Angelica standing so close to the edge, even though she was secured by a glass wall railing, was giving Rofiki heart palpitations. Reaching forward pulling her off the glass railing trying to lead her inside asking, *"Yo ma, ya ready to roll out or whad?"* Puffing the cigarette, she waved him off saying, *"I'm not allowed to smoke cigarettes inside. I mean, I don't smoke inside. Plus, I just left a message for Mr. Major Leagues attorney to inform me immediately of his release."* So, with the news that Mr. M. L. would not be home anytime soon, they chilled. Both exhausted, but intrigued with each other and feeling the chemistry and attractions.

MARA HRUBY "The Panties" FROM HER EYES

Babe slow down, just take your time, Rofiki and Angelica gonna be there for a while, oka-ay? There was no rush, but he didn't want to be standing outside and he pulled Angelica back inside with her cigarette still lit, Rofiki was checking out her swollen eye and had flash backs of the fights he had with STARR, he could proudly say he never gave her a black eye.

RAHEEM DEVAUGHN *"Black & Blue"* THE LOVE AND WAR MASTERPEACE

Rofiki just wanna speak from the heart to a friend in need, he hope Angelica get this. Love ain't two in the morning walking the highway. Then wondered what Angelica did to make Mr. M. L. flip his lid and go upside her head. The cork popping knocked him out of his thoughts. Opening a bottle of champagne Angelica's robe slipped open showing her slim curves through tight black body wear. Sipping and listening to all the jazzy music playing in the background Rofiki could feel the chemistry was there just horrible timing.

The sun was rising up over the city and they were engrossed in conversations about everything from city pollution and learning, she didn't have any diseases or children. So tell Rofiki what type of love is to love her till she's black and blue. That's something he would never do. He'd never put his hands on Angelica. Relaxed Rofiki's head was reclined resting on the sofa with her showered and smelling sweet, fresh and clean, sitting next to him. He had to taste her. His lips where wrapped around hers as she pulled on his dreads, he was rubbing her small breast. Rofiki had his pants off ready to make love when her house phone rang.

J. SPENCER *"If It Feels Good"* BLUE MOON

It was the attorney calling to inform Angelica that Mr. Major League was released hours ago and arriving home within minutes. She hung up the phone and immediately called the front desk to have valet parking have Rofiki's car ready. She hung up explaining everything to Rofiki and wrote down his phone number promising to call and practically pushed him over all her luggage at the door and handing him the LV sunglasses.

Rejecting the designer sunglasses, Rofiki told Angelica they were a gift. Just as he was getting on the elevator, Mr. Major League was stepping off another elevator wearing dark shades and talking on his cellphone saying, *"Yeah they had some nigga's pimped out Hummer parked out front and for some reason they thought it was mine."* When Mr. Major League noticed Rofiki, he quickly ended his phone conversation and before the elevator doors closed they made direct eye contact with each other.

Excited to see White -Gyal ready and waiting for Rofiki. He drove away from the scene thinking of the incident at the waterfront condo and checking his rear view mirrors, and looked at the Rolex on his arm. Thinking about the crazy scenario that just went down. He thought about when Angelica asked him if he had any children. He wasn't lying when he said, *"No. Well not yet."* What if he told her about STARR'S pregnancy? Checking on STARR and his seed growing in her belly was his whole purpose for coming back to Philadelphia.

After driving a few miles and double checking and checking again to be sure he wasn't followed. He did expect his phone to ring with Angelica screaming that Mr. Major League was about to throw her ass off the 18th floor. Just the thought made his stomach squeamish with the fear of height. Driving on and leaving all that drama behind he knew before dealing with STARR he had to get some sleep and freshen up. He started to head over to North Philly to check on the house, though he didn't want to roll up on the block and nigga's touching and peeping inside all day and night, especially when he was asleep. So, he headed over to the nearest motel with secured parking.

LIZZ FIELDS "Ride On" PLEASUREVILLE

"Ride on put the metal to the petal..." Checking into a motel room, Rofiki showered and laid across the bed butt naked listening to JAZZ1CAFE Radio, estimating STARR had to be about 4 – 5 months pregnant. Wondering if her belly was big and swollen enough to be rubbed. He was really interested in seeing what she has been into the last couple of months, he kinda missed her. He needed to see for himself and squash all the rumors.

Ready to boast and brag and ride his new whip through the hood, but Rofiki knew once he pulled up in the Hummer 'White Gyal,' he would shut the hood down. Also the new car would show he was about business. He was planning to help, STARR out with the rent and talk about finding a new spot before the baby was born. And most importantly to give her the important personal paperwork. Puffing and puffing thinking about all the shit that just went down in the last few hours had him sidetracked and exhausted. He fell asleep awaiting Angelica's phone call.

TRACK 7: #1 VIDEO VIXEN

BEYONCÉ "Partition" BEYONCÉ

"Driver roll up the partition please, Big Tank Monica Lewinski'd all on Kandice's gown. Oh there daddy, d-daddy didn't bring the towel..." Pacing the floor and looking out the window waiting for the next limousine Big Tank was sending for her. No stranger to danger, Kandi Gyal feeling conceited and taking selfies photos of her booty through the mirror and posted the pictures on social media sites.

Kandice Perez A.K. Kandi Gyal did her homework and Goggled all about Big Tank and read all the urban hip- hop magazines and knew he had the money to make and turn her world around. She recorded her first single and now they were ready to promote. Big Tank told her to dress especially nice for this event, even giving her $10,000 cash to shop. Making her feel like a *"Million Dollar Bill"* She never had a man give her that much money.

WHITNEY HOUSTON "Million Dollar Bill" I LOOK TO YOU

"If he makes you feel like a million dollar bill
Say oh, oh, oh - Say oh, oh, oh!"

The limousine was running late and Kandi Gyal wondered if she could call Big Tank, maybe he was back with Lil' Pam like all the tabloids said. Keeping tabs and running behind men was not usually her style. However, she was used to men with bitches on the side, but she had to be the main bitch. Though they had hot steamy and hours long sex sessions, she knew Big Tank would probably rather lose her than money. So, she kept her eyes and ears alert and ready. Seeing his money hungry desires and crazy mood swings and the malice in his stories told, she knew what she was dealing with.

There was something that Kandi Gyal couldn't put her finger on, but she assumed, he was still involved with Li' Pam. Because he talked about her too much not to be. He talked about her and didn't have to say her name. Kandi Gyal knew who Big Tank was referring to when he talked about to many plastic surgeries and sexy gangsta style. Funny, because Rofiki said the same thing. Still sitting and waiting and now thinking of Rofiki who was on his way back to Philadelphia, and now Kandi Gyal didn't have to sneak out to meet Big Tank. Their new affair was made clear that it was to remain private. Kandi Gyal wasn't sure what to do with sneaky Rofiki is what she called him.

SADE "Punch Drunk" PROMISE

There was something very sexy about sneaky Rofiki's Rasta swagger that reminded her of Kymani Marley's character in the movie 'Shotta's.' His words were Rasta- hip – hop – natural movements that could talk any chic's panties off. For fact Kandi knew he didn't have to chase pussy, pussy chased Rofiki. JAZZ1CAFÉ flash back...

Reflecting back to JAZZ1CAFÉ the night in Philadelphia when Kandi ran into Rofiki. JAZZ1CAFÉ was filled with folks getting down bobbing their heads and jamming to SoulShine Sessions. It had been awhile since she checked out the Philly scene of men. Red lights, Strobe lights, neon lights and everything was looking right. She was hanging out with her cousin Abigail Perez, and Abigail's best friend Nene, who was not fond and no fan of Kandi – Kandi Gyal, "whad eva'." Abigail and Nene were big music lovers of all genres and Jazz, Neo Soul and spoken word poetry, were their passions.

SPACESTAR "Cosmic Odissey (Remix)" NU: JAZZ ITALIA

Bored, Kandi Gyal listened to them talking about some chick named 'S-T-A-R-R spelled with 2 R's' the winner of some open mic contest. They sounded all hyped about this chick 'STARR' spelling her name out. She could care-less about some contest winning chick. Kandi Gyal was really only there as a layover, she needed somewhere to go until her man Black Mike, was ready to come pick her up.

Known in the Philadelphia and New York area for being notorious in the drug game and Black Mike was also married and that was known.

Kandice was no stranger to danger and knew her place. So, she didn't get mad when he called and said he would be late picking her up. So, why not chill with Abigail and get caught up, something to eat and plenty to drink.

ALEX BUGNON "Around 12:15 AM" SOUL PURPOSE

Walking through the crowd and passing many tables, Kandi knew all eyes were on her big bouncing booty prancing across the floor in white Manolo Blahnik Strittina Stiletto's. Dressed the sexiest in the place and confident she wore her size 4 Versace white dress, as she inspected other women to see who could out shine her?

Exactly, nobody could out shine her, she was the star! Not even the competition at the table. Including her cousin Abigail looking vintage chic from consignment stores fashions couldn't compete with her a high class designer diva, nope. Inspecting the crowded place, she was now mad that she didn't know about the contest? This could have been her chance to show Philly what *'Kandi Gyal'* got.

Throwing back her head and letting out a burst of laughter, Abigail's friend Nene was asking, *"So, Miss Kandi why didn't you enter the contest? And when is your CD coming out?"* With a quick nonchalant response Kandi said, *"Who has time for silly little radio contest when you're negotiating major record deals like me."* She rolled her eyes ignoring them and glad her phone lit up with a text from 'Black Mike.'

BLACK MIKE: *Yo babe U ready?*

KANDICE: *I'm ready.*

BLACK MIKE: *U @ JAZZ1? 20 minutes come out. I can't be fughing around I gotta get back to N.Y. I got shit to do!*

KANDICE: *I'm ready!*

Yes, Kandice was ready to be with a tall and big glass of water, Big Mike quenched Kandi Gyal's thirst. She was also hungry, and ready to go roll with the Big Dogs! Pop champagne, eat prime rib instead of sitting around chick's sipping Pina-Coladas and eating mozzarella sticks all night.

Nope, especially not with Abigail's corny friend dressed like she borrowed something from Abigail's closet. Of course she did, Kandi recognized that corny flea-market jean jacket with the fringes down the arms anywhere.

At this point Kandi Gyal was beyond intimidation and holding her pose, sipping white wine and wearing a spandex white hip and ass hugging dress from Neiman Marcus. Bring their hands up to stifle the giggles, Abigail and Nene were complimenting her, *"Girl you wearing that dress!"* A faux smile ruffled, Kandi's lips wanting to call them bitches and haters, wishing they could be her.

LAURYN HILL *"Social Drugs"* UNPLUGGED

"These social drugs -These social drugs
These social drugs - These social drugs"

Over the loud music, Nene was now trying to act proper addressing Kandice by her full government name and asking stupid questions, *"Ms. Kandice Maria Perez, since becoming this Kandi Gyal have you perform unplugged yet?"* What was this chick talking about? Asking people to repeat things wasn't Kandice's style and having her full name shouted out. But since she was curious she asked, *"What do you mean unplugged?*

A shadow of annoyance crossed Nene's face looking at Kandi Gyal and asking more questions, *"Okay Ms. New York – New York. You're actually playing unplugged now, playing dumb, as much as you have been performing."* Then Abigail jumped in the conversation and put in her 2cents. Her response held a note of impatience explaining, *"Unplugged, musicians perform acoustic or unplugged versions of their familiar electric repertoires like Alicia Keys, Lauren Hill and Mariah."* Instantly humiliatingly conscious of their scrutiny Kandice was irritated and damn sure ready to go. She hated envious bitches.

ALICIA KEYS *"If I Ain't Got You"* UNPLUGGED

Some people live for the fortune. Some people live just for the fame. Some people live for the power. Some people live just to play the game and Kandice Perez wanted it all! Abigail asked Kandice again, *"Do you play unplugged? Do you know what I mean?"* The only time Kandice heard of unplugged was on MTV like these two and they were sitting there telling jokes like they had their own camera crew.

Getting up from the table to go powder her nose, Kandi Gyal was ready to ditch these haters. Showing off her Anna Nicole smile flashing her veneers and tucking her white Prada clutch under her arm and strutted her stuff like a runway model to the bathroom. She overheard Nene say, *"Who she think she is Lisa Raye? Wearing all that white!"* Kandi didn't give a hoot, she knew who she was the shit! Throwing her shoulders back and pushing her pelvis slightly forward, a book could be balanced on her head, perfect posture.

Coming from the bathroom Kandi Gyal was headed straight to the front door, until she seen Rofiki standing next to the stage. Handsome, golden skin, beautiful sexy smile, long dread locks and the 18kt gold lions head ring with the carat diamond in the mouth was on his finger. How could she forget the ring, she once had appraised. Prancing up to him she greeted. *"Hello it has been years since I've seen you, but you haven't changed. Marley, right?"* She smoothed out the white dress displaying how it clings to every curve of her body, landing her hands on her hips.

ALICIA KEYS *"You Don't Know My Name"* UNPLUGGED

Baby, baby, baby, from the day Kandi Gyal first saw Rofiki. She really - really wanted to catch his eye. Round and round and round they go, will he ever know? Mystified, Rofiki had no idea who she was, but it was blowing his mind thinking who is this beautiful woman that all the men were staring down and mentally licking? And thinking she knew him?" He smiled and said, *"Right, Marley. Wad good wid ya?"* Kandi Gyal didn't get a chance to say anything else.

The band was in intro on stage and some brown skin chick with dreads was coming out the green room toward them. She watched as Rofiki whispered in the chick's ear and handed her a bottle of spring water. The girl rejected the bottle and kicked off her shoes and walked up to the stage and the audience clapped harder. Kandi was paying attention to the response that STARR was getting.

J-KWON "Tipsy" STILL TIPSY

"Everybody in the club gettin' tipsy..."

Introducing and starting the show SoulShine Sessions was on stage and welcoming STARR to the platform. Retreating to a fake smile, Kandice checked out STARR wearing a pair of jeans and a simple white T-shirt that read, 'JAZZ1CAFÉ PARTY' singing and dancing, her long dreads swung freely. She walked up on the stage waving and blowing kisses. Dancing barefoot and freely, she went right into song. Kandi Gyal was not trying to pay any attention to the chick on stage, where she should be. But, she did take a few mental notes checking out how STARR was connecting with the audience.

JAZMINE SULLIVAN "Round Midnight" OLD SOUL (ELLA FITZGERALD)

"At midnight it gets so bad." Assuming the audience must have been all of her family, because everyone was clapping and feeling her vibe. Again she noticed the ring on Rofiki's finger as he was clapping too. Instantly Kandi Gyal's ego exploded feeling that she was just as good, in fact better. Still standing next to Rofiki who was now clapping with the audience, she began to feel awkward.

Midnight it get so bad, midnight it gets so sad. Midnight Midnight – Midnight it gets so bad

Checking out the show, Kandi Gyal thought STARR was okay, if you like that ERYKAH BADU, JILL SCOTT or INDIA ARIE kind of stuff." She nudged Rofiki and said, *"So you with her?"* Rofiki smiled and said, *"Meh de manage."*

ROMINA JOHNSON "Boogie" SOUL RIVER (House Remix)

Caught up in Rofiki's smile Kandice knew that if she hung around any longer, she would want to "Boogie" with him. Her cellphone began to vibrate meaning that Black Mike was outside and she had to go. Feeling the pressure of her phone vibrating again, meaning he was calling her twice. If she didn't answer he would leave. She wasn't a groupie, she was an artist too. She handed Rofiki her calling card and said, *"If you are interested in managing someone who is negotiating a record deal with Clay David give me a call."* Then she stepped away and was gone. She didn't even say bye to her cousin or what's her name?

ALICIA KEYS "Love It Or Leave It Alone / Welcome To Jamrock" UNPLUGGED (Featuring MOS DEF, COMMON, DAMIEN MARLEY, and FRIENDS

"Wad' up Philly!!!
Freak, freak you'll and you don't stop
Mad love for the culture since the days of Adidas and hip hop posters."

Rastafari stands alone. Welcome to Jamrock! Rewind Rofiki held the business card tight in his hand, as he watched Kandi's hips and big ass bounce out the door, shaking his head because he could have forgotten that booty. Remembering he thought, Wow Clayton David that signed Aailyah Kelly and many other top recording artists. He looked at the card and read her name out loud *"Kandice Perez."* Sticking the business card in his back pocket looking throughout the crowd several times hoping to get another glance at Kandice, he had been caught completely off guard. Knowing she assumed he forgot all about her.

KEISHA COLES "A Different Me (Intro)" A DIFFERENT ME

A FEW MONTHS LATER... What's going on? Kandice would like to introduce a different side of Kandi Gyal. She would like to introduce a sexier side of her, a different gyal. Everything was going her way. Ready to rock the world with her 'Big-Big-Booty.' She was ready for her new single to be released. Rofiki was her manager, though they were keeping their sexual relationship under the microscope, he was still up her ass every move she made. Everyone even Big Tank had their suspicions. So they made sure to keep it business in public.

Though Kandi had her suspicions about Rofiki heading back to Philadelphia to handle some real estate business, he claimed. She was glad to put some space between them, plus this gave her the opportunity to float like a butterfly – sting like a bee and spread her wings and prepare to take off with the invitation to a weekend photo shoot. Big Tank and her manager Rofiki have made all the plans.

Ready to rock study, Big Tank's assistant Cheryl called to inform Kandice that a driver was arranged to pick her up and drive her to Big Tank's Play Palace. Still pacing the floor awaiting the limo and making sure she looked picture perfect, she spent most of her time in the mirror thinking about the night before. Just after Rofiki left for Philadelphia. Big Tank called and asked her if she was hungry. She got dressed thinking they were going to dinner. He came over with 2 large greasy pepperoni pizzas and 2 bottles of Moet and plenty of blow.

COOLY'S HOT BOX "Let Me Get Some" TAKE IT

"Let Me Get Some..." The night Rofiki went out of town driving away in the new white Hummer, Big Tank picked her up in a limo and the night on the town turned into an after-party of wild sex at her apartment. Big Tank sweaty heavy and unable to get an erection due to the drugs and alcohol. But Kandi Gyal was entertaining enough for him to get cheap thrills.

Now 24 hours later dressed in a Kimmy beaded striped black and white dress, Rachel Zoe Blake – Linen and Suede Forzieri pumps, Salvatore Ferragamo satin red clutch, she stepped out the limousine. It surely looked like a party was going on with several custom limousines and SUV's, pulled up one by one to the lavish gated multi –million dollar estate looking like 'The Playboy Mansion' known as 'Big Tanks Play Palace' located in Englewood, NJ, just 10 minutes from Manhattan. With the gracious honors, Big Tank gave Kandice a personal tour showing her the bowling alley, theater and recording studio. There was also a full-size indoor basketball court, (2 pools) outdoor and an indoor pool, elevators and a carriage house with gym.

DRAKE "The Real Her" TAKE CARE
(Featuring LIL WAYNE & ANDRE 3000)

People around Big Tank should really have nothing to say. Big Daddy, he's just proud of the fact that Kandi done it her way. *"Vixen girls, love the way it goes down..."* But Big Tank gotta say, *"Oh, baby, oh baby, why is this so familiar?"* Just met Kandi, already feel like he know the real her. As they stepped outside to where the guest had congregated around with champagne flutes and little delicate appetizers being served were the most recognizable faces of beautiful woman in the world of urban – hip hop – and R & B music videos today.

AMERIE "Can't Let Go" ALL I HAVE

"All I know, all I know, all I know
I know, I know
Is I can't, I can't let go"

There were no rappers or chart topping singers, just booty popping, large silicone and natural 40D's breast bouncing on the video models that will become the new faces of the new reality television show 'The Next Top Video Vixen.' In a celebrated pilot shoot for the reality television show produced by Big Tank, he had 20 of these unique women gathered at the stunning location to sit back, relax, and get to know one another with the cameras rolling and the girls giving brief introductions.

The cameras were rolling and Kandi Gyal was standing back watching her future flash in front of her eyes. She felt like Paul Abdul most have felt next to Simon Cowell and was ready to give her solicited opinions or Tyra Banks looking for "The Next Top Model." Emotions on top of the world until Big Tank spanked Kandice on the ass and told her to go chill with the girls, because he also wanted to see how she looked on camera. She wasn't sure what he wanted her to do, talk to the vixens' or the cameras?

KEYSHA COLE "Make Me Over" A DIFFERENT ME

"Come on make me over - Baby make me over
I wanna look nice now - I wanna look real pretty"

Eye-hustling the whole scene, Kandice stood around sipping a glass of champagne listening to one of the prettiest video vixen's, who had a sticker that labeled her #10. Kandi Looked around and noticed all of the girls were wearing numbers, no names. #10 continued bragging about all her accolades and giving big shout outs to producers who were not there. She was talking to the camera as all the other girls labeled with numbers were listening and posing for the cameras.

Interrupting the conversation 'Video Vixen # 7' alleged, *"Not to be confused with the video ho, the video vixen is a woman of a different and astonishing nature. A video vixen is capable of causing multiple jerk off sessions during the period a day. A video vixen is not thought to be easily attainable even though her skin bearing appearance may lead one to assume otherwise. Video vixens are known to cause premature ejaculation."*

Then Vixen #18 talked about how many 'Video Vixen's' transition into higher ranks, and how she played in one of Tyler Perry's stage plays and in Kanye West's video 'Gold Digger.' Kandice started to walk around checking out the girls #2 through #20 she thought for sure they were all beautiful enough to be beauty pageants. Judging the girls they just kept getting prettier and prettier, Kandice judged them as if she was there to judge. *"She's Cute – She's Pretty – She is Prettier – she is gorgeous."* She thought they were all brilliantly polished and put together, eyelashes long, fingernails and pedicure polished, Brazilian waxed and bikini ready. Now seeking out who had the #1 sticker.

JILL SCOTT *"One Is The Magic Number"* WHO IS JILL SCOTT?

So many times Kandice define her pride through somebody else's eyes la, da, da, la, da. There's just her, one is the magic number...

"One Is The Magic Number"

Out of nowhere Big Tank reappeared handing her a sparkly pearl-white thong bikini and slapped the #1 sticker on her booty, telling her to hurry and get dressed. She instantly pulled the sticker off and said, *"I have to talk to my manager. I'm not doing this I'm a singer!"*

Slapping Kandice on her ass, Big Tank put the #1 sticker on her ass ignoring the other girls watching. Then he whispered for her ears only, *"Stop playing with me and get your phat ass out there if you want to be touring and modeling for various fashion and pop culture companies including BET 106 & Parks and, Channel, Versace, Moscino! My time is money and I'm giving you the #1 chance and only 1 chance."*

AALIYAH *"One In A Million" I CARE 4 U*

"Love it babe, love it babe, love it babe"

Totally surprised Kandice thought, she was there observing with the rest of the VIP's off camera. She had no plans of being part of some silly reality television contest, or she would have brought her own bikini. She didn't want to blow her 1 chance, Kandice put the bikini on venting, she would only shoot the pilot, and so she could see and prove how good she looked on camera.

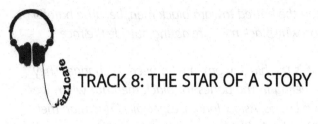

TRACK 8: THE STAR OF A STORY

GRENIQUE "The Star of A Story" BLACK BUTTERFLY
(HEATWAVE)

Angel come to Bluesy, let him be, part of all the love you are. 'Cause Angel they could fly, him and her, ride a rainbow to the sky. Sunday was Bluesy's official day off and the coffee shop was closed. Exhausted from working days in the coffee shop and nights on the buildings renovations and running between his parents, exhausted. Knowing his mother would be upset if he missing a Sunday family dinner and she was making Lasagna and Antipasto Pasta Salad, more of his favorites. But all he could think about was being with STARR.

Finding his second wind and thinking about STARR and their day plans. Thinking about her always brought on heart palpitations and butterflies in his stomach that were more than just nerves. With him working days and nights and her long hours at the recording studio, he hadn't seen her in a few days, but he was happy to know she was sleeping better and in a new bed.

They drove to South Philly to an Italian restaurant and everything was going fine until dessert when they happen to notice the stares they were getting and over hearing the conversations of 3 African - American men sitting at the bar talking about them.

Man #1: "If black woman want to date outside their race let them because most of us black men don't care. If a black man date outside the race, he hates black women but when a black woman dates outside the race, she is looking for love."

Man #2: "There is plenty of great black men out there but black women are too stupid to see that because they are blinded by hate for black men and then want to get mad when good black men start to date white women.

Black women need to stop the hatred toward black men, because hateful black women is the reason why black men are dating outside the race."

Man #3: "Amen, exactly it is the black women who need to change. They always have this hatred feeling in the bones for black men but when we date other races of women Latino, Asian, Indian, especially Caucasian then they all of a sudden want us back. Black women need to step their game up for real."

MARVA KING "Sistah" SOUL SISTAH

Okay, so this sistah's got a white boy and that brotha's got a white girl. For sure were inside a mixed world, so let the truth began to unfurl. After dinner and irrespective of the ignorant conversation they overheard, they both were bothered by the prejudice, regardless. Though Bluesy knew STARR was troubled before they even got to the restaurant, when he picked her up and she didn't kiss him was the first warning sign.

During the drive back to STARR'S place the car ride was silent, another warning. Instead of beating around the bush Bluesy asked sounding like he was begging, *"Can I spend some more time with you this evening? I'm not sure if you have rehearsal or something else to do."* She looked at him as if she was rejecting but she said, *"Stay awhile."*

MIKE PHILLIPS "Stay Awhile" M.P.3

There was nothing else for her to do since it had been months since she heard from Rofiki and a couple of days since she heard from BearLove. Still linger in her mind was the kiss. Thinking back to the narrow escape with Mina and having to sneak out of BearLove's house, she was pissed he hadn't called her. She was still thinking about what could have happened if Mina didn't come home. Now, she knew she couldn't go back to rehearse until they straighten things out. But, she couldn't let that stop the show. Categorizing the kiss as a friendly thank you very - very - very much.

CONYA DOSS "You Are My Starship" POEM ABOUT MS. DOSS (NORMAN CONNERS)

Bluesy's was STARR starship. Yes, he was her starship and don't be late, and don't he come too soon. Reaching out to hold hands Bluesy knew that the comments they overheard about interracial relations must have touch a nerve and upset her. Speaking out on the subject he said, *"I'm not racist but I could have kicked their ignorant asses. Please don't let those ignorant guys get to you. Honestly this shit pisses me off the human race has the same red blood. This society is full of bullshit we should not be treated any different because of white, black, and red, yellow, brown or black skin, why can't we just be people of the human race."* Finding comforted in his words STARR said, *"Wow finally someone who gets it. There is no such thing as colored; we're all of a color."*

PSYCHE OF SOUND "Burning Up" PSYCHE OF SOUND

"Burning up! The roof is on fire!" Whenever someone starts a comment with *"I'm not racist,"* She knew there's a 'but' coming next. But, she commended him for politely calling them dumb asses, instead of ignorant nigga's. There she said it for him, gladly! At the end of the day the only things that really exist is them, so fugh it. Annoyed she reclined her seat and close her eyes.

Bluesy was eyeing her, just as she assumed he would. Both were very tired and the drive was oddly quiet back to her place. His mind was full of confusion. Did he turn off the coffee pot? Does STARR want to be bothered?

Between thoughts he admired STARR'S dreadlocks pulled back seductively looking like a sleeping black beauty, she had drifted off to sleep

KAZZER "Pedal To The Metal" GO FOR BROKE

Just wanting to bring STARR peace, Bluesy knew it was time to tell her the truth about all that was going on in his life. He wasn't fibbing, he just didn't mention a few things and needed time to explain his plan. Bluesy noticed there were no parking spots in front of her house. That is when, he noticed the big Hummer driving away. She was still asleep and his instincts were to put the pedal to the metal and making a quick left turn onto the exit I-76 Schuylkill Expressway and as predicted the Hummer turned left and followed. Checking his rear view mirrors, right – left and center, making sure he had good views. He put his hand under his seat and felt for his gun and it was still where he left it. Without STARR noticing he brought it to his side.

> *"I'm like a 454 with the four on the floor*
> *Hummer comin' at ya avoiding the capture*
> *Rebuilt the motor 'cause she decided to blow*
> *And what do you know someone stole my stereo"*

Relieved STARR was not alarmed or suspicious of them being followed. Bluesy picked up speed switching lanes noticing the Hummer picking up speed. Bluesy noticed the traffic light was yellow about to turn red. He sped up trying to make the light and went through the red light, so did the Hummer. Now they were neck and neck both automobiles with tinted windows obstructing the views. Bluesy was prepared to drag race it out and go through the next traffic light but he seen a cop and slammed on his breaks, which startled STARR. His hand was up to secure her from going forward, even though they were wearing seat belts.

RUBEN STUDDARD "If Only For One Night" THE RETURN (LUTHER VANDROSS)

> *"Let me hold you tight if only for one night*
> *Let me keep you near to ease away your fear"*

Apologizing to STARR and eyeing the halogen lights of the hummer that went through the light. Bluesy began to feel that he may have been over acting, until ahead he seen the Hummers trying to make a U-turn. Bluesy was quicker and now a few blocks away and out of sight explaining, *"I'll get you home safe. I just have to make a stop."* Tired and unaware she mumbled *"ok"* and then closed her eyes and laid her head back. *"Dumb ass trying to follow me in a big ass Hummer,"* Bluesy mumbled under his breath. Though he wasn't sure who it was and sure he was being followed.

THE INTERNET "You Don't Even Know" FEEL GOOD
(Featuring TAY WALKER)

STARR don't even know... The white Hummer was now nowhere in sight. Bluesy drove around an extra 15 minutes to make sure he was safe heading towards North Broad Street. But the only safe place he could protect himself was the coffee shop. STARR tossed and turned a little but was still asleep when he parked. Before getting out the car he secured his gun on his hip. He got out the car and opened the passenger side. Startling STARR awake. Helping her out the car, he pulled her close. His deep voice held challenge as he said, *"I have something to show you."*

Confused STARR wondered why they were at the coffee shop. Looking at her surroundings a bright sign outside of the coffee shop lit up read 'BLUESY'S CAFÉ' in fancy calligraphy fonts and neon ocean blue frosted lights. STARR stood motionless and in shock. It was stunning the ambiance would pull anyone inside the café.

The re-grand opening was a week away. He even had coupons printed for free cups of coffee. She loved the hues of blues painted on the walls. Bluesy showed off his skills of interior designed paint faux finishes of marble and special paint finishes throughout the store.

The coast was clear and there was no sign of the white hummer. Bluesy felt safer when he was on his own turf. STARR was overwhelmed and impressed! She kissed him for what seemed like forever. Bluesy needed STARR like flowers needed rain. He was working on the problems in his life that was keeping him from cuddling under the same blankets with her electrifying body heat and tight hugs.

FRANK SANATRA "The Coffee Song" MAGIC OF OLD BLUE EYES

Satisfaction pursed Bluesy mouth, as he walked over to the portable stereo and began playing "The Coffee Song" and picking up a hat his father left and placing it over his bald head. He became a strong visual and vocal resemblance to a young Frank Sinatra. Transforming into his impersonation and doing a surprisingly wonderful job. For a few brief minutes STARR was being entertained by Frank Sinatra.

"Way down among Brazilians
Coffee beans grow by the billions"

(instrumental break)

During the instrumental break Bluesy shared some of his fondest memories waking up in the morning hearing this song. Still dancing around and pointing at the new coffee machine, new espresso machine, new cups and mugs and the many flavors of Brazilian coffee, Cuban Coffee, Coffee and Coffee and loose teas. Educating STARR about the song he said, *"The Coffee written by Bob Hilliard and the Music by Dick Miles in 1946. It was introduced at a stage show at the Copacabana Night Club in New York. The song caricatures Brazil's coffee surplus, claiming that no other beverages are available and that a politician's daughter was fined for drinking water."*

"You date a girl and find out later
She smells just like a percolator"

At the end of the song Bluesy turned off the lights inside the café on cue. Leaving them in the pitch black he was still singing and now joking around in a Spanish accent, *"Hey, Pedro get the flashlight - I cannot find the sugar."* He grabbed a heavy flash light and led her up the back steps to the second floor.

CARMEN RODGERS "Love" FREE

"It's all about Love..." It was like discovering a completely new person inside the person STARR thought couldn't dance or sing. Still laughing and tickled at how good Bluesy sounded and danced, STARR allowed him to guide her by flashlight to the back of the café and up the steps. She stopped and asked, *"What is this? I didn't know there was a second floor."*

Almost hesitating but proceeded to follow Bluesy as he unlocked the door, not answering her question, but showing her. The door opened to a dark room. Bluesy ran around with the flash light and began lighting candles explaining, *"The electric on the second floor will be on in a few days. I wanted to wait until everything was done, before surprising you with the apartment."*

Rambling around the 2 bed-room apartment that was now fully lit with candles. STARR praised his work, *"Beautiful! You've been working hard."*

KENYA SOULSINGER *"Lovetopia"* THE LOVE YOU TO LIFE ALBUM

It was *'Lovetopia'*, STAR pictured them time is erased and their souls are free. It's not too far, just beyond their fantasy and he is her brightest star. She admired the apartment covered in saw dust and newly dry walled and a beautiful hardwood floor. Noticing a cot in one of the bedrooms with lots of his clothes lying around. STARR instantly knew that Bluesy brought her a bed while, he slept on a cot all these nights after working blood sweat and tears on his dreams. Her tears fell with love, admiration, respect for Bluesy who interrupted her thoughts, *"I want you to live here with me. I just need a couple weeks after the grand opening and then I will have everything inspected and functioning."* Puzzled, confused and not sure, but sure he was sincere.

Holding her head down not wanting to look Bluesy in his ocean blue eyes, because the only thing STARR would see was that he was telling the truth. She did believe he loved her, but she wasn't sure what love was. After all she had been through, she wasn't sure if she was afraid to face the truth. But this was the first time she felt like somebody is being truthful with her.

The truth was Bluesy was blowing her mind with the thing he was saying, the things he was doing, the feelings she was feeling. She never imagined a man could have so much love to give. He was a walking inspirational Hallmark card. Running away with her emotions looking into his blues eyes, she kissed him.

FARNELL NEWTON *"The Bluest eyes Revisited"* CLASS IS IN SESSION

Bluesy showed her around the big spacious gourmet kitchen. She laughed to herself about not missing her old microwave and hallways full of cats, then about who would take care of the cats. Then she thought about where would she smoke? Yes, she was still trying to hide her dirty little habit. Maybe, she should stop smoking weed altogether. Bluesy must have read her thoughts. He said, *"If you have to smoke, during business hours open the back bedroom window, come let me show you."*

STARR wanted to object, but didn't. She couldn't believe she was seriously thinking about accepting his proposal and living there. The bare windows were big and tall and exposed them to the traffic on North Broad Street. But no one could look directly in with the big tree blocking the view. She had to admit it felt like a place she could call home.

V "Born Again" THE REVELATION IS NOW TELEVISED
(Featuring JILL SCOTT)

Feeling '*Born Again*' feeling baptized by Bluesy's spirit, STARR can feel it. She's captured, she had to write it down page for page, and she was so satisfied. Book after book could not possibly feel our capture this love. Candles burning and soft sexy sounds of their breathing, she reached up and touched his clean shaved balled head. His arms were now up her shirt cuffing her C cups and releasing her bra.

Caressingly, Bluesy held STARR'S exposed breast giving the nipples the attention they needed, and her wetter. Taunting and rubbing his lips against her nipples and gently kissing the new heart tattoo that read 'Diva' that covered up the old 'Rofiki 101' tattoo. In the candle light shadows of their bodies danced off the walls. Their tongues twisted and tasting like Red-Hots cinnamon candy mixed with M&M's with peanuts.

Bluesy: *I'm LOVING you!*

STARR (moaning into her response): *I'm LOVING you too!*

Reaching for the top button of STARR'S jeans, she let Bluesy release all her clothes to the floor. Wildly kissing and biting him, helping him remove his clothes. Moans of sweet ecstasy echoed all through the empty apartment. Kissing Bluesy's reddish brown chest hairs covered in sweat, his husky moans only she heard. There was no furniture and the floor was dusty. She held on with her arms wrapped around his neck. He carried her into the bedroom. As soon as the both of them laid on the single size cot it collapsed to the floor. They laughed and continued making love on the floor.

ABNIQUE "Reminisce" THE WAY HOME

The next morning hours before the coffee shop was to open, Bluesy drove STARR home. As she sipped on a new protein smoothie of spearmint, organic honey, wheatgrass, vanilla bean raw sugar syrup and soymilk. A drink Bluesy created, he calls it the 'Morning STARR,' and had it on the new menu. She loved it and he promised to make her one every morning.

After dropping STARR off at her place, he noticed the note book on the floor of the passenger seat. He seen the book before and knew this was STARR'S poetry journal. Picking up the journal to put it in the glove compartment and noticed pictures sticking out of the book. He put the book away and locked the glove department. He was actually locking it away from himself. There was so much he wanted to know about her. He thought about turning back around to give her the book. But, he couldn't take the not knowing.

CHRIS GODBER "Ain't No Stoppin" MY OFFERING
(MCFADDEN & WHITEHEAD)

Finding a secluded parking spot watching the sunrise welcoming Philadelphia into a new day, Bluesy sat in his car and began flipping pages. There were 2 pictures in the book. The first picture was a picture of her mother $hantey Money, reminding him of Queen Latifah with a twist of Missy Elliott. He couldn't believe the candid resemblance between STARR and her mother $hantey Money in their eyes and smile.

The camera caught their laughter and there was no mistaken it showed their love. The second picture caught him totally by surprise. He didn't know she had a picture of him. He was standing on the side of the stage. The camera caught him STAR(R) gazing. It was a picture of STARR on stage doing what she does best and he was caught up in it. There were lip-stick prints over his face. He smiled knowing she had been kissing the picture often. He opened the book marveling how STARR'S cursive handwriting gracefully flowed in black ink across the pages. He went directly to the page that had a black ink pen stuck between the pages.

MARCUS JOHNSON "Potomac Ridge" THE PHOENIX

Digesting STARR'S words, Bluesy thought she could literally sing or write about 'cows eating grass' and it would be a hit song. Holding on to her verbs and pronouns trying to find clues, but feeling guilty and immediately he closed the book. But each word echoed in his head making him want more. Holding the book closed tight fighting to keep it closed, he chuckling at the lyrics 'Bull – Shit ain't nothing but chewed up grass.' He sighed wanting to be her world of peace, and not bring her any grief. Even if he put the book down her words and voice still was ringing in his ears.

Later that evening after the coffee shop was closed, he headed over to his parents' house with STARR'S journal locked in the glove department. Thinking about how much he was feeling and needing more of her. He had never felt this way about any woman. He had thought by now he would have had a battle with the Rasta boyfriend showing up.

Being among the few, the proud, a Marine, Bluesy was ready for the battle, yet pleased that he wasn't in another war. He had so much going on in his own life working nonstop trying to get the new café in order, along with the renovations of the apartment on the second floor. There was so much to talk to STARR about, before they go any further, he had to come clean and be honest. He couldn't go a day without seeing her, smelling her or calling her countless times. He was glad he decided to come back to the United States after leaving the Marines. If he hadn't he would have never met her.

WYNTON MARSALIS "I Guess I'll Hang My Tears
Out To Dry" STANDARD BALLADS

The thoughts almost made Bluesy tear. Wishing he could take STARR willingly to England, so she could experience with him the views of the Siena. They could live in a villa in Tuscan, awakening to crowing roosters and opening the shutters to watch the mist burn off the fields. He was sure STARR would love vegetating in a rustic retreat of hiking trails and pools. He thought of the Tuscan Restaurants that served golden huge pastas, sausages in all shapes and sizes and cheese that's seldom found in the United States. Bluesy savored his memories of Europe but there would never be a better memory then STARR.

TORTURED SOUL "Fall In Love" INTRODUCING TORTURED SOUL

"Come on baby lets fall in love
Don't you be scared"

Falling in love, Bluesy locked up the journal before going into the house. He seen a shooting star a common name for the visible path of a meteoroid as it enters the atmosphere, becoming a meteor. He closed his eyes and made a wish on that star, *"I wish for peace on earth!"* He felt it was a clear sign that he was in love with STARR. He opened the front door to his parent's house and ciaos awaited him, as expected. He went straight to his bedroom locked the door wishing for STARR.

Yes, they had their differences but, instead of judging STARR, Bluesy judged himself. He was not perfect, but he was a good man. All he wanted was to be happy and at peace with GOD, his parents and the universe. He knew without a doubt that no other woman could attract him the way STARR did. She had a smile that lit his fire. He knew of the pain from her past relationship, and he never wanted to resurrect it. That was why he knew it was time to tell STARR the truth or never be forgiven.

ERYKAH BADU "Annie" BADUIZUM

Good thing Santa Clause didn't bring a lot of sexy draws, because STARR don't wear no panties, she don't wear no panties, no panties. After the amazing evening with Bluesy and seeing all the hard work he has been putting into the newly renovated 'Bluesy's Café.' STARR was happy for him, for them, feeling more secure in their relationship, she relaxed. Bluesy told her all night that the apartment on top of the coffee shop would be just as much her place. They spent the night on a single cot on the floor, happy and starting to feel secure, planning their future. She wanted to move out since the day she moved into the Junky - Jenki's third floor apartment. But, she would have moved into a cardboard box to get away from Rofiki. She didn't want to think about Rofiki anymore.

Then next morning STARR was feeling nauseas and vomiting with her head hanging over the toilet with throbbing temples, emotionally all together FUGHED UP! She was blaming it on her nerves replaying words and faces of her past, old remarks Rofiki made and even Mina's actions when she is around BearLove trying to work (sing). Life was feeling half crazy, just a little better than the insanity she came out of. After Bluesy dropped STARR off in West Philly and making sure she was alright before rushed back to open the coffee shop.

Knowing BLUESY was serious about her moving in with him. She was seriously thinking about it. Though, she was working and paying her own way through life now and not really sure if it would be a good move for her at the moment. And like Badu, she didn't need anyone telling her the time when she woke up in the morning.

ERYKAH BADU "Certainly" BADUIZUM

The world is STARR'S when she wake up. She don't need nobody telling her the time. Certainly, certainly not STARR, no. Running around looking for her journal, STARR'S whole life was written in those pages. A flash from her past was written on each of the pages, worn years old with ashes and tear stains. Assuming it must have dropped out of her bag. She called Bluesy, no answer. That is when she stumbled upon the 'Black Book' that Bluesy gave her the day they met in his coffee shop. Feeling guilty for forgetting all about the book, assuming it was a small Bible she open the pages.

Immediately noticing Rofiki's handwriting. The first page had his mother's Haile's address and phone number. The next few pages had a few phone numbers, her name or number was not listed. Immediately she closed the book not wanting to be a part of his world, because she wasn't. Exhausted by the thoughts of Bluesy finding her journal with stories from her past that she didn't share. STARR's past life haunted her and told Bluesy a few stories, but not the ones written on those pages. Wondering after telling him about her past life and her mother M.C. $HANTEY MONEY disappearing without a trace if he would use the information to hurt her too. She fell asleep into haunted dreams that played back old lyrics and memories.

$HANTEY MONEY "Bullshit" (Lyrics)

J. DILLA (Jay Dee) "Bullshit" (Instrumental)

"I came tonight to rock the Party... Party... Party...
I came tonight to rock the Party... Party... Party...

Now wave your hands in the air...
Wave them like you just don't care!

I'm $hantey Money
Ain't a damn thing funny
Don't try to play me - Pay me!

Bullshit ain't nothing but chewed up grass
Ask me how I know? 'Cause you showed me your ASS!

I'm a real fly honey
Like a bee to money
Rocking your body into a jerk

It takes 4 fly brotha's to make me a man
That's the whole idea of Shantey's plan

Can I get a Hey!
Can I get a Ho!

But the Bullshit you serving I do eat though!"

"I came tonight to rock the Party... Party... Party...
I came tonight to rock the Party... Party...Party...
I came tonight to rock the Party... Party... Party...
I came tonight to rock the Party... Party... Party....

Bullshit ain't nothing but chewed up grass
Ask me how I know? 'Cause you showed me your ASS!

Telling me you you'll be right back
When in fact I helped you pack
I'm cool no need to write back

I'm Shantey Brown and that's how I get down!
Can't be found - Never lost – What's cost?
Always BOSS!

YO!

Now you wanna be my friends *(Bullshit)*

It'll never happen again *(Bullshit)*

Now you wanna borrow ten *($10 - Bullshit)*

Still puff and don't pass *(Bullshit)*

Now you wanna fuck my friends *(Bullshit)*

Now you wanna hear me rap *(Bullshit)*

Can you borrow a pen *(Bullshit)*

You got my lighter again? *(Bullshit!)*

I came tonight to rock the Party... Party... Party...
I came tonight to rock the Party... Party...Party...
I came tonight to rock the Party... Party... Party...
I came tonight to rock the Party... Party... Party....

Bullshit ain't nothing but chewed up grass
Ask me how I know? 'Cause you showed me your ASS!

So now you hear me – And you know I'm the shit
My homies love it when I roll that shit
Stick around you may catch a whiff

I'm know you love it when you smell Bull-Shit!

I keep a blade - Can't be played!
Walk around in purple haze
Spark it up and get it blazed!
Let's get a taste (drink)
Don't let it waste
No need to hide - It's me inside

Never settle for less - I'm the best!
Turn up the bass – I'm in the place
I know I'm black - And yes I'm proud
No regrets - I kept my seed
Best believe - It's me she needs
I am not greedy – but I'm needy
I can't sleep - I always eat
I feel so high – I reach the sky
May never come back till' 4th of July
There is lust in his eyes
I know, I make his nature rise
I'm pulling back - that's a fact
Not giving up shit – Yes there is a twist
Not spitting Bull - Shit

Bullshit ain't nothing but chewed up grass
Ask me how I know? 'Cause you showed me your ASS!

FLASH BACK to the age of 15, STARR and $HANTEY MONEY, last day together. Music was blasting through STARR'S head phones as she sang along and sorting through piles of Right On! Essence, Ebony, Jet and Sister2Sister magazines. Listening to the music and flipping pages and observing her mother $HANTEY MONEY.

With only 15 years between them, STARR wasn't raised to call her, mom. STARR knew $hantey Money was leaving again, watching her stuff clothes in big green trash bags. While the dude in the car, a new boyfriend from North Philly waited. STARR overheard earlier that day Shantey and Auntie arguing, before Auntie left for church choir practice. When Auntie wasn't around STARR took advantage of the moments to call Shantey, mom. *"Mom where are you going and tell me the truth?"*

"Bullshit ain't nothing but chewed up grass
Ask me how I know
Caused you showed your ASS!"

Bullshitting STARR, because she wouldn't understand the truth. There was a 15 year difference between them and their youth kept them close, but STARR couldn't go with her.

Refusing to be a one hit wonder for having one signature song 'Bullshit' that over shadowed $hantey Money's other work. So when STARR asked again, *"Mom! Why you leaving me here?"* her mom explained as she gathered her belongings, *"I'm going to work in the studio. On a new project, I'm trying to get to with Jazzy Jeff. I could open up for The Fresh Prince and Salt & Pepa tour."*

SALT -N- PEPA "Push It" HOT, COOL & VICIOUS

"Oooh, baby, baby
Baby, baby"

"Get up on this! Ow Baby, $hantey Money is here." STARR's eyes lit up wanting to hear more. Her mother was a true blue hip – hop queen and known locally for winning contest for best female rappers, back in the 1980's. Shantey was initially regarded as one of the most promising female rappers to emerge out of the suburb of Norristown. Female rappers from Philly, Jersey and New York have lost the battle trying to free style against her. $hantey Money was also known for being a regular dancer on the television dance show that came on channel 17 'DANCING ON AIR.' But couldn't perform due to the lyrics in her song.

Also once a member of the Philadelphia dance group "The Pop-Along-Kids.' Yes, $hantey Money had big dreams about her rap career and every time, she got close to be signed by a major record label disappointment followed. Being told she was too raw and soften up, too big, too dark, and too smart, too many things the industry didn't want. STARR was Shantey's biggest fan and would make money on the side in school selling old school underground hip-hop mixed tapes with different rap artist.

UTFO "The Real Roxanne" UTFO

"I'm the real Shantey and I'll rock your world
And I'm all stuck up
Well you say that
Cause I wouldn't give a guy like you no rap?"

There was no female out there that could dress as fly or rap like $hantey Money, besides herself, being born and taught by the best, but STARR only wanted to singer Soul, R&B, Jazz. Her mom was famous for her swift rap flow, sharp and raw poetic lyrics, and Hip – Hop fashions.

Rocking the latest fad and wearing brightly colored name-brand tracksuits, sheepskin and leather bomber jackets and sneakers such as Pro - Ked, Puma, Converse's Chuck Taylor All-stars and Adidas Superstars often with oversized shoelaces. $hantey Money also sported the popular 'Jheri Curl' hair style, Kangol bucket hats or Kente cloth hats, designer jeans, 14kt heavy gold rope chains, Kemetic ankh, and nameplates, name belts, and multiple rings on her fingers, an oversized 14kt gold door-knocker earrings.

ROXANNE SHANTE "Bite this"

"Tell them Marley – Mar what to do..."

"Bite this..." Noticing how Shantey was trying to hide the big bulge in her belly. STARR heard her Auntie screaming at her mother a few days prior, *"Shantey you dumb ass! Now who gonna raise this baby! If you leaving STARR you betta sign over some papers and still send money!"* Just as confused, STARR knew that her Auntie had no idea that Shantey was taking all her belongings as she remembered Shantey walking out the door and never returning. Shantey lived with Auntie (her foster mother) since she was 9 months pregnant with STARR. Auntie was supposed to adopt STARR once she was born. But Shantey would never sign over the papers. So Auntie felt forced to let Shantey come and go, because of her love for wanting a baby and her hate for not having her own.

The mother daughter relationships between her and Auntie never bonded because STARR always knew her mother SHANTEY BROWN! Shantey called her Auntie, and naturally so did STARR. Auntie was not sweet or sour, but always ready to be fair and give and take no mess, or she would take off her church robe and curse you out so ever politely. The lyrics from $hantey Money were Auntie's quotes.

QUEEN LATIFAH "U.N.I.T.Y." BLACK REIGN

"U.N.I.T.Y.
You got to let him know - You ain't a bitch or a ho!"

Rumor was that $hantey Money pissed off somebody and got blacklisted in the industry, having her tied up in court and broke, but her one hit, "Bullshit," kept her name alive. People compared her to the likes of Queen Latifah, Missy Elliot, M.C. Lyte, and Bahamadia with a dash of Salt & Pepa. Shantey's lyrics were notorious and unchristian like to the ears of Auntie, so her rap career dreams were never supported, but the money was accepted. STARR was used to her mom coming and going. Remembering Shantey hurrying out the house with arms full of belongings explaining, she needed a few weeks to get settled. Running out the door blowing kisses and telling STARR she had an old soulful heart and to keep singing, because she sounded outstanding singing and that she would be back for STARR to rock on her next track.

JEAN GRAE "My Story" JEANIUS

In STARR'S story, she would swim a thousand lakes to bring her mom back, she would write that, but infinity can't rewind facts. Chasing the same dreams and still saying the same raps had them still living with Auntie. Shantey claimed that Auntie was the nicest of all foster mothers. STARR knew that her mom continued to come back and forth, because of her. Though Auntie didn't have custody, STARR was still in the system as a foster child.

So legally, Auntie was her guardian that received the check. Auntie came busting in the door from choir practice out of breath and looking for someone to help her with her coat and pocketbook, she discovered Shantey and things gone, she went off screaming, *"Where is your - that two-faced Shantey? Did she wash the dishes and scrub out the tub and get up all that dang-on weave glue. Did Shantey leave my money?"* STARR didn't answer avoiding the high pitch voice of the heavy woman.

URSULA RUCKERS "Philadelphia Child" SUPA SISTA

A Philadelphia child, Shantey Money was wild, mild, mind all filled with fresh city, foul city, fiery city. A wild flower and STARR would walk to her mother if she could. But, no matter how far she walked away, Auntie could be heard yelling, *"I know Shantey's pregnant and back on those drugs. Got my basement smelling like marijuana?"* STARR turned the volume up high on her headphones. Hoping $hantey Money wasn't pregnant, and just fat from fast-food like she claimed.

Though it had been 6 months and STARR was still hearing Auntie walking through the house cursing out Shantey for not returning. *"Bull – shit ain't nothing but chew up grass and still no heads or tails. Shantey out there running the streets want to be a rapper and having babies and smoking weed and you had better pray you don't end up just like her."* Was the last thing Auntie was saying when she dropped dead of a heart attack in the kitchen, while cutting up collard greens. After the ambulance came and took Auntie away and the church member left. STARR curled up on the sofa looking out the window terrified until sleep took her by surprise.

DIANNE REEVES "Better Days" DIANNE REEVES

Silver gray hair neatly combed in place. Heaven sent angels down and gave Auntie her wings. Now she's flying and sliding and gliding in better days. STARR remembered hearing Auntie saying, *"Be patient, be patient."* The following morning STARR awoke to women dressed in business attire and brief cases, knocking at the door. They didn't give her a chance to wipe the sleep out her eyes before saying, *"Get dressed were here to take you to a home."* Her heart sang with delight and face lit up like a Christmas tree.

STARR'S mouth spread into a thin-lipped smile asking, *"Are you taking me to my mom $hantey? Where did they take Auntie?"* The woman didn't say anything they took her by the hand and led her to the car. STARR looked out the car window and wondered how many more blocks. They pulled up to a street full of kids playing kick-ball and jumping rope. Checking out the nameless faces of boys and girls playing in the front yard, as she got out the car.

ALEX GOPHER "The Child" NU-JAZZ DIVAS VOL. 2
(BILLY HOLIDAY)

"Them that's got shall get. Them that's not shall lose... God Bless the child..." They rung the door bell and a middle aged woman answered the door and inviting them inside putting out her cigarette and turning down her jazz music. STARR was introduced to Mrs. Baker and that's when the confusion began. She asked, *"Where is my mom? Where is Shantey?"* The case managers and Mrs. Baker gave each other signals that STARR didn't understand.

The case manager bent down to bring her face leveled to STARR'S as she explained. *"Well, honey you have to stay here until we're able to contact your mother Shantey Brown. You're too young and can't stay home alone. "* Tears ran down STARR'S cheeks as she mumbled, *"But Auntie is dead. I need to be home if Shantey calls!"*

ZOÉ "City of Love (Philadelphia)" LET'S FLY

Emotions were pulling STARR down to the floor in tears. Unsympathetic Ms. Baker looked around for her belongings. When she realized there were none, she said to the case managers, *"Y'all brought me another child with no clothes? This is the third one this week. Where am I supposed to get the money to clothes these here children? I can't wait no month for you to send me a check from the foster care agency. Bad enough I have to feed them a month before you pay me."*

It didn't make a difference what Mrs. Baker said to them. They still left STARR there standing with just the clothes on her back. When the door closed Mrs. Baker peeked out the windows watching the social workers drive away. She turned her music back up and relit her cigarette. She watched Mrs. Baker's poker face sweet smile turn into a cynical grin. She walked over to STARR and gripped her up by the shoulder.

Nudging STARR towards the steps sighing, *"Get up there and get your butt in the tub. You kids can't sit or sleep in my house unless you clean."* STARR noticed that the upstairs of the house was a mess. The hallway had green trash bags filled with dirty clothes piled high outside of the bedroom doors. She had to step over them to enter the bathroom.

JILL SCOTT "GOD Bless The Child" JILL SCOTT COLLABORATIONS
(Featuring AL JARREAU & GEORGE BENSON)
BILLY HOLIDAY

"Momma may have, Poppa may have,
But GOD bless the child that's got his own, that's got his own."

The bathroom was dingy and trash was everywhere, except the trash can. Mrs. Baker locked the bathroom door and filled the tub with steaming hot water and added bleach. STARR was horrified but didn't know what to do but obey. STARR was forced into the scolding hot water. Mrs. Baker took a bristled brush and scrubbed as she repeated. *"Child, I don't know if you are that black or dirty, but we is going to get you clean."* STARR got out the tub scratched up by the abuse of Mrs. Bakers scrub brush. She had to remain standing in the tub until all the water was drained.

Then Ms. Baker took cups of peroxide and splashed it all over her freshly scratched body that was already irritated by the bleach. With her body feeling like it was on fire, she pushed Mrs. Baker away from her. When Miss Baker noticed that STARR might fight her back she took it easy, though Miss Baker was 100lbs heavier. Humiliated STARR knew when they found Shantey, she would tell her about Mrs. Baker and they would both jump and kick her ass!

Standing in the middle of the bathroom floor butt naked STARR grabbed a towel off the floor. She was so angry she wanted to run out the door with just the towel. But she had to be smarter than them (them being the system). Shantey had always warned her about 'DHS' the system (Department of Human Services).

As STARR watched Ms. Baker's eye travel over her body, a lump formed in her throat. Ms. Baker barked, *"Child ain't nobody here going to hurt you. But if you swing at me I will kick your ass! Now get your head to the zinc."* STARR was confused. Ms. Baker snapped, "What *is wrong with you? Child you must be slow. Don't you know what a zinc is?"* STARR shook her head no. Ms. Baker pointed and STARR said, *"I didn't know you were talking about the sink."*

MARY MARY *"Yesterday"* MARY MARY

STARR had enough heartache and so many ups and downs. Don't know how much more she can take. See, she decided that she cried her last tears yesterday... Dragged to the sink and nearly drowned, as STARR got her hair washed. Next, Ms. Baker sat on the toilet seat and nestled STARR between her thick pork chop thighs. STARR held her breath from the stench that came from the toilet and between Ms. Baker legs.

Aggravated, Ms. Baker was preparing to yank her hair free of naps, but was surprised how freely the comb slid through STARR'S hair. Instead of complimenting her long black thick hair she said, *"Hmmm – You gotta perm? Your hair can't be this long and not nappy."* Ms. Baker threw STARR'S clothes in the trash and gave her a dress that was tight. STARR felt self-conscious about not having on any underwear and after her bath she felt like Ms. Baker was trying to put a voodoo spell on her. Coming down the steps with Mrs. Baker the other children were coming in the door.

Recognizing a few faces from getting out of the car. Immediately a little girl attacked STARR screaming, *"That is my dress!"* Ms. Baker grabbed the child after she threw a few punches at STARR. She could have easily beaten the girl up, but she knew Ms. Baker couldn't be beat. Ms. Baker grabbed her daughter looking at STARR and snickered, *"This is my daughter Keisha and you're wearing her dress. I was nice enough to let you have some of her stuff, so be grateful."* Ms. Baker led Keisha away explaining, *"Child let them kids have your old stuff. When I get the check you get all the new stuff."* Keisha dashed away happily.

TRIN-I-TEE 5:7 *"Won't Turn Back"* TRIN-I-TEE 5:7

No, STARR 'Won't Turn Back' now she has come too far... Placed in 10 different foster homes until she was 17 years old. She was fully developed and that had been nothing but trouble for her. Some foster mothers cursed her, foster fathers eyes molested her, their sons tried to rape her and their daughters hated her.

The end of the straw came was when she was in her last foster home. She was placed with a woman that had no husband or children or other foster children. Ms. Nancy who slightly reminded STARR of Auntie, maybe it was the Christian lifestyle. Ms. Nancy loved gospel music and loved getting dress to go to church, just like Auntie.

But STARR didn't have to go to church with Auntie. But with Ms. Nancy she had to get up and go everywhere, because she assumed she wasn't trusted to be left alone. So, off to Agape Nondenominational church of GOD and visiting other churches and listening to the Agape Choir. STARR found her spiritual side being lifted in gospel music.

The one thing that was bringing STARR and Ms. Nancy together was the music. Travelling and visiting different churches all around the Philadelphia area and going to gospel concerts featuring Tremaine Hawkins, Hezekiah Walker, Barbara Ward Farmer & the Wagner Alumni Choir and The Wilmington Chester Mass Choir, and many more gospel choirs.

WILMINGTON CHESTER MASS CHOIR "Stand Still"
STAND STILL (Until His Will Is Clear)

Day and night STARR wondered, what do she do? What do she say, when she don't know what to say? Oh, oh, oh, she'll stand still. Until. GOD'S will is clear to her. Things were starting to feel safe and Ms. Nancy lived a discreet life, but there was one visitor that came by more than often.

The first time Deacon Frank Wayman stopped over to Ms. Nancy's house, he aggressively gave STARR a bear hug and his deep snarling laugh sound intimidating. Holding on to her tight with his big hands saying, *"The Agape Non-Denominational Church needs more youth like you. When I come here – I'm still your Deacon, but I visit as a friend. You can call me Mr. Frank when I come to visit. But, in church you make sure you call me Deacon Wayman. Amen."* Coming to her rescue Ms. Nancy waved him away saying, *"Leave that girl alone. She already been anointed and we had prayer."*

STARR hadn't been there a day and already and Ms. Nancy had olive oil dripping off her forehead and prayed over countless times. Mrs. Nancy stayed in church 7 days a week. Sunday morning church service was the kick off for the weekly events that followed. Monday night prayer, Tuesday night woman auxiliary's meeting, Wednesday night bible studies, Thursday noon day prayer and Friday night gracious women meetings. On Saturday afternoon STARR sat in the back of the pews listening to the choir rehearsal, while Ms. Nancy visited the sick and shut in with Deacon Wayman. STARR enjoyed her time writing in her journal and singing along listening to the choir.

SMOKEY NORFOLK *"I Need You Now"* I NEED YOU NOW

"Oh not another second. Not another minute, Lord. Can't wait another day, oh. Oh Lord, I need you now! Mmmmm, Yeah." Humming the different melodies, STARR was overhead by the first lady Mrs. Jazilyn Williams, the pastor's wife sitting a few pews behind coughing, sneezing and sipping tea to nurse her sore throat. When the choir director called out for Mrs. Williams to come practice her solo part, she insisted STARR try singing it. She could barely talk trying to convince the director, *"This girl can sing. I'm listening to her harmonize, I can't talk or sing, so who gonna do it?"*

After Mrs. Williams made a big deal about it and the choir was clapping and calling STARR up to take the microphone, she had no idea what was going on shocked out of her private thoughts of running away. Singing and thinking about running away consistently occupied her thought and time. The only thing that kept her from running away was remembering Shantey's warnings about the system. *"Don't run because if they find you they keep you longer. And if you keep running away they will put you in a place that medicates you. And if that happens they can keep you until your 21. If anything ever happens stay until I find you!"* She had been waiting in foster care for 2 years and still no signs of $hantey Money.

Sunday morning, STARR had a solo and the Agape Church was a full house. She came forward to the microphone and the fumbling could be heard through the speakers. A screech came as she tried to pick up the microphone. Stepping back to bring the microphone into range. The screeching and shuffling of the microphone made Ms. Nancy slumped down in the front pew embarrassed and mumbling, *"Lord. Please don't let this child embarrass me."*

KIRK FRANKLIN AND THE FAMILY *"Real Love"* KIRK FRANKLIN

"He loves me, he loves me, he loves me..."

Have STARR ever loved somebody? Will STARR ever love somebody? The way that Jesus loves her? STARR closed her eyes, opened her mouth and let out the sweetest voice that enveloped the congregation. The choir director knew STARR was good, but was nervous at practice. Standing with the microphone in her hand and the sea of smiles encouraging her, she transformed into a song bird. The whole congregation were on their feet including her foster mother, Ms. Nancy was shouting. STARR lit up the place with the glow of her voice. They shouted and wanted more. They had only rehearsed one song with her, so at the Pastor request she sang the song again. After service she saw a side of Ms. Nancy that she never saw before. Ms. Nancy took her out to dinner. Brought her new dresses and gave her money to get a fresh perm.

HEZEKIAH WALKER "I'll Make It" LOVE FELLOWSHIP CHOIR

"It's alight now, I'll think I'll make it anyhow," Two months later the choir made it to the National Gospel Choir Competition. *"Everything is gonna be a'ight now!"* After church one Sunday after everyone kept telling STAR over and over how good she was they were heading home when Mrs. Nancy murmured satirically, *"I made you what you are. I put you on the choir. I brought you new clothes. Don't think your cute because some snotty – nose boys are smiling at you."* She could put up with the name calling and smart remarks. She was just happy that Mrs. Nancy never physically touched her. STARR learned how to block out Ms. Nancy. But she was smart enough to know that Ms. Nancy couldn't block her voice when she sang.

CHERYL PEPSI RILEY "Stephanie" ALL THAT

Just a little girl thinking everything she ever done was wrong and you may ask STARR, how she know, because STEPHANIE is STARR... The day will come when she would leave Ms. Nancy's house too, and STARR would always remember. 6 months away from her 18th birthday and she had $50 saved. Then there was the pressure of the choir entering the Gospel competition.

To enter the competition, she needed a copy of her birth certificate. Something she never thought about it until it was requested. When she asked for the copy Mrs. Nancy unlocked a file cabinet she kept in her home office. When she learned it was for STARR to register in the Gospel Competition, she locked the drawer back. *"That is private information that you can't go giving to just anyone. I don't trust anyone. I will look into it."*

KIM BURRELL "I Come To You More Than I Give" EVERLASTING LIFE

The only thing STARR could do was pray and keep singing. *"I come to you more than I give. Always with my hands out instead of lifting them up."* STARR kept her eyes on the drawer that was locked with her paper work. She had to get in the locked drawer. She could see that Ms. Nancy was deliberately holding her back from registering. She wondered what other papers she had and any update info on her mom, Shantey.

YOLANDA ADAMS "I'll Always Remember" SAVE THE WORLD

When STARR would lay down to sleep. She would always pray, *"Dear Lord my soul please keep."* Later that night after Mr. Frank came over and Ms. Nancy assumed STARR was asleep. STARR heard them behind the closed bedroom door giggling as she tipped – toed downstairs. She knew they were in Ms. Nancy's bedroom drinking Vodka and smoking cigarettes, she could smell it. Plus she was the one who had to take the trash out and Ms. Nancy didn't do a good job at hiding the liquor bottles or empty Newport boxes.

"STARR remember, yes she remember
Oh yes she will, she will always remember"

STARR went straight to the file drawer that was locked. She sat on the floor trying to work the lock with a hair pin and fingernail file. It just wouldn't work. Disgusted she fell back in a chair sitting on Mr. Frank's coat with jiggling car keys. She picked up his coat to find his car keys, thinking maybe one of his keys might work on the lock. What she found was his wallet filled with credit cards and lot of $20 bills. STARR didn't count them all, just the five she took.

A week later when STARR heard Mr. Frank & Ms. Nancy in the mist of mad passion behind closed doors. Tip-toeing again down stairs and found Deacon Frank Wallet and took another $100. STARR was nervous that she would be caught, but she was never questioned. She knew that Deacon Frank parked around the corner to hide his car. In case his wife would notice or anyone else for that matter. Deacon Frank could stay out overnight a couple times a week because his wife would stay over her parent's house to help take care of them, because both of her parents were elderly sick and bed ridden.

LISA MCCLENDON" Grace Grace Grace" SOUL MUSIC

The night had come when STARR knew she had to escape before they moved her into another foster home. In that transition there would be an inventory of her belongings and her money could be found. She had gotten up in the middle of the night to go to the bathroom. Ms. Nancy could be heard snoring as she passed her bedroom door.

Rubbing her eyes, STARR entered the dark bathroom and turned on the lights and found Deacon Frank leaning over the toilet pissing and finishing up. He smiled glad to see her. He closed the door and turned the lights back off. Startling STARR, she closed her eyes tight and whispered. *"Oh, I am so sorry Deacon Wayman – I mean Mr. Frank. I didn't know you were in here."*

Smirking with a mysteries snicker Mr. Frank stood there with his penis still in one hand and shutting the door and holding it closed with his other. *"I guess that means that I should still have money in my wallet. Don't think I don't know you've been taking my money."* Mr. Frank had actually thought it was Ms. Nancy dipping into his wallet. Figuring it out when one night he had money missing and Nancy never left his side.

LEJUENE THOMPSON "This Too Will Pass" METAMORPHOSIS

Feeling like all hope was lost, STARR kept standing until her prayers for Mr. Frank to disappear were answered, trusting this too will pass. Before She could object Mr. Frank whispered as stroking himself, *"Don't worry I'll give you some more money, but first you have to earn it."* He locked the bathroom door and STARR began praying in a whimper, *"The blood of Jesus"* as he tried to force her to perform falacio. She was sickened by his strong stench of stale alcohol and cigars on his breath and the funk of Ms. Nancy, STARR began to gag. Then they both heard a BANG! In Ms. Nancy's bedroom.

Pushed away, STARR was released from the grip of Mr. Frank a child molester. He looked at STARR and mumbled, *"Forgive me, I thought you were someone else."* He opened the bathroom door and seen that the coast was clear and stumbled back into Ms. Nancy's bedroom. STARR was left kneeling on the bathroom floor that turned into a praying position. She cried out silently afraid to open her mouth and scream, because no one ever came to help. Deciding it was defiantly time to leave. She knew she had to find a way to get into Ms. Nancy's drawer and get her birth certificate and any other information she could find about herself.

LEJUENE THOMPSON "Like A Butterfly" METAMORPHOSIS

Changing right before her eyes, STARR isn't the same girl she used to be. Like a butterfly she is going to fly and soaring so high. There was no way she was going into another foster home and no one was going to make her do that to them again. She knew that Deacon – Mr. Frank was the devil and would eventually start sneaking into her room. She thought she heard him a few times outside her bedroom door. She slept with her bedroom door locked every night after that. She had gotten in trouble for locking the door before. Ms. Nancy said if you don't pay any bills in her house, you didn't own a door to lock.

The next morning STARR prepared for church wondering how she was going to make it through the service without screaming out all of Ms. Nancy and Deacon Wayman's business. She was planning to step up to the microphone and instead of singing, she was going to tell it all. She looked around her bedroom and gathered her personal belongings including her journal. Because she knew once she told the truth, she wouldn't be able to come back and collect anything. STARR even put on 5 pairs of underwear and stashed her money between the layers in a small purple Crown Royal pouch, she found in Ms. Nancy's trash.

DEBRA KILLINGS "Without HIM" SURRENDER

"She can't sing without HIM
She can't think without HIM
She can't give without HIM
She can't live without HIM"

Trying to act as if everything was normal, STARR prepared for church. Once they were in the car, she made up an excuse about having to go to the bathroom. Thinking fast she told Ms. Nancy that she forgot feminine pads and it worked. Exasperating Mrs. Nancy gave her the house keys that also had her desk key. STARR ran into the house and went straight to the desk drawer and began searching for her papers. They were gone. STARR almost lost it as a tear escaped her eye. Just then she noticed a thick folder in the back of the drawer. STARR pulled it out and locked the drawer. Ms. Nancy was blowing the horn repeatedly.

PAUL OWENS & APC "He Reigns" COMFORT ME

"GOD is an assume GOD
HE reigns forever
From Heaven Above"

The folder was too big to stuff in her bag or between the layers of underwear. She ran to the kitchen and found a trash bag and placed the folder in it. She was able to go unseen placing the bag in the outdoor trash can. She would return later to retrieve it.

On the choir stand fully covered in her choir robe, STARR'S heart was pounding through her chest. Keeping her hands clutched to the secured pouch, she touched her stomach so many times choir members noticed assuming a tummy ache, not that she was holding on to her stolen life and savings.

YOLANDA ADAMS 'The Battle Is Not Yours" YOLANDA LIVE IN WASHINGTON

"This battle is not yours, no, it belongs to the Lord! Hallelujah, yeah!"

The time came for STARR to step up to the microphone and sing. She looked over and seen the dull expression of Ms. Nancy's face. She took a quick glance over at Deacon Wayman who was sitting with his wife on the other side of the church, as usual. The eye contact caused Deacon Wayman to drop his head. He acted like he was reading the church program for the tenth time. He hung his head in shame. The choir director seemed extra happy that Sunday morning playing the piano like they were already in competition.

Listening to all the different voices shouting, *"Sing - Girl sing!"* As much as STARR wanted to hurt Ms. Nancy and Deacon Wayman, she didn't want to hurt his wife. She grabbed the microphone and for GOD, she sung. She sung like it was a competition, she could feel the spirit moving in her gut. She was singing like it would be her last time and last chance. Everyone was on their feet clapping except Deacon Wayman and Ms. Nancy. STARR thought when she was finished singing, *"I guess it is true. GOD has a way of sitting people down."*

NATALIE WILSON & THE S.O.P. CHORAL "When you need a friend" THE GOOD LIFE

"When you need a friend, right to the very end, GOD is on your side!"

The ride home was silent. STARR continued to hold onto her stash. She became conscious that she didn't actually have a plan or any clothes and her paper work was still hidden in the trash. Once they were in the house STARR went straight to work doing her choirs washing dishes, sweeping floors before Ms. Nancy could bark any orders.

Adrenaline running high, she needed to keep busy and from thinking of ways of harming Ms. Nancy in her sleep. As STARR was putting towels in the linen closet, she noticed the luggage set that Ms. Nancy brought with one of the checks that the foster care agency gave her to buy STARR some clothes. Instead of buying STARR clothes, Ms. Nancy brought herself a Louis Vuitton duffle bag and cosmetic case. Ms. Nancy kept it in the closet awaiting the promised vacation with Mr. Frank.

Leaving the bags in the closet STARR returned to her bedroom complaining of cramps. Ms. Nancy went about her business hoping, STARR would fall asleep early, so she could invite Mr. Frank. STARR locked her bedroom door and began to gather enough stuff to pack in a duffle bag. She put everything under her bed until ready to put it in the Louis Vuitton duffle. STARR stretched across the bed and dosed off.

Hours later waking up in a panic. She tried focusing on the digital clock. She tripped over the bottom drawer that she had forgotten to close. She waited to hear if she was heard.

It was 3 A. M. she went to the linen clothes and pulled out the bags. She made sure that the bags were easily accessible. She returned to her room and began to pack. She went into the bathroom and took all the aspirin, face cream, tooth paste, shower gels and body lotions she could fit in the cosmetic case.

TAKE 6 "If We Ever Needed the Lord Before (We Sure Do Need Him Now)" TAKE 6

"We need HIM in the morning
We need HIM in the night
We need HIM in the noonday
When the sun is shining bright."

Tiptoeing STARR made her way down the steps with bags packed, swung across her shoulder. She still had her money stashed in between her 5 layers of underwear. Noticing Deacon Frank's coat folded across a chair. She stuck her hands in his coat pockets looking for his wallet. This time she was going to take all of his money and maybe even a credit card. There was no wallet, but there were car keys.

Taking the cars keys to keep Mr. Frank stranded. STARR planned to throw them in the trash when she retrieved her paperwork. She stuck the keys in her pocket thinking, Let him explain why his car is parked around the corner from Ms. Nancy's house. He might have to call his wife to pick him up.

Thankfully, Ms. Nancy never set the house alarm when Mr. Frank stayed over. STARR was glad, because she didn't know the alarm code. Sneaking out the back door she went straight to the trash can for her paper work. Once she was a few houses away, she felt the load of her bags taking a toll on her. She turned the corner and noticed Deacon Frank's car parked on the corner. She still had his car keys in her pocket.

Approaching the car she thought about finding a big rock to smash the window. Thinking about the sound and possible car alarm, she changed her mind. She looked in the car and noticed Deacon Frank had a CD player on the passenger seat.

KIERRA SHEARD "This Is ME" KIERRA "KIKI" SHEARD

"This is me, in my entirety
This is me, a person saved by grace"

Reaching for the car keys in her pocket. Sitting the designer luggage on the sidewalk STARR opened the car and reached for the portable CD player. She needed to rest a few minutes before picking up her heavy bags, she thought about the bus schedule and knew it would be a few hours or more before the buses started to run. Her mind fluttered away in anxiety.

The clicking sound of shoes and a dark shadow crossing the street coming towards her direction alarmed her. She grabbed her heavy bags and swung them into the car and shut the door. The pounding of her heart was so heavy, she almost forgot to breath.

DEITRICK HADDON "Love Him Like I Do" LOVE HIM LIKE I DO (Featuring RUBEN STUDDARD and MARY MARY)

See, STARR gotta testimony. How her soul was just a sinner left in the cold and given a second chance... Sheer black fright swept through her thinking it was Deacon – Mr. Frank and she was caught. She had just enough time to lock the doors with fearful images built in her mind. She began to shake as the tall man dressed in a long black coat and black cowboy boots waved trying to get her attention.

Noticing it was a strange white man didn't make her feel any better. Terrified she put the key in the ignition and started the car. She thought that would make him turn around and go away. He knocked on the window.

Not looking at the stranger, but STARR could hear him asking, *"Hey which way are you heading?"* STARR shifted the car into drive and pressed her foot hard on the gas. The car pulled off fast and both of her feet slammed on the breaks. Coming to an abrupt stop, her heart was jumping in her chest. She could hear the man shouting, *"Hey girl let me handle that wheel. I can swing us both out of here."*

So scared she almost peed on herself putting her foot to the gas pedal, STARR pulled away in a screech that burned rubber and leaving the man behind her in the middle of the street still trying to wave her down. She was lucky that the car was parked in a spot that she could just pull out of. She put more pressure on the gas to escape further away.

Terrified with both hands on the wheel, STARR swayed to keep control of the car. She was too afraid to look behind to see if he was out of sight. She felt trapped in a horror flick like the 'Shining' with Jack Nicholson right behind her and if she turned around, he would be in the back seat. She didn't know anything about the rear view mirrors.

DEZZIE "You'll Never Hurt Me" HERE I AM

Never will STARR allow anyone to hurt her the way they did before. She has a new beginning and with it there is so much more. *"You'll never hurt me, never – NO!"* Each mile she drove, she got better at driving. All she needed to know was stop and go. Accidentally she discovered the turn signals and windshield wipers. Having no idea where she was going, STARR just drove. Panic was rioting within her, as she followed the lead of other cars. Turning when they turned, stopping when they stopped. *"You'll never hurt me again. NO!"*

15 minutes later, she was following a red jeep that turned into a gas station. Getting out the car she noticed that the red jeep was being driven by a young black dude of about 20 years old, STARR thought she seen him at church before. When she got out the car he immediately spoke, *"Whad up Shorty you following me?"* Caught off guard, STARR didn't know what to say. After a short pause she said, *"No!"* The young boy responded, *"Oh I was about to tell you church girl to follow me to this party."*

URSULA RUCKERS "Church Party" MA'AT MAMA

"They all stand in a buffalo stance. B-Boy posin' skin and style pressed up against the church wall, 3-D graffiti hit. Somebody say, "Exotic! Exotic!" The word church and party caught her attention and confused STARR. She knew she wasn't dressed for church or a party. She had on a pair of jeans, a gap t – shirt and a pair of Nikes. She thought maybe if she went to the party she could find Shantey. Excited she asked, *"Will M.C. $hantey Money be there?"*

Perplexed the dude responding, *"How the hell would I know? Wrong party this ain't no old school party. I'm taking you to be the party!"* STARR left fast not wanting to be a part of his mess and knowing all too well about his kind of 'Church Party.'

AMANA MELOME "Searching For Myself" INDEGO RED

Searching for directions purple - peach now paints the sky a super natural electric light. Tears swelled up inside STARR'S eyes and she's so sick of asking why? Searching for herself quickly trying to drive off, she wanted to get far away taking the first exit to the Schuylkill Expressway (I-76) east towards central Philadelphia, yet she was lost.

The sun is nowhere to be found behind the clouds. Supposed to rain, she hardly doubts. She's speeding, just like her heart. The wondering road, the little car and her bags. She's hoping to see the day when she'll become strong again and know her way.

"Know her way – Find her way"

Unfamiliar with the city of Philadelphia, STARR followed signs that read South Street and turned off the exit and drove until she came across Broad Street, and turned left heading North on Broad street until she was on the other side of City Hall. She could feel her bladder needing relief. She turned into an alleyway happy that it was empty.

Jumping out the car and leaving it running, STARR squatted beside the open door to release her bladder. A flicker of apprehension went through her noticing someone passed by. She almost most pissed on her foot, not sure, but kept peeing. Ice fear twisted around her heart as she hurried to pull up her jeans. From nowhere a man approached the car. She paused briefly turning in his directions.

It was a police officer on a bike. STARR stood completely still thinking of what direction to run. The tight knot within her begged for release. The cop parked his bike and walked towards. *"I was just checking to see if everything was okay. I see the car lights on and a young woman in a back alley is dangerous, especially in areas like this."* All she could think to say was, *"It won't happen again."*

AMEL LAURRIUEX *"Searchin' For My Soul"* INFINITE POSSIBILITIES

"Somebody tell her where to go - Searchin' for her soul"

The cop seen the trail of piss by the car and began walking off telling her to be careful in her travels. He stopped to observe the back of the car. STARR was so scared, she thought it was all over her face. The cop asked, *"You go to Temple University, I'm an alumni."* She managed to smile wondering what made him think she went to Temple University and what is an alumni? The tense lines on her face relaxed watching the cop cycle away as the sun was now smiling upon her face.

STARR's life, her life, her life, her life. Immediately, she tried backing out of the alley bumping into trash cans and then the car cut off. She was out of gas and had to hurry along before the cop came back. The sun was bright and she was sitting in the car looking up at buildings with beautiful art murals that she had read about and seen on the news that covered the side walls of buildings. Philadelphia is truly 'The City of Murals.'

Thanks to the City of Philadelphia's *'Mural Arts Program'* that began in 1984 as a component of the Philadelphia Anti-Graffiti Network, an effort spearheaded by then Mayor Wilson Goode to eradicate the graffiti crisis plaguing the city.

MARY J. BLIGE "My Life" MY LIFE

"If you looked in my life and see what I seen"

Ooh when STARR'S feeling down she would never fake it. Saying what's on her mind, STARR'S life, her life, her life, her life. She began fiddling with the glove department looking for anything, finding Mary J. Blige 'My Life' CD, candy, gum, anything worth taking before she ditched the car. Her heart jumped when she found Deacon Frank's wallet with credit cards and a thick envelope with a $1,000 and deposit slip with the church's name. She had never seen that much money before.

Saying a prayer for forgiveness, STARR also asked GOD for punishment for Mr. Deacon Frank Wayman and Ms. Nancy. Grabbing her bags and strolling up North Broad Streets, she admired the extraordinary works of arts that provided a fascinating window into the diversity of the Philadelphia neighborhoods.

LEDISI "Lost & Found" LOST AND FOUND

Always alone, someone come for STARR. Here on her own feels like the pain lasts an eternity. Please someone find her. No strength to walk she found a coffee shop a block away and hurried looking for the first available seat where she can organize her bags and her thoughts. The sun was full of energy and she was languorous and feeling hopeless. She wasn't sure where she was going. She was on her second cup of coffee when the real cute guys with dreadlocks grinned towards her, again.

KEZIAH JONES "Hello Heavenly" LIQUID SUNSHINE

Hello heavenly come along with Rofiki, *"Meh will show it all."* Show STARR how to be free in captivity. How to know it all... The strange cute guy with dreads smiled at her as she opened the newspaper on the table pretending to read, thinking of her next steps. She was lost and not a clue what to do. She was between pages when he walked up asking, *"Yo ma is dat ya car back in da alley?* She was confused, but then again she wasn't. But who was he? *"Not a parking spot ya ride will be towed."* With a quick response and looking hopeless she replied, *"I'm out of gas."*

JIMMY ABENY "Star of The Story" RETURN TO FOREVER (HEATWAVE)

'Cause STARR is the star of a story, Rofiki will always tell. She is the star... Feeling his own embarrassment unable to offer to buy gas. Rofiki seen the keys on the table and could only ask, *"Ya have cash fa gas?"* He was delighted to her response, *"Yes."*

Introductions were made and STARR was confused about her own name stutter S - STA - STARR with 2 – R's." She knew she must have sounded corny. He replied, *"With 2 – R's? Meh like – Meh like!"* Rofiki was handed the car keys. He stood there with his hand out for the gas money. STARR wasn't sure if she was being played and it was if Rofiki was reading her mind. For security he took a gold lion ring of his finger and put it on hers grinning. *"Rofiki is my name. Meh cool ma, hold on to meh gold ring, meh treasure, meh be back."*

MARY J. BLIGE "Be With You" MY LIFE

"I just wanna be with you
Nothing else I'd rather do
I wanna be with you
I want to spend my life with you"

"Turn – Turn the music up!" Pulling up to the coffee shop blowing the horn and banging the music loud, STARR actually could hear him coming down the street playing Mary J. Blige. Rofiki noticed STARR earlier peeing in the alley, but he also noticed the cop on the bike. He seen her walk

in the coffee shop and followed wondering why she left her car? Now, STARR sat wondering why she let Rofiki put gas in the car when she was supposed to be ditching the car.

Turning the music up louder Rofiki didn't move from the driver seat, *"Meh can drive!"* She happily sat in the passenger seat feeling she was getting closer to her mom, $hantey Money. She also didn't want him to see that she really didn't know how to drive.

MARY J. BLIGE "I'm The Only Woman" MY LIFE

Helping STARR put her things back in the car she listened word for word to the song. If only she knew it would become her national anthem 'I'm The Only Woman.' She started to object until Rofiki said, *"Nice ride, pretty gyal meh need ride to the other side of North Philly?"* "Yes!" She would have leaped with glee if she had the strength on her way to find $hantey Money.

INTERMISSION: JAZZY SMOOTH LOVE SESSIONS

D' ANGELO "Really Love" YODA THE MONARCH OF NEO-SOUL

DEBORAH BOND "Love's Been Waiting" DAYAFTER

WILL DOWNING "Run Away Fall In Love" CHOCOLATE DROP

BEVERLY KNIGHT Send Me, Move Me, Love Me" PRODIGAL SISTA

ERIC ROBERSON "Punch Drunk Love" THE BOX

KEM "Nobody" PROMISE TO LOVE

PHIL PERRY "Ready For Love" READY FOR LOVE

EMERALD JADE "I Found Love" A NEW CLASSIC

MARK BAXTER "Love Is True" MARK BAXTER THE LADIES MAN

BRIAN MCKIGHT "Don't Take Your Love Away" TEN

IMPOMP2 "The Definition Of Love" THE DEFINITION OF LOVE

BILAL "Love Poems" 1st Born Second

DA TRUTH 'New Found Love" MOMENTS OF TRUTH

TRACK 9: "BULL SHIT AIN'T NOTHING BUT CHEWED UP GRASS"

BLACK BEAST RECORDING STUDIO, LLC owned and operated by C.E.O. BearLove. With over twenty years working as a professional in the music industry, BearLove's studio lingo and terminology span from analogue to digital recording as well as live sound engineering. Through his career as a drummer performing with the group 'The Organics' and releasing albums worldwide and touring the United States many times, his heart, body and mind was in the studio.

There was no course book needed he could do more than the general navigations of the recording studio. He could teach the subjects of vocal recording techniques, full band, single room, isolated multi-track recording, recording with compressors and limiters, room acoustics and sound development, DAW and outboard gear routing, condenser and ribbon microphones, and of course recording drums and percussions.

THE ROOTS "Act Won" THINGS FALL APART

The talented drummer, composer, arranger BearLove credits his mother Khadijah-Love with helping him develop an ear for the type of music he makes. At an early age BearLove displayed a talent beyond his years drumming on everything in the house and making his own drum set out of empty paint buckets, mop buckets, pots and pans. His mother signed him up at the age of eight years old to begin his musical training playing drummers at 'The Settlement School of Music' Germantown branch.

The young BearLove eagerly listened to anything his mom put on the stereo. Their Germantown home was soulful with the Philadelphia sounds of Patti Labelle, Frankie Beverly & Maze, and McFadden & Whitehead.

"Ain't no stopping us now!"

By his freshman year in high school, he was experimenting with the Kurzweil Mark 10 electric Piano with 8 tracks, familiarizing with audio outputs, inputs, modifiers, and mixers, audio. He started getting into MIDI sequencing and synthesizers creating hip-hop – soul - funk beat and recorder tracks in the basement of his home. His dedication earned him student awards. After graduation his mother brought him the Simmons SD1000 5-piece electronic drum set.

The philosophy of millennium music was too focused on live instrumentation in concerts and in the studio. Hooking up with friend and rapper 'Dark Mind' their friendship developed into a musicianship and lyrics comprised winning talent shows with BearLove's drum kit backing Dark Mind's rhymes. The pair began to earn money and moved from the street to local clubs, becoming an exceptionally versatile house band they met up with other musicians and became 'The Organics' a highly underground act around Philadelphia and New York.

THE ROOTS "Dillatude The Flight of Titus" HOW I GOT OVER

Forsaking usual hip-hop protocol their album was produced without any samples or previously recorded material. BearLove has appeared in several music videos and a can be heard on a host of recordings and movie soundtracks. Along with playing drums, he has added production and engineering to his repertoire.

BLACK BEAST STUDIOS was in full effect. BearLove had his own production company and label up and running. Along with STARR to break out as THE FIRST LADY of BBS. The plan was to record everything during the next few weeks and scheduling days to mix the songs, which involves taking all the individually recorded instruments and vocals and mixing them into the final sound.

After months of writing, rehearsing, performing and late nights it was all coming down to these final recordings. The one thing he knew for sure about music recording sessions usually turned into after parties and jam sessions. They actually involve considerable work and planning and a true test of stamina.

The Studio was full of folks. Not only were the band members there, but a couple of well-known producers and record company representatives. BearLove was a business man and knew that mainstream had no choice but to come to him. All will have varying degrees of input on the final mix based on their working agreements. But the emphasis will be on creativity and marketability of the music.

THE ROOTS "The Next Movement" THINGS FALL APART

"Word up!
We got the hot, hot music the hot music"

"Yo, 1-2, 1-2, 1-2." That's how they usually start, "Word up!" The engineers were good friends of BearLove and along with him they had the technical background to set up and operate the recording equipment. They knew which microphone to use in each situation and how to organize a mixing board. They were also there to troubleshoot the monitors with digital inputs and any technical problems that wouldn't disturb BearLove while he was playing.

The recording booth was dimly lit with red lights making it a comfortable environment to groove in. The recording and monitoring spaces was specially designed by an acoustician to achieve optimum acoustic properties. Everyone was there to make sure they understood the full concept of the mission of making timeless music that music - historians will be raving about for years to come. The mission of the group is to produce music that fans will play over and over.

THE ROOTS "A Peace of Light" HOW I GOT OVER
(Featuring Amber Coffman and Angel Debadoorian and Haley Dekle)

'THE NEOSOUL STARR' music was a compilation of songs written by all the musicians and STARR the vocalist. Their mission is to make music that make you want to tell a friend and that makes them want to tell a friend. Making music that makes babies and touching generations of music lovers with sounds of new songs and retelling old rooted deep life stories. Making timeless music fans will love and enjoyed always. They wanted to be that song you just had to hear again.

Everybody was busy with all the musical instruments and special equipment, as well as microphones, effects boxes, sound mixing boards, amplifiers and lots of cables. Joe Daddy was hooking up his bass and guitars. The white aged and signed electric guitar, Don Felder 'Hotel

California' EDS-1275 known for the "world's greatest guitar solos" and to honor this legendary pairing of artist and instrument, Gibson Custom introduces the Don Felder "Hotel California" SG Double Neck guitar, in a strictly Limited Edition with only 50 aged and signed units and 100 aged units produced. Joe daddy happened to be 1 of the 50 blessed with a signed guitar, as he played chords up and down the strings. Joe Daddy was playing and turning the tuners for each string the lifeblood of the instrument to their proper pitch.

Each tuner consists of a nut and cog to tighten or slacken the strings. Joe Daddy also explored his music spiritual side and given a vision to build a new instrument. The result is a one-of-a-kind acoustic hollow bodied, arched top and back, seven string bass guitar. With this instrument, Joe Daddy began to write music for an entire spectrum of genres including pop, rock, R&B, and classical, folk, and country, yes country.

DJ CAM "Afu Ra (Interlude)" SOULSHINE

Ron Glasshouse was hooking up the Midi cables to his electric keyboard-style synthesizer Kurzweil PC3K8 – 88 Key Production Station. He plugged the keyboard directly into the mixing board and recording apparatus (a group or combination of instruments) and the microphone for his back ground vocals. Not many jazz pianists can give you such broad range and ear-pleasing sounds as Ronny G running his fingers across the black and white keys warming up playing Arabic sounds. A traditional Arabic scale includes quarter notes, but these are not available on Euro-American-style keyboards.

However, Ronny G's Arabic sounds were attained by him playing scales, but not in order. Skipping around on the scale gave countless Arabic-sounding combinations. He was switching his settings from piano to clarinet to strings, playing the Locrian Major Scale *C, D, E, F, G flat, A flat and B flat*. The Double Harmonic Major Scale *C, D flat, E, F, G, A flat and B* or the Double Harmonic Minor Scale *C, D, E flat, F sharp, G, A flat and B*. Looping one of the note sequences over and over and recording and looping in hooks and sequences that are looped throughout.

DJ JAZZY X had his 2 turn tables. Stanton ST150HP Super High Torque Digital Turntables w/ S-Shaped Tone arms and 680.V3 Cartridge set up and ready to old school vinyl scratching in his intro of $hantey Money's song. Along with his other special sound effects he was hooking up his Mac laptop computer and Numark 'MIXDECK' iPod DJ mixing console. The complete system to blending different kinds of music sources, whether he play his CDs, MP3 files, USB flash drives, iPod, or even other analog players, he mixed and perform all with using MIXDECK.

QUESTLOVE "Mind Diving" (www.youtube.com)

There were drum sticks and drum keys, guitar picks and extra guitar strings and any items needed for quick repairs. BearLove was tapping on his Granite silver sparkling Pearl Drums in the customized isolation booths to accommodate loud instruments like his drums and keeping the sounds from being audible to the microphones that are capturing the sounds from other instruments. Warming up and following the notes of the Bass player Joe Daddy, who was doing a lot of staccato finger movements. Laying behind the beat BearLove took the stick over the top stick and making sure his rim shot went splat!

The splat was the fringe of the snare. BearLove tapped away on the 8x8 tom, 10x8 tom, 12x9 tom, 14x14 floor tom, 16x16 floor tom, 22x18 bass drum, 14x6.5 snare drum, 13x6.5 snare drum. Making sure the drum rack, rack joints, snare stand, hi-hat stand, remote hi-hat stand, Throne, Tom holder x 3 and Demon Drive Double Pedal, were all secured. Warming up he banged out triplets and a shuffle leading into 16th notes.

JSOUL "Intro" URBAN RETROSPECTIVE

Neumann is the Rolls Royce of microphones the quality is top notch and with the headphones on STARR was ready for "Microphone check 1 -2 - 1 - 2." In the vocal booth standing at the Neumann TLM49 Cardioid Condenser microphone which she found very - very appealing. The sound through the microphone was awesome! It has a very crisp and clear. It was a microphone exclusively for vocals designed to give her voice that richness and depth in the low frequencies.

It was a wow factor for STARR'S lips to be so close to the sexy microphone (she found the $1,600 receipt on the floor.) Not only was it sexy, but Charismatic. The solid metal color, the heavy (over 2lbs) weight, the shape and its large grill gave it an attitude and invitation for STARR'S voice.

Excited and of course nervous, STARR was ready. She was especially nervous about meeting 'Dark Mind' for the first time. He was in the U.K. recording music for his upcoming album titled 'M&M 'Mysterious Mentality. Immediately the title made her think of Bluesy eating candy. She was happy to know Dark Mind came back to the states to record with THE NEOSOUL STARR. He also apologized for the phone conversation she overheard and he even gave her a big hug.

ROBERT GLASPER EXPERIMENT "Lift Off / Mic Check" BLACK RADIO (Featuring SHAFIQ HUSAYN)

Though STARR couldn't play an instrument or read musical notes, she had perfect pitch singing the correct notes and perfect timing. She easily recognize the keys played and sang the notes within the chords or scales without sounding sharp or flat, unless that is the effect required for the song. Like a maestro, she directed with perceptive details instructing the musician. Displaying her vocal percussions, she could beat-box using her mouth, lips, tongue, and voice, letting BearLove know every pit – pat, she wanted him to hit. Articulating her vocals to whistle swirls of riffs and raffs.

The TLM49 Microphone was acting a little hyped in the 4k to 5khz range. But being that they had a good channel strip like the Avalon VT737 they were able to raise the 15 kHz by about 3 db to balance the mic out for great vocal recordings needed to get that professional sound.

The lights in the studio were low. The remixed track BearLove composed by $hantey Money's hip hop song was flipped and remixed into a fly dance groove that will start any party off. Loving the pitch of her vocals and melodic motions, the engineer gave STARR a thumbs up and a little more reverb. Everyone reminded each other how music was supposed to be enjoyed. Everyone was jamming and it was just mic check and they were in choirs with rich thick warm voices to crisp crystal - clear musical sounds.

J. DILLA (Jay Dee) "Bullshittin" (Remix Instrumental)

They did every song in one take just like they were in concert. The flow was inseparable even though they were divided by recording studio, vocal booth, isolation rooms and the control room, everything was flowing together perfectly. Every musician was on cue, even with background vocals. During the recordings they were all being videotaped for the upcoming video.

THE NEOSOUL STARR "Bullshit Ain't Nothing But Chewed Up Grass"
(Featuring STARR and Dark Mind)

MUSIC: *J. Dilla (Jay Dee) "Bullshittin" (Remix Instrumental)*

(STARR)

Bullshit ain't nothing but chewed up grass
Ask me how I know
Caused you showed your ASS!

Telling me that you'll B – Right – Back
When in fact I watched you pack

I'm telling you that I don't concur
'Cause I know your fucking her

No compromise
I've open my eyes
No need to hide
Stop telling lies

You're full of shit
You showed your ass

You're full of shit
You showed your ass

You're full of shit
You showed your ass

You're full of shit
You showed your ass

Keep Your Bullshit
Sorry I asked
Keep your Bullshit!

(DARK THOUGHTS)

Yo Boo!

DARK THOUGHTS ain't trying to play ya
Blow smoke and Purple Haze ya
I'm as black as the Boogie Man
And the Afro-pik with the fist in my hand
U Understand?
I got music on my mind and my mind is on my music
Come just let me hold you - Squeeze and console you
YEAH!
I'm rocking it – Non-stopping it
Every day in every way

I went to court
I BEAT da shit

If he pay me back
We'll squash that shit

I know love you me
I'm the shit

Hear me when
I Rap my shit

Of course I loved it
Touch this shit

Come around
Puff on some shit

Best believe I
I handle shit

I know you hear me
Talking shit

I'm out of cheddar
Get off my shit

(STARR)

You're full of shit
You showed your ass

Bull-shit ain't nothing but chewed up grass
Ask me how I know
'Caused you showed your ass!

You're full of shit
You showed your ass

Bullshit ain't nothing but chewed up grass
Ask me how I know
Caused you showed your ass!

You showed your ass
You're full of shit

You showed your ass
You're full of shit

Telling me this
Telling me that

Always fiction
Just give me facts

I'm not like this
I'm not like that

I got feelings
I'm not over that shit

You showed you ass
You're full of Bull - Shit

TRACK 10: PREVIOUS CHICKS

MUSIQ SOULCHILD "Previous Cats" JUSLISEN

"I am not to blame for the pain that was caused by previous cats
You gotta see me for me"

It had been 3 months since the unexpected house guest arrived at Bluesy's parent's house. Yet he still hadn't been honest and forthcoming about his living situation to STARR. But tonight he had to tell her everything. It had been a long day at work and he couldn't wait to see her, closing early. His truck was at the mechanics due to someone putting sugar in his tank, so he borrowed his father's car.

Now, pulling up to STARR'S in his father's car eating M&M's with peanuts and trying to find courage. He was feeling completely miserable because of the information about his past withheld. He thought it would be easier to take care of his problems without involving her. He needed a glass of wine to calm his nerves, before he sat STARR down and told her everything. Just as he was looking for a parking spot, he noticed the white Hummer pulling away from her house.

It was all confusing Bluesy, the unexpected guess at his parents' house, the sugar in his tank and now a few cars behind following the white Hummer that was driving East on Girard Avenue. Driving past the Philadelphia Zoo feeling like a Gorilla as big as King Kong. Checking out the New York license plate. He could see the Hummers left turn signaling flashing and then turn left onto 29th Street. Bluesy was laughing at the fool who wanted to play this cat and mouse game. Laughing inside for all the mistakes already made. Just as he was having wicked thoughts his Saint Christopher medallion fell to the floor. He had no time to look for it or pick it up.

STEPHEN SIMMONDS "Killing & Religion" THIS MUST BE GROUND

"Whatever you be singing, I ain't listening rabbi. Wicked mind loving tongue Bible and a loaded gun. But Jesus never killed no one," Bluesy sang along to the music following the white Hummer observing the New York license plate and a target that can be spotted miles away with Bluesy's trained military eyes. He followed the Hummer to 29th & Lehigh Avenue and watched it park and noticed the guy with dreadlocks.

The same guy from the coffee shop, STARR'S ex-boy the Rofiki dude jumped out of the Hummer. Bluesy was sure it was him, watching Rofiki greeting with fist pounds with a few guys that were hanging out on the corner before entering a house. Judging from the location, Bluesy assumed it was the house were STARR used to live. He also knew not to hang around in a neighborhood in North Philly where an odd car circling the block could easily be noticed. He took his time cruising around the block planning to go into action. Remembering he was no longer at war, yet he would be for STARR.

ASOTO UNION "Make It Funky" (We've Got Funky Jazz) ASOTO UNION

Now Bluesy was ready to make it funky as soon he turned the corner passing the house again, noticing the white Hummer was gone. This made him sit straight up and adrenaline running high. The first thing he did was reach under his seat for his gun and remembering, he was in his father's car. Then Bluesy noticed the Hummers halogen lights trailing behind him. He kept driving straight down 29th Street ready for the chase. But that didn't happen noticing in his rear view mirror the Hummer stopped and was parking in front of a bar.

At this moment Bluesy's funky feeling were right. It was Rofiki following him in the white Hummer, he seen everything he needed to see for now. Still wondering, *"What's was going on?"* He drove back to STARR'S still confused about seeing Rofiki at her house.

MOONCHILD "Misinterpretations" BE FREE

After knocking forever on the door only to be told by Ms. Freda that STARR wasn't home. He quickly asked about the man in the white Hummer. Ms. Freda replied, *"Lawd hamercy! Now dat ain't none of my* business. He just left some papers here for STARR. But since you're her boyfriend – her rent is due!" Embarrassed but liking the fact that Ms. Freda acknowledge him as such and still standing out on the porch, he reached in his pocket asking, *"How much $400?"*

Embracing his hand Ms. Freda took the money and said, *"Now I just need to give STARR an extra key for you. But she ain't here right now!"* Ms. Freda closed the door and left Bluesy still standing on the porch. He pulled out his cellphone to called STARR who was walking up on the porch returning from a studio session.

When they passed by the Jenki's door Ms. Freda came to the door holding a big manila envelope and a spare key. Meowing louder than usual Frisky was desperately trying to get everyone's attention running in between their legs frantically. Big G was responding with thunderous purrs trying to force his big body out of the door and with all his might trying to push past Ms. Freda.

CONYA DOSS "Friends" BLU TRANSITIONS

Searching and searching, STARR found her lover and friend in Bluesy, she hope to never to see the rain again. Before closing the door Ms. Freda Handed STARR the manila envelope and pushing back the fat cat and whispering, *"Your ignorant old boyfriend – the one that wear them dreadlocks like you – he dropped this off.* Then she handed STARR an extra set of keys saying, *"I don't mind if you give this here new nice white boyfriend of yours a set of keys – since he paid your rent."* Confused and embarrassed, but before STARR could respond Mr. Jenki was screaming, *"I cants hear the TAVIS SMILEY show - close that damn door and shut them damn cats up!"*

Shoving the loud meowing Big G back inside Ms. Freda closed the door. Still in the hallway Frisky purrs were earsplitting and deafening and the cat almost tripped them running in between their legs, as if she was trying to warn them. They noticed Midnight was at the top of the 3rd floor steps sleeping, which was unusual, since Midnight was too old to go up or down steps. STARR called out his name *"Midnight!"*

Reaching out and petting his rough-coated head lightly, she noticed his scar-nosed and tattered-ears and lifeless body. STARR began screaming, *"Oh my GOD Midnight is DEAD! I'm sorry Midnight I wasn't here for you."* Assuming the old cat had climbed to the 3rd floor apartment for her help.

KYLE JASON "Cat-O-Tonic" REVOLUTION OF THE COOL

"Ha-Ah!" Ms. Freda ran out into the hallway hearing STARR scream and noticing Bluesy carrying Midnight's lifeless body dangling in his hands. Mr. Jenki came yelling, "Hold on let me get a green trash bag. The trash men are coming in the morning." STARR yelled, "Oh no Mr. Jenki you can't just toss Midnight in the trash like that." Mr. Jenki screamed back, "Why not? If y'all find my ass up in here dead, I suggest y'all do the same for me. Don't spend all my money on a funeral!"

Boohooing Ms. Freda yelped back, "All what money? You ain't got no money - You old fool! And when you die I'm gonna get me a nice white man like this one." Mr. Jenki replied holding open the green trash bag, "Woman you keep talking like that I'm gonna put you in this trash bag too!" Bluesy spoke up saying, "Don't worry I got a box in the car and STARR and I can go bury Midnight respectfully." As they left out the door with Frisky, Big G and Tyson trying to follow Ms. Freda was crying, "Good bye rest in peace Midnight!"

CLARA HILL "Morning Star" RESTLESS TIME
(Featuring THIEF)

Waiting, STARR was waiting on her morning star to guide her all through the day. Silent as a ghost Bluesy was her faith in time. Feeling like the fingers sliding on the neck of the guitar, followed by the smooth bass line came morning sickness and queasiness. She ran into the bathroom vomiting and gagging for air. She could hear Frisky purring and scratching at her door. She knew that Frisky was still mourning the loss of Midnight.

Frisky and Midnight spent a lot of time together on the second floor. Though he was neutered and without the sexual urges, still he was one of her companions. The only thing to do was to get up and tend to Frisky, who was pregnant and due any day. She feed Frisky and Tyson and slid cat treats under the door for Big G and changed the litter boxes. Harmonizing and grooving to the tunes pumping through her head phones.

Watching Frisky getting fatter and fatter, STARR now believed Ms. Freda when she said Big G wasn't neutered. STARR would not have believed that the obese cat could even manage to get his fat ass on top of Frisky without crushing her. Until she seen it with her own eyes one of the reasons why Big G wasn't allowed out. She still had the vivid image of catching Frisky and Big G mating.

The cats were making so much noise that STARR was surprised the Jenki's didn't hear. She remembers seeing Big G lying flat on his back spread eagle and Frisky perched right on top of him riding like a woman would be on top of a man. She had no idea that cats could fuck like that until she seen it with her own eyes.

SLAKAH THE BEATCHILD "Living For The Rush" SOMETHINGFOREVER

Living for the rush of the puff and the huff of the good-shit, no bullshit. Living in the moment of green chronic dreams with no seeds. Smoothing sailing of the mind, reclined puffing one more time. Living for the rush and busy cleaning up, STARR was cleaning and thinking and of course listening to JAZZ1CAFÉ and freestyling. She was now on the second floor putting Midnights old litter box in the green trash bag Mr. Jenki left in the hallway.

Tying up the trash bags still shaking her head at the thought of Mr. Jenki wanting to throw Midnight in the trash. She was carrying the bag downstairs when someone was knocking on the door like they were the police. It startled STARR for a moment, she waited and listened for either Ms. Freda or Mr. Jenki to come to their door, but there was no movement coming from the Jenki's apartment. She could hear the television on 'The Wendy Williams Show.' Making her mad since STARR didn't have a television.

QUINTESSENCE "Sticks & Stones" TALK LESS LISTEN MORE

"He had to be out there somewhere – He had to be out there somewhere..." The knocking continued and grew into a banging as Tyson hissed and hunched his back ready to attack or get out. Thinking it could be Bluesy, but STARR could see through the curtains the profile of a woman. The closer she could see it was a woman. Assuming it was someone at the wrong address, she opened the door unalarmed and without asking who it was and Tyson ran out.

Holding the trash bag of soiled funky kitty litter and Midnight's old litter box STARR was ready to tell the chic, she had the wrong address. From the expression on this woman's face, whoever she was looking for she had to be mad at them. The strange woman swung her long blonde hair around looking like a Marilyn Munroe wannabe. She stood back and removed her designer sun glasses and placed them on top of her head, as she inspected STARR from head to toe. STARR asked, *"How may I help you?"*

After showing a disapproving look the woman puckered up her red lipstick stained lips and pointed her extra-extra-long blue finger nails at STARR saying, *"So this is STARR?"* STARR had no idea who she was and her expression showed it. The woman said, *"I'm Karen! Is my husband and son here? I figured he brought our son J.R. as in Junior, here to finally meet you before taking him to the zoo!"*

MUSIQ *"Halfcrazy"* JUSLISEN

Mind's gone halfcrazy 'cause STARR can't leave Bluesy alone and she's wondering if it's worth her holding on. Her mind's gone halfcrazy 'cause she can't leave him alone. Not in the mood for any craziness STARR was already nausea and now feeling her head spin with confusion, her stomach churned tight as she spoke, *"I have no idea what you are talking about. I don't know you- your husband or son."*

Watching the crazy chic growing angrier and reaching in her hand - bag, STARR thought she was going for a gun and swung the cat litter bag and knocked whatever she was pulling out of her bag out of her hands. STARR was ready to kick her in the face until she noticed that she was just picking up a piece of paper. She started to apologize until she heard the woman calling her *"CrAzY!"*

After shaking cat litter off her grey cashmere dress and black leather high heel boots and screaming, *"Are you CrAzY!"* Karen bent down with a million bracelets jingling on her arms, sounding like the clattering of noisy wind chimes. She picked up the flyer STARR knocked out of her hand and opened it showing STARR the paper that read 'Free Kittens to loving homes. The owner STARR says the mother cat 'Ms. Frisky' is due any day! Please call Bluesy's Cafe for more information...'

ALEX BUGNON *"Giant Steps"* SOUL PURPOSE

Taking giant steps forward to see the flyer and apologizing STARR said, *"Okay, this is the flyer my boyfriend has up in his coffee shop."* The crazy white chick began screaming, *"He may be Bluesy to you, and I'm Karen his wife! He is my husband and we have a son and planning to have more. We live together and I help take care of his parents."*

Feeling her skull gyrate, STARR shrugged her shoulders to try to hide her confusion. Karen knew that STARR was ready to shut the door in her face and that would ruin her plans. She needed to talk to STARR and keep her from telling that she was there.

Softening her voice, Karen a few tears slid down her cheek and reaching in her handbag to get a tissue and showing STARR it was just a tissue and dabbing her eyes. Using all her drama acting skills Karen wiped tears pleading her case. *"I'm sorry that I came here. It's just that he took our son out today and I felt that he might have brought him here since or son wants a kitten and then he said they were going to the zoo. I know about the two of you messing around, but I don't want to lose my son too. Please don't tell my husband I came here. I will have to deal with his crazy side, he hasn't been right since returning from Iraq. Did he tell you he was seeing a psychiatrist? Yes he has a shrink! And we started family therapy, but can't take his lies."*

JILL SCOTT "Gettin' In The Way" WHO IS JILL SCOTT?

"You're getting in the way of what I'm feeling"

Everything was beautiful between STARR and Bluesy and here come Karen and her big mouth talking bullshit. If she keeps lying on her man? Girlfriend, STARR is going take her out in the middle of the street and whoop her ass for all it's worth. Better back down, before Karen get smacked down, she better chill.

Leaning against the door frame STARR tried to keep her balance. She started to invite her in to learn more, but realize she couldn't stand to hear more. She listened and didn't say anything until Karen was finished. STARR said, *"You have no more worries. I won't disrespect you and please don't disrespect me by come here again."*

"You're getting in the way of what I'm feeling"

Ready for the show down, Karen wasn't going to let STARR have the last word saying, *"I was wonder why my husband would put his phone number on these flyers and say he was helping a friend. Now I see by all the cats running around you and the smell you really do need help."* Before STARR closed the door Karen raised her voice and handing STARR the flyer, *"Well here, we won't need this, I hate cats!"*

"You're getting in the way of what I'm feeling"

Closing the door STARR fell out in the hallway listening to the crazy white chic named Karen - Bluesy's wife walking away. She didn't know what to do, go after her and asked more questions or dump more kitty litter on her. Nothing would change the fact that Bluesy had been lying to her all this time.

The thought of Bluesy being a married man brought tears to her eyes as she sat there and cried like a baby next to the trash bag until she got tired of Frisky rubbing her pregnant belly against her. With Frisky trailing behind her, STARR practically crawled up the steps to the third floor and closed the door. Though Frisky was the only cat she let in, not today.

LIVE TROPICAL FISH "Breathe Again" THE DAY IS TOO SHORT TO SELFISH (Featuring: LAURNEA)

Breathe again, STARR wanted to breathe again. She needed the way they were, she needs the time they had, she was trying to breathe again. Hoping it was a nightmare and that she could wake up instantly. *"Breathe again,"* Singing along listening to JAZZ1CAFÉ blasting through her headphones. She picked up the phone to call Bluesy and noticed she had just missed his call. She assumed he was calling to warn her about his wife? Afraid to hear the truth, because what would happen next? Bluesy was supposed to pick her up for a dinner date. Fingers trembled and tears wet her cheeks. Answering her phone that was now ringing. She answered planning to stop Bluesy from coming over.

ANGELA HAGENBACH "You Keep Calling Me" POETRY OF LOVE

It was Rofiki pleading on the other end breathing deep and sorrowful, *"Me fughed up and me sorry. STARR, meh needs to see ya. Meh need to talk to ya personal."* He seems to have the knack for calling her, when she is down. How did he know? How did he know, her last lover messed up? He had the audacity to call, STARR couldn't believe Rofiki had her new phone number. The pressure of her voice was meant to be heard when she growled, *"How did you get my number?"* Rofiki knew he had to take his gangster heart and put it in his back pocket and sit on it hard.

Using his punk bwoy please forgive me voice Rofiki pleaded. STARR was familiar with all of his voices as she listened. *"STARR meh know meh da problem. We be together fa eva years. Meh no when meh gyal is mad and when meh fughed up chasing green and azz. Meh cumming ova to see ya."*

EUGENE IV *"Voices"* STARVING ARTIST

Ear-shots of Rofiki's voice transported through the phone speakers brought back recollections of his cantankerous behaviors. Like fussing because she left the microwave plugged in running up the electric bill. He complained about STARR washing her hair and hands in the kitchen sink, and not the bathroom only. So, that was Rofiki's story chasing money and ass.

Hearing Rofiki's voice was like hearing a song STARR never wanted to hear again. The thought of seeing him was repulsive as her stomach tumbled a 1000x's remembering his demons, irritated by the sound of his voice she replied, *"Lose my number!"* (Click) She turned her phone off. Trying to take it all in remembering the words about chasing green and azz!

Just when STARR had the chance to curse him out, she realized it wasn't worth her breath. Rofiki left her for dead. She knew instantly she was changing her number, it would be that simple. She didn't wish him dead, but knew there were many nights when, she thought he might be, or needed to be. Then she started a mental hate campaign listing all the things she hated about him.

Double checking to be sure her phone was turned off, STARR looked for the manila envelope from Rofiki. However could she forget all about it and where was it? Opening the closet, looking under everything and now looking in the trash?

LAURNEA *"Trash"* I REMEMBER

If you were sifting through STARR'S trash, what would you find? Would you find the orange that she cut so precise? She hope you don't find no maggots or flies? Pulling the manila envelope that Rofiki delivered out of the trash. She didn't get a chance to look thoroughly through it because it reminded her of her past and the stress. It was all her paper work that she took from her last foster mother, Ms. Nancy house in Norristown.

Looking through her old foster care home placement and psychological evaluations papers always made STARR hurt all over again. So what was Rofiki trying to prove by dropping off some documents? She thought of the 'Black Book' he dropped and would be willing to give it to him for her other belongings, he put in storage.

THE SAXPACK "Falling For You" THE SOUND OF FM RADIO

In STARR'S anger and rage and ready to attack, she could hear Bluesy turning his key in the door. Yes, she gave him a key since, he paid the rent. She hurried and put the manila envelope of personal information away. She tried shaking it off and not let things pop off in her head and prosecutes Bluesy without letting him explain his wife and son?

Unaware of the situation with Karen, Bluesy came in the door smiling and talking, *"Hey I found Tyson outside and let him in and there was a bag of litter all over the porch I cleaned up."*

Was STARR in love with Bluesy or not? The thoughts drove her emotionally into rage and she wanted to shout, but knew the Jenki's would hear. So, she barked, *"Good! Now - Get - Out!"* Immediately Bluesy ran to STARR trying to figure out what was going on. He called out to her, *"STARR babe. What is wrong? Are you hurt, did someone hurt you?"*

Observing the place, Bluesy looked around to see if anything in the place was disturbed. She sobbed harder refusing not to let go of the pillow holding on tight. Bluesy kneeled on the floor and reached out to rub her back.

JAZZYFATNASTEES "The Lie" THE ONCE AND FUTURE

"She'll sacrifice, and she wants the life, she wants the lie"

Speaking through tears with a true change of heart, STARR didn't want the lies anymore, *"Please just go and leave your keys. I can't take another person coming in my life lying."* Bluesy couldn't understand where all this was coming from. But he knew that he needed to talk to her about everything that he had not shared with her. But he didn't know what was going on and didn't want to add to what was going on. He tried rubbing her back, only for her to push his hand away hard. Managing to give him a questionable glance STARR moved his hand. Quickly Bluesy asked, *"I don't know what is going on, but I would like to know. There is nothing we can't work out. I love you more than my own life. I never felt that way about anyone and I want to spend the rest of my life with you."*

FLOETRY *"In Your Eyes"* FLO'OLOGY

Ooh, STARR think she fell for Bluesy, from the day that he arrived into her life. She believe it's true, when she look into his eyes. She see, love in his eyes, she see love in his eyes. But STARR'S red swollen eyes didn't blink looking him in his royal - blue eyes asking, *"What about your wife and son?"*

Shamefully, Bluesy dropped his voice gasped speaking, *"STARR you will be my wife and you will give me sons and daughters. I love you and I want to marry you."* STARR loved hearing him say that even though, she was emotionally in pain. Shaking her head in disbelief softly she said, *"Please leave Bluesy. Go home to Karen. You can't lie and say you don't live together."*

LYNN FIDDMONT *"Lover Man"* LADY LYNN FIDDMONT

"Lover man where have you been?" Beginning to panic, Bluesy felt that life without STARR would be meaningless. He began to stutter as he spoke, *"Pl-pl-please let – let me explain and prove something to you."* Bluesy stood up and stumbled through his pockets pulling out paperwork from his attorney and the Red Cross. Just as he pulled the papers out his pocket they heard a car horn blowing several times.

Viewing out the window, STARR seen Rofiki standing next to a white Hummer double parked in the street looking up at her in the window. He began waving his hands for her to come open the door. She couldn't believe the nerve of him. Bluesy was ready to lose his mind. STARR had no intentions on opening the door for Rofiki, but Bluesy thought that it was a planned visit.

THE RURALS *"Save It"* RURAL SOUL

"Go, save it, save it, save it. Save it all for someone who cares?" STARR acted like she didn't want to know what Bluesy been doing. *"Go save it! Save it, save it, save it, oh, save-it!"*

Grabbing STARR ready to begged, she could feel his whole body shaking trying to hold her. The last thing she would ever want to do is to see Bluesy hurting, and she wasn't trying to hurt him. The horn blowing followed with Rofiki now banging at the front door. She said, *"We can talk first let me just tell him to go away."* Rofiki's continued to knock. As STARR walked down the steps to open the door she could hear Bluesy behind her snarling, *"Tell him to go away for good or I will."*

ATJAZZ *"Before"* FULL CIRCLE (Featuring CLARA HILL)

Glad Mr. Jenki and Ms. Freda didn't come to the door and had their television playing THE REAL HOUSEWIVES OF ATLANTA louder than usual. She decided not to open the door or peek through the curtains, instead she shouted through the door. *"Rofiki please go away."* Rofiki didn't like the rejection hollering back through the door, *"STARR babe open up. Ya know meh and ya solid like a rock - like Ashford and Simpson!"*

Walking away from the door, STARR was hoping Rofiki would get the message and just leave. Nope. Now he was banging on the door down screaming, *"STARR cum now open up!"* Bluesy was now coming down the steps yelling, *"She doesn't want you around here – You heard her get away from here now!"*

Posting her body against the door. STARR had to stand in front of the door to keep Bluesy from going out to confront Rofiki. Bluesy was so forceful that she was practically fighting him back. Rofiki and Bluesy were arguing with each other through the door. Mr. Jenki and Ms. Freda were now standing at the top of the steps looking down at them with fear. The cats Frisky and Big G were looking like scaredy cats peeking their heads through the banisters. Tyson was standing by Bluesy ready to help attack if the door opened.

THE RURALS *"Relax Your Soul"* RURAL SOUL

Exhausted and hurting STARR began to scream at Bluesy, *"Relax your soul and if you don't stop fighting me to get out this door. There will be no us – please just go back upstairs."* Bluesy heard what she said and knew he would be putting their relation in more risk if, he didn't listen to her.

Hesitating, Bluesy went up the steps walking past Mr. Jenki and Ms. Freda. STARR screamed at Rofiki, *"I will call the cops if you don't go away."* Rofiki could hear police sirens from a distance thinking she already called them. *"Meh need to talk to ya STARR! Meh be BACK!"* He screamed walking away and noticing the shadow of a big male figure looking out the dark windows of the third floor. Rofiki looked up and yelled, *"Ya blood-clot. When meh see ya, meh gonna get ya!"*

ESTELLE *"So Much Out The Way"* SHINE

They got so much things to say right now. They go so much things to say and if a bwoy don't know what he's dealing with Rofiki need to move out the way. They got so much things to say right now. They go so much things to say and STARR knows what's she's working with and Rofiki get his ass out the way.

Not forgetting her visit from Bluesy's wife Karen. STARR pulled him away from the window, who was fuming and watching Rofiki drive away. She could feel the heat of his body temperature and his bright red face alarmed her. He was literally shaking with anger and sweat was dripping off his bald head. She wanted to scream and tell him to just go and leave her alone. Unable to pull herself away and witnessing for the first time a man cry real tears, she was almost hesitant to speak.

It was breaking STARR'S heart to see Bluesy in the state she was in earlier. Bluesy picked up the papers from the floor and showed STARR that he had filed for divorce years prior when he was in the military and that he was legally divorce, and had his doubts about J.R. as in Junior being his son. He further explained his parents, the grandparent's role in inviting Karen, so they can be with their grandson. He also explained the 72 hours paternity results and all the hearts that would break if it was negative like he expected. He admitted and apologized that he wasn't forth coming with the information.

ERRO WROTE THIS "Previous Cats" ERRO WROTE THIS
(Remix: STARR "Previous Chicks")

"I'm not to blame for the pain that was caused by previous chicks
You gotta see me for me"

First things, first Bluesy needs to recognize, who is with him now. Second thing, can't blame STARR for how, he were treated before, she is not the blame for the pain that was caused by previous chicks, Bluesy gotta see STARR for her. Explaining that he never loved Karen. Well not enough to marry her. But right before leaving for Iraq, she told him, she was pregnant. So he married her to be sure his child would get all the health benefits needed. A few months after he deployed, she sent him a letter telling her she made a big mistake, but never stating what the mistake was and he never heard from her again.

Then she shows up with a 5 year old son – 6 years later. She didn't interrupt Bluesy who was talking and still looking out the window worrying about Rofiki returning. Bluesy explained, *"It has been difficult spending as much time as I wanted with you due to my long work hours, and parents. The situation with Karen was my parent's invitation to stay, since her and J.R. had no other place to go. Karen has never kept me from you. Me living back home made my parents feel more secure in their neighborhood. That is why I recently had an alarm system installed, so now with me gone they will still feel safe."*

FRANK MCCOMB "Actions" THE TRUTH

Coming with more than just adjectives and talking nouns and verbs, Bluesy learned that *'Actions speak louder than his words.'* Handing STARR the paper work from the Red Cross, showing he went for paternity testing earlier that day. STARR was past his wildest dreams and the thought of losing her because of Karen brought on deep chest pains. The last time he felt this kind of pain in his chest was when he lost a friend in a road side attack in battle.

Just wanting everything to go back to the way it was with them. They spent the rest of the night into early morning holding each other - afraid to talk – afraid to pull apart - afraid. Bluesy left at sunrise, STARR remembered hearing him leave pretending to be sleep, as he kissed her good-bye.

MUTLU *"Damage"* MUTLU

Damaged, Karen it's not her, it's her fantasy. 'Cause all she really do-o-o is damage Bluesy, she'll say they're through. But it's him, still him, she keeps coming back to. A few weeks before Bluesy met STARR, he came home proud with the surprise news of just buying the coffee shop, he found Karen his ex-wife at his parent's house at the dinner table claiming he fathered, her 6 year old son, 'J.R.' He planned on telling STARR everything, but he wanted to be positive and have paperwork to prove his facts were not fiction.

The following sunrise after burying the cat Midnight and the emergency call from his parent's house changed everything for him and he couldn't go on living a lie. Walking into the house he found Karen sitting on the sofa flipping channels as her / their son played with some many toys scattered across the floor. He couldn't believe how lazy she was. She complained unable to find a job and wanted to work with him at the coffee shop.

In Karen's mind, she had it all planned for his parents to baby-sit, so they could work together. There was no way on earth Bluesy would ever work side by side with her. He had told her to stay away from his business, because she caused too many problems. One day she came by the Coffee shop when he wasn't there announcing that her husband was the owner and their son J.R., and she were joint owners of the establishment. She even complained about the JAZZ1CAFE radio station playing in the store and asking questions about the flyers for free kittens posted.

JEFF BRADSHAW "Lookin'" BONE DEEP

Looking for answers, though dog-tired from working. Bluesy went home and walked past Karen and picked up J.R. Telling her that it was time, he spent some alone time with J.R. Karen started to object but instead said, *"I wouldn't mind spending the day with the both of you."*

Walking out the door Bluesy said, *"Sorry this is a boy's only day at the Zoo."* He didn't say father and son, Bluesy had J.R.'s birth certificate in his pocket and his name was listed as father and headed to the Red Cross for a paternity test. Explaining to J.R. that they were just getting a check-up before going to the Zoo. Bluesy was told he would have results within 24 hours. Bluesy felt bad the innocent sweet boy that called him daddy had to go through this, but he needed to know the truth, the boy needed to know the truth.

THE MANHATTAN TRANSFER "The Zoo Blues" BRASIL

"I'll turn you on, Tell me, what, what's the trip? To turn you on quick"

Bluesy's a rational fella, but he thinks he's going nuts. Just wanna be, wanna be, left alone and unwounded. Keeping the promise even though he had a headache, and took J.R. to the Zoo. Not long after they got to the zoo Karen found them and ruined any opportunity he had to get to talk and know Junior outside of Karen and his parents' influences.

Disappointed, but Bluesy was sadly relieved watching junior run open arms happy to see his mother. He made an excuse about an emergency at the coffee shop and left her and Junior at the Zoo. Hating being this way towards Junior, because of his distaste for Karen and her actions. But still Bluesy couldn't bond or even part his lips to call junior son.

A Caucasian catholic woman his parents approved of Karen, but Bluesy never got the explanation on why she disappeared for almost 6 years. Her only explanation has been she was young and foolish and now mature and never stopped loving him. But showing up with no explanation and a little boy who keeps asking, *"Are you my daddy,"* had him puzzled. From the start he ignored all her advances not wanting to step back into the past.

JARRROD LAWSON "Think About Why" JARRROD LAWSON

"Thinking about why?" Noticing Karen's was still well molded and feminine, she dye her jet black hair to blond, since the last time he seen her. There was no attraction to her lies. Seeing how pleased his parents were with having a grandchild, he didn't push the subject to hard and hoped her stay was temporary.

Junior was an extremely shy kid that looked just his mother, nothing like him. His parents loved their first and only grandchild. They continued to tell them how they thought they would never get a chance to see a grandchild with both of his parents being in their 70's. A blessing and change of life baby for Bluesy's parents. His mother had him when she was 42 years old and his father was 46, he was their miracle child.

After leaving STARR, Bluesy went straight to his parent's house to straighten out things and to put Karen out! He found Karen dressed in lingerie in his bed. She had been waiting there all night waiting for him. Things were getting out of control and just as he was telling Karen to get out of the house all together and that he would send her child support, his parents entered the room after ease dropping.

Everyone sat around him with their robes tied tight. He felt like he was being ganged up on. His mother showed him a warm smile and spoke first, "*Honey Junior is too big to still be sleeping with his mommy. We turned the guest room into Junior's room and now this is yours and Karen's bedroom. You need to spend more time together and be with your wife and son, and give us more grand kids.*"

Missing STARR and witnessing his parents happy, Bluesy realized that they were selfish enough to make him suffer, just so they could be happy. His father patted him on the back and gave him a wink as his mother said, "*Grand kids.*" Karen blushed as she sat in silence. Bluesy spoke up and said, "*Karen is my ex-wife and now, I see what the three of you do when I'm not around. You plan my life.*" He got up and left.

THE MANHATTAN TRANSFER "So You Say" BRASIL

So they say it's a feeling, Karen will get over someday. So they say, so you say. She should try, just to let the flame inside her die. Against the wind with her face turned to the empty side of loneliness. Midnight black and blue. So they say that the world will keep on turning. So they say, so you say.

(Sax solo)

TRACK 11: THE B-SIDE

Nothing was erased from their minds and hearts, but they were both able to bandage their pains and nurse off each other's company. THE NEOSOUL STARR were a few days away from their listening party at Bluesy's Café's grand opening. STARR wanted to tell BearLove that she wanted to cancel, but then she would have to explain and look like a fool.

CHOKLATE "Suns Out" TO WHOM IT MAY CONCERN

Alarm buzzing and phone ringing, STARR woke to the morning thinking, she was going to sleep in. Then she peeped out the window and the sun said, "*Hello.*" The sun was out for her today. Guess she'll get up and go-go-go. Climbed out on the right side of the bed adjusting her attitude. Getting into it and before she knew it, she was knee deep in some good ole goodness.

Today is going to be one of those yummy sunny days. Though STARR tossed and turned in the bed an hour longer, after Bluesy left, knowing he was going home to her. She was actually awake all night thinking, though she acted like she was asleep when he tried to snuggle up tight and even when he kissed her good – bye before leaving in the morning. Nauseas and vomiting and head hanging over in a bucket feeling woozy with throbbing temples, emotionally all together messed up! Blaming it on her nerves and replaying every word, every action, every remark and every pose of Karen.

QUEEN AAMINAH "Keepin' It Real" LOVE REIGNS

"*Keepin' It Real- Keepin' It Real- Keepin' It Real...*" After all STARR been through with Rofiki, she couldn't believe that Bluesy didn't trust her enough to tell her the truth. She never asked questions about him dating anyone, because she didn't want to answer questions about her relationship with Rofiki. Assuming he was single and only living with his parents, no siblings, no wife, and no kids. She wanted to paint fool in red lipstick all over her face and take a picture, print it out and use it as a dart board, so she could throw darts at herself.

Mumbling out loud pleading out her prayers, *"Oh GOD... Oh... GOD I have been so disobedient with my prayers. I know- I don't pray like I'm supposed to. I think it is because I'm not sure how to pray. Should I be on my knees? Should I be on my face? Should I stand with my head to the sky and my hands open wide?"* The phone rang. Assuming it was Rofiki or Bluesy, she was about to turn the phone off. Until noticing it was BearLove.

BEARLOVE (voice sounding sad): *As-salaamu 'alaykum* (Peace be unto you)

STARR (fighting back tears): *Wa'aleichem ashalom* (and upon you be peace)

BEARLOVE (sounding even sadder): *Yo whad up? You Busy?*

STARR (lying): *I'm cool – what's up?*

BEARLOVE: *I'd rather not rap on the phone. Can you come over?*

STARR: *I'm on my way!*

BEARLOVE: *As – salaamu 'alaykum*

STARR: *Wa'aleichem Ashalom*

ERYKAH BADU "Rim Shot" BADUIZM

"I came to hear my drummer play"

When STARR arrived she found BearLove's front door wide open, as she entered taking off her shoes and calling out, *"Bismillah"* and finding BearLove stretched out on the white plastic covered vintage sofa that was once his grandmother's, then his mother's and now his. It's where he always went to be close to them. Stretched out on the sofa with his arms covering his face and the place was silent. There was no music and no barking.

"Get your stick up against that drum
I wanna hear it
I want my rim shot"

Noticing the empty bottle of Hennessey, STARR immediately began asking questions, *"Bear why the door open? Where's Negro?"* Closing the door she waited for him to respond or Negro to start barking. She tapped BearLove hard to be sure he was still breathing and aware of her presence. Looking around at the mess on the table, STARR started to clean up, picking up an empty glass off the floor, she started to clear off the coffee table removing the empty cognac bottle. Reaching for a brown cardboard box he bawled, *"Don't touch that box!"* Startling and confirming that Negro was nowhere around, or the dog would have attacked her by the alarming tone of BearLove's upsetting voice.

URSULA RUCKERS "1 Million Ways To Burn" SUPA SISTA

Looking upon, BearLove with eyes burnt from tears. Searing the meat of STARR'S heart with memories. Slow burn, slow burn, slow burn, slow burn 1 million ways to burn choose one. Assuming he might be sick, she kneeled carefully beside him greeting with peace, *"As – salaamu "alaykum."* She watched his chest breath heavy and then heard him mumble low, *"Wa' aleichum Ashalom."* He took long pauses to catching his breath before removing his hands from his face. She assumed from the looks of his blood shot eyes, he too had been up all night crying. She reached out and hugged the big guy, because she too needed a hug.

Observing the place STARR curiously asked, *"Where is Negro?"* Tears slide down his cheeks, pausing before his fuming response, *"The bitch killed my dog! She let him out the yard and he was hit by a car."* Bear was in tears biting his lip and trying to hold it together. STARR

Reaching out rubbing BearLove's back and hugging him. STARR knew how close he was to his dog, she found herself crying with him, *"I'm so – so – so sorry. Oh My GOD I'm sorry!"* Standing up and trying to gain his composure he said, *"At least you're sorry. That bitch said it must have been his time to go. Can U believe that shit?"*

VISIONEERS "Smoker" VISIONEERS

Now sitting up BearLove and preparing to roll a blunt, he didn't answer her reaching for a Phillies blunt that was on the table. Slicing the cigar with his thumbnail and emptying the tobacco, he licked the tobacco leaves along the edges to seal them, before speaking. *"Word up STARR, I have a lot of respect for you. You mind your own business. You don't be tripping on money. You're just mad cool. I'm just fucked up and going through changes. My chest is full of pain and my mind is going wild wanting to fuck up the whole world. Right now I need a friend. I don't want to do nothing but chill and try to get my mind right!"*

Lighting the blunt, BearLove passed it to STARR. Thinking of the cat Midnight, she shared the story, though knowing Negro and BearLove had a longer and closer relationship. She tried explaining that some people are insensitive to other people relationships with their pets.

Sharing the sad news, STARR explained how Mr. Jenki wanted to put Midnight in a green trash bag and put him out for the trash men. BearLove pointed to the cardboard box that was on the table and said, *"In that box is Negro's remains. I cost me $100 for 'Taxi Cab' ride home, because Mina had a hair appointment. She said I could have used the car, knowing my phobias about driving, and I can't see that well. I took my house keys and told her to keep the car as a gift, I'm done!"*

KIM HILL "Taxi Cab" SUGAHILL

Huffing and puffing and passing, lost in the clouds of hemp STARR knew like a *'Taxi Cab'* Rofiki keep passing her by? Passing her, passing her. Just like a *'Taxi Cab'* her light was off and she wasn't letting him in. She wasn't letting him inside, her mind. She will not be in that situation no more. Finally walking!

It was the first time, STARR heard BearLove openly admit, his phobia about driving. That would explain why, Mina drove him everywhere in his car. Changing the subject she said, *"I had an unexpected guess come to my house the other day."* She almost told him about Karen, but she didn't even want to think or talk about her or Bluesy right then. She continued since she had his attention, *"Rofiki dropped off some of my personal paperwork that he had been holding hostage. I didn't see him thank GOD or I would probably be in jail right now."* Still trying to find words of comfort she said,

"We have to keep moving forward and wait for the happy chapters of our fictitious book life to shine through the pages."

QUESTLOVE, HERBIE HANCOCK, LIONEL LOUEKE, AND PINO PALLADINO *"Culture Freedom"* BONNAROO

Talking to BearLove, STARR watched his expressions of hate change into desire. Open hearted she spoke, *"I know it's crazy my mind still thinks of music at a time like this. But I count my blessing and music is one of them. I'm grateful that I have a friend like you in my life at times like this. I don't look for trouble or want to be in any, though it seems to want me to be right in the middle of the mess. Pain is going to come, but there is always my faith in GOD holding me up. I'm blessed to have a friend like you. When I was going through and still going through my break through, you have always been here for me too, with a new song, a new beat, a new reason to continue. When I met you things changed instantly and I'm still here ready to sing about some more love, some more pain, some more, so we can't give up."*

SMOOTH JAZZ ALL STARS *"A Long Walk"* A TRIBUTE TO JILL SCOTT

"You're here, I'm pleased
I really dig your company..."

Taking heed to everything STARR was saying re-lighting the blunt BearLove's phone rang signaling Mina's ring tone. Ignoring the phone call and turning his phone off he said, *"Come on let's go"* grabbing the box with NEGRO'S ashes and placing them in a big shopping bag and they were out the door for a long walk.

"Maybe we can talk about Surah 31:18"

Taking a long walking along Germantown Avenue BearLove was the tour guide and history buff exposing his knowledge and stories of Germantown, a thriving neighborhood of culture and history in Northwest section of Philadelphia. The cobblestones of Germantown Avenue distinguish the busy street from the rest of the neighborhood. Teaching the history of these jagged rocks, and the streetscape and how the current construction affects area businesses and just how residents feel about the rocks that makes their unique homes.

"Maybe we can talk about Revelation 3:17"

Taking a long walking through the 'Brickyard' section of Germantown, BearLove's hood. He lived on his block of Germantown Avenue all his life. Everyone respected him, even the local corner hustler knew not to disrespect and sell drugs on his block. No one ever tried to rob him they already knew the deal, his cheap ass never had money in his pockets. He kept all his money in the bank and only used plastic.

LIZZ WRIGHT "Walk with Me Lord" SALT

Holding hands and walking down Germantown Avenue on the combination of the trolley track and cobblestones and watching cars tremble while driving down the avenue. Neither of them were concentrating on music. They stopped at the corner of Germantown Avenue and Haines Street and froze as if forcefully hit by an invisible wall. BearLove could barely speak pointing up at the street sign explaining that Quadir lived on Haines Street.

Finding strength to continue the journey and changing the subject. BearLove pointed at 'Germantown High School' introducing his old school before transferring to 'The Philadelphia High School for Creative and Performing Arts', commonly known as CAPA. After graduating he studied experimental theater at New York University.

Walking a few more blocks and were now standing there at the corner of Germantown Avenue and Washington Lane and BearLove was pointing and teaching the history of the *'Johnson House'* and telling STARR that his mother took him there often. The historic Germantown home had a relaxed, backyard feel. Strongly urging STARR too follow him inside to check out the history about the Philadelphia Underground Railroad station and museum built in 1768.

D'NELL "This Thing" 1st MAGIC

"This thing" STARR held on BearLove had him wide open in with feelings just being with her. Keeping his cool and educating and

explaining, *"This is a center of three generations of Quaker families who worked to abolish slavery and improve living conditions for freed African Americans. This is where Philadelphia's only Revolutionary War battle was fought. This place tells the stories of every kind of freedom, religious, racial, political, economic, and artistic of the everyday people who fought for them, from the 1600s to this present day. Look it up at johnsonhouse.org."*

After the *'Johnson House'* history lesson still holding hands they walk up Washington Lane and took the long walk letting plenty of buses and taxis pass enjoying the walk. BearLove knew that he wanted to be more than just a friend, more than just a fellow musician, more than he ever wanted, he wanted her. It took everything he had not to reach out and touch her. She satisfied the urge, when she squeezed his hand harder crossing the streets and he never let go.

ZHANÉ *"Crush"* SATURDAY NIGHT

Seeing the gentle side of Bearlove took STARR'S heart and made it sing, she love him and he doesn't know... Enjoying the new sights of being somewhere new walking in parts of Philadelphia she never knew existed. STARR also seen a more intelligent and sensitive surface of him that she didn't know. Seeing him care to help an elder woman cross the street, which they ended up walking home and carrying her groceries. He also pulled on her dreads a few times playfully and unaware it was turning her on.

Yes, STARR wanted to feel good and she went with the feelings enjoying a day of peace and quiet and walking, just being away and learning something. No questions they just walked and talked about things in general leaving everything and everyone behind, while both held onto the bag with Negro's Ashes. 5 miles later they were entering the gates of Chelten Hills Cemetery on Washington Lane in the Mount Airy section of Philadelphia.

BOYZ II MEN *"It's So Hard To Say Goodbye To Yesterday"* LEGACY GREATEST HITS

"How do I say goodbye to what we had? The good times that made us laugh outweigh the bad. I thought we'd get to see forever. It's so hard to say goodbye to yesterday!" Realizing she had never been in a cemetery or seen

a dead body before, STARR began thinking of Auntie who raised her and remember the foster mother not taking her to the funeral.

Now STARR'S heart was mourning her first foster mother 'Auntie,' and Midnight the cat, Negro the dog, and sadly thinking of her mother $hantey Money. Walking across the cemetery lawn. BearLove was chanting, *"As-sa-laa-mu `a-lai-kum wa rah-ma-tul-laah. Peace be upon you and the mercy of Allah."* Walking and talking in Arabic and English to greet someone and as if someone was waiting.

They walked until they came across the large tombstone with a picture of his mother and grandmother together. Watching BearLove bending down in prayer position and making 'Duaa' prayer for the deceased. Kneeling and followed his lead silently, she listened to him pray.

DUAA PRAYER

"Bismillah! O Allah! Shower your mercy upon Muhammad and the followers of Muhammad, as you showered your mercy upon Ibrahim and the followers of Ibrahim..."

There was a fear of death building in STARR as she looked around at the many tomb stones and still trying to concentrate on praying. She never asked BearLove how his mother or grandmother died, She overheard Mina saying he would die of a heart attack too if he kept eating cheese steaks. So she had assumed they both died of heart attacks. After Praying BearLove lifted a vase out of the ground and began pouring some of NEGRO'S ashes down the hole, before putting the vase back.

Now crying unable to hold back emotions kneeling in front of the grave as STARR rubbed his back consoling BearLove. Standing up he kissed the tombstone and began walking away without saying a word. Following and unable to count the many rows of graves and wondering where he was going. As he walked deeper into the cemetery still chanting, *"As-sa-laa-mu `a-lai-kum wa rah-ma-tul-laah. Peace be upon you and the mercy of Allah."* Walking until they came across another tomb stone.

DUAA PRAYER was recited again and they prayed for Quadir. STARR stopped and looked at the tomb stone that read Abdul 'Quadir' Raquib July 25, 1984 – February 26, 2011. Reading the dates STARR realized it was the same date, but the year before Trayvon Martin (Feb. 26. 2012) was also Murder. Looking at the handsome young face on the tombstone, she knew it was SoulShine's son 'Quadir' A.K.A. 'Duce' the 26 year old rap artist and friend that BearLove was working with before the tragedy.

27 people in homicide and not one person would say who did it! Still no justice for Quadir or Trayvon, or families living with grief and no politically correct answers or justice. BearLove reminded, *"Allah see all and no one gets away from GOD!"* Rumor is that the owner of the club came out shooting. 3 people were shot and 1 stabbed. Quadir was shot in his back 3 times trying to run away and a bullet hit his heart. Quadir was the only one that didn't survive. BearLove had all his music sitting in a vault keeping it safe until he could get his mind right. Again they made prayer and afterwards BearLove explained that Muslims were not supposed to mourn it was not good for the loved ones spirit, but he couldn't stop.

Remembering the story all over the news and FATIMAH ALI'S article in the Philadelphia Daily Newspapers May 1, 2011 'A Mother's Bleakest Moment.' She also heard the interview on the talk radio station WURD/900 AM, Philadelphia, PA, with FATIMAH ALI, the host of 'THE REAL DEAL' with Iyanla Vanzant talking with his mother. About how her son went to a birthday party and then walked a young lady home that wasn't feeling well. Upon returning to the party a fight broke out outside the North Philly club and 3 bouncers were beating up and stabbed his friend. Quadir tried to stop the fight with words hollering, *"Get the fuck off of him, he'll give you a fair one."*

Yes, Bearlove agreed speaking fondly of Fatimah Ali, *"She's a Philly gal who kept it real, produced thoughtful commentary in written and spoken words, and gave back to the community and she suddenly died almost a year after Quadir."* Then BearLove sat down on the ground in front of Quadir's grave and dug a small hole and poured out the last remains of NEGRO'S ashes, telling STARR how much his dog and sons loved Duce. Before breaking down in tears he pulled out his cellphone and called the Germantown Cab company to take them home, he recited the lyrics to a song Duce A.K.A Quadir wrote about how the cops would just mess with young black men for just walking down the street (Haines Street & Chew Avenue), *'Twisted in a Web.'*

QUADIR "Twisted" DUCE

"The streets got me twisted up and twisted in its web
And when I get out I hope I ain't dead
They got me running down the block screaming fuck the cops
But when I get out I hope I ain't dead..."

THE EXTENDED BEATS...

ZAMA JOBE "Taxi Ride" NDAWO YAMI

Deep in thought STARR never knew how she would be touched in that *'Taxi Ride,'* in that taxi ride, in that taxi ride. In conversation with BearLove, he told her that everything would be okay, knowing nothing. In that *'Taxi Ride,'* in that taxi ride, in that taxi ride. Caught up in the emotions of the moment and the rain pouring down, they rode back to BearLove's in a taxi cab and headed straight to the studio.

TAFE FIVE "Permanent Midnight" NU-JAZZ DIVAS VOL. 2 (Featuring YULIET TOPAZ)

Feeling like it was permanent midnight, STARR noticed it was after midnight when they finished recording and running through music. After singing all evening and her voice needed a break, though she was feeling a second wind of adrenaline. Sipping on a cup of honey and lemon tea, she noticed that she missed 12 phone calls from Bluesy before turning off her phone. She wasn't ready to see or talk to him, she needed time. BearLove announced after taking the last puff, *"Shit I'm out of weed."* STARR was feeling a nice buzz and smiled back, *"I'm all out too!"*

Then BearLove exclaimed with intense pleasure, *"Oh wait I do have something. But it's not that usual bud we be smoking. It's some exotic bud and needs to be smoked right. Straight up! Now let's get our heads together with killa' and let me see if you can handle this shit."* She was no stranger to marijuana – ganja – Kush - hash, Rofiki was a weed-ologist, so she wondered what BearLove had that was so exotic. BearLove turned down the lights in the studio and it gave the room more of a chill – out – relax – your – mind – kind of feel.

A TRIBE CALLED QUEST "Find A Way" THE LOVE MOVEMENT

Now STARR caught BearLove's heart for the evening and kissed his cheek, moved in and confused things. Should he just sit back or come harder? Help him find his way. BearLove pulled out a glass bong. Giggling and admitting she never smoked out of a bong before. Simply because it was against Rofiki 101– He was against her using anything that looked like drug paraphernalia of a junkie, though Rofiki kept a glass and wooden pipe.

Blissfully happy, fully alive and shaking away the thoughts of Rofiki, STARR was eager to inhale as BearLove explained everything. *"First, I have to fill the bong with cold water. The cold water cools down the smoke so that more can be inhaled. Some folks fill their bong with ice. Okay now adding just enough cold water so that the bong makes a bubbling sound when inhaled through. Some folks prefer very hot water because the steam helps bring moisture into the lungs. The drying effect of smoke, not the heat of the smoke is the main reason people cough while using a water bong."*

DAVID ANTHONY "Smoke One" THE RED CLAY CHRONICLES (Featuring EARL KLUGH)

"Smoke one with your folk
Drink one with ya boy
I know it's been a little while
Since we had a little fun"

Basking in the knowledge of his powers and having a little fun, BearLove continued with the lesson. *"We have to check the water level to make sure that the water isn't up too high. It should be low enough so that it doesn't spill water out the carb as you bend down to take a hit. The carb is a small hole located right here on the side of the bong. Okay pack the bowl, but make sure no buds fall out of the bowl. You want to get as much in the bowl as possible while still being able to pull air through it with each inhale."*

FERTILE GROUND "Take Me Higher" SEASONS CHANGE

Ready for BearLove to take her higher and paying close attention, STARR did as he instructed, and bending her head and studying her mouth and hands. Nervously she moistened her dry lips and put your mouth against the opening and forming a seal with your lips. Make sure that the entire opening is covered. Otherwise, she won't be able to draw any smoke out. Gripping the bong, she covered the carb with one hand and resting the bong on her breast. She watched as Bear held the lighter up to the bowl and she inhaled. The chamber filled up with thick smoke, she inhaled until he instructed, *"Uncover the carb and inhale the smoke. Breathe all the smoke into your lungs."*

Coughing uncontrollably, STARR was surprised by the amount of smoke, she inhaled. Lightly beating and smoothly stroking, BearLove patted down her back. He was still giving Bong lessons tutoring, *"Hold your breath and try to suppress your cough. It is normal for first timers. The longest I held my breath was for 20 seconds, tonight I'm going to break that record!"* STARR was counting in her head *"1-3--5"* and having a good time *"4 – 7 –5 –6."* She was messed up from the first hit and couldn't count straight. BearLove was slowly exhaling until there was no more smoke coming out of his lungs, relaxing and enjoying his high.

JILL SCOTT "Crown Royal"
THE REAL THING WORDS AND SOUNDS VOL. 3

Sipping *"Crown royal on ice, crown royal on ice, Crown royal on ice, crown royal on ice,"* and heads bobbing music jamming to JAZZ1CAFÉ Internet Radio Station and the both of them relaxing in the recording studio. STARR was upside down with her head hanging off the edges of sofa and newly polished red toes danced up the wall.

"I catch that thrust, give it right back to you..."

Sitting in the upright position BearLove looked down at her head dangling off the sofa. They looked at each other upside down, smiling. They were having a good time and it turned out to be a good evening. In a cloud of smoke, STARR'S mind was feeling lighter and lighter until all her thoughts were tucked away.

"Down on the floor 'til the speaker starts to boil..."

"Crown royal on ice, crown royal on ice, crown royal on ice, crown royal on ice," Still singing, STARR was high and feeling tranquil and horny. It started with her begging BearLove to let her braid his hair. *"No you can't braid my hair. I don't like little plaits all over my head."* Giggle giggles she pleaded, *"No come on, I will just give you cornrows going straight back. It will be easy to take out."*

Hiking up her wrap around skirt, STARR didn't have to convince him to squeeze tight between her warm thighs. She could feel his hot breathe blowing on her knees felt like kisses between her thighs and making her nipples hard. *"Got ya on ice, baby."*

JAZMINE SULLIVAN *"Braid Your Hair"* GILLES PETERSON THE BBC SESSIONS VOL. 1

STARR can feel BearLove everywhere, can he feel her too braiding his hair-air-air! When she braid. When she braid his hair it's such a grand experience (*experience*). She can feel BearLove and not wanting him to stop. She went willing letting her body twist until his head was between her legs sucking her like she was a human bong. She had hands full of his black long strong breads, pulling on - holding on. Moaning and groaning and pleading, moans, giggles and begging it was just what he wanted to hear. There was a tingling in the pit of her stomach and the tip of her toes and ready to explode.

FOREIGN EXCHANGE *"Sweeter Than You"* LEAVE IT ALL BEHIND

"Nothing better to do, there's nothing better
What could be sweeter than you?
What could be sweeter?"

Doors slamming and hearing BearLove and Mina upstairs fussing and things being thrown around awoke STARR. She could hear Mina screaming, *"What they fuck did you do to your hair?"* Bear explaining that STARR did it. Then STARR could hear rumbling, cursing and BearLove blocking the door screaming and not letting Mina down to the studio. She scrabbled for her clothes and realized she was already dressed. She was confused about the night before unsure of reality or wet dreams. Mina managed to barge her way down the steps. Mina looked around and noticed the bong and knocked over the bong and the atrocious smelling water spilled on the floor and splashed on STARR.

FOREIGN EXCHANGE "Valediction" LEAVE IT ALL BEHIND

No need for Mina to remove her coat, no need to take off her shoes. Usually she could stay, but not today, not today. No! Standing speechless STARR didn't know what to say or do until Mina shouted accusing, *"Bitch I knew y'all were fucking all along! You can have him and I hope y'all make enough money, so you can help him pay child support! You dirty black bitch!"* STARR couldn't take Mina disrespecting and stepping close enough to smell her morning breath and BearLove wasn't stopping her.

So when she pointed her finger in STARR'S face calling her a 'dirty black bitch' and poking her in the nose. STARR swung her right fist and did a LALAH ALI upper cut to the chin and knocked Mina on her ass. BearLove ran to Mina's aide yelling, *"Yo, STARR chill out that's my Baby Momma!"* She might have got away with calling STARR a bitch, but dirty and black? Mina needed more than a slap.

ESTELLE "Dance Bitch" THE 18TH DAY

Yes, it's STARR like you never seen before, she paid her dues and now she is ready to break it down. *"Dance Bitch"* Running out the door angry with the morning sunlight right in her face, STARR was venerable enough to walk into that trap. She ran in the opposite direction of the bus stop, she didn't want anyone chasing after her, still wondering if they really had sex or was it all a wet-dream.

LEDISI "Trippin'" TURN ME LOOSE

BearLove can do what he want, be how he be. But STARR gotta fall back, boy 'cause this ain't her. Ooh baby, baby, she ain't tripping over him. Nauseas and vomiting and head hanging over in someone's yard feeling woozy with throbbing temples, emotionally destroyed and embarrassed. Blaming it on nerves replaying every word, every action, every remark and every pose of Mina. Now STARR felt that everything was ruined and her music career was squashed. Out of sight a few blocks away she tried waving down a 'Taxi Cab.'

AQUANOTE 'Waiting" THE PEARL

Looking for Bluesy in every strangers eyes. We all need a little loving in our life time, but until he brings his loving back in her life, she was waiting for him. Only for him, only for Bluesy. When STARR arrived home getting out the cab, she noticed Bluesy sitting in his car *"waiting"* and Tyson outside on the porch. Bluesy jumped out of his car and paid the taxi driver happy to see her. Not wanting to admit he had been sitting out there all night. He walked alongside her into the house asking if she was feeling okay.

Intentionally, STARR didn't answer not wanting to start a conversation in the hallway or wanting him to smell the atrocious bong water that disappeared into the air of funky cat litter when she opened the door. She made it past the Jenki's door without it opening, but found Frisky lying at the top of the 3rd floor steps breathing heavy.

EUGEE GROOVE "Café De Soul" BORN TO GROOVE

Forgetting all about Frisky due to deliver any day and it looked like today was the day. When Frisky saw STARR, the cat began purring in pain and repeatedly licked her bottom preparing for the birth of her kittens. STARR unlocked the door knowing Frisky was trying to get inside to retreat to the nesting box made for her.

STARR found a cardboard box with sides that were somewhat tall so that the kittens couldn't wander off after they were born. Tearing rags into strips to provide soft and comfortable padding for the box and make small air holes around the sides, so that the cats can breathe easily.

Making sure the holes were not large enough that the kittens could get their heads stuck and suffer injury. Cutting another larger hole, part way up the side so that the Frisky could get in and out to use her litter box.

DON E "You Got a Friend" THE COLORED SECTION

Following behind Frisky who was wobbling into the bathroom, STARR closed the bathroom door not inviting Bluesy, she jumped into the shower to wash away 2 days of funk from a long walk, cemetery dirt, sweating and possibly sex. Scrubbing off the lust and all its possibilities she was glad to smell the scent of cucumber melon, as the bong water washed away. All along while listening to Frisky giving birth.

Knocking on the door Bluesy was asking, *"Is everything okay in there? Do you want to take her to a veterinarian?"* STARR just wanted him to leave them alone. She just wanted some silence, but Frisky wouldn't let her have it as she pushed, grunted and whining louder. STARR was drying off with when the third and last kitten was born. She was so excited she opened the door and let Bluesy peek in and noticed Frisky getting upset wanting isolation. Bluesy wanted to keep the peace and closed the door and left Frisky and STARR to privacy.

Coming out the Bathroom STARR announced that Frisky gave birth to 3 kittens, 1 black male, 1 white male, and 1 orange female kitten. When she came out the bathroom with the exciting news, she found Bluesy eating M&M's for the hundredth time and picking out certain colors to eat first. She finally asked, *"What are you doing."* It seemed like the question he had been waiting for her to ask him. Most people asked him immediately as if it bothered them how he chose to eat his candy.

ERIC BENET *"News For You"* THE ONE

"I got news for you
I still got work to do
And you're thinking that I'm done
That's just when love just begun"

Don't you worry about Bluesy leaving, no, no, girl! He valued STARR'S ability to see the world from a unique prospective and not have to questions about his differences. But after doing it as often as he did, he knew one day she would ask. *"Oh, I always pick out the brown ones. Then I eat the primary colors first. Then I go back and eat the brown ones. Save the best for last?"* Star laughed, *"Oh you're a sick man. The Mar's candy company has no special formula they all taste the same."*

Handing STARR a pharmacy bag Bluesy said, *"Now it your turn."* STARR pulled the pregnancy kit out of the bag and her mouth fell open. She didn't want to know if she was pregnant. Because she knew that it would not grow in her belly. Holding the home pregnancy test Bluesy was being very persuasive and challenging. STARR threw the test at him huffing,

"This is not funny!" Picking up the test up off the floor, Bluesy handed it to her again saying, *"It wasn't meant to be funny. I know my woman's body."*

Insulted STARR handed it back to him stating, *"I am fine!"* He sat it on the bed and said, *"You sure are FINE, but I want to make sure our baby is fine too!"* She didn't want any of his charm and she couldn't think about a baby right now, she was still mad at him and he knew it.

GWEN BUNN *"A Baby"* THE VERDICT

"Oooo – Oooo," As STARR belly grows, she don't want it to be her turn. Well, not right now anyway. 'Cause she's just a baby, a baby, a baby, a baby. Changing the subject Bluesy said, *"I hope you remembered the grand opening is in a couple of days and I will be busy around the café. You're welcomed to hang out with me, unless you have to be here for Frisky or do you have rehearsal?"* He was trying to figure out her schedule and she cut him off answering, *"I have things to do don't worry about me."*

Bluesy didn't think, his words registered asking, *"I need BearLove's phone number?* STARR'S brain was in tumult. She jumped up screaming and hollering, *"What the hell you want his number for?"* He was momentarily speechless before responding, *"I just wanted to ask him if there were any certain electrical outlets he would need to set up the sound equipment. Calm down everything is going to be okay."*

AMARIE *"Outro"* ALL I HAVE

Looking back, STARR knew that everything was exactly how it should have been. Going through, the ups and downs and the blessings. Calming down, so overwhelmed with everything and sleep deprived, she cuddled up on the bed next to the pregnancy test. Falling asleep with Bluesy cuddling next to her, watching her sleep.

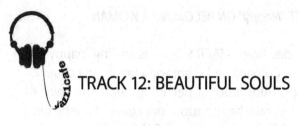

TRACK 12: BEAUTIFUL SOULS

MARY J. BLIGE "A Beautiful Day" NO MORE DRAMA

STARR doesn't have a complaint in the world. Even though it's cloudy, she can see the sun's rays. It's a beautiful day. No matter what nobody say. After a week of using hair-kits for removing dreadlocks, she washed her locks thoroughly with shampoo and with water hot as hot as she could stand. This helped melt the wax or whatever greasiness that built up on her scalp and hair.

Working large amounts of shampoo into each section of each dreadlock, STARR gently pulling her hair apart and getting the soap in the middle and on every strand, before rinsing. Then she poured quality conditioner on each lock soaking her hair completely and using a metal comb she gently picked each one out. Sitting for hours daily with hair conditioner in her hair and carefully combing beginning from the bottom and working her way up to her scalp. This took a LONG time – but she had nothing but time – wanting her hair free strand by strand.

ALISON CROCKETT "Everything Is Beautiful" BARE

"Everything is beautiful when there is nothing going on. But is everything beautiful when things are going wrong?" Admiring her new look and natural waves and curl patterns in her hair, STARR beamed. Yet, wondering what she was going to do with the newly released long head of hair. Pulling out her scissors and cutting off inches of split ends, questioning if she should get a perm or add human hair extensions to make it even longer.

Once STARR was finished clipping and picking out her natural afro, her head felt lighter but full. Her hair flowed between her fingers long, soft and strong. To the new free thick hair and new growth, she gently rubbed Moroccan Argan oil to the roots twisting and twist, twist, twist, and twisting, until she was at the end of the strands.

ALISON CROCKETT "Nappy" ON BECOMING A WOMAN

Café Ole beauty and Indie. Now, STARR'S body is smiling, happy to be nappy. Today, she rain like Cumana and embracing her ebony beauty. Happy with her new look, STARR studied her image that the mirror projected and also nursing her new heart tattoo that covered up the old 'Rofiki 101' with Aloe Vera gel from a fresh piece of aloe leaf.

Hurrying to the store to get 'Top' papers, a new lighter, incense, spring water and a bag of chips and newspaper. Though she hated reading bad news, she had to stay current with events. Going out the door, she noticed the steps and halls had been swept and the citrus fresh aroma of the first floor.

BAHAMADIA "Beautiful Things" BB QUEEN
(Featuring DWELE)

"Talk about beautiful things a little bit"

Coming back inside from the store, STARR noticed the mail was delivered with the new issue of Essence Magazine. The lemon-lime renewed fragrance of the first floor made her linger longer. Picking up the magazine and cheering happily observing the cover owing and awing at 'LL Cool J' on the cover, when the door to the first floor apartment opened. A woman stood in the doorway wearing a pink silk robe with her hair pulled up seductively and holding a cup of tea asking, *"Is there anything for T. Vernell?"*

So many times, STARR wanted to knock on the door and ask, excuse me what music artist are you listening to, what is the name of that group? Normally, Tyson would want a boxing friend and start fighting her for being in his space for too long, if she didn't have food for him. Or Bluesy would be trailing behind her, or she would be rushing in to go to the bathroom trying not to pee on herself and trying to make it past the Jenki's door unnoticed. But there were a few nights that she did sit on the steps and listen to the music.

Speechless seeing the mystery person for the first time. The surprise siphoned the blood from STARR'S face. She handed over the magazine and bills that would normally slide under the door, before read the magazines first. Closely observing and handing it over to the mystery of person T. Vernell, who reminding STARR of the beautiful actress Jackée Harry from the television shows '227' and 'Sister – Sister.' When invited inside the 1st floor apartment, STARR felt welcomed hearing my voice, my vibe, my words, sounds, parables, and most of all happy to meet me. Never in the apartment before, STARR was curious to learn more and didn't object wanting to discover the other side of my 'Intro.'

AYANNA GREGORY "Intro" BEAUTIFUL FLOWER

The door squeak opened wider to let STARR in and I closed it telling hear my 'Intro.' *"As a little girl, I didn't understand life had seasons... That rain was just as necessary as sun. I spent a whole life time trying to avoid pains and struggles. Only to find transformations waiting for me on the other side..."*

DJ KAWASAKI "Intro" BEAUTIFUL

After our introductions, STARR felt a bottomless peace of satisfaction never imagining me to be young enough to about the same age as her mother, $hantey Money. When invited to come into the apartment in renovations, she wondered if, I was real. Because she assumed all this time some old spooky ghost had lived here. When STARR first moved in the Jenki's told her to stay away from my door – unless it was to put mail under it. Ms. Freda told her to mind her business and just put the mail under the door, so that Tyson didn't urinate on it.

JOY JONES "Beautiful" GODCHILD

"I am beautiful, yes I am despite the lies I've been told, I still am"

Now on the other side of the door and sitting in the large sunny clean kitchen sipping on ginger tea (good for the throat) admiring each other. STARR never envision a person like me living on the 1st floor, though the inside of her apartment reflected my personality. It was clean and artistic and whimsical and relaxing. Inquisitive STARR asked, *"Miss- Mrs. Vernell how long have you been living here?"*

CAROL RIDDICK *"Beautiful"* LOVE PHASES

The heavy lashes that shadowed my cheeks flew up happy to answer. *"Please just call me Theresa. Meeting you up close and personal STARR, I must say you're beautiful and your name fits you perfectly. You have beautiful clear skin and your soulful voice. I've been hearing singing in the hallways, you should be singing. I Love the new natural hair style – You are rocking it well."*

Sipping the tea, STARR was trying to make it last smiling and happy to hear a compliment especially about her hair, wondering how I knew the hair style was new. So she asked, *"You saw my locks?"* Looking STARR in the eye's the way a mother would a daughter, the way a sistah should a young sistah, the way a friend would look at a friend and responded, *"Yes, trust and believe I see everything. I loved your locks too. You're organically beautiful and not everyone can embrace their natural beauty. You're beautiful."*

RA-RE VALVERDE *"RV Intermission"* A BEAUTIFUL MESS

Not to change the subject, but still on subject I continuing talking to STARR, *"I know we have not personally met in the months you've been here. But, I thank you for cleaning up. Ms. Freda said you were a nice girl. You noticed that there is no privacy and trust me, they're watching out the windows even if she doesn't come to the door. They just don't want traffic, which is understandable since the Jenki's are too old for mayhem. I've been here a month longer than you. I brought the building and been waiting for the Jenki's to move. Then they decided they didn't want to move back down to South Carolina. But it looks like they want to remain tenants and I'm selling the building."*

Confused about the deception STARR looked shocked as I finished explaining, *"When I moved in I was going throw financial hardships, and nowhere to go and no other place I could afford. I needed a place to clear my head, write and create without the phone ringing and folks knocking at my door. I brought this building with tenants 'The Jenki's whom you have been paying rent for."*

RHONDA THOMAS "Peaceful Blessings" BREATHE NEW LIFE

"Peaceful Blessings from within, peaceful blessing." Watching me talking and studying my confident body movement. It smelled good inside the apartment and STARR complimenting that the candles burning were the best she ever smelled.

"Trials come to make you strong"

Wait! Did STARR hear me correct? She had been paying the Jenki's rent? Seeing my questionable puzzled expressions as I explained, *"I just caught on and I just want you to know the deal. If you stay your rent is $200 and the Jenki's Rent $200 month before renovations. After renovations I don't plan to rent, I only agreed to keep the tenants so no one is homeless and the cheap rent was to give the Jenki's time to save money. Giving everyone time to find a new place."* STARR was happy her rent had decreased by half, but to think that the Jenki's robbed her blind. She hugged me, catching me by surprise saying, *"You have a beautiful soul."*

"Hold on – Hold on – Hold on"

Knowing how STARR was feeling wrapped in a silken coon of pain, I explained. *"STARR I believe I'm a good judge of character and I should have met you sooner. But the time is now and I'm glad, I had this opportunity to meet you. If you would like to take the Essence magazine upstairs and read it first, like you usually do, be my guest, and if you need anything knock. But, I don't get involved with domestic disputes, so the next time the chic come around scare her off with kitty litter again and when that cute Rasta friend come back around acting a fool – you will have that handsome big Mr. Coffee as security. Oh, and about BearLove, a drummer with fly beats you'll figure him out. I know it's complicated. But, you have a beautiful soul too."*

RA-RE VALVERDE "Complicated" A BEAUTIFUL MESS

Just like STARR was lonely and they weren't talking again. It's a new day, but same ole story. Much easier to be lovers then friends. When did it all get so complicated? Astonish, dumbfound and flabbergast STARR asked, *"Wait you was here all those times?"*

Grinning cleverly, I winked my eye saying, *"I mind my own business. I didn't hear anyone screaming for help. Then I would have called 9-1-1. But, those were also the times I was in here alone going through my own bull-shit. In fact the day the white chick showed up, I watched her pacing up and down the sidewalk for 15 minutes, looking frantic chain smoking before knocking on the door. I was going to answer and then you came down the steps and answered the door. I had your back and grabbed my baseball bat hoping, I didn't have to come out swinging. But, you took care of that swinging kitty litter."* Finding humor in her own pain STARR was enjoying the girl talk about being *'Caught Up and listening and relating.*

DJ KAWASAKI "Shooting Star" BEAUTIFUL

I, also reminded STARR of the beautiful comedian Kim Whitley from the movie *'Friday After Next'* and *'Raising Whitley.'* Well that's what she said. Caught up and carrying on the conversation, I continued expressing myself. *"I don't announce my comings and goings and would rather not."* I might of sound harsh, but my smile said different as I continued talk. *"I come here to think and write and sleep and think and write. I'm learning to understand my purpose for being here too. I thought I would be long gone from here, but I sleep very well here nothing haunts me here. Here I am free to be. I don't want to be on an island, but I like being left alone if you don't come in peace."*

Understanding from experiences with the Jenki's, STARR listened and surprised at all I witnessed. She was also wondering what kind of writer? What did I write? But, she never asked. The more she listened to me talk the more familiar I felt though we just met.

It was my style that intrigued STARR the same old school hip – hop Philly swag similar to her mother's $hantey Money. She had so many questions, but more of a listener. Enjoying my compliments, *"STARR you're a natural beauty and you should be off in New York, Paris somewhere modeling, because you're eye-catching and easily you could be on the cover of Ebony or Essence."* She dropped her head feeling maybe the compliments were just nice jesters and said, *"I'm too dark – or probably too plain – or probably."*

BRENT JONES AND T. P. MOBB "Beautiful" WOW GOSPEL 2003

Can GOD take STARR and make her something beautiful. Something tight something bomb something really dope. Don't want her ugliness to embarrass you, so she's begging you can you make her something beautiful. Though STARR was feeling bad saying the things that were really on her mind instead of just saying thank you, she was puzzled watching me laugh.

Laughing and shaking my head that turned into a serious of nods and understanding as I explained, *"I'm fair skinned, light skinned and I always wanted to be darker. You want to be lighter? I wonder what we're doing with ourselves, wanting to change everything from our skin tones to our hair to our nose, lips, breast, belly, hips and ass. We're all naturally beautiful and you can't buy or want to change that."*

Handing STARR the Essence magazine to take up stairs I said, *"Just keep singing and loving who GOD created you to be. Study the winners in life and stay away from the whiners. Take it one day at a time and focus on the promise for your future. Even though you may experience resentment or resistance from others around you, remember the biggest battles you have are with yourself. So be aware of any of your sabotaging habits and attitudes."*

Not sure if I would see STARR again, but knowing I must encourage. I spoke from the heart, *"Acknowledge your strengths. Look how far you have come. Instead of putting yourself down, lift up your head with self-worth. Give yourself credit for what you have endured, what you have overcome, what you have learned, what you have given and for all the times you didn't give up. Stay in the light, because you truly are a star. A word of advice, pray for even the enemy and watch how you too will be blessed."*

BLUESIX "A Beautiful Tomorrow" A BEAUTIFUL TOMORROW

"You'll have a beautiful tomorrow
A beautiful tomorrow yea
A beautiful tomorrow
If you just pretend the world has gone away"

After the pep talk, I was now ushering STARR to the door and late for an appointment saying, *"Keep singing because you sound better than any next American Idol and also I like your new tattoo."* STARR laughed inside remembering when 'American Idol' came to Philadelphia, Rofiki messed that up so she couldn't go. There was a knock at the front door snapping STARR out of her past and before closing my door we said, *"Peace!"*

The door closed with STARR bewildered and confused about how I knew about the new tattoo? Bluesy was knocking at the front door as she was leaving out of my apartment, and that's when I, reminded her of the beautiful *'SoulShine Sessions'* of JAZZ1CAFÉ.

PHUTURISTIX "Beautiful" FEEL IT OUT
(Featuring Jenna G)

"How you doing today Bluesy?" Mmm, Bluesy was looking good and was he feeling it too? STARR is thinking about how good it is to be there, another day with him in that way. Now let her give praise to the sun and the moon, and the stars, 'cause her man and his love and what they are. Beautiful together, beautiful forever. Beautiful, so beautiful.

Confused STARR'S was now wondering why Bluesy was knocking and remembered, he no longer had a key. Overwhelmed by the surprised bouquet of roses, she hurried out the door pushing Tyson back inside with the Essence magazine. Wanting to talk about me the mystery woman on the first floor, but decided not at this time enjoying her man.

Beautiful, so beautiful. In awe and actually stumbling back, Bluesy loved STARR'S new hairdo flowing free and naturally curly. He complimented her right away, *"WOW you look amazing!"* She had heard for the first time that she looked amazing. Bluesy had been working day and night on renovations at the coffee shop and needed a break from all the chaos and needed to have a heart to heart with STARR.

PRINCE "The Most Beautiful Girl In The World" THE GOLD EXPERIENCE

Could STARR be the most beautiful girl in the world? It's plain to see she's the reason that GOD made a girl. Oh yes, she is! Eyes sparkling more and reflecting the shine of her ebony black hair. Her lips looked fuller and smile brighter, framed by long dark curls. He loved the new look and wanted to kidnapped her for the day.

As Bluesy drove across the Atlantic City expressway. STARR stuttered in questioning, *"R – Are - R we going to Atlantic City?"* The whole drive he played with her hair or she was rubbing his bald shaved head. She was a little embarrassed to admit that she had never touched the ocean.

Quickly the memories of the bus trip to A.C. with Rofiki and the fight they had because STARR wanted to play in the sand. He only wanted to gamble and had a holy fit and stopped her when she went to go touch the water. He told her that it is a fact the Atlantic Ocean has large amounts of plastic contamination and chemicals, particles, industrial, and a lot of other shit in it.

Claiming she could touch the water when he takes her to Jamaica to meet his mother. Also he claimed in the Caribbean seas the pollution problems come from cruise ships dumping their solid wastes. Then they had a big argument that caused STARR to find her own way back to Philly on the bus that night. She prayed it wouldn't be a repeat of an evening like that.

JEFF BRADSHAW "Beautiful Day" BONE DEEP (Featuring FLOETRY)

It's a beautiful day, STARR wanna do her thing. They could get together. 'Till the sun goes away, and back again... It was a beautiful day the sun was bright and the board walk was full of folks and many of the people they did pass complimented her hair. She had never had so many compliments on her hair and she was feeling beautiful.

The sand felt like quick - sand slipping between her toes, STARR listened to the tranquil sounds of the waves kicking the salt water and licking the salt off her lips. After confessing that it was her first time touching the ocean, spitting out the atrocious tasting salt water with delight. They played in the water and then walked the board walk until dry. Not caring about gambling they felt they hit the jackpot of love.

DAVE MCMURRAY "Beautiful You" I KNOW ABOUT LOVE

Why else would he do all the crazy things he do? (Well, alright!) Because of beautiful STARR. She makes him do the things he do. (Well, alright!) After dinner since it was getting late they drove back to the café, Bluesy still unknowing to STARR was making sure they were not being followed. Bluesy was glad that she was looking beautiful and relaxed. He parked and double checked to be sure no suspicious people were lurking around. He escorted STARR around to the side door of the coffee shop.

Unlocking the big Steele doors, Bluesy explained that it was an additional entrance to the 2nd floor apartment. Once they were at the top of the steps he unlocked the door to the apartment announcing, *"Welcome Home Baby. Welcome Home!"* He unlocked the door and handed her the keys. She opened up the door to the renovated apartment.

ANITA BAKER *"Perfect Love Affair"* COMPOSITIONS

"Uhhh - uhhh," There's a picture in STARR's memory of the days when they first met. When solo became duet and the words Bluesy spoke compelled her. It's a perfect love affair. Wanting to touch the freshly wet white walls, STARR squalled with delight, *"This is truly amazing! Just last week this place was an unfinished."* She was in complete shock. She heard what he said when he unlocked the door *"Welcome home baby."* She wanted to believe it could be her home. But could she? Or was this all just another trap? Bluesy chose his words carefully, *"I know we have not known each other long enough for some folks to understand how I feel for you. Heck I don't even know if you understand what I feel for you. But there is nothing I wouldn't do for you."*

Wondering if they were moving too fast. But all STARR'S life - life moved fast. Changing from one scenario to the next and if her life was going to be a fast life of change.

Why not embrace it? Bluesy was a good man, he never raised his voice, he never cursed at her. He always made sure she was taken care of and did extra – extra things to let her know, he was sincere. Or should she move slow and marinate in the pains of her past? But this felt different, this felt right. He was like a favorite song.

QUEEN LATFAH *"Simply Beautiful"* THE DANA OWENS ALBUM (AL GREEN)

If STARR gave Bluesy her love, she'd tell him what she'd do. She'd expect a whole lot of love outta him. He gotta be good to her. She's gonna be good to him...Taking a deep breath Bluesy paused before continuing, *"I know- I too came at you not telling about my chewed up grass. Then I met you and want to chew and chew and chew unto I smell like your shit! That is how much I am into you. My purpose is to be with you. You are as true as every breath I take and I need you to know that. I care about everything you eat, feel and where you sleep. If you're not sure."*

A warm glow flowed through STARR, interrupting and talking fast. *"Oh I had plenty of time to think too and I've been waiting to love and be loved, I'm just scared. What about your parent's?"* She knew talking about his parents was a sore discussion. Glad he didn't answer, because the truth always hurt. She continued to walk around looking in awe and revelation of the transformation.

"Beautiful... WOW!" She praised his carpentry skills that transformed the stark white box of 1,500 square feet into intriguing shapes, sensuous textures, soothing colors. There were hardwood flooring throughout the entire place, exposed brick walls, wood beams, soaring ceilings, and oversized windows filled the rooms with natural lighting.

YAMAM'NYM *"Beautiful"* DUE TIME

Beautiful that's what Bluesy was to STARR. Shinning eternally that's how she want this love to be. Animated she jumped up and down as Bluesy pointed out the central air and heat. She danced around the new modern kitchen with black granite stone countertops that she danced her fingers across. Playing with the light switches as the polished chrome rotational ceiling fan fluttered blowing air.

PHONTE *"Gonna Be A Beautiful Night"* CHARITY STARTS AT HOME

And Bluesy can tell by the look in STARR's eyes it's gonna be a beautiful night. He said, *"It's gonna be a beautiful night baby doll, baby doll. And I can tell by the way that you're looking at me it's gonna be a beautiful night"* Skip the bojangling, just be his Lena Horne.

Overwhelmed with the beauty and elegance of the gourmet kitchen Furnished with state of the art stainless steel appliances, 6 burner gas range, dishwasher, microwave, garbage disposal, and stackable front loaded Bosch washer/dryer, subzero refrigerator which she played with the ice machine because she never used a refrigerator in her life that had an ice maker.

Designed for chef Bluesy to bake his wonderful pound cakes. He made it quite clear, he wanted to specialize in only pound cakes, and known for the best. STARR never really cooked our baked and was ready to learn everything as Bluesy shared his recipe for 'Bluesy's Sour Cream Pound Cake.'

BLUESY'S SOUR CREAM POUND CAKE

Ingredients:

1/2 pound (2 sticks) butter
3 cups sugar
1 cup sour cream
1/2 teaspoon baking soda
3 cups all-purpose flour
6 large eggs
1 teaspoon vanilla

Optional: Whipped cream and Blueberries.

Directions

Preheat oven to 325 degrees F.

In a large mixing bowl, cream the butter and sugar together. Add the sour cream and mix until incorporated. Sift the baking soda and flour together. Add to the creamed mixture alternating with eggs, beating each egg 1 at a time. Add the vanilla and pour the mixture into a greased and floured Bundt pan. Bake for 1 hour 20 minutes. Topped with whipped cream and fresh blueberries.

BRIAN OWENS "Beautiful Love" MOODS & MESSAGES

The bathroom back-splash fully tiled with mosaic white marble and glass tiles, double vanity and double Shower with multiple shower heads. There were lots of closets with plenty of storage space. *"It's Beautiful Love!""* She dashed through the apartment like a little kid happy on Christmas morning. Touching the freshly painted walls of every room, she could smell the new paint in the air. Walking into the master bedroom Bluesy and found STARR looking out the window in a daze. Feeling bad for lashing out at him about his parents, she apologized, but she need to let him know what was paining her.

JILL SCOTT "Epiphany" BEAUTIFULLY HUMAN

Watchin', watchin' the fire in his eyes, hands getting bolder STARR responded, "Mmm." She felt for the rock and sure enough for a North Philly sister, she reppin' hard. Yes, they were in an interracial relationship, even if they were secure with it, or was she? And was he? But, she would not be shut behind closed doors, not any more. He admired her facial structure delicately curved with exotic high cheek bones. His voice velvet – edged and strong, "It's for you my Beautiful Love." As she turned to embrace him, she had an 'Epiphany' and knew just what she needed. He may not have a song, but his recipes were an instant cure.

SOULSHINE SESSIONS: INDIE IS THE NEW MAINSTREAM

ADRIANNA EVANS "Walking In The Sun" NORMADIC

Greetings from JAZZ1CAFÉ and welcome to SOULSHINE SESSIONS... Remembering the past when reading the credits on the back of record albums, was just as important as listening to the record. Reading cover to cover and the inside sleeves searching for lyrics, musicians and song writer names. I remember playing songs over and over again until, I heard every melody and lyrics.

In the turn of the new millennium, new music, new artist, new soul emerged, Neo-Soul grew in popularity filling airwaves and MTV and BET when they still played music videos. Neo Soul artists and groups have taken its place among the circle of Jazz, Funk and Hip-Hop music genres, but it has taken a dissimilar road from practically every other popular music style before it.

MONDO GROSSO "Star Suite III – North Star" MG4

The trouble with the mainstream music industry is that they're missing one vital ingredient that can't be faked and that's passion. Passion! Desire is the root of all creativity and good music. The reason people enjoy Indie music is because it is like being in a candy store and your ears can hear and taste the variety without having it being overplayed on the radio repeat over and over and over and over and over again, and again.

PHUTURISTIX "Sunshine Lover" FEEL IT OUT
(Featuring AMMA)

The responsibility for that lack of popularity is largely due to a broken music industry without the central methods of distribution that have supported commercial music sales for decades. Despite being talked about in magazines, parodied in late night television appearances, most indie artists remain basically anonymous to the general public.

Indie is 'NOT' a genre. It means the artist or group is on an independent label, or distribute music themselves. You may have noticed that progressively Indie acts are taking over the charts while less and less mainstream artists are getting notoriety. This an evolution of decision about who to listen to everyday is due to more choices with technology.

DIONNE "Move (DUB Mix)" HELIUM

@ JAZZICAFE, we further our commitment to the industry, as well as the consumer, by bringing you the best the music industry have to offer without propaganda. When was the last time you turned on the radio or picked up a book that gave you information about the hottest movements in the industry? Also a playlist committed to bringing the grassroots exposure to the artists?

The music industry has changed over the past several years. Corporate greed increases while the record stores close at an alarming rate. Even music is affected by government policies.

JAZZ1CAFÉ believes that you have the power to help make a difference. Please tune in and help support the station and become a V.I.P. Member.

Just A Few Clicks Away from JAZZ1CAFÉ...

1. Download 'LIVE365 RADIO APP
2. Launch the LIVE365 RADIO APP
3. Type: JAZZ1CAFE (Click GO!)

BECOME A V.I.P. MEMBER!!! FREE 5 Day Trial Membership and No Credit Card Required!

Please become a V.I.P. Member and help support JAZZ1CAFÉ Internet Radio Station and the music artist. Portions of you subscription go towards the royalties for the songs played.

Enjoy zero commercial interruptions, no banners or ads, just you and the music. Listen on multiple devices, tablets & desktops. Go anywhere with the LIVE365 Mobile APP for. Listen in the comfort of your home on devices such as Sonos, Roko, WDTV, Grace digital wireless radio, Tangent, TIVO and more.

TRACK 13: PLAYING MY SONG

TIORAH "Got It Going On" NOONDAY CAFÉ

"Ooh, he got it going on, going on. Ooh wee, ooh, ooh, ooh, mmm..." It is the grand opening of Bluesy's Café! A private event and folks were showing up hours before the doors opened. Folks were raving about the gourmet, organic, and imported coffees, and teas, personalized coffee mugs, and Bluesy's famous sour cream blueberry cream cheese pound cake was being put on the map, as #1 lip smacking delicious. There was so much excitement going with the addition of "THE NEOSOULS STARRS CD listening party and video recording of STARR performing Unplugged, *"Bull-shit ain't nothing but chewed up grass."*

DAVE MC MURRY "Radio Days" I KNOW ABOUT LOVE

Reaching for the phone to call STARR repetitively, Bluesy felt that something was wrong when she didn't answer the phone or return any text messages. Everyone in the group showed up except for her and BearLove. They were the only two missing. Mina had asked Bluesy several times if he heard from them.

When Bluesy got tired of Mina asking, he started hunching his shoulders. Furious she spitted out, *"They're probably somewhere fucking!"* Then grabbed her purse and left. Bluesy continued to call and still no answer. When he noticed the band members were inquiring about STARR and BearLove, he felt the knot in his stomach getting tighter.

Bluesy's smile was without humor. He spoke to BearLove earlier on the phone making sure the electrical outlets could hold the power and they talked about where everyone would set up. Now an hour before the doors open and two hours before show time, he was pray that everything was okay. It was a delight to have such an opportunity to have BearLove suggest videotaping STARR'S performance at the grand opening.

Of course, Bluesy had hunches about BearLove due to all the time spent with STARR in the studio. He knew that music was very intimate to her and having her share that with someone else had him trying to understand her art. Her art of passions never made him feel like she would leave him for another man. But he knew a man was a man and wanting to believe BearLove had STARR'S career in good interest.

JAZZANOVA "Coffee Talk" REWORKS FROM JAPAN
(Yukihiro Fukutomi Remix)

"Talk about Bluesy's Future?" Everything was beginning to feel almost back to normal? STARR was sincerely happy to see Bluesy's accomplish, his dreams and goal coming to light. He did such an exquisite job on the renovations of the café.

Now pondering the words of Mina felt like punches to the head, Bluesy knew he should have picked up STARR. She insisted that he stay and make sure all the coffees & teas were percolating –and the sour cream pound cakes baked. He had everything in order and glad he had the time to concentrate and make sure everyone else was right. So, he didn't object when she insisted on taking a cab. A tear slid, Bluesy caught it just hoping it wasn't what Mina had insinuated. He needed a drink of something other than coffee!

RADIO CITIZEN "Density" BERLIN SERENGETI

Almost ready, STARR was charging her cellphone and enjoying the silence before the big event. She received countless messages from BearLove apologizing and asking her forgiveness and they spoke briefly. She knew that incident was just another that she had to learn to overcome. She wanted to look perfect before calling a taxi. Because ready or not it was 'Bluesy's Café' grand opening.

Combing and rubbing oils to every hair strands, STARR teased the spirals of natural curl patterns. Phone was fully charged and she turned it on ready to tune into JAZZ1 CAFÉ and get the party started. Before she could launch the LIVE365 Radio APP, she was interrupted an incoming call.

The familiar voice of BearLove had more thickness, concentration and density. Asking if STARR was listening to the internet radio station

JAZZ1CAFÉ. Because they were playing her song, their song *'Bull – shit ain't nothing but chewed up grass'* and it wasn't STARR singing.

Next, Bearlove was blasting the music in his background, so STARR could hear too. Listening and asking the questions, she was thinking. *"How could this be and who could this be?"* After the confusion BearLove made a few phone calls with STARR on the phone and they were informed it was Kandi Gyal. A new artist with Vicious Heat Records.

Trying to understand the confusion BearLove told STARR to come outside, but she hung the phone up on him afraid. She sat in the middle of the floor holding her head in her trembling hands. She felt like if she removed her hands, her head would fall off. STARR didn't want to be bothered with anyone. But, within minutes BearLove was at her front door which was wide open, cats outside, and up STARR'S steps (for the first time) and picking her up off the floor. They got in the car that he took back from Mina, and drove to the destination of the interview.

ROBERT GLASPER "Calls" BLACK RADIO 2
(Featuring JILL SCOTT)

"You always come
You always answer calls
When I call you come
You always answer my calls"

The JAZZ1CAFÉ Restaurant building was still destroyed by the fire, but the radio station was still running smoothly. They pulled into the station parking lot of the Philadelphia Airport hotel and STARR noticed the white Hummer parked in the parking lot with New York license plate.

On the way to the hotel BearLove called the program director explaining that the song being played is not an original or authorized song. He let them know he was on the way with information for SoulShine Sessions and bringing her a special guest and that will have social media buzzing. Internet Jockey, SoulShine Sessions isn't a devious gossiper and would rather play music than talk and entertain rumors. She didn't want to gain a bitchy reputation for on - air spats with producers, labels, rappers, R&B artists or personal affairs. Asking questions about sexual activities and religious practices just wasn't her thing. But, SoulShine would never backing down from a juicy story. Since she was now twisted up in the drama playing the song.

LYFE JENNINGS "Radio" THE PHOENIX

"Said when my song comes on the radio
I forget all of my troubles"

"That's my jam." On the air with 'SoulShine Sessions.' Who was having a good day and she loved the song. Though she never mentioned to Kandi Gyal or her manager Rofiki about the special surprise guest coming. So she went on as business as usual, but she had a feeling about this interview. Making small talk with the guest to get a feel of their character traits. SoulShine asked simple basic questions checking out Kandi Gyal. *"So what artists inspired you to sing and how did you hook up with Big Tank?"*

Feeling comfortable with the simple basic questions, but Kandi Gyal heard a twist of sarcasm when asked about Big Tank. She also refused to answer if she was a true 36 DD? SoulShine Sessions was truly heterosexual and knew Kandi Gyal was wondering if, she was flirting. Not. SoulShine didn't hold her tongue nor did she hesitate to judge if HOT or NOT! Checking Kandi Gyal's overly Botoxed lips puffed and glossy, as the new artist pranced around in a glittery gold mini dress with cleavage running over.

Yes, Kandi Gyal was wearing the same dress she wore to Big Tanks 40th birthday bash. Nobody in Philadelphia saw her in it and on radio who could see? SoulShine Sessions already got word that Kandi Gyal was a fake. So just wondering what else was fake she asked again, *"Silicone or pushup bra?"* That is when Rofiki injected his coolness answering for Kandi, *"Yo meh Kandi Gyal iz all real."*

CHRISETTE MICHELE "Mr. Radio" I AM

"Thank you for your tone to make love true I heard it before
Thank you for your love song, Mr. Radio"

The radio stations program director was waiting in the hotel lobby for STARR and BearLove. They gave 'THE NEOSOUL STARR' new CD to the director. They were told SoulShine Sessions had been updated to what was going on. STARR made it clear she was there to prove her music was stolen. They were asked to give them a few minutes to check with SoulShine to see how this was going down.

Dressed in a simple pair of jeans and white hoodie and a pair of white sneaks and long wavy hair bouncing, STARR was ready to rumble and kick ass. She should have been dressed in the sexy outfit brought for Bluesy's grand opening. She almost forgotten the grand opening, BearLove told her that he didn't and they would be on time. Wishing that she had changed into her new pretty outfit.

All of the sweetness Kandi Gyal heard in SoulShine's voice turned cynical after she watched her reading text messages. SoulShine curled her lips covered in bright pink bubble gum lipstick and jumped right into asking questions. Speaking in a cool, sweet deep welcoming voice into the microphone, SoulShine began the interview that was also being videotaped. "Welcome to SoulShine Sessions! *Today's special guest is a new artist from Vicious Heat Records. A Latino - Philly sistah, Kandi Gyal you have a sweet sexy voice. We're getting great reviews from emails and inbox messages, but this is what I can't understand.*"

ANGELA JOHNSON "On The Radio" IT'S PERSONAL

Ooh, SoulShine Sessions can tell you where all the good music is being played. Ooh, the kind of stuff that makes you want to hum it all day long. Making you feel so good inside, emotions like a roller coaster ride. On the radio where SoulShine play that kind of music. Yes, @JAZZ1CAFÉ.

Ooh, Kandi Gyal noticed it was chillingly silent and she sense that something's was wrong. Ooh, something's surely was wrong. Ready to clarify the confusion, SoulShine didn't give Kandi Gyal a chance to answer still asking questions. *"What made you chose $hantey Money's song 'Bull – Shit'? This song is well known to the old school Hip-Hop lovers in the Philadelphia area.*

Puzzled, curious and still asking questions SoulShine rattled on, *"But it has been brought to my attention that another group called 'THE NEOSOUL STARRS' also released the same exact song, same drum introduction and guitar riffs, and the same lyrics. The music is identifiable though the opening* *lines are the same the two songs split immediately following the bridge. But no matter how you say Bullshit, it's the sampling of $hantey Money."*

Dominating the interview, SoulShine's style was not normally brash but curiously asked, *"So were you paying homage to $hantey Money?"* Kandice looked at Rofiki bamboozled. Almost forgetting they were recording the interview mumbling, *"Who is $hantey Money and who the hell are THE NEOSOUL STARRS'?"* Then SoulShine's eyes narrowed suspiciously and said, *"You don't know $hantey Money? As far as 'THE NEOSOUL STARRS', I know them very well."*

ESPERENZA SPALDING *"Vague Suspicions"* RADIO MUSIC SOCIETY

"On the radio, Kandi Gyal knew they won't be talking about these lies that were stealing..." Tilting her eyebrows, becoming wide awake, Kandi Gyal looked at SoulShine not understanding what was going on. Then noticed the program director coming into the room handing SoulShine a note and whispering in her ear, which Kandi Gyal thought was very rude.

Squirming in his seat, Rofiki felt something was up. When the program director left, STARR was able to peek into the room. Seeing who she assumed was Kandi Gyal and the back of his head – his extra-long locks and knew it was Rofiki. Her heart dropped, she wasn't sure but now, she was sure.

Recalling where she seen Kandi Gyal before. Okay, she was the chic that was standing at the edge of the stage with Rofiki, the night STARR won the radio contest and performed @ JAZZ1CAFÉ. Seeing beautiful woman around Rofiki was nothing new. It was just that she had woman's intuitions about that one. Now she was confused about how Rofiki hooked up with this bitch and giving her permission to record her music.

Unable to hold back STARR screamed out, *"What is going on Rofiki!?"* Pushing pass the producer, STARR and BearLove hurried into the interview. This is when SoulShine thought they may need hotel security. Still recording and ready for what could happen, SoulShine was going for it. Her interviews were about being real and unscripted. Kandi Gyal was standing behind Rofiki who was screaming, *"Whad da fugh iz dis?"*

KYMANI MARLEY *"One Time"* RADIO

"Let mi tell it to you one time
You violate mi even one time..."

Recording every word SoulShine Sessions spoke into the microphone, *"This is the music business. Please sit down and redeem yourself because we're still recording. This could make or break you. Now you have a chance to tell you story."* Kandi Gyal stormed out of the room knocking over chairs with Rofiki chasing her and intentionally bumped into STARR. Causing STARR to swing her fist, but he was not close enough to connect. But they could hear her behind them furiously yelling, *"My songs are not for sale! You recorded my music without my permission."* Kandi Gyal yelled back without turning around and heading for the front door, *"I'm the one with the record deal – You hating ass jealous bitch!"*

"Girl if I give to you one time
It's for sure you'll be back more than one time..."

Walking fast Rofiki's kept it moving noticing, STARR'S new hairstyle. His voice broke with huskiness, *"Remember da papers yu signed? Meh on da copy rights and meh still ur manager 'member dat!"* Quickly, SoulShine Sessions played THE NEOSOUL STARRS' version of the song. BearLove intervened and stopped STARR from chasing them out into the parking lot, as he shouted to Rofiki, *"We will let our attorneys handle this Bullshit!"* They calmed downed and agreed to go back and tell their story.

On normal circumstances STARR would be have been delighted to be interviewed on her favorite radio station, but it was all feeling like a test. Though she thought it was funny remembering how Rofiki's always claimed, he dislike the station, because not enough Reggae played. The producer signaled for SoulShine to ask more questions. STARR stood up and was stepping away from the microphone. Waving her hands signaling no, she was done and ready to go, boiling inside this was not what she wanted.

RADIO CITIZEN "Test Me" HOPE AND DESPAIR
(Featuring URSULA RUCKERS)

"So you want to test me, test me, see me bleed..." Not wanting to lose the surprise guest STARR and BearLove, SoulShine stuck to her end of the bargain announcing, *"Welcome to SoulShine and tonight is the Grand Opening of Bluesy's Café on N. Broad Street at 7 P.M. Where you can check out the listening party for THE NEO SOUL STARR. In the studio now we have the lead singer STARR of the NEO SOUL STARR and BearLove the drummer, who we all know also as the drummer of the jazzy, electrifying hip hop group Philadelphia's own The Organics. So, tell us BearLove what is going on with the Organics?"*

No! BearLove didn't plan to be interviewed under these conditions. But, he knew SoulShine had him and listeners were waiting for the reply. He said, *"The Organics are cool. But I'm here on behalf of Black Beast Records and THE NEO SOUL STARR. The reason we're here is because Kandi Gyal wasn't given permission to record STARR'S music. Now if you wanna know what's up for real – for real, please join us tonight @ Bluesy's Café on Broad Street @ 7PM sharp for the listening party and more events please check out www.jazz1cafe.com."*

LUPE FIASCO "State Run Radio" LASER
(Featuring MATT MAHAFFEY)

"State run radio, state run radio"

The social media sites and bloggers were now spreading the news like wild fire and SoulShine continuing with the interview. *"For those missed it you can rewind, but let me brief you real quick. We had a new artist named Kandi Gyal with Vicious Heat Records. A Big Tank Production, debuting her new single "Bull - Shitting" and then we got visitors from the group 'THE NEOSOUL STARR'S claiming Kandi Gyal did not have permission to record their song. All hell has broken out and Kandi Gyal has left the building, but here with me now we have the lovely lead singer STARR and the drummer of 'THE NEOSOUL STARR' BearLove, who is very well known from the group THE ORGANICS."*

Even though STARR took off her head phones they were still on the recording. SoulShine puzzled STARR asking, *"Explain how Kandi Gyal also recorded your song?"* STARR was trembling ready to fight wishing that she had broken out every window on that white hummer, remembering Rofiki pulling up to her house trying to flaunt. She had been so stupid trusting Rofiki.

Reading messages from the social media sites SoulShine waited for their responses. *"I love Neo Soul music and I actually love both versions 'Bullshit ain't nothing but chewed up grass." But maybe we can do a battle of the songs and let the listeners be the judge?"* Pushing past the anger STARR answered, *"I am not one of those out of touch artist who is upset about their music not being played on the Radio. This is about my rights to protect me. It is unfortunate when everyone in this business seems to be a snake."* SoulShine smiled and licked her lips, because she was giving the listeners just what they wanted and countered, *"Well I see you're feisty. But I tell you that my venom is poison-less.*

ROBERT GLASPER EXPERIMENT *"Black Radio"* BLACK RADIO (Featuring MOS DEF and YASIIN BEY)

*"Ha! You're rocking. Yes, you are rocking with the fresh
You are rockin' with the Def, you are rocking with the best"*

There was a critical tone in BearLove's voice interrupting and not giving SoulShine Session's a chance to read another message. *"Let me tell you my opinion about radio stations. Once upon a time mainstream radio was the' showcase' for the record industries. However, it appears now that the 'showcase' is money controlled, talent is not necessary and most of the time a total disregard for the wellbeing of the listeners. What I enjoy about your show is that you hand pick good music to play. The song 'Bull – Shit' by Kandi Gyal might be a good song. We're not here to hate. The problem is that Kandi Gyal and the people over at VHRecords have used it illegally. They made the bad choice in recording our song.*

THE ROOTS *"Radio Daze"* HOW I GOT OVER (Featuring BLU, P.O.R.N., DICE RAW)

*"Never leave you alone
Never, never leave you alone
Never, never leave you alone"*

The radio daze kept us in the dark and the satellite age brings us to the light. Interrupting SoulShine spoke directly to STARR and pointing, *"Speaking of choices. You chose a song by a very dear friend of mine, from back in the day and I must admit you also have a very strong resemblance to her. My homey and would come through the parties and get on the Mic and rock the house right! I asked Kandi Gyal this question and now I'll ask you STARR, Why did you choose to sample $hantey Money's song Bull – Shit?"*

> *"Bull Shit ain't nothing but chewed up grass*
> *Ask me how I know*
> *Cause you showed your ass!"*

Instantly STARR became nervous and teary eyed looking at BearLove not sure to answer the question. BearLove's eyes swept over her face approvingly. This is the chance, she waited to tell the world. Looking straight in SoulShine eyes she replied, *"$hantey Money is my mother!"* SoulShine screamed, *"Bullshit ain't nothing but chewed up grass!"*

ROBERT GLASPER "Trust" BLACK RADIO 2
(Featuring MARSHA AMBROSIUS)

"Trust" And 2 hours late Bluesy's heart was relieved to see STARR and BearLove and SoulShine Sessions making their way through the crowd trying to get in the café. Immediately STARR rushed to Bluesy needing him now and giving him a big hug. Apologizing and briefly telling him what happened. The music was flowing and STARR had just enough time to change into her new outfit and smile for the camera's. She was in her zone singing along with Joe – Daddy playing the guitar, Ronny G also showed off his Xylophone talents and BearLove on drums.

After the day STARR had, she performed like the incident earlier at the radio station had no effects. Noticing Bluesy eyeing her, she fashionably embraced the microphone. This would explain to Bluesy the growing number of people on the sidewalks trying to get inside and the traffic stopping trying to look inside, 'Bluesy's Café.' The folks inside were sardine tight. He was glad Mina was way off base with her accusation about STARR and BearLove.

TRACK 14: "'CAUSE YOU SHOWED YOUR ASS"

N'DEA DAVENPORT "Bullshittin'" N'DEA DAVENPORT

Unbelievable, Kandice didn't see that coming at the JAZZ1CAFÉ Interview. She couldn't believe the demo tape Rofiki gave her was STARR singing. That was her story and she is sticking with it. Signing Rofiki on as her manager had her understanding, *"Bullshit ain't nothing but chewed up grass"* and Rofiki was manure.

In an uproar over the embarrassment having her talents compared to the likings of Millie – Vanilli, Fab Morvan and Rob Pilatus who formed the popular German duo pop group back in the later 1980's and early 90's that had all their Bull – Shit was exposed. Their Grammy was revoked when revealed that the lead vocals on the record were not actually theirs, they were lip –synching.

Though Kandice wasn't lip - synching it didn't matter when mocking just about every lyric and harmony of STARR'S. After the radio interview and on the ride back to New York Kandice and Rofiki argued like cats and dogs. They were actually ready to go to blows until she had a flash of back of Chris Brown and Rihanna's situation. No-No-No, she wasn't about to let anyone bruise her pretty face. They quieted down when her cellphone started ringing.

Immediately from the ring tone they knew it was Big Tank. He was cursing and screaming, *"Shut the fuck up and listen! Where your Rasta boy at?"* Kandice gave Rofiki a quick glance and mumbled humiliated, *"Right here!"* Big Tank growled, *"Fuck it put me on speaker phone."*

(Speaker Phone On)

BIG TANK: *"YO! I'm all the way in Fucking - Cali hearing about this Bull-Shit! What the fuck happened? You walked out of the fucking interview and caused a disaster giving that bitch freedom to exploit VICIOUS HEAT RECORDS!"*

ROFIKI: *"Na' Man we was set up – Meh have de copyrights. Meh work wid da Gyal STARR dat sing with dat group 'Da Neo – Soul Starz' and she laid down some tracks for Meh. But meh manage her and meh have da copyrights."*

BIG TANK: *"Fugh copy rights – Right now I have to save the fucking image of VHR – the Fucking Empire, I built fighting haters and bitches! But if the Bull-Shit is true about this other fucking group 'THE NEOSOUL STARR' having copy rights – both your asses are done! My ass is not going down for this Bull-Shit. This will literally make you chewed up grass with Vicious Heat Records.*

ROFIKI: *"YO! Chill mon meh fix de fugh'n problem!"*

BIG TANK: *"Yo fuck you dready! You see that's just it, Vicious Heat don't and won't have any problems. You're signed on as Kandi Gyal's manager, not an employee of VHR. So, what you and Kandice do is between you, don't call us and the money already advance to you for your services and call it even. Oh and leave the Hummer at the door, I'll have my business associates waiting at Kandice's apartment, please hand over the keys. Let's do this the easy way Kandice take me the off the speaker phone!"*

(Speaker Phone Off)

Shaken and in shock after hearing Big Tank talk to Rofiki with such bark and authority. Petrified, Kandi Gyal Kandi was positively sure fear appeared in a few of Rofiki's expressions. Also noticed Big Tank call her Kandice. He didn't like her stage name Kandi Gyal, he said it didn't sound mature and would only be good for her first single title. Trusting him and his marketing directors to take her in the right directions.

In the background being overheard Rofiki was yelling, *"Fugh dat blood clot!"* As she listened to Big Tank roar, *"I will be in New York late tonight. I'll call you, don't call me! Lay low until, I figure something out! Yo and get rid of that dread-loc nigga, I don't care how you do it. But he better be gone by the time, I call you back! And tell him I said no, he is fucked!"* Enraged, Rofiki spit the lyrics of 'Prodigy' from the group 'Mobb Deep.' *"Illuminati want meh mind soul and me body. Secret society tryin' to keep their eye on meh."* After a series of denials, accusations, speculations, and rumors regarding Big Tank being gay, yes gay and involved with the Hip-Hop Illuminati.

VISIONEERS "Hip Know Cypher" DIRTY OLD HIP HOP

It was noticeable that VHRecord artist reference the secret society by throwing up the hand signals and subliminal messages in their songs. Then play dumb or act offended when they get asked about their involvement. After Big Tank hung up, Rofiki began yelling. *"Whad da fuck dat lizard eye nigga say?"* "Adding words Kandice yelled and immediately jumped out of the passenger seat of the car and just in time. *"He said fuck you too Blood-clot!"*

Just like Big Tank said there were 2 big dudes waiting at her apartment to greet them. Big dudes, Rofiki seen before. The same dudes from the coffee shop, before going to Big Tank's birthday party. As they got their personal things out of the Hummer, Kandice screamed like security was there to secure her too. *"I want you out!"* Rofiki didn't show any expressions nonchalantly snarling," *No problem meh out!"*

KYMANI MARLEY "The March" RADIO

"Yeah, yeah, Ha-ha. Rise to his feet little soldier. Times are changing, yeah. He got to go out there and get it. Yeah, take his mark. Let's go soldier! Yo left yo left yo left right left." Immediately Rofiki went into the apartment with his heart pounding afraid they may have already been in the apartment and found his stash. He was relieved to see that nothing had been touched. He began grabbing his shit and stuffing it in the same bags he came there with. Cursing under his breath about how tired he was of her trifling ass. He kicked hairweave out of his way laying all over the bathroom floor, wigs on the closet floor, black weave glue droplets wasted on the bathroom sink.

The furniture was a basic 3 piece brown leather sofa set abused with dirty laundry, new clothes, a pizza box with 2 slices of pepperoni pizza, her ass was eating pork. His heart settled when he discovered his home security camera system with 4 digital wireless cameras. Never asleep, Jah Na' Sleep, so why should Rofiki.

DAMIAN MARLEY "Pimpa's Paradise" WELCOME TO JAMROCK (Featuring STEPHAN MARLEY and BLACK THOUGHT)

"Pimpas' paradise that's all she was..."

"Kandi Gyal loves to party, have a good time. She loves to smoke, sumtime sniffin' coke!" She's always laughing when there ain't no joke. Discreetly keeping surveillance on the situation the whole time viewing Kandi-Gyal's recorded actions. He had his eyes on what went down and around Kandi Gyal's loft- apartment with a 9-inch LCD monitor connected through an APP. This gave him the ability to view live video and record from anywhere in the world using internet connections. When motion is detected, the system will trigger the cameras.

FREEWAY "What We Do..." PHILADELPHIA FREEWAY

"This that real shit! Rofiki still hustle till the sun go down, crack a 40 when the sun go down..." This is what Rofiki do. The surveillance monitoring featured a picture frame mode that actually recorded and uploaded photos to a SD card from any PC computer. The same security system, Rofiki set up in North Philly to observe if nigga's was messing with his property or STARR trying to get more of her belongings. Double checking because he still didn't have his 'Black Book,' but had his laptop and everything packed and was O-U-T!

ADRIANA EVANS "7 Days" NOMADIC

"Baby, Baby, Baby, baby, baby." 7 days away from Big Tank (*Baby*) and 7 nig – ig -ights without loving him. (*Baby*) Like nights and days without no food. The week went by slow as Kandice sat sluggishly in the lonely apartment stressing. Cellphone cut off due to non-payment, no food and no money to order out, surviving off of romaine oodles of noodle and dry Cheerios cereal. Drinking water from the faucet was once taboo, now she was drinking glasses full as if it turned into wine.

No call from Big Tank and Rofiki was gone. Kandice remembered watching Rofiki go in and out the closets retrieving the vintage shabby black duffle bag, he kept locked with all the things he had of value and importance. Kandice didn't care, she had already been through it all and seen the envelope with STARR'S contract too. But one thing for sure, he was heading back to Philadelphia with an envelope filled with blank papers, she had all of the originals.

RHIANNA 'Rehab" GOOD GIRL GONE BAD

It's like she checked into rehab and Big Tank was her new drug. Popping pills to sleep the blues away, only to dream about it all over again, Rofiki, Big Tank, STARR, until Big Tank's personal assistant Cheryl *'The Pearl'* of Vicious Heat Records came banging at the door with informing that there was a pending lawsuits. Due to the sex video tape released that was all over the news and tabloids. Also, informing her that her #1 Video Vixen contract had be canceled. Everything was put on hold until things were straightened out legally.

There was also a new cellphone delivered and some money. The two huge security goons that also picked up the Hummer were right behind Cheryl. This looked like a good time for Kandice to hand her eviction notice with less than 24hr to evacuate. Cheryl looked at her and rolled her eyes not caring and handing it back, *"I am not here to collect bills, just delivering a message and care package."* Kandice tried smiling and bating her lashes at the big fine thugs that didn't crack a smile barking, *"Lay low and don't call Big Tank. He'll call you!"*

Now Kandice understood what Big Tank meant when he said he would get in touch. That meant other people will come by or call her, not him. She would do as instructed and stay out of sight, off the phone and away from Rofiki! Baffled after everyone left Kandice crawled out of her funk and got dressed regretting not having a home computer. She dressed in baggy jeans, a plain black hooded sweat jacket that Rofiki forgot to take (because it was in her dirty-clean clothes) and hurried to the nearest cybercafé. Her moment of fame was feeling like her moment of disaster.

DRAKE "Cameras / Good Ones Go Interlude)" TAKE CARE

Word on the road, it's the clique about to blow. Kandi Gyal ain't gotta run and tell nobody they already know. The internet was flooded with stories of the sex tape that had been released with Kandi Gyal and Big Tank! She thought Big Tank had set her up, but she knew who ever was involved would pay with their life for trying to destroy hers. She sat in shock with her mouth wide open. Browsing and reading social media sites and blogs on the internet made her feel nauseas.

The articles on the internet compared her to other celebrity's sex tapes that were released without consent. However, she also read how many celebrities benefited from the publicity of the release of a sex tape. The release of Pilar Hampton's sex tape in 2003 as well socialite and store-keeper Kay- Kay's sex tape in 2007 made by then-boyfriend Jay - Jay brought them to a new level of fame, leading to magazine covers, book deals, and reality TV series.

CIARA "Body Party" CIARA

Ohh, oooh, ohh, ohhh. Yeah, right there. No, right there (giggles) Kandi Gyal was having fun. She hope Big Tank was having fun too. Her body was his party, baby. Nobody's invited but him, baby... "Ohhhh," Continuing to read Kandice was oblivious of her surroundings and learned the surfacing of sex tapes have become so common that some are 'leaked' as a marketing tool to advance or establish a media career.

Reading and reading until her eyes burned, Kandice read that most celebrities try fighting the release in court to maintain deniability while still feeling their career benefits. Some celebrity took the route of openly releasing their tapes and benefiting directly from royalties as well as indirectly from the publicity. She also read that in 2004 professional wrestler Asia and her husband entered a distribution deal with Blue Light Videos for their home video collection. Asia later was cast on the VH1 reality show 'The Unreal Life.'

TREY SONGZ "Sex For Yo Stereo" TREY DAY

When men see Kandi Gyal in the videos, babe. Do she make their body go crazy? Or when they catch her in a magazine, baby. Do they rip her out and save her page. Engrossed in reading and headphones on and listening to JAZZ1CAFÉ to keep up with what was going with THE NEOSOUL STARR. Captivated in the articles Kandice didn't notice the stranger that was now gawking at her. Eyes glued to the computer screen she continued reading that Tammy Anderson and then-husband Tommy B. is known to have been in two different sex tapes. Tammy Anderson had various interludes from their honeymoon placed online by an adult internet entertainment company.

There was footage of many celebrities' sex tapes that had been circulating on the internet for many years. Photos of J. L. White engaging in unprotected sexual acts with another man published by gossip columnist Pierre Hampton's. Her mouth dropped watching videos of the former Senators sex tape that surfaced in early 2010, reportedly while his wife was pregnant.

MIGUEL "Vixen" ALL I WANT IS YOU

"She always said she wanted to become an actress"

Let's play a little game. Just between Big Tank and Kandi Gyal. Obviously physical. To please and entertain. Kandi Gyal can be Big Tank's vixen… Still reading Kandi Gyal was unaware of the time and that the cybercafé was closing. The next story fascinated her because she had seen the video and had been compared to Montana Firstborne, daughter of actor Laurence Firstborne. Who claims the rehearsal footage leaked which was never intended to be released. She performs again in an hour long features in a car, a hotel room and a shopping mall. Subsequently, at the age of 21, Firstborne started her own porn site, released a pay-per-view adult film titled Firstborn: *Catch Me On Video,* and commenced to tour the United States as a stripper.

JHENE AIKO "Hoe" SAILING SOUL(S)
(Featuring MIGUEL)

"I hope she don't think that I think that she's some kind of hoe"

Finally Kandice noticed the man a few seats away starring. When they made eye contact he smiled and said, "*I hope you don't think that I think that you're some kind of hoe. 'Cause I don't care I just bought your hot sexy DVD this morning - can I get your autograph!*" Moving fast Kandice didn't even reply hurrying past him and out the doors making sure he wasn't following. Basically running to call her cousin Abigail whom she hadn't spoken to since all the craziness at the JAZZ1CAFE interview.

It was now time to call Abigail in Philly, she answered on the first ring yelling *"Chica why you just calling mami?"* Abigail swiftly began telling Kandice about the sex tape with Big Tank sold at every other corner in Philadelphia. Also informing about the tabloids where Lil' Pam gave an interview saying Big Tank was a little tank in the pants and the video proved it and then there was the clip with her and Rofiki showing the Mandingo, Jamaican proud and bigger than any porno king.

KELLY ROWLAND "Kisses Down Low" TALK A GOOD GAME

Kandi Gyal liked her kisses down low making her arch her back. When he gave it to her slow. Baby just like that and now she was ready to kill him. Now everyone knew what they did behind closed doors and the fact that someone videotaped her every move. Now, desperately Kandice wanted to hang up the phone after hearing no pity in Abigail's voice that grew into laughter talking about Lil' Pam's interview about the mirrors in the video scenes. Kandice went dashing out in the pouring down rain without an umbrella. Stopping at the nearest news stand and was able to quickly grab the last tabloid that had a picture of her with Lil' Pam and Big Tank between them.

After paying the newsstand man yelled loud enough for all to hear, *"Hey you're Kandi Gyal– with Big Tank and Lil' Pam in that tabloid you just brought!"* Instantly Kandice was in the middle of some Bull- Shit over Bull-Shit! In front of her apartment building paparazzi popped out from behind cars and a man driving by yelled obscenity. Soaked and wet from the rain and fumbling with her keys unable to get in the building fast enough. A few cameras flashed multiple times and people were hurrying towards her with microphones, just as she unlocked the door.

NEYO "Mirror" IN MY OWN WORDS

"Love making love in front of the mirror
So that I can watch you enjoying me"

Back inside breaking mirrors and crying heavier then she had before. She know Rofiki and Big Tank loved making love in front of her big vanity mirrors. It was so unbelievable and stressful that a few hours later she escaped out the back alley with Abigail helping her stuff her stuff in her cousin's car and heading back to Philadelphia to rest. She assumed Rofiki must have found his way back to Philly to his STARR. After the embarrassment on 'SOULSHINE'S Radio Show' she had a score to settle with his ass.

TRACK 15: MOVE INTO MY GROOVE

The grand opening was a huge success and a high volume of customer after all the publicity behind the controversy at the JAZZ1 CAFÉ Internet Radio Station interview with SoulShine. And with all the ciaos behind STARR'S and Kandi Gyal's legal battles over their songs, Bluesy has been swarmed with work too busy to keep up. STARR was busy with rehearsals, meetings with lawyers and countless phone calls for interviews, studio work, performances, special guest appearances, and plenty of people trying to take her picture.

Everyone wanted the scoop and advised not to talk about the lawsuit, STARR'S attorney sent out the press releases. She had no problems keeping silent not wanting to be any part of the circus. Paparazzi was hanging around the coffee shop and following her and Bluesy everywhere. She was afraid to go to the café, because there were always someone blinding her with their flash of lights and asking her questions about her relationship with Rofiki and Kandice. She read an Article that insinuated that STARR, Kandice Gyal and Rofiki were in a love triangle fusing over some bullshit music.

ALICIA KEYS "Listen To Your Heart" GIRL ON FIRE

Bluesy says, 'Have no fear open up let me in." He say, "Take a chance here's your song time to dance." What STARR gonna do when it comes for her? Listen to her heart. Oh, she gotta listen to her heart. Listen to your heart. Oh, why don't she listen to her heart? He says, "Here's your sky don't look down we can fly". She said, "You're a little bit scared just hold on we're almost there." What she gonna do when it comes for her? Listen to her heart? Oh, she gotta listen to her heart!

After reading the articles, STARR needed to talk to someone. She thought of calling BearLove, but lately Mina had been answering his phone and she didn't want to hear the two of them fighting, because she was calling. She went against her better judgment and called BearLove and just as she assumed, Mina Answered. But before STARR could ask for him, Mina growled, "*Stop calling my man bitch!*" STARR hung up just needing some peace and quiet. Since the interview with SoulShine Session's things were even crazier. The publicity was good for the group but with the lawsuits no one could sell their music.

ERYKAH BADU *"Fall In Love (Your Funeral)"* NEW AMERYKAH PART 2: RETURN OF THE ANKH

Bluesy better go back the way he came. Run away, if he stay. Prepare to have his shit re-arranged. Before going to his parents, Bluesy drove over to Kelly Drive listening to JAZZ1CAFÉ and sitting on the edge of 'The Strawberry Mansion Bridge.' Yes, he could easily jump off the steel arch trust bridge and swim across the Schuylkill River in Fairmount Park and live to tell it all like a proud U.S. Marine, he would survive. He did all he could to keep everything from falling apart. Trying to handle Karen, JR, his parents, the business, STARR, and all while neglecting his health and over exhausting himself to conquer, fix, cure to help heal everyone else.

Making observations of automobiles driving east and west on Kelly drive, Bluesy admired the beautiful view of all the lights lighting up the houses on boat house row. Thinking of STARR made him reflect back to the first time she walked into the coffee shop, and then Rofiki. He inspected Rofiki too from head to toe. As a Marine would and looked him right straight in the eyes. Hearing Rofiki speaking Patwa the language Rasta's are especially known for. But, Jamaicans are not the only ones who speak Patwa. Most Caribbean people speak the language, so Bluesy didn't want to assume. He had also heard non Jamaicans speaking the language, but when he shouted, "*Jah Rastafari!*" Bluesy knew he was Jamaican.

ANGIE STONE *"U Lit My Fire"* RICH GIRL

If, Bluesy's cool with his loving dipped with STARR'S loving, they could do something and work it out. It would be so nice his turn, he'll just rise. What if her sweet walking walked into his sweet talking? The first time that he met her, baby. He knows she lit his fire. She lit his fire. Never asking any questions about STARR past and was glad she didn't talk about Rofiki or wasn't like most women comparing the world to their ex-boyfriends. He admired her for being brave enough to survive. She was the most amazing experience a man could experience in a woman, he was sure of that. Though it was all happening fast, he was holding on and not willing to let go. Then there was her friendship with Bear Love. A hellava wicked kick ass drummer, like no other drummer Bluesy ever seen. He had never felt anything distrusting about this man.

Knowing STARR'S magic was contagious, her beautiful lips that curve perfectly with each lyric, word, and syllable spoke or sung. BearLove had always been genuine in their greetings and never showed a prejudice sign. Not wanting to read too deep into their relationship, he put aside his Marine tactics. He assumed it would be the *same as dating an actress letting her go and play her role / part. He was happy to be blessed with happy new images in his mind rather than the bloody war daydreams and* nightmares.

GERD "Fire In My Soul" PERSPECTIVE
(Featuring MARILYN DAVID)

On fire, Bluesy soul and his body was burning hot, and it was like that for STARR. He entered his parent's house and they were sitting in the dining room with Karen, who was very high. He heard rumors about her hanging out in the local 'Rudy's Taverns', he witnessed her tip-toeing in the door with the day-light.

They were all sitting there waiting for him to come in the door. Bluesy's mother was the first one screaming at him. *"How could you do this to Karen? Blame her for going to that girl's house for a kitten for your son. The same woman dancing and singing in the café all and all over the news about some radio station! All this for a woman that wiggles her and sing to other men!"* His father joined in, *"You have a good woman waiting here for you every night and now you don't come home at all."*

Shaking like a leaf getting ready to get blown off the branch and far away from the tree, Karen took a long swig of her morning hot toddy. Black coffee laced with Sambuca hitting the spot before intervening and pleading, *"Please everyone let me talk to my husband alone."* Bluesy spoke up, *"No I am not your husband and conversation finished!"* Karen began to cry, *"How can you do this to me. Why did you divorce me? What about your son!?Our son!"*

Miserable, Bluesy never meant to hurt J.R, but he wasn't his junior. He believed STARR was carrying his junior though she was denying and hiding it and everyone needed to hear the truth. Karen stood up moaning into a cry and into a song letting him know that he did not know what love is.

MARILYN SCOTT "You Don't Know What Love Is" HANDPICKED (BILLY HOLIDAY)

Bluesy don't know what love is. Until he has learned the meaning of the blues. Until he has loved a love he had to lose. He don't know what love is. Remaining to stand Bluesy voice was firm and final! *"Karen I know my parents are fond of you. But, we have not been together in years. Then you pop up because of whatever reasons. But I had to find out the truth about what I wanted for me. Not what my parents want to for me. I am in Love with STARR and I will marry her as soon as possible."*

Hysterically Karen began to cry and ripped up the copy of divorce papers she received. *"I will never let you be with that Black Bitch! When I leave you will never see your son again."* Bluesy didn't like threats and especially towards STARR. Lashing out he shouted, *"If Maury Povich was reading the results he would say - In the case of 5 year old Junior – I AM NOT the father! J.R. is not my son he is your son! Here are the paternity test papers and your copy will arrive today. You will never be able to threaten me using an innocent child."*

ZO! "Black Cow" JUST VISTING THREE (Featuring PHONTE and SY SMITH) (STEELEY DAN)

"So outrageous - So outrageous - So outrageous"

So outrageous Bluesy can't cry anymore while Karen run around, while his family and friends in the neighborhood see it too. Break away, just when it seems so clear that he is in love with STARR. That it's over now Karen, and she can drink her big black cow and get out of there.

Leaping up Karen and knocking breakfast plates off the table, sending scrambled eggs everywhere screaming like 'The Diary of a Mad White Woman' shouting, *"You're lying! You had someone make up false papers so that you don't have to be responsible for your son."* His mother began cleaning up the eggs and trying to calm down Karen. His father became silent watching the women feuding with his son. His mother scowled low and deep in her South Philly Catholics beliefs praying, *"Oh St. Andrew protect our family. My son you could never marry a Negro and take my grandson away from me I would die!"*

MICHAEL FRANKS "I don't Know Why I'm So Happy I'm Sad" THE ART OF TEA

So happy Bluesy is sad, he's in trouble seeing double. Their like a scene from the 'African Queen.' The night Bluesy met STARR he became unglued. He is so happy and sad, yes he is, and yes he is. Head spinning and Bluesy's heart hit the ground hearing his mother calling STARR a Negro and claiming death! He had to push the emergency button that would save him from hurting his mother's feelings forever. He knew his words would be felt deeper than his actions and he already made up his mind.

Nothing could be said that could stop Bluesy from being his own man. Trying to be respectful as he spoke, *"Please call me when you have made it welcoming for me to visit and when I come back with my new wife you will respect her and your future African American grandchildren."* His father spoke up and it wasn't often his father intervened surprisingly shouting, *"Semper Fidelis! You're my son darnit! I understand you have to live your own life – go live it!"* Bluesy was about to intervene with an outburst of obscenity. But, choked back hearing his father's approval.

Then his father turned to Karen responding with sympathy and impatience, *"We'll help you find a place by the end of the week. Leave my son to have peace in his life that is what he went to WAR for. I can't let my son not enjoy his life after the wars he already fought for us serving the United States Marines. He didn't come home to fight against his parents and lies. Please stay away from his coffee shop – and stay away from the girl - No need for embarrassment – You have a great kid. Nobody will be against my son – my flesh and blood!"*

AMY WINEHOUSE *"Tears Dry On Their Own"* BACK TO BLACK

"He walks away, the sun goes down
He takes the day but I'm gone
And in your way in this blue shade
My tears dry on their own"

It was endearing when his father once a Marine too stood up for him saying, *"Semper Fidelis."* Agreeing and remaining faithful to the mission at hand, to each other, to the Corps and to his country, no matter what Bluesy loved STARR. He turned to leave with his mother consoling Karen's tears and yelling, *"Son please come back!"* He left fast not believing his mother chose to side with a woman that cared nothing about him. He would never understand everything, but he loved his parents and knew they loved him too.

INCOGNITO *"Blue (I'm Still Here With You)"* WHO NEEDS LOVE

"I could talk 'til my face turns blue
But do I have the heart to breakaway and make a change"

Back at the new apartment on top of the new coffee café, STARR paced the floors of the Philadelphia stylish apartment in the historic section of North Philadelphia, neighboring Temple University. STARR couldn't believe she moved in for good. She was now living right there on top of the café and in the middle of it all.

Until the 'For Sale' sign went up on the building, STARR hid out a few hours during the day in West Philly to feed the cats and played with the kittens until T. Vernell the mystery woman from the first floor sold the building and surprisingly the Jenki's were gone. They moved and left all their trash and cats behind, including Big G. Leaving her no choice but to take all the cats to the S.P.C.A.

Stressing and blue, what's a girl to do? STARR'S stressing and she's blue, but still she's still with Bluesy. It's easy to say that she's leaving, but harder to ignore the feeling. They both know they don't want nobody else. Growing tired of all the reporters and paparazzi stalking around the coffee shop trying to get her to talk about the lawsuit against Kandi Gyal and now there was a sex tape with Big Tank and the reality television show '#1 Video Vixen' had lawsuits from all 19 of the other contestant claiming they were unjustly represented, since Kandi Gyal wins on the final episode not yet televised. STARR had nothing to do with that 'Bull – Shit' she had her own bullshit.

Trying to relax and clear the way for new energy STARR sat on the new hardwood floors spread out a Yoga mat. In a relaxing 'Zen' pose remembering everything she learned from the Yoga videos on 'YouTube.' Kneeling on the mat STARR lowered her buttocks onto the soles of her feet. Bringing her big toes together and she lowered her arms down and placed her hands on her knees with her palms down. She read that yoga increases efficiency of digestive system, strengthens the pelvic muscles, directing sexual energy to the brain for meditation purposes and introduces tranquility into her mental and physical body.

ANANDA PROJECT "Many Starred Sky" FIRE FLOWER

In a seated pose, STARR allowed her spine and head to straighten, but not tense. Noticing not to arch backwards or slumping forward keeping balanced. Relaxing her entire body, she closed her eyes and concentrated on her breathing and following the gentle stream of air passing in and out of her nostrils. Feeling how sweet and smooth the air felt coming into her lungs and feeling how her ribcage and diaphragm was expanding. After stretching she was feeling a little better.

Earlier in the day BearLove canceled the rehearsal so STARR assumed he was still going through his Bull – Shit with Mina. Looking at the time counting every tick it had been a couple of hours past the time Bluesy was expected back and she was tired of worrying, so she called his phone and no answer. He said he was going to pick up something from his parent's house, she couldn't recall what he was picking up.

In deep thoughts, STARR thought about the incident with Karen and the son Bluesy almost had. She knew Bluesy loved his parents and pained him not to be able to talk about them. She wished she knew a better way to communicate and not hate them for hating her, so she could enjoy the stories about his past that make him smile. She tried to understand their point of views, but *"Bull shit ain't nothing but chewed up grass"* they should be respectful too.

MARSHA AMBROSIUS "I Hope She Cheat On You (With A Basketball Player)" LATE NIGHTS & EARLY MORNINGS

STARR hope Kandi Gyal cheat on Rofiki with a NBA basketball playa. Hope that she Kim Kardashian'ed her way up. Don't know the difference 'tween a touchdown and a layup. She may sound bitter, she's a little bitter, just a little bitter because he was with her. The sun went down and darkness entered the living room, STARR didn't turn on the lights, but lifted the shades allowing more moonlight in the new place.

Listening to JAZZ1CAFÉ and curling up on the new sofa. She couldn't help but have flash backs of Rofiki and his new chick Kandi Gyal. The sofa was delivered in the late afternoon and she was there to sign for it as planned, but didn't plan to be sitting in an empty apartment with bare walls projecting flash backs of the past running through her mind. Remembering all the nights Rofiki left her waiting.

EDDY MEETS YANNAH "Take A Little Trip" FICTION JAR (MINNIE RIPERTON)

"Take another trip on a magic carpet ride
Take a little trip through your mind and explore it
Take a closer look at the you, you're tryin' to hide"

Watching the shadows of the trees dancing on the newly painted golden walls, she got up and lit candles, though there was now electricity. She was feeling under the weather blaming it on her nervous and missing a couple of periods wasn't unusual. She noticed her weight gain was 10 pounds heavier since Rofiki left. Yeah that was all due to Bluesy's delicious pound cakes and the countless dinner dates. She also had her own money and making her own food choices to eat whatever she wanted and when she wanted. This is what freedom taste like to her. Rubbing her belly still ailing from lunch, she felt nausea.

"Do-dodo-do-dodo-do... Dah-dahdah-dah... Ha-Ah!" Wanting to puff, but no weed. *She wondered if this was just another trap, another world of restrictions with no place to run.* She thought about her parents knowing she never knew who her father was, a subject taboo to $hantey Money. Though all the publicity with the song, STARR thought by now, they would have found her mom. She needed talk to Bluesy about hiring a private detective. Her thoughts were interrupted when she heard him unlocking the door.

WALTER BEASLEY "Barrack's Groove" FREE YOUR MIND

Confused watching Bluesy enter the apartment smiling like he just been elected president or hit the lottery. STARR joked about it. Bluesy spoke eagerly, "*Yes I have hit the lottery of Love and I come to claim my prizes.*" He was holding up a white paper bag in his hand. She looked closer and noticed it was a pharmacy bag. Concerned and still confused she asked, "*What do you need medicine for?*" His happy expression explained he wasn't sick. He said, "*It's not for me it's for you.*" Now, she was really confused opening the bag and pulling out another home pregnancy test.

Yes, Mother Nature has not visited and her period was very late. Blaming it on the stress with everything going on, she had been feeling the morning sickness and was starting to blame paparazzi, but she had these symptoms before and just like before she would never be able to carry a baby. Hysterical – upset and mad she jumped up off the new sofa shouting "*A BABY? Who said I wanted a baby? What is wrong with you? Why would you keep giving me pregnancy test like it is some damn joke? I don't have time for this! I am not pregnant. I can't get pregnant. I don't want to be pregnant. I won't get pregnant. And if I did get pregnant I would not...*"

Now, Bluesy jumped up hysterical and nervous stopping STARR from saying it. He would never want to hear her say, she didn't want to have is baby. He didn't want to hear her say that she would abort their baby.

BEBEL GILBERTO "Baby" BEBEL GILBERTO

"*Baby- baby,*" With Bluesy, he felt everything would be fine it was time for STARR to make up her mind, he loves her! Choking back tears and with a heavy heart he shouted back, "*Don't say it STARR. I would never let you abort our child.*" STARR calmed down softening her voice with empathy for the subject of abortion. Explaining with the compassion that she held for each child she lost or could not conceive. "*I would never abort my child. Don't say that again I am totally against that too. Let me finish explaining - if I did get pregnant I would not be able to carry full term. I have been to the doctors about this because of the 3 previous miscarriages. I had the last miscarriage a few weeks before I met you. I...*"

Cutting off STARR'S sentence off with a kiss. Bluesy loved STARR and was ready to live a clean and open life with her. No skeletons in their closets. He handed STARR the pharmacy bag and she didn't say anything since, she really did have to pee bad. She took the test to the bathroom and did as instructed peeing on the stick. They watched the two blue lines appear that meant the test was + she was pregnant. Bluesy was tearfully cheering, *"I'm gonna be a daddy!"*

GREGG KARUKAS *"Soul Kisses"* GK

After long soul kisses Bluesy rubbed STARR'S belly and said, *"Hey Bluesy Jr. this is daddy."* STARR put her hand over his. Though she wasn't happy about the moment with BearLove though, she wasn't really sure what happened. Shaking the thoughts out of her head saying, *"What if it is a Bluzette?"* Bluesy kissed her stomach and began to talk to their unborn baby, *"Well, little Bluesy, Bluzette, blue, black and brown, pink, red, yellow or white I will always love you all right."*

MOET *"Jr. Butterfly"* MOET MEETS BLUEY

Feeling the fluttering of butterflies in her belly as if a baby was agreeing to Bluesy's hand rubbing her belly, he felt it too. Bluesy kneeled next to her saying, *"Let's pray together - Let's pray for a healthy baby."* It was all so emotional. After praying and getting their emotions together Bluesy held on to her stomach feeling her smooth skin and then wrapped his fingers around her long strands of hair. STARR enjoyed the attention of his fingers and kisses so passionately. When they came up for air with smiles reciprocally they sang, *"I Love you!"*

LIZZ WRIGHT *"Fire"* SALT

Is Bluesy frightened by the fire in her eyes? It burns for him and she know he see it too. Take the fire, he don't have to give it back to STARR. The following morning Bluesy found that someone had smashed his truck window. He didn't let that stop him from moving forward. He called his insurance company and contacted his attorney and went to the police station to file a restraining order against Karen, who was no longer living with his parents and they didn't know where she was. After getting his window fixed Bluesy hurried back to the café and found everything running smoothly. Jonathan the new assistant manager was doing just fine and was the help Bluesy's cafe needed.

BILL LAURANCE "Swag Time" FLINT

Later that evening Bluesy unlocked the apartment doors to find STARR in the empty kitchen fussing on the phone with Karen, who now had their new home phone number. Now on the other end Karen was trying to sound threatening. *"Look sister girl, what make you think? I'm going to sit back and let you take my husband. I love him and I'm pregnant again!"* STARR was not ready for this conversation, but she needed to put an end to this woman's nonsense saying, *"Well I have a revelation for you too sistah -wanna be girl. Not you or his mother or father can change that. I think it is time for you to move on and use common sense."*

KYOTO JAZZ MASSIVE "ME Outroduction" SPIRIT OF THE SUN

Losing her mind and heart broken Karen was screaming at STARR, *"I will bury you before I let you have him."* STARR had enough of the conversation shouting back, *"Think about your actions before you try to bring it to my house. Let me make this clear I'm right here!"* Bluesy heard enough and took the phone and with red face and fury screeching, *"Don't call again I already filed a restraining order against you."* Karen hung up.

Holding each other not letting anything stand in the way of their future. STARR'S head was against Bluesy's chest thinking how good it felt knowing, she would be a mother. She didn't need a diamond ring or big house to prove it. She would raise 10 babies in that apartment if she could. Feeling the energy of each other Bluesy said, *"I'm sorry to bring this on you and get you involved. I won't let our baby be born into this nonsense, please trust me. We're family and I want you to know our children will not be born out of wedlock. We have to go in city hall."* STARR smiled loving the sound of children – her family.

MAYSA "Feel The Fire" FEEL THE FIRE
(STEPHANIE MILLS)

Something that STARR told Bluesy. Stayed in his head all night long. *"Feel the fire, feel the fire, feel the fire."* The next morning they woke up to a hard knock on the door. Bluesy didn't expected the delivery men to come so early. STARR was brushing her teeth when they delivered a new baby crib and changing table.

Flat screen televisions and more. With a mouth full of tooth paste she stood confused. She had no idea what was going on. As the men brought the boxes into the 2nd floor apartment Bluesy said, *"Your new furniture arrived."* STARR looked at him as if he was crazy. She began really beginning to think he hit the lottery and joked about it. Bluesy replied reading her mind jokingly replied again, *"I hit the Lottery of Love."* Sincerely, STARR looked at Bluesy and asked, *"Bluesy how are we going to afford this stuff. We don't need a crib this soon – It's bad luck to buy stuff like that."* Bluesy was in a good mood explaining, *"More coming soon."*

GREGG KARUKAS "Believe In Me" GK

Watching STARR'S expressions turn puzzled that scared look Bluesy was now familiar with. He announced, *"We have a doctor appointment tomorrow maybe that will make you feel better."* Affection was new to her and she was amazed at how Bluesy immediately responded to caring for her with such sincere love and affection. She spoke aloud to GOD, but for Bluesy to hear tilting her head towards the heavens (ceiling) saying, *"GOD I know I prayed for this special man and I appreciate him, thank you!"* She kissed him a million times. The delivery men were even laughing and enjoying and addressed her as Mrs. That tickled her pink.

After all the boxes where in the 2nd bedroom Bluesy announced that until the baby was born STARR could use the bedroom as a home studio. Looking around at all the boxes feeling like she hit the lottery too and asking, *"How did you know what to buy?"*

KENNY LATTIMORE "Never Too Busy" KENNY LATTIMORE

More than a lover, Bluesy was a friend and he was *"Never too Busy"* for STARR. He wanted to be a blessing too and confessed, *"A few months ago I brought a book for home recording studios for dummies. I thought I would try to figure out what exactly you would need to be able to have a space where you could go and create. Also in the book was an inventory list for recording studios and I shopped around in music and computer stores."*

Remembering everything he learned from the how to recording studio books, he walked into the big walk in closet and turned on the light showing her that the closet was also sound proofed and could be used as a vocal sound booth. This way she could come in the closet and sing even if the baby was asleep. The glass front door was now explainable. Pulling STARR out the closet Bluesy opened her new laptop computer explaining the programs downloaded. *"The program is a streamlined digital audio work station and music sequencer that can record and play back multiple tracks of audio."*

YAHZARAH "Fire Fly" HEAR ME

Searching for a higher meaning. In what really makes no sense. Yeah – eah, work for higher living. She's waiting for a *"Fire Fly"* to shine some light on her. Wow, how Bluesy was shining light on STARR. Shocked with her mouth wide open exposing her tonsils – speechless and of course still listening wanting to hear more.

Excitedly Bluesy continued, *"Wait I'm not finished and you can easily edit audio, MIDI and music notation. The home studio is the complete solution for creating professional quality music."* After sounding like a commercial and helping STARR close her mouth with a kiss and a big hug she choked back tears and kissed his bald head, before sitting next to him so he could explain more. He even brought a keyboard that she didn't know how to play, but knew she would learn, microphones and stands, books and more.

MAYSA "I Can't Help It" FEEL THE FIRE (MICHAEL JACKSON)

"I can't help it if I wanted to
I wouldn't help it even if I could
I can't help it if I wanted to
I wouldn't help it, no..."

Later that evening STARR stood in the doorway looking around at everything and the baby crib in the corner sitting and waiting to be put together, but may never be used, though the doctor visit in the morning would assured her that she was pregnant. STARR was feeling the effects of the Lottery of Love. She hurried back to bed where Bluesy was already asleep.

LIZZ WRIGHT "Wake Up Little Sparrow" DREAMING WIDE AWAKE

"Wake up, wake up little sparrow
Don't make your home out in the snow
Don't make your home out in the snow"

7 O'clock in the morning snowflakes were fluttering and building up against the window panes, and Bluesy and STARR awoke to FIRE ALARMS! Instantly they jumped up out of the bed running into the living room noticing the smoke coming in from the café entrance. Rushing they immediately grabbed their clothes from the night before, STARR also grabbed her new laptop, She knew Bluesy wanted to grab the crib, but they ran down the back steps, praying everything would be safe, only to be greeted with smoke, they choked their way out the door seeing nothing but blue flames and black smoke.

It was a horrible 5 alarm fire, but thank GOD no one was hurt. In an hour everything was gone, the café, the second floor apartment, the new crib and home recording studio. Their new life all up in smoke. They were not allowed back into the building to see what could be salvaged. But, Bluesy would be allowed to return later to board up the first floor windows that were broken out by the firemen, in case of looters. They had to reschedule STARR'S doctor appointment to meet with his Insurance Company representative and were told not to worry.

Materialistic things were the last thing on Bluesy's mind, but there was one thing he had in the café hidden and had to get. He was told that there was no reason for him to even come back to the café. The building would probably have to be demolished and built back up from the ground. After hearing that he knew he had to get into the cafe.

SADE "War Of The Hearts" PROMISE

"It's a war of the hearts (It's a war of the hearts) It's a war of the hearts"

Bluesy got a bullet to spare. Don't wanna send it Karen's way. Who's calling the shots? One of us must make the peace *(One of us)*. To have or to have not. The fire has got to cease. He already ended it. It was a little after midnight and Bluesy's hadn't heard from STARR since he dropped her off at a rehearsal at BearLove's, were he felt she would be safe with the whole band and Mina there patrolling her man. He got caught up with trying to salvage things in the building, hunting people down, making phone calls and then a late talk with his parents.

THE ROOTS "The Fire" HOW I GOT OVER
(Featuring JOHN LEGEND)

There's something in STARR'S heart and it's in her eyes. It's the fire, inside her, let it burn. She don't say good luck she say, *"Don't give up. It's the fire, inside you, Let it burn."* After not returning any of Bluesy's phone calls, STARR finally texted she was rehearsing for the grand reopening of JAZZ1CAFÉ RESTAURANT. He texted back that he was with parents and if she need he, he was available. Exhausted and happy that his bed was still upstairs in his parent's house. Though he found it hard to sleep knowing STARR was not with him.

CHAKA KHAN "Through The Fire" I FEEL FOR YOU

"Through the fire, to the limit
Through the fire, through whatever"

The following morning STARR assumed they were going to the coffee shop to see the damages, but noticing they were driving in a different direction she asked, *"Where are we going?"* He looked over and winked at and started singing and begging, *"Please sing for me STARR."* He never asked her to sing for him and she appreciated that about him. He didn't love her just for her voice. But she knew he enjoyed good music. She gladly sung for him at his request.

After singing Chaka Khan, STARR turned the music down and asked, *"Where are we going?"* Bluesy smiled and said, *"We're here."* Pulling into a parking lot STARR looked around having no idea where she was. He got out and walked around to open the car door for her, *"We're at the doctor's office."* STARR had completely forgot about the appointment with the OGBYN Dr. B. As Bluesy assured her that everything would be okay, he held her hand letting her know he was going to be there every step. *"I want to be sure that our baby growing in your belly is taken care of."*

Speechless and scared to face reality, STARR didn't want to hurt from losing another baby. She agreed, *"Okay daddy, and our next* stop is *your doctor's office to get your headaches checked out.* He grinned and said, *"Come on and let's take care of our family."* Hearing her call him *'daddy'* was all he wanted to hear. As expected STARR was very pregnant and Bluesy called his doctor at the Veterans Hospital and was scheduled for a MRI. They drove off happy and ready to be a family.

TEENA MARIE "Marry Me" CONGO SQUARE

STARR don't think Bluesy heard her, She's gonna say it once again, *"Marry me, marry me, marry me, baby, yeah. And make a respectable woman out of me."* She noticed that they were heading towards center city. They parked and walked towards City Hall. STARR followed Bluesy not having any idea what he was doing. Holding a tight grip to STARR's hand, Bluesy walked her to 'Love Park.' Located across the street from City Hall began telling the history. *"The plaza, designed by famed City Planner Edmond Bacon, father of actor Kevin Bacon, was originally constructed over an underground parking garage in 1965. The plaza expanded in 1969 with the addition of beautifully curved granite steps and a majestic fountain."*

IMPROMP 2 "I Wanna Marry U" IT IS WHAT IT IS
(Featuring JUDITH HILL)

"I want to marry you, I want to be with you, do yo feel the same way I do?" Finding the nerves to propose, Bluesy didn't have a ring, and of course STARR said yes! Strangers looked upon and clapping could be heard as they kissed forever. After the kiss Bluesy took STARR by the hand again leading, her across the street into City Hall. They went into

an office and Bluesy told the person at the counter, *"We are here to apply for a marriage license."*

Leaving City Hall they stopped in front of jewelry store windows looking at all the beautiful rings, Bluesy tried to go inside the stores to pick out something. STARR smiled and said, *"You are my diamond."* Bluesy kissed her and they heard a few school kids giggling at them. Then Bluesy blushed, *"We will have matching wedding bands. I will wear mine like I wear my soul."* STARR began to tear. Bluesy words were so moving to her. She said, *"Surprise me, I like your surprises."*

TRACK 16: DON'T DISTURB THIS GROOVE

THE SYSTEM *"Don't Disturb This Groove"* DON'T DISTURB THIS GROOVE

"Hang the sign upon the door, say, don't disturb this groove. Just a way to say that, STARR is so into Bluesy and the feelings so real, so don't disturb this groove!" It was the day of the big concert @ JAZZ1CAFÉ the grand reopening after the fire renovations and 'THE NEOSOUL STARRS' have been working none stop, all day, all night and now the clock was ticking. STARR slept in late tired and exhausted from rehearsals, nauseas and life, but excited about the big concert and live video recording was going to take place regardless of the pending lawsuits. Her garment bag was ready and hanging in the closet.

Weak and still tired Bluesy woke having funky feelings and hurried to get dressed, moving about quietly not wanting to disturb her sleep. He kissed her forehead while taking deep sniffs of her scent. Wanting her to get all the rest she needed, because it was her big night! He hurried out to the door to his attorney's office to pick up some confidential information.

KIM HILL *"Sunny Blue"* SUGAHILL

Oh Sunny, Sunny, Sunny, Blue. Oh those eyes make STARR sticky just like glue. Before she knows it, she won't have a clue. Bluesy's eyes were looking at her. She wanted to have his baby. No one else in this whole wide world could make her feel this such. Bluesy retuned and couldn't wait to show the information received from his Attorney. He explained, *"I stopped by my attorney's office and have information about your family."*

Sitting motionless, STARR wondering if she heard Bluesy. Watching her intently as he spoke, *"I haven't looked at the information. If you want to look at it alone that would be fine."* She replied softly as her eyes narrowed in on the folder. *"My family? We're family, I have family? We can look at it together."*

URSULA RUCKERS "L.O.V.E." MA'AT MAMA

"On this day there will be no talk of war or politic or disaster or death. Love is alive today, so speak only of L.O.V.E." They looked over all the paper work as STARR showed no expression. Bluesy told her that the attorney did inform him that they should have some more information soon. STARR closed the folder and began flicking channels with the remote like nothing ever happened. There was no need to ask her any questions, because he read the information too. Watching STARR become busy with trying to get herself together for the big night, Bluesy worried she showed no expressions and went about as if she didn't just read the information about her family. He did reach out to give her a hug, but said she was alright moving away.

Putting the envelope in a safe place STARR knew it was a few hours away from sound check and she couldn't let nothing new mess up her head. Yes, she read the information and the first thing in the morning, she will deal with it. But there was nothing she could do about it now. Tending to Bluesy and giving him a few ibuprofen to stop the migraine, before falling asleep, he asked start to remind him to send money to his employees as severance pay and thanking them for their love and support.

THE BAYLOR PROJECT "More in Love" THE BAYLOR PROJECT

"How can I be more? How can I be more? In love with you?"

Tear drops stained the folder as STARR privately wept in the bathroom while taking a shower. She loved Bluesy and every day she was falling more and more in love. "But, why GOD?" She pleaded in prayers, *"GOD I'm so confused. Why do pain keep haunting me?"* Hearing Bluesy calling her name she dried off and came out the bathroom.

Noticing Bluesy's eyes open when she came out the bathroom, she slid behind him snuffling up to his warm back whispering, *"Are you feeling better?"* Bluesy rolled over to face her and held her tight. Let her know he was happy to have her next to him, but he was upset. His voice broke with huskiness, *"I'm – I'm messed up in the head! Yes, I'm stressing about the fire and my parents who are in their seventies and though they don't complain, I know they're both ailing. I'm concerned about your wellbeing,* our baby and where we're going to live?" Knowing, I should be thankful we're all still here with lungs full of air."

JANITA "I Only Want You" SEASONS OF LIFE

"I only want you, I only want you, I only want you, you, you! Why can't I just have you?" Turning around to face STARR so he can look into her alluring earth brown eyes and managed a small tentative smile as he continued, *"Babe, I can't put my emotions into material things and a building that can be rebuilt. I'm upset because I feel the fire was deliberately set while we were both in the building!"* His facial expressions turned into a worried explaining, *"STARR, I have a plan and it is a great plan. I am not going back into the coffee business. We're going into the music business."*

Shocked to hear him rattling on about how to make her dreams come true after he just lost his. Bluesy sat up on the side of the bed and wouldn't let STARR get a word in stopping her every time she tried to talk or ask a question. Bluesy continued, *"They told me there was no reason for me to even return to the cafe and I got the few personal things I could savage. In fact I picked up the insurance check, since it was declared an electrical fire and condemned. But, my gut feeling are telling me it was arson, I plan to find out. In the meantime, I want to start looking for a house that will also have enough space for you and the baby and a home recording studio."*

BEADY BELLE "Tranquil Flight" BELVEDERE

Tell STARR a tale and lull her to sleep. She'll walk into 'The Vale of Wonderland' so deep. Quickly, STARR had to interrupt because Bluesy was talking fast about the things that would make her happy. All she wanted was for him to be happy. There was a slight tinge of confusion in her voice, *"Bluesy there are other options we can make. That is if we are making decisions together. Right now I want you to relax and let's just start making plans and decisions that are not rushed."*

Touching STARR'S shinny long wavy strands of hair Bluesy purred out his heart. *"You have no idea how much you mean to me. I want to be a happy family."* Getting up and walking over to his coat, Bluesy pulled something out his pocket and as he was saying, *"This is the most precious thing I was able to save from the fire, STARR will..."*

Interrupted by a knock at the door was the pizza delivery man interrupting them and the excitement of curing STARR'S cravings for Hawaiian pizza, pineapples and diced turkey ham and slivered slices of toasted almonds and black olive, she craved day and night. After she ate, she noticed, Bluesy had quickly fell asleep. STARR turned the music up in her headphones playing JAZZ1CAFE Internet Radio to escape his snoring. Happy to see him finally resting. She had plenty to do getting ready for show time @ JAZZ1CAFÉ.

ZERO 7 "In the Waiting Line" SIMPLE THINGS

"Everyone's saying different things to me - Different things to me..."

Kandi Gyal, Kandice, Kandi was wait in line 'till her time. Ticking clock everyone stop. Everyone's saying different things to Kandice. After weeks of having funky feelings, Kandice finally got the call she was waiting for and Rofiki had been located. It had been confirmed that he was inside the bar and 20 minutes later Kandice pulled up and now they were all outside parked and just waiting.

While following and driving solo in Abigail's car and talking on prepaid phones to Noriega and Jorge, Kandice was orchestrating the plan. Rofiki was caught coming out of a corner bar on 29th Street in North Philadelphia. Kandice listened to every word Rofiki said, when he used to brag about his hang out spots in North Philly.

N'DAMBI "Imitator" PINK ELEPHANT

"So go on see you later
You're not the man I used to know
You're an Imitator"

Thinking of the trust she had for the imitator Rofiki, Kandice was absolutely positively sure that Rofiki he would be close to the bar. She didn't know exactly where his mother lived, and he kept that a holy secret. But she remembered him mentioning the bar was close to his mother's crib. Kandice didn't know anything personally about STARR. Once or twice she tried asking questions, but Rofiki would just cut her off replying, *"Na STARR meh homey – just business."* But now she knew it was more than business, she heard everything STARR said while crashing the radio interview.

TRIBALJAZZ "La Tormenta" TRIBALJAZZ

Parking a few cars in front of Kandice sitting in a van was Noriega and his cousin Jorge. They were friends they grew up with and would do anything for Kandice, but more interested in making money. Noriega always had a big crush on Kandice and she was using that to her advantage.

They watched Rofiki exit the bar and as soon as he walked past the van Jorge asked him for a light and when Rofiki handed him a lighter they used a stun gun subduing him with electric shock disrupting Rofiki's muscle functions. Before he could comprehend what was going on, Noriega knocked him out with one punch. Everything was going according to plan. They tossed Rofiki in the back of the van and drove off.

In the back of the van Noriega bragged about his one punch knockout, as he tied Rofiki's hands and feet together, they put a pillow case over his head. Adrenaline was flowing as Kandice stayed on the phone talking to Jorge and trailing behind the van. Jorge instructed her to drive ahead and meeting at the spot and let them handle things alone.

There was no need for Kandice to be any more involved, but she refused to stop following them yelling in the cellphone, *"Hell no! I'm staying right behind you in case that nigga tries to jump out. I will be sure to run over his ass and every one of his dread – locks!"* Keeping an eye out making sure they were not being followed by anyone and no cops. They made complete stops at every stop sign and yellow lights. Proceeding with caution they turned into the cemetery.

ROLAND KOVAC ORCHESTRA "Northern Lights" SOUND OF THE CITY BERLIN

Turning off the van lights Jorge and Noriega knew from experience to be very careful in the cemetery. That was where the police brought you when they wanted to whip your ass for 'GP,' General Purpose. Kandice followed their lead and turned off the car lights. It was so dark they almost couldn't see their hands in front of their face. She didn't have to question her own actions, she was sure she wanted him dead after finding out he was the one involved in recording and selling the sex tape. She knew there was no turning back with Noriega and Jorge.

Adjusting her eyes in the darkness Kandice watched them pull Rofiki out the car. She stayed in the car listening to Jorge arguing with Noriega, *"Don't turn into a bitch now! It's too late for that. Let's just shoot his ass so we can be out!"* Rofiki was now conscious and trying to speak. Every time he spoke, Jorge punched him up side his head. Noriega came over to the car and opened the door to let Kandice out. She was now having second thoughts about being in the cemetery it was spooking her. He wrapped his arm around her waist and said, *"You wanted to be here and you want it done so you're going to pull the trigger!"*

THE CINEMATIC ORCHESTRA "Familiar Grounds"
CITY LOUNGE VOL. 4 DISC 3

Out of the car and standing a few feet from Rofiki, Kandice was whispering to Noriega, *"Fuck no, I paid your asses to do this shit."* He put his gun in Kandice's hand and held on too. He insisted, *"You want reality TV, well this is your initiation into the Philly Rican Bad Girls Club."* Kandice began to shake but she didn't let go of the gun. Wondering what if the information she got was wrong. What if Rofiki had nothing to do with the sex tape? But she knew he had everything to do with it. She figured he had set the camera up in her apartment and taped them together too.

Barking demands Jorge pushed Rofiki to walk further into in to the grave yard. Rofiki started begging for forgiveness. Jorge yelled, *"Walk until, I tell you to stop and don't try to run."* He pushed Rofiki to step further and then moved so Kandice wouldn't accidentally shot him as Noriega fussed, *"Stop bull-shitting and shoot his ass."* Kandice pulled her hand free from the gun saying, *"I'm paying you both and one of you better do it."* Rofiki knew instantly when he heard the voice it was Kandi Gyal.

Praying for a miracle to come his way, Rofiki was scared and pissing out all the Heineken beers that was in his bladder. He had no idea where he was or where he was walking. He felt the ground unleveled in many areas as he continued to walk. He was confused and could feel that he was walking on grass. He could hear their voices a few feet behind him. He made a nervous attempt to speak. He needed to plea to Kandi Gyal for help and for reconsideration about what she was doing. He spoke again begging to JAH and her, *"JAH have mercy - Please Kandice not dis meh not want to end like dis' leave meh where ever meh is."*

THE TAO GROOVE *"Cha Cha Cha 57"* FRESH GOOD

Telling Rofiki to walk was like a dance step, 2-3-walk-walk-walk-2-3- cha-cha-cha. Then Jorge's voice came fast behind Rofiki growling thuggishly, *"Your ass is in the cemetery your new home!"* Rushing him to the ground causing Rofiki to hit his head on a tomb stone. Blood oozed out of a large gash on Rofiki's forehead. Rofiki was unconscious or dead, they weren't sure.

Hearing something that sounded like a loud car engine that was in a short distance. Jorge pulled out his cellphone trying to use the light and spotted a fresh grave that was dug and prepared for a funeral the following morning. They drug Rofiki's body to the open grave. Mad they didn't get a chance to shoot him. Shinning the light down the six – feet hole they noticed that a cement crate had already been placed into the ground. Hearing the car engine growing closer they pushed Rofiki's body into the grave.

Sprinting back to their cars as they nervously could see a car with bright lights coming towards them. As instructed everybody got in their cars like a couple with the alibi that they were there to celebrate a friend's birthday by pouring wine on the grave. In case it was the police. After the car pasted and realized it was a couple looking for a spot to make out. Hurrying back to the grave only to find Rofiki was gone. They all knew then it was time to get out of there and ran back to their cars, Jorge and Noriega with their guns out leading the way.

TOURTURED SOULS *"We Like Tequila"* DO YOU MISS ME

"We like Tequila!" Drinking Pink Pussy Tequila drinks trying to lay low, Kandice and Abigail waiting in a Pub in the North –East section of Philly for Noriega and Jorge to return. Before saying anything, she observed Abigail's questioning eyes then said, *"Don't worry nothing happened to him or your car. They just beat him up and left him out there."* Noting the expressions on Abigail's face, Kandice could tell that what Abigail needed to hear that none of them were going to jail for murder. She knew her cuz always had her back. They were thicker than water.

ADINA HOWARD "Buttnaked" THE SECOND COMING

"Don't ever put your clothes on again stay buttnaked
Baby, baby, baby"

The sex tape with the producer Big Tank & Kandi Gyal was the hottest black market porn and Abigail knew her cousin's career would probably blow up. Now sitting next to her popular cousin, Abigail wondered if it was all worth it. She assumed that Rofiki must have been the best lover Kandice ever had because he had her turned out, answering her phone, driving her new Hummer and had her head full of bullshit.

XSCAPE "My Little Secret" TRACES OF MY LIPSTICK

"You're my little secret
And that's how we should keep it
It's on everybody's mind, about you and I"

Smirking, Abigail wanted to know Kandice's little secrets with these men asking, *"Who was better Rofiki or Big Tank?"* Kandice looked at Abigail puzzled wondering was she really asking that question? Abigail didn't back away from the question asking, *"You know – who fucked you the best. Because judging from that video tape, Big Tank ain't all that big. But you were hollering "Yes! Yes!" Rofiki is hung like a horse and you just moaned and groaned."*

Kandice hadn't laughed in weeks and she enjoyed that moment laughing at the size of Big Tank's penis. *"She take his money when he's in need. Yea, she's a trifling friend indeed. Oh, she's a gold digger way over town. That digs on Big Tank!"*

KENYA WEST "Gold Digger" LATE REGISTRATION

Kandice is not saying, she's a gold-digger, but she ain't messing with no broke niggaz. *"Get down Kandi Gyal, go ahead and get down,"* Abigail sang out. Then she asked again, *"Which one was better?"* Sipping her drink Kandice blurted, *"Isn't that what every bitch wants to know?"* A little tipsy and rambling on Kandice revealed the past, *"I met Rofiki back in the day when I was on one of my missions and he was on one of his. I went to Atlanta to visit this dude, you know the NFL dude that played for the Atlanta Falcons football player. What his name?*

Sipping and talking like nothing ever happened earlier, Kandice rambled on. *"Whatever, anyway shortly after I get there, he is rushing me out the house and quickly to a hotel, because of some ex-girlfriend on the way over. I decide to leave and hopped on a greyhound bus, and Rofiki was on that bus."*

MISSY ELLIOT "Get Ur Freak On" MISS E... SO ADDICTIVE

"Gimme some new shit, yeah
Gimme some new shit, yeah"

Engrossed and sipping slow Abigail listened to another one of Kandice interesting stories. *"Well, Rofiki was carrying a lot of weed, but when he seen me, him wanted to mix business with pleasure."* Always loving attention, Kandice posed curving her lips around a shot glass, no hands on the glass tilting her back and swallowing in one gulp the Tequila. All while eyeing the guy at the bar that kept buying them drinks.

"Go, get ur freak on
Go, get ur freak on"

Pausing for the cause and sizing up the guy as her next victim, Kandice continued. Blabbing to Abigail about how she met Rofiki. *"We sat together in the back of the bus boo - loving and talking all the way back to Philly, as I played in his locks. He was so fly reciting rhymes and rapping about silly stuff. I told him my dreams of being a singer and even sung for him. Before we got off the bus he took his gold lions head ring off his finger and put it on mine."* Impatiently Abigail just had to interrupt and ask, *"Do you still have the ring?"* Kandice sucked her teeth complaining, *"Damn you gonna let me tell the story? Hell no! He took it back."*

JAMMIE FOXX "Blame It" INTUITIONS

"Blame it on the a-a-alcohol..." Feeling the pain of love and betrayal, Kandice was now a scorned woman, and didn't want to be called Kandi Gyal ever again. It seems every man that seen her was now lusting over

the sex-tape of Kandi Gyal. Ordering another drink before letting Abigail into any more of her innermost thoughts. She knew Rofiki wasn't violent, never man-handled her, but words hurt too.

"Blaming it on the a-a-alcohol..." While sipping her drink, Kandice didn't miss a beat observing who may be eases dropping and whispered to Abigail, *"I used to like watching Rofiki watch porn and masturbate, seemed like the only way he could off. He liked to fuck every day, but no passion, just punch and literally fucking crazy. Complaining about money hungry bitches! Gold diggers and materialistic hoes that want to be, but won't be without Rofiki 101."*

RAHSAAN PATTERSON "Water" WINE & SPIRITS

It was time to start drinking water and put down the glasses of spirits. Familiar with Kandice blunt honesty and vivid descriptions, but Abigail sat in shock with her mouth wide open. Kandice told her to shut her mouth because if Rofiki walked in the door, he should would stick his dick in it. Abigail knew, Kandice had too many drinks and was becoming belligerent. That too she was familiar with when Kandice's voice went pitches higher lecturing, *"YoU HaVe to know what a MuthA - FughA GoTs!"* Kandice sung out slurred remixing words to Gwen Guthrie's song, *"Nothin' goin' on but da rent. U need to be C.E.O to be with me."*

JAGUAR WRIGHT "One More Drink" DIVORCING NEO TO MARRY SOUL

"One more – one more..." Ordering another drink, Kandice was still talking shit and enjoying the attention from the guy, now looking cute after drinks, and still buying. Tipsy Kandice continued the conversation trying to keep her mind off what just happened in the cemetery. Giving Abigail some food for her thought, Kandice growled the 3 requirements to be her man. *"Fuck that Steve Harvey shit. I think better than men and I'm always a lady. I call the shots and I need big bucks and any woman that says she wants a broke man is a liar!"*

#1 He got to have a six – figure income or more? Rofiki looks like he got a little money, but it is hard to get him to spend a dime, other than on himself. Big Tank is MAKING it and spending it!

#2 He must lick - Rofiki didn't eat pussy, but he had the biggest dick. Since you saw the video then you know Big Tank is a licker! And...

 # 3 He must have his own shit – His own crib – his own house – AND LIVE ALONE! Rofiki claimed he lived alone in his mother's house. But, Big Tank has a mansion, but he also has a girl friend."

Flipping and flipping and whipping her hair and reapplying bubble gum pink lipstick, Kandice wondered cousin was so obsessed with her. Basking in self-knowledge of gold digging powers asking Abigail, *"You watched the sex-tape didn't you?"* Drinking another 'Pink Pussy' Tequila drink, Abigail giggled thinking about how Jorge and Noriega commenting on how Big Tank was a 'Nasty Boy' eating Kandice's 'Pink Pussy' for what seemed like hours, and now Abigail was sick of her drink, and interrupting spitting her words and pink liquor, *"First of all, I refuse to watch the video but, I did glance at it and seen home boy Rofiki was packing."* Kandice said, *"Well then you already know."*

NUSPIRIT HELSINKI *"Seis Por Ocho"* NUSPIRIT HELSINKI

Kandice almost spit her drink instead of sipping. Her thoughts went back to Rofiki laying beat up in the cemetery. She didn't feel a morsel of sympathy for Rofiki or Big Tank for that matter. Since the sex tape Big Tanks people were not calling her back and even Big Tank changed his number.

Still at the pub waiting, Kandice listened to Abigail still asking questions. *"So Kandi Gyal- al - al tell me how was the video tape made without you knowledge about it?"* She didn't answer sipping her drink and letting Abigail talk, wondering the same thing. She responded sarcastically, *"We're grown! Abi –Abi - Abigail tell the truth did you watch the video?"* Abigail lied quickly answering, *"NO!"*

Though Abigail lied, she still told the word on the street. A few days after the radio incident and after Kandice fired Rofiki the sex tape surfaced with Kandi Gyal and Big Tank turning it up and going buck wild! They say she played the role as cute and innocent as Kay - Kay, but nasty and Kitty squirting like Firstborne. Rumor has it that Rofiki sold it for $$$ to some young boys who worked for TMZ.

SOUL'N SODA "Tomorrow" BARLOUNGE CLASSICS / LATIN ADDITION

Kandice came up with the conclusion that Rofiki set the video camera to spy on her. She explained, *"One night Big Tank stopped when Rofiki went to Philly to go check on his mother's house. Once I opened the door it was on from the first step in the door. He came in kissing me complimenting and calling me his main squeeze. I was on Big Tank like hot butter on popcorn. Telling me, he wanted to give me everything I wanted. He was a freak and did whatever he could to make me feel so good."*

Looking at the time and getting impatient waiting to make her next move, Kandice had not forgotten about 'THE NEOSOUL STARR.' She was ready to get on with plan B and that was to take care of STARR. There was no turning back not after they destroyed her life. Abigail was envisioning the sex tape with Rofiki's round brown ass bouncing in between her cousin's thighs. In fact the same thoughts and images were now on Jorge and Noriega's mind as they rushed in the pub to tell them somebody found Rofiki and an ambulance arrived.

SLAKAH THE BEATCHILD "The Cure" SOMETHING FOREVER

"You're my cure, cure,
I'm a chase you, you're my pill and I'm like water
Just what the doctor ordered, that's f'sho
f'sho, f'sho, f'sho, f'sho"

MEAN WHILE BACK @ the motel as Bluesy slept, STARR tried to get herself together. Tip toeing around the motel room. She retreated to the bathroom to get ready for the big night and started grooming the new growth of her hair. Trying to keep her mind from wondering in the wrong directions. Trying not to disturb Bluesy, who finally was asleep, after hearing him pacing the floors now suffer from insomnia. Opening the bathroom door she smiled to see him peaceful and not snoring. The air conditioner was on full blast, she hurried to turn it off. After turning off the cold air, she noticed outside on the windowsill was a dead blue bird.

ADRIANA EVANS "Blue Bird" EL CAMINO

"Little blue bird, blue bird, sing me a song..." STARR wiped her eyes to be sure she was seeing a dead blue bird. For a second she thought the bird looked familiar, like the same blue bird that visited her in North Philly and the same blue bird that followed her to West Philly has found her in a motel by the Philadelphia Airport. She hurried to wake Bluesy to tell him about the dead blue bird and also let him know that they had an hour before they needed to leave for sound check.

Observing the peaceful smile on Bluesy's face, STARR didn't want to disturb him, glad he wasn't snoring. Nudging him softly and then a little harder noticing he didn't want to wake up. *"Come on Bluesy get up we're going to be late."* But he didn't respond. Forcefully STARR began to shake him harder and after he wouldn't move from her shaking and screaming, immediately she dialed 9- 1-1. Screaming, *"HELP!"* She ran outside in one of his T- shirts hugged tight around her swollen belly. The ambulance was there in minutes finding a traumatized STARR crying, *"Please somebody help him."*

KIKI SHEARD "Faith" THIS IS ME

"Faith - I gotta have
Faith - Can't make it without it
Faith - Where I wanna be I gotta have faith"

Faith is all STARR had to hold on to as the ambulance rushed Bluesy out the motel room with an oxygen mask on his face. They asked was she, his wife, she was too hysterical to answer. A female E.M.T. Grabbed Bluesy's coat and put it around her so she could ride in the ambulance to the hospital. On the way to the hospital, she called his doctor. Sitting in the emergency waiting room seemed like forever. She noticed Bluesy's doctor rushing into the E.R. He promised that as soon as he heard anything he would be out to tell her.

Mustering up the nerves STARR called, Bluesy's parents. His mother began to curse in Italian and his father took the phone explaining they would be there immediately. Not knowing what to do pacing the floor and sobbing and looking for tissues, STARR put her hands in the coat pockets. Realizing it was Bluesy's coat, she was wearing and pulled out a little blue box tied with a silver ribbon that contained an engagement ring. Then Bluesy's words echoed in her head, *"This is the most precious thing I was able to save from the fire, STARR will you."* And then they were interrupted by the pizza man knocking at the door. Without hesitation STARR slid the ring on her finger and a perfectly fit.

CARLEEN ANDERSON "The Preacher's Prayer" SOUL PROVIDENCE

As STARR marveled at the beauty of the size 6 ring, police officers and 4 paramedics came rushing in the ER doors causing total confusion and havoc. Doors were immediately buzzed opened and code blue was announced over the intercom as a man bloody on a gurney and also wearing an oxygen mask and hair wild and dreadlocks released and dragged on the ground as they had the paramedic hurried through the doors. With all the confusion STARR'S heart jumped and thumped worst then heart burn as she recognized every dreadlock that hung off the gurney and dragged on the floor.

Like a rocket STARR jumped forward to get a closer look. She knew the lion head ring on the hand of the man, she knew his smell, she knew his silhouette, she knew every hair particle – every hair thread – every strand – every dread lock. STARR tried to hurry through the doors and immediately stopped by police. Rofiki's eyes were locked to hers as he struggled with paramedics and pointing at her with the lion head ring towards her belly.

Unbelievable, STARR didn't have time to get her thoughts together as Bluesy's parents came rushing in the Emergency Room. Wearing Bluesy coat, STARR was unaware it was wide open and her little round belly was poked out for all to see. Bluesy's mother's mouth dropped opened when noticing the belly. His mother screamed, *"Oh my Jesus – Mary and Joseph she is pregnant! Is this what you called us for? Where is my son and why do you have on his coat?"*

RACHELLE FERELL "Prayer Dance" SOMETHIN' ELSE

"Lift my knees from the ground
I will put my feet down
I will dance all my prayers
Unto God..."

After explaining what happened, his mother started to yell for them to open the door and blaming STARR. The doctor appeared and informed them of Bluesy's condition.

"1/3rd of people with ruptured aneurysm die before they get to the hospital.
1/3rd die after they get to the hospital.
1/3rd survive after they get to the hospital.
Some survivors end up with neurological problems that make life difficult."

Bluesy's mother stopped the doctor from further explaining anymore in front of STARR, she wasn't his wife and demanded to know about the ring. STARR snatched her hand away forgetting she had on the ring. She didn't reply as his mother shouted, *"It's your fault!"* Leaving in a hurry because there was no way STARR could be at the hospital with Rofiki and Bluesy's parents that didn't know she was pregnant, but now they knew. In fact no one knew she had managed to keep it secret from everyone. She hurried out knowing if she spoke to his parents she would say something that would make them hate her forever.

LEELA JAMES "Prayer" A CHANGE IS GONNA COME

"What would I do if, I didn't have you to be there for me?" Eyeing and twisting the ring on her finger on the taxi ride back to the motel room. Mental images of the past year of her life flashed in front of her face. The taxi driver couldn't drive fast enough. She lost track of time and had completely forgot about the concert and realized she had missed sound check. STARR had the cab wait while rushing in the motel room, noticing the dead blue bird was gone.

Swiftly, STARR dressed and grabbed the garment bag and carefully hung up Bluesy's coat. Hurrying back into the taxi she noticed her cellphone and Bluesy's was completely dead, so she couldn't call BearLove and she knew they were just about to start the show without her.

"I just wanna thank You, Lord
I, I just wanna thank You, Lord"

Rumbling around in an old bag of make-up, STARR pulled out a set of keys with a Jamaican flag symbol that belong to Rofiki's North Philly house. They both had the same keychains sent straight from Jamaica from his mother Haile. She grabbed the keys and sheltered them as if they were something illegal. Her heart pounded as she quickly put them in her pocket.

TRIBALJAZZ "Blues For Bali" TRIBALJAZZ

Just when STARR had muscled up all the power to forget about Rofiki. There he was covered in blood looking like he was in a bad car accident or someone tried to beat his ass until they killed him. Yet, It still puzzled her how cold his heart was. The question that haunted her most was how, he could leave her without an explanation, and betray her with no hesitations.

SOULSHINE SOUL SESSIONS:
INTERNATIONAL UNDERGROUND RHYTHMS

INCOGNITO "Everybody Loves The Sunshine" BEES + THINGS + FLOWERS (ROY AYERS)

"Everybody Loves the Sunshine" Welcome back to another session of SoulShine, and thank you for supporting the station JAZZ1CAFÉ and becoming V.I.P. Members keeping the grooves flowing commercial free. It's all about the music!

JAZZ1CAFÉ Internet Radio Station is intended to provide a platform for music artists, songs, and events. We are dedicated to keeping the underground music above ground and the music scene alive and kicking for many years to come. Showcasing the next generation, and the next culture of music in all of its different Jazz, Soul, R&B, Hip-Hop and inspirational roots.

BRAND NEW HEAVIES "Music" GET USED TO IT

My forte is also the United Kingdom's, acid jazz movement. Acid jazz, also known as club jazz is a musical genre combining elements of soul music, funk, and disco particularly repetitive beats ad modal harmony.

Defining acid jazz is like describe what your favorite candy taste like. It's better just to hear the sweet juicy jazzy beats yourself to know. The walking bass lines, syncopated rhythm, wah-wah effects on guitar, brass sections, and vibrant soulful vocal improvisations. Acid Jazz is also like the stepchild of the R&B and Funk birthing jazz fusions, combining elements of funk and hip-hop, and looped beats chord structures straight from jazz (sometimes including sampling or live DJ cutting and scratching).

JAMIROQUAI "Cosmic Girl" TRAVELING WITHOUT MOVING

Originating in the London club scene in the mid-1980s, the Acid jazz movement has spread universal and became a popular subgenre of club music during the 1990s. Using danceable grooves and samples from earlier jazz albums to create a sound that had people shaking their hips in clubs. Though the genre spread through the US, Japan, Eastern Europe, Africa and Brazil, acid jazz dissolved out and nowadays, the best acid jazz artists are often regarded as jazz rap or neo soul, but not acid jazz.

US 3 "Make Tracks" HAND ON THE TORCH

The most popular major artist including Incognito, Brand New Heavies, Us3 and Jamiroquai from the UK. From the U.S.A. we have such groups as, A Tribe Called Quest, Buckshot LeFonque, Digable Planets, Groove collection, and US 3. But there are many more acid jazz artist to name, and you can tune into JAZZ1CAFÉ to hear more of the experience.

A TRIBE CALLED QUEST "Jazz (We've Got)
Buggin' Out" THE LOW END THEORY

The fussy criticizers slid Acid Jazz back into the clubs and parties where jazz originated. The style is characterized by danceable grooves, and long, repetitive compositions. Its vibrant improvisations, exciting, passionate, and crazy sounds expressing the thoughts and feelings of the artist and better than any candy I ever ate.

BUCKSHOT LEFONQUE "Music Evolution" MUSIC EVOLUTION

Acid Jazz is also the name of a recording label in the United Kingdom founded by Gilles Peterson & Eddie Pillar. DJ Gilles Peterson formed the Acid Jazz record label, the first single Galliano's "Fredrick Lies Still" a cover of Curtis Mayfield's "Freddie's Dead," from the film 'Superfly' was a club hit. Gilles then announced in the late 80's that the term Acid Jazz was dead, and that no one wanting respect would dare call themselves acid jazz anymore. Despite Gilles' pronouncement the term Acid Jazz the term has stuck.

Acid Jazz has even derived into Tri- Hop!!! Trip hop is a genre of electronic music that originated in the early 1990s in the United Kingdom, especially Bristol. French hip hop developing from post acid jazz, and acid house music. There is even 'Mushroom Jazz' a series of musical compilations by DJ Mark Farina. Originating in 1992 and on cassette tape, then in 1997 the commercial CD and vinyl releases.

Music makes my world go around and I am forever thankful for the internet and being able to connect with music globally and the wonderful invention of mobile devices and the new headphones created. Whatever they come up with next, I'll admit, I'm waiting for it!

DIGITAL PLANETS "Rebirth Of Slick (Cool Like Dat)" REACHIN' (A NEW REFUTATION OF TIME AND SPACE)

Just A Few Clicks Away from JAZZ1CAFÉ...

1. Download 'LIVE365 RADIO APP
2. Launch the LIVE365 RADIO APP
3. Type: JAZZ1CAFE (Click GO!)

BECOME A V.I.P. MEMBER!!! FREE 5 Day Trial Membership and No Credit Card Required!

Please become a V.I.P. Member and help support JAZZ1CAFÉ Internet Radio Station and the music artist. Portions of you subscription go towards the royalties for the songs played.

Enjoy zero commercial interruptions, no banners or ads, just you and the music. Listen on multiple devices, tablets & desktops. Go anywhere with the LIVE365 Mobile APP for. Listen in the comfort of your home on devices such as Sonos, Roko, WDTV, Grace digital wireless radio, Tangent, TIVO and more.

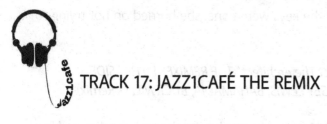

TRACK 17: JAZZ1CAFÉ THE REMIX

ANGELA JOHNSON "Be Myself" REVISITED, EDITED & FLIPPED
(KERMIT & JALON Remix)

THE REMIX... The night STARR had been waiting to sing her face off, singing songs of liberation, peace, and love and now faced with more drama, she was out of her mind. She didn't want to disappoint anyone and knew the sweat, blood, tears and hard work, BearLove put into making this happen for her, him and everybody. She wanted to tell the cab driver to turn around and take her back to the hospital, so she could be with Bluesy.

Thankful, Bluesy was always there as STARR's friend, her man stepping into the position with such ease and flow. With his is mild temper, compassionate manners and big marine blue eyes always ready to please. Though she knew about the previous chick and the negative paternity results. He was always there regardless of her bullshit. Now he was in the hospital and she was on her way to perform. There was no turning back and he wouldn't want her to sing.

JILL SCOTT "Breathe" THE REAL THING: WORDS AND SOUNDS VOL. 3

"Breathe, just breathe..." Driving down Main Street she could see the lit up marquee outside the newly renovated JAZZ1CAFÉ that was counting on 'THE NEOSOUL STARRS'. As the taxi got closer to JAZZ1CAFE. STARR asked the driver to drop her off around needing to get herself together. Wiping tears from her eyes and feeling the difference in life was much different and an enjoyable difference due to Bluesy.

Thinking of Bluesy and the dead blue bird had tears dropping again. STARR knew that it was her time to shine. Stepping out the taxi and tossing the keys to Rofiki's house in the trash can, but missed and hit the ground, she kept on stepping. Just as she turned the corner and walked a few steps, and thinking about her belongings still at Rofiki's, she went back for the keys, and the keys were gone, she hurried on not trying to figure it out.

GURU 'Respect The Architect" THE REMIXES by HILLSIDE (Featuring RAMSEY LEWIS, BAHAMADIA, BUCKWILD - Remix)

Trailing behind STARR and keeping close to the taxi, Kandice and her crew followed STARR coming out of the Emergency Room. They were following the ambulance to the hospital to keep closer tabs on Rofiki. Noticing STARR exiting the hospital, made Kandice's job easier. Following the taxi to the motel by the Philadelphia Airport and noticed the taxi waiting. They followed her to JAZZ1CAFÉ and Kandice was glad to see STARR get out around the corner near an alley.

Handing them the gun, Kandice hurried Noriega and Jorge out the car to take care STARR. They refused to handle her unpaid personal business, she had to handle it. Shaking and pleading Abigail begged her cousin to stay in the car. Kandice got out the car and was footsteps behind STARR when noticing her throwing away keys. She picked up the keys unnoticed and reached in her pocket for the gun, there was no gun, but her cellphone lit up and vibrating. Instantly her face lit up looking like she won the lottery, because it was Big Tank. She hurried back to the car to talk, as they sped off.

BIG TANK: *You back in Philly with that dread lock nigga?*

KANDI: *I haven't seen him and hope he isn't breathing and I'm in Philly with my family.*

BIG TANK: *Get your ass back to New York tonight. I will make the reservations and will text you the info. There is too much shit going on to explain over the phone, but the lawsuit has been settled out of court and you just need to get your ass back in the studio.*

Ignorant, but Big Tank called. He didn't say hi or bye on the phone. Kandice didn't care sharing the good news with her cousin and quickly gather her belongings and having Abigail drop her off at 30th & Market to hurry and catch the express Amtrak train to New York.

THE ROOTS "The Coming" ...AND THEN YOU SHOT YOUR COUSIN
(Featuring MERCEDES MARTINEZ)

"I'm coming
Take my chance my footsteps in the road
No one sees and no one knows"

"I'm coming - I'm coming - I'm coming..." JAZZ1CAFE was the place to be. Gazing up at all the lights that lit up the marquees, seeing it with her own eyes, her name 'STARR' was in lights. She should be feeling like a superstar on her way to living her dreams, which were feeling like a nightmare all over again. It was like someone had sprinkled magic dust on her and was now blowing it all away. Then she noticed by the crowd.

Cameras were flashing at some of Philadelphia's finest singers and musicians mingled among the exclusive crowd. Majority of the ticket holders were well known recording artist, A&R people, music reviewers, bloggers, movie stars, and industry folks, and happy fans were all mixing and mingling, one big happy JAZZ1CAFÉ Party!

CITY LOUNGE "Still In Time" CITY LOUNGE
(Featuring MICATONE)

"Don't go so fast, I'm in my full circle standing still in time... Slow down... Slow down... Don't go so fast..." CONCERT SOLD OUT! Everyone in the place would be a part of the live recording. After the concert snippets of videos will be streamed from the www.jazz1cafe.com website on the internet. They were going global and reaching their international fans.

Security at the café was turning folks away at the doors yelling, *"The concert is sold out – guest list and ticket holders only – the concert is sold out!* After the fire that destroyed everything, but the mahogany red polish *'Young Chang'* baby grand piano. If you fancy an aficionado of jazz, then you were in the right place. JAZZ1CAFE had a jazzy new-school, cool and hip vibe. The venues consisted of an array of bands, trios, pianists, vocalist, divas, trumpeters, saxophonists and spoken word artist.

In fact, JAZZ1CAFÉ'S signature 'Young Chang' baby grand piano bares the autographs of many of the performers who've played there over the years. As if the music isn't enough the joint also scores big with its 'Jazzed

Up' Tapas menu of soul & seafood appetizers, prepared by the best and special guest chiefs.

JAMES PERRI "The Power" NUDE DIMENSIONS Vol. 2 (ATJAZZ REMIX)

The re-grand opening was just in time to venue the special event and live recording presenting 'THE NEOSOUL STARRS' featuring SOULSHINE SESSIONS and special guest artist. Observing the crowd, she tried to keep her emotions together and want to be part of the night. There was 12,000 square feet of pure entertainment in an opulent lounge setting that provides a unique experience not found elsewhere in the Philadelphia area. The millions of dollars that went into the renovations showed in the multi-level space that included 26' x 8' slate bars with cocktail waitresses dressed for the part dancing on top pouring and serving electric - blue vodka drinks with round balls of ice, no square cubes.

LIV WARFARE "Groove DJ" EMBRACE ME

SoulShine Sessions, already had the JAZZ1CAFÉ party started. Folks were in full swing dancing and drinking and having a merry good time. A 14-foot-wide staircase furnished with sleek seating built into the steps and over 50 LCD TV's, including the 10 - 72" plasmas televisions displaying colorful abstract computer graphics that swooped and pulsed with the music. There were 2 V.I.P. Rooms *'Hookah Lounge"* and *'The Black'* room for the mystifying minds. The rooms were fully equipped with their own personal entertainment centers controlled by touch-screen remotes, plasmas, Italian leather wrapped furniture.

There was no time to enjoy any of it. Instantly STARR was recognized trying to make her way through the doors. Fans called her name, STARR! STARR! People were trying to get her autograph and take her pictures. Luckily security came to her rescue, and escorted her safely to the green room. The capacity was filled and it was a standing-room-only venue.

ZHANE "Hey Mr. DJ" SATURDAY NIGHT (Remix)

"Hey DJ keep playing that song all night on and on and on"

Behind the stage 5x's DMC World Champion DJ Jazzy X was setting up and ready to take over and take the party to the next level with his new turntablism routine, using Traktor Scratch Pro and the Kontrol X1 controller. Using the X1, Craze simultaneously triggers cue points on both decks, while still staying true to his roots with some serious beat juggling switching from left to right – super fast. Watching him was very entertaining and attractive, he drove the women crazy with his olive clear skin and European accent and long blond dreads locks that danced to the beats.

"Everybody move your body! Now do it" Ready to show off his turntable trickology, DJ JAZZY X was balancing headphones from one ear to the next setting up the next blend of beats ready to be mixed in. Prepared to keep the party people dancing and entertained juggling - flipping and spinning vinyl records and flicking the switch on the mixer from side to side. He razzle and dazzled them with his mixology and blend of music. Watching him was very entertaining and he was very attractive with his olive clear skin and European accent and long blond dreads locks that drove the women crazy.

DJ CAM "The Show" SOULSHNE

Paparazzi, along with the fans, were flashing cameras at some of Philadelphia's finest singers and musicians who mingled among the exclusive crowd of well-known recording artists, movie stars, A and R people, music reviewers, bloggers, and promoters. Many music industry people were there along with radio contest ticket winners and fans.

A nervous wreck since leaving the hospital, STARR couldn't think of performing after all she had been through, but a super force of nature was pushing her forward, knowing Bluesy would insist that she perform as if he were right by her side.

Rushing into the green room STARR found the band members pacing the floor, just like she did in the Emergency Room. Her appearance brought the sign of relief to their faces, especially BearLove's and before she could explain, SoulShine walked in announcing, "Show time!"

Lights were low the band was playing the intro for STARR to hit the stage. She inhaled through her nose and exhaled through her mouth praying and dedicating, *"This is for you Bluesy!"* Dancing on stage her hips swayed to the music, trying to release her mind, body and soul into the music. She gradually converted over into her world of harmony, melody, lyrics, music a world where she felt understood.

THE ROOTS *"Proceed 2"* HOME GROWN
THE BEGGINER'S GUIDE TO UNDERSTANDING THE ROOTS, VOL. 1

They had the variations in sound needed to PROCEED! STARR looked gorgeous in a colorful eccentric dress that was sexy, though it hid her plumping figure. Her long dark strands of hair flowed naturally free heart beating fast looking out at all the faces. Embracing the microphone eyeing the crowd and over whelmed by the love and support and all the joyful faces cheering and smiling. Well, not everyone was cheerful and merry. There was Mina with her lips turned down and the only one in the front row not clapping. The music was playing and since STARR had missed microphone check 1- 2 – 1 - 2.

STARR: *I SHALL proceed AND continue TO rock THE mic!*

BEARLOVE: *I shall PROCEED and CONTINUE da ROCK the MIC!*

RONNY GLASSHOUSE: *I Shall Proceed - Continue To Rock!*

JOE DADDY: *I shall proceed to ROCK the mic!*

DJ JAZZY X: *I shall Chicka - Chicka - Chicka rock the mic!*

(Audience clapping)

(STARR closed her eyes thinking of Bluesy)

The stage light dimmed and hues of blues from the spot light danced off the slow turning mirrored disco balls that swept glittery blue lights softly throughout the crowd. The opening musical bars of the song shimmered and lifted the song, as STARR'S seductive body movements sent visual scenes that didn't need to be spoken.

Turntablist D.J. JAZZY X added his art of scratching records and manipulating the sound creating music using mixing in the old school classics. He watched STARR'S hips swaying right into rhythm of the sensual strumming pattern of Joe – Daddy's fingers plucked out a groove on his tenor guitar. The place was standing room only and silently caught up in the sexual healings of the bands harmony to STARR'S storytelling lyrics.

The sultry urban – jazz tempo was hypnotic. A slave to the music, she obeyed and surrendered. Posing seductively in the middle of the stage, the microphone was so close to her lips, she looked like she was kissing it. BearLove was lightly tapping his cymbals keeping the pace.

KINDRED THE FAMILY SOUL "Meant To Be" SURRENDER TO LOVE
(KING BRITT Remix)

Clinching fist full of flowing hair falling in her face, STARR embraced the music listening to the switch up to a funkier beat. STARR danced to the left side of the stage and pointed to the crowed, letting them know she was feeling them. Then she danced to the middle of the staged and pointed out to the crowed that was clapping and singing along. She paid no attention to Mina's middle finger, and danced over to the left side and knew they were feeling the music too.

Laying the microphone down on the stage and walking away, still singing. STARR did what she witnessed Patti Labell, Jaguar Wright and Lady Alma do when on stage. Proving they didn't need a microphone to project their vocal powers. She could be heard singing among the many in attendance even if they were singing along with her, her voice stood out in the crowd as she sang tearfully, *"I'm feeling you! Ya, I'm Feeling you!"*

SUPER-PHONICS "P.A.R.T.Y" INTERSTELLAR

Picking up the music off the floor, and on cue ready to keep the party going STARR was set to give more. DJ JAZZY X on the wheels of steel showed his vocal skills as a human beat box, and scratching out a funky rhythm version of SLICK RICK & the human beat box DOUGIE FRESH on the turn tables. BearLove's heavy hands switched up the pace banging out a jazzy Hip - Hop beat.

Embracing the music dancing STARR's size 8 bare feet wiggled her freshly red painted toes across the stage. Joe Daddy was playing the bass right along beside her. Boogie-oogi -ooging her way over to BearLove. She grabbed the big black afro-pic with the black fist out of his afro and began picking her hair. Holding the afro -pic up in the air and rapping, *"Let me hear you say Ho! - Let me hear you say Ho - Ho! -Let me hear you say Ho – Ho - Ho!"* The crowed was earsplitting back, Ho – Ho - Ho!

Singing into screams STARR was excited, *"Somebody - Anybody - Everybody scream!"* The crowed went off screaming!!! STARR was in her zone and now not feeling anything but the party giving shout out to the Philadelphia neighborhoods, *"North Philly – South Philly – West Philly- Germantown is in the house! Mt Airy – East & West Oakland –Olney and North East Philly is in the house! To my home town Norristown is in the house! New Jersey through to New York is in the house! Delaware to Maryland to D.C. to the dirty South is in the house! THE A- T – L and Tampa is in the house in the house! YO stop playing everyone in PHILADELPHIA is in the HOUSE!"*

LIZ FIELDS "It's Ok T Love Me RE-PRODUCED (HOT COCO Remix)

The crowed was fixated voices high pitched hooting and hollering. BearLove knew that was the cue to switch up the beat watching STARR on fire putting all her energy into the performance. Repositioning her body, relaxing her mind and getting back to feeling Ronny G pounding out the keys on the piano. Clenching the mic STARR tilted her head back and letting her hair bounce to the beat. BearLove was lightly beating the high hats slowing down the tempo. STARR closed her eyes, opened her mouth and sang.

It sent the audience to their feet, clapping and screaming. As STARR relaxed her breathing the band brought the beat to a slow tempo. The band continued to play while STARR talked to the audience and video cameras. Spacing her word evenly she spoke, *"Can I talk to you for a second? Bullshit means nonsense and is commonly used to describe statements made by people more concerned with the response in truth and accuracy. It is impossible for someone to lie unless he/she thinks they know the truth. I got a song for all you bullshitters, but first!"*

"Chicka - Chicka - Chicka
Bull- Zigga – Bull - Zigga
Bull-Shit"

DJ JAZZY X was scratching in the bridge from $hantey Money's song, 'Bullshit.' The band was fully exploded and people were cheering and clapping to the jazzy beat. The DJ was on the wheels of steel scratching out a funky rhythm on the turn tables, STARR imitated using her vocal skills. Champagne flutes and smiles, wine glasses and cheers the vibe was incredible Party goers were synchronize to the beat.

ERYKAH BADU *"Next Lifetime"* HEARTACHE & MORE
(LINSLEE Remix)

The hypnotic sassy funky vibe and STARR'S powerful purrs, had all ears alert. Even though she was caught up in the music she scanned the crowd of faces and races, among the international fans. Because of the lighting on the stage it made it hard to see the audience faces clearly. Everyone seemed so happy, noticing a few Rasta's, she was just happy that none of them were Rofiki, swaying there dreads to the texture of the music. Embracing the music and bringing sparkles to people's eyes, singing and performing for the world. No more running because there was no place to hide, STARR had to step out in no disguises, no interruptions, no intermission and no technical problems.

FLOETRY *"Say Yes"* FLOACISM
(Remix)

Observing the audience, STARR noticed a full – figured blonde hair white chick almost knocking her off beat thinking of Bluesy's ex-wife Karen, because if it was Karen, she would jump off the stage and beat her ass. She relaxed into the music ready to sing her favorite song. The song that had brought so much controversy and the crow was ready for. The fans had been chanting all night, *"Bullshit ain't nothing but chewed up grass!"*

The drums in that song are off the chain and when BearLove began rocking, STARR could only think about was Bluesy. She began feeling nauseas with a horrible feeling in the pit of her belly that wasn't the baby. But it was the cue to sing. The audience was clapping and whistling.

THE NEOSOUL STARR "Bullshit Ain't Nothing But Chewed Up grass" (Featuring STARR and DARK THOUGHTS)

The room grew dark as DJ JAZZY X was mixing and scratching as the flat screen televisions darkened and then began displaying snap shots of the group in the studio and then it played right into a short video clip of STARR'S studio sessions @Black Beast Studio jamming and then when DARK THOUGHTS part came up on cue the band picked up the beat and the television monitors switched into black and white visuals patterns as he strolled out on stage, tipping his Kango hat performing his part live – never missing a beat.

"YO Philly!
DARK THOUGHTS ain't trying to play you
Blow smoke and Purple Haze you
I'M AS BLACK AS MY AFRO PICK WITH THE FIST
AND THE BOOGIE MAN
U Understand?

On cue the band picked up the beat and STARR came back on stage introducing DARK THOUGHTS and finishing the song performed live. Together they ripped the song alive, sounding great. The crowd were out of their minds cheering and dancing.

"Bull Shit – Ain't Nothing But Chewed Up Grass!"

Singing STARR had the song under control sounding amazing. She improvised with random vocals and syllables or without words at all as Ronny G let his fingers roll across the ivory and black keys exemplifying his style. They were bonded together by the power of their musical souls and independence. *"Bull – Shit ain't nothing, but chewed up grass!"*

"Boom - Boom
Pat -ah
Boom - Boom
Pat!"

STARR relaxed into the music and her hips were swinging left to right and her belly troubled. She demanded, *"Put your hands together for BearLove! Let the drummer get wicked!"* Sticks in hand BearLove's heavy left hand made the cymbals ting. His right hand dropped his drum stick and allowed his bare hand to tap on his high hats. The audience loved it. Bear Love ended with a room hushed drum tapping solo. Standing up he tapped out the rhythmic beat with his bare hands on the drums.

BAHAMADIA "Philadelphia" BB QUEEN (Featuring DWELE)

"Shout outs to all of Philadelphia!" The crowd sung back, *"Bull-shit ain't nothing but chewed up grass!"* STARR was standing next to BearLove shaking a rain stick. She didn't know how to play an instrument, but she could shake the shit out of a rain stick. He could feel the music that poured out in her lyrics. STARR was very gifted and animated when she performed.

Whatever the direction the universe was pulling STARR, she was moving and going with the flow and growing eager to get back to the hospital. She was exhausted and praying to GOD that Bluesy was okay. Also remembering, Rofiki on the gurney bleeding and then she remembered the information Bluesy's attorney had about her family. Actually she didn't forget any of these things, she just kept trying to push them back in the corner of her mind until after the concert.

J. DILLA (Jay Dee) "Bullshittin" (Remix Instrumental)

This was the debut that would make them, because nothing could break them. The chemistry within the band was a relationship of understanding each other's grooves and moves, pitches and scales, lyrics and they respected each other's art. BearLove was disappointed that he didn't get a chance to talk to STARR or apologize and explain all the crazy bullshit that Mina had him going through.

Tapping on the drums BearLove couldn't stop thinking of tapping her ass, STARR was looking real fly. He knew he had to put his emotions in check. Because he knew she moved in with the dude Bluesy, who he respected. It was also noticed that Bluesy wasn't there and maybe something happened like an argument? Was that why she missed the sound check? But, she dedicated a song to him. With all the thoughts going on in BearLove's head, he didn't miss a beat. Needing tonight to be the night, he tells his feelings.

Unable to erase that night, though a few months have passed and they barely talked about it, but it did put a little distance in the rehearsals. He thought mainly because Mina was there. Observing Mina in the audience as jealous, as she was beautiful. Things were feeling good regardless to what was going on off stage with Mina gritting on STARR. But there was for sure a strong musical connection going on – on stage as they were finishing the last song of the night.

LAURYN HILL "The Sweetest Thing" MS HILL (Remix)

Bear Love ended with a room hushed drum tapping solo rhythmic beat then shouting, *"Peace Quadir!"* Exiting the stage as the band continued playing, STARR was blowing kisses to the audience pretending everyone was Bluesy. The host SoulShine Sessions was on the mic announcing, *"Put your hands together for THE NEOSOUL STARR featuring the lovely vocalist STARR! Isn't she just amazing!"*

The crowd was still singing in harmony, *"Bull-Shit ain't nothing but chew up grass."* The band stopped playing and the crowd sounded like a football stadium of fans cheering *"BULL SHIT – BULL SHIT!"* Proud that she made it through the evening, STARR knew she had to stick around to meet and greet and autograph CD's and Poster, but she really needed to get to the hospital.

The host SoulShine Sessions was now on stage talking to the crowd, *"You heard it! Right here @ JAZZ1CAFÉ. The rest of the evening we'll party and flow with Neo Soul tunes. Check us out the website and stay updated on upcoming events. Again put your hands together and give it up for Philadelphia's Own THE NEOSOUL STARR and the voice that has touch us all and there is no way after tonight you would forget STARR!"*

THE ROOTS "Waok (Ay) Rollcall" PHRENOLOGY

Immediately after BearLove came off stage Mina grabbed his arm ready to go. He had a feeling this would happen. They had been fighting all day and got into a physical altercation in the car on the way to sound check. The argument in the car had gotten so bad that he had to pull the car over, he refuse to let her drive his car anymore and slap the 'Bull – Shit' out of her. He never hit a girl. Never, his mother KadijahLove raised him better than that. But he had to because Mina was biting his finger and wouldn't let go. He pointed his finger at her telling her to chill out, she bit his finger. Which caused him to perform all night in excruciating pain from a swollen right index finger.

The end of Mina. BearLove didn't have time for Mina's bipolar behaviors, her psycho baby momma drama, and her actions showed her ass over and over again. Not even Mina could stop his flow powerless to STARR'S musical control. He was on a musical high, so high even Mina couldn't fuck it up.

Still holding his drum sticks in his hands, BearLove walked Mina outside. Past all the many faces of fans and cameras, waving and hollering at him, he had to ignore, but plastered a smile on his face, as he walked Mina's outside the café. To her surprise, he was sending her home in a cab.

YAHZARAH "Black Star" BLACKSTAR (Remix)

Back in the 'Green Room' they were celebrating their wonderful night. THE NEOSOUL STARR tossed and drank champagne. DJ JAZZY X made the toast in his bloody English accent, "STARR U R bloody fucking Amazing! "Bull shit ain't nothing - I Bow to you! To you other fughing bloody amazing musical bastards that rocked the house – I've never had more pleasure. I could do this 'Bull – Shit' every night all night! Drink up we still have a party going on and I want to go buzz around and enjoy the minxy and sexy peaches (women)!"

Now in the mix of the celebrations, BearLove finally got the moment he was looking for. He had to thank STARR for being there like M.C. Micstro, "Through rain or shine or even a blizzard." All of the other band members left the 'Green Room' to joined the party guest and get ready to sign autographs, CD's, posters, and ticket stubs. STARR was ready to slide out the side door and head to the hospital to check on Bluesy when BearLove stopped her.

This was the moment BearLove had been waiting for the whole night. He would do anything for STARR. Alone with STARR again, he wrap his arms around her proud. She held such admiration for him and seeing all his hard work was for her too to be able to live her dreams. Still holding on and glad nothing physical went on between the two of them this way they could still move on as friends too. BearLove handing her a beautiful bouquet of roses cheering, *"Congratulations you were wonderful tonight. I have roses for you!"*

THE ROOTS "Don't Say Nuthin"
BEST OF THE ROOTS: J. PERIOD PRESENTS (Remix)

Thanking each other in an embrace, BearLove said, *"STARR, please I need to talk to you later."* STARR was in no mood to talk thinking about Bluesy, though she really needed to talk to BearLove too. Now BearLove was holding her tighter and not letting go of the embrace. Before she could pull away, BearLove was rubbing her small round hard belly. She didn't flinch, she reached out and touched his swollen bruised finger that looked like a dog bite asking, *"What happened?* He didn't answer or remove his hand from her belly as she announced, *"I'm almost due."*

Unknown to them, Mina was standing in the doorway listening and witnessing everything. Seeing BearLove's hand on STARR'S stomach sent her in an uproar. Mina picked up an empty champagne bottle and hit BearLove over the head. Seeing all the blood squirting out of his head, because of a main artery hit, STARR quickly put a towel on his head and they hurried out the exit door to get help, as Mina ran away

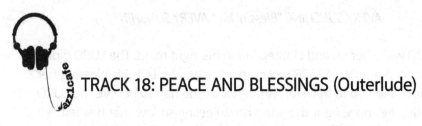

TRACK 18: PEACE AND BLESSINGS (Outerlude)

RACHELLE FERRELL "Peace on Earth" RACHELLE FERRELL

"How can we heal the wounds of the world?
If we cannot heal our own?"

Arriving early in the morning to the 'Munroe Funeral Home' on North Broad Street in Philadelphia. In the wee hours cars and people were scarce. All she could think is 'he is gone' and feeling like a black and white movie with no sound, STARR stood in the middle of Broad Street eyeing the building.

"And where does this peace on earth begin?
If not in the home?"

Eying the brick interior, STARR Wondered if she was at the right place, knowing she was. Goose bumps covered her body as she walked towards the doors. Thinking of him laid stretched out dead in a casket and ready to be viewed in a few hours, had her head pounding with the aftermath and trying to grasp reality.

DJ CAM "He is Gone" SOULSHINE
(Featuring CHINA)

"We gonna murder this one and murder that one"

Leave STARR alone, she don't care anymore. *"He's gone."* The drops of rain started to fall heavier and she didn't have an umbrella. Wishing she had a joint and finding shelter on the porch of the funeral home. The winds picked up slapping her face wet. Even if she smoked 10 pounds of weed it wouldn't get her high enough, plus she had stopped smoking.

AVERY SUNSHINE "Blessin' Me" AVERY SUNSHINE

GOD woke her up and clothed her in her right mind. The LORD didn't let her sleep too late, STARR woke up on time. The LORD is blessing her right now, she had to believe. Through it all she had to believe the LORD is blessing her now, right then and now. Feeling so low that hell felt like it was above her. Puffing on wind she thought, *"To feel HIGH as HELL, Do you know how low you have to go? Damn!"* Her heart jumped when the lights on the first floor of the funeral home came on.

The wet chill of the morning didn't faze her numbed body and mind. Now, standing at the double mahogany doors with watery eyes and awareness of her now being wet and him dead, she wanted to run. A deep scared grunt came from her, as she rang the bell reading the gold plague on the door.

"Welcome to Munroe Funeral Home"

Forced to read the sign on the door over and over and over again. Until, a woman dressed in black answered the door with greetings. *"Welcome to Munroe Funeral Home."* STARR wanted to snarl, don't fucking greet me to see the dead. Have some damn sympathy. But, instead speaking in a suffocated whisper, *"I'm here to view. Please, I won't be long."* Inside the funeral home there was another welcoming sign. This is not a place for welcoming signs, she thought.

Still trying to hold it together, she walked into the foyer wanting to turn the sign over, but immediately stopped. Her eyes focused on M&M's on the floor. The woman's eye traveled to what had startled her. Walking over to the candy on the floor the woman replied, *"Sorry it is just candy, no rodent droppings or whatever you thought it was. My husband Mr. Munroe's loves M&M's."* Keeping the smile on her face and throwing away the candy the woman extended her hand. *"How are you? I'm Mrs. Munroe."*

LEJUENE THOMPSON "This Too Will Pass" METAMOPHOSIS (Reprise)

This too will pass, STARR's pain won't last always. A tear dropped, STARR tried not to cry, eyeing her surroundings. She didn't want to be surprised by any unwanted family members, paparazzi, old friends or strangers. Almost instantly the clouds crashed and hard rain knocked on the windows and doors. It was eerie enough to make her want to run, but she was tired of running.

Noticing a dim lit room and all she could see was the end of a black casket. Mrs. Munroe stared at the dark rings around STARR'S swelled eyes and asked, *"Can I get you a cup of coffee."* Coffee was not what she needed and almost vomited from the faint scent of coffee on Mrs. Munroe's breath. STARR replied offended, *"No coffee! Please let me get it over with!"*

THE ROOTS 'A Peace of Light" HOW I GOT OVER
(Featuring AMBER COFFMAN, ANGEL DERADOORIAN, HALEY DEKLE)

Following the shocked Mrs. Munroe as she walked toward the dim room and turned up the lights. STARR with a praying spirit observed him lying stretched out in the ebony black casket and many flowers. She became more nervous than ever in her entire life. Her stomach twisting was proof of her emotional state. Forgetting that Mrs. Munro was beside her, STARR was startled when she spoke, *"My Husband did a wonderful job. He looks good doesn't he? He is at peace."* STARR looked at her bewildered and blurted, scarcely unaware of her own tone, *"He looks dead and is there peace in death?"*

S.O.U.L. "Praying Spirit" SOUL SEARCHING

Walking slowly up to the casket with a *'Praying Spirit'*, STARR wanted to stop, but it felt pushed. Standing at the foot of the casket, she thought his hand moved. Panicking and losing her mind or was she just that delirious? Looking closer, he almost looked like he was smiling, and she would remember every detail of his dead face. His lifeless body dressed in a charcoal gray pinstripe suit. She wondered if he could be dreaming. She reached out to touch him, stopping and reading his name, 'Ralph B. Urbany' on the gold plaque inside the casket and the date, March 1st... The same exact date, 1 year prior that she walked into the Coffee Shop.

SOUL TEMPO "Trust In God" TRUST IN GOD

Really needing to put her trust in GOD and watching her thoughts, because STARR knew GOD could hear them too. Spooked, she backed away startled into Mrs. Munroe announcing. *"What a good man he was. The viewing is in an hour you can wait, because your family STARR?"* Puzzled, but still confuse not remembering if she told Mrs. Monroe her name or relationship STARR replied, "Yes, *I am family!"*

LISA MCLENDON "Go" SOUL MUSIC

Cradling her growing belly, feeling to the pressure of the baby's head on her bladder. She was feeling the need to run back outside in the rain. But, she didn't want to leave her father's side, not just yet. She looked at all the empty seats and more flowers being delivered. She knew that she was supposed to be on bed rest, but she needed to be there too. Sitting in the first row. Staring at the man in the casket, the man she never knew to love. She thought of her baby who may have never known his father. She needed to hurry home, which was now Bluesy's parent's house.

CECE WINANS "Everlasting Love" EVERLASTING LOVE

"Where there is grief, there will be hope...
Know that the peace that comes from above
Is the same everlasting love"

After Bluesy underwent surgery to correct an aneurysm in an artery that supplies blood to the right side of his brain. Then he was transported to a rehabilitation center and now home recuperating. So thankful and remembering the times when STARR couldn't close her eyes. She would lie awake despairing, don't know how many nights. Afraid of death that her chest would give way to the fear. She now knows that the peace that comes from above is that same everlasting love. Before coming to the Monroe funeral home, she cared to Bluesy needs, and he was awake and alert, oriented, moving all extremities. Well his parents, have whole-heartedly apologized to her. And as for their living arrangements, she found them to be respectable and very devoted.

CYNTHIA JONES "Gotta Soul" SOULOLOGY

STARR gotta soul, Bluesy gotta soul, and Rofiki's soul was beat up and in a coma, but recovered and left the hospital against doctors' orders.

This is what STARR learned when she called and asked about him. And Thank GOD, Rofiki's little 'Black Book' had more information in it then she thought. The extra numbers under his mother's Haile phone number were to the combinations to his storage unit and the code to the safe in the storage unit. It was easy finding 'Montego Bay Storage' and getting her few personal belongings like her music, song books, pictures and more.

SAUNDRA WILLIAMS "Hidden" BLESS THE DAY

"Everything that is beautiful is sometimes overlooked
And the real treasures are found in the most obscure places."

The lawsuit against VHRecords and Kandi Gyal was being settled out of court and STARR cared to hear no more about them. That was a relief and the blessings keep rolling in after praying for BearLove. After a few stitches, he dropped all charges on Mina, though he still had a restraining order against her. Which the rest of the band member say is stupid since, she already hit him in the head and he was letting her get away with it. Thankfully BearLove and STARR are content with their new music (only) relationship.

SUE NEIL "My First Love" THROUGH THE FIRE

Again STARR read the name 'Ralph Urbany' and date. It was crazy that the same exact date she met Bluesy, she meets her biological father, a dead man. While searching for her mother $hantey Money, the detectives found her biological father on her original birth certificate.

Only to found him a day late, he died of natural causes. STARR looked at his face and wonder if there were any similarities in her face. She had his nose maybe and the same exact skin complexion and rounded chin. She wanted to know more about him. Did he have any more children and who was his family and was now the right time to meet them? What if they didn't know about her? And what if they did?

SHEREE BROWN "A Lil' Mo' 2 Go" FIRST FRUIT

Just a lil' mo' 2 go. Keep it moving, keep it moving until the end, just a lil' mo' 2 go.... Nothing was making any sense when Mrs. Munroe returned with her husband, introducing Mr. Munroe who was explaining, *"We know this must be a difficult time for you. Your father Ralph Urban, A.K.A. D.J. Urban, $hantey Money's DJ."* Continuously eying the dead man from head to toe reading the name again. 'Ralph Urbany,' but that didn't make any sense. He was her father? Quickly asking questions, *"Do you have any information about my mother?"*

Entering the room, Mr. Monroe ready for business and requesting to take pictures and selfies and autograph. He explained that they have been keeping up with the media and know about STARR looking for her mother. So, they assumed she would be sure to lay her father to rest properly. All while talking they handed STARR the bill for the funeral. $10,000. She felt the knot in her stomach pop and the trickling of pee running down her leg, knowing that her water broke. She ran out of there as fast as she didn't want to give birth next to a dead man in a funeral home, she would never be able to shake that Omen.

CYNTHIA JONES "No Apology" SOULOLOGY

If you're looking for an apology, you won't get one from STARR. Running out the funeral home she was greeted by flashing lights and news reports sticking microphones in her face, and just as she made it to Broad Street to try and wave down a taxi. Bluesy father, Yes Mr. Francesca was pulling up to rescue her, knowing that GOD heard that prayer. When he found out where STARR was, he knew his son was not in good health to accompany her. He was pulling up as she came running out. They headed to the hospital, feeling the cramps of labor pains and the strong kicks of the baby try to escape.

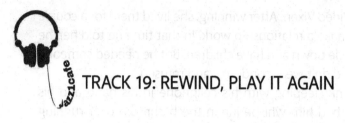

TRACK 19: REWIND, PLAY IT AGAIN

AARIES "Baby This Love" ALWAYS REMEMBER
(MINNIE RIPPERTON)

"Baby, I'm trying to show you that I love you
Baby, I'm trying to show you- you – you- you..."

The things Kandice say and do may not come clear through, her words may not convey just what she's feeling. But she, hoped Big Tank recognizes what's right before his eyes. Oh, his heart should realize from where she's dealing.

ERYKAH BADU "Bag Lady" MAMA'S GUN

"Bag lady you goin' hurt your back. Draggin' all 'em bags like that." Out of breath and exhausted from carrying luggage and bags, Kandice arrived at the busy downtown Manhattan coffee shop fearing she would be recognized. But this was the where Big Tank told her to meet him. She was becoming embarrassed assuming the people inside recognized her through the disguise of scarves and wide sunglasses and all her bags. Thinking everyone could read the neon lights on her forehead that read, "Fool!"

Head throbbing and anxiety feeling like a best friend. Kandice sat waiting for Big Tank, her producer, and manager and supposed to be man. He was running late, as expected. She was panicking and at the end of her ropes and not a strand of mercy for him, but needed him. She was feeling like an emotional tear jerking song rewinding and playing again.

MAJAHBA "Womanizer" SOUL UNSIGNED VOLUME 1

Woman's intuition had Kandice's eyes wide open. She was seeing all the signs in Big Tank's bull-shit. Like when they were at his mansion famously known as 'Big Tanks Play Palace' after the filming of the reality television show #1 Video Vixen. After winning, she lived there for a couple of weeks trying to make a relationship work. In that time he told her, he was not ready to settle down and have children. But he needed someone special like her, and didn't wear condoms, and refused.

Recalling Big Tank sleeping with his cellphone in his hand and his late night calls that had him whispering in the bathroom over running water. He said it was all business, she knew there were other women. He probably had sex with all the girls before being cast for the show, she should know.

SLOW TRAIN SOUL "Sexing The Cherry" SANTIMANITAY

Asking how Kandice how she feel, she don't know, Big Tank left her high and dry. After the sex tape scandal Big Tank's big ego has inflated back to 'Bigger' after their steamy bathroom scene with her holding on to the shower rode. Home supply stores sold out of shower rods because of them. She could hang on a rode like it was a stripper pole, even at that height and angle.

Don't get it twisted, Big Tank C.E.O. of Vicious Heat Records is still a big man with big pull. Kandice seen he meant business, and when you're down with him, his is down with you. If you step out of line and don't follow directions, he will drop you cold. After things cooled down Kandice went back to New York to record, but she has done nothing but been kept in different hotels - motel with him coming to get high and fuck and talk shit, *"If you don't hear back from me the next day, the next week or longer don't mean shit. Just means I've been busy and never give me something (STD) that I can't wash off."*

SHAUN ESCOFFERY "Break Away" SAINT GERMAIN DES PRES CAFÉ IV (KOOP Remix)

"Break Away!!!" It would be normal for Big Tank not to call her for a week or two. But, he dropped out of sight for a month, he still paid the motel bill and had his goons watching. Since then Kandice's cellphone was cut off for nonpayment and she could only receive calls on the motel room phone.

Finally, Big Tank called telling Kandice to check-out, pack up and meet him. Yes of course, she knew the coffee shop, but couldn't object. It was the same coffee shop and the same table she had sat with her last manager, boyfriend Rofiki. The one she held responsible for the bad business deals that got her fucked up. She knew she had to be there on time.

YAMAM'NYM "My Life" DUE TIME
(MARY J. BLIGE)

"My life, my life, my life, my life in the sunshine"

If you looked in Kandice's life and see what she's seen. Life was really starting to feel like it was someone else's. All the fame and all the money had come and gone and feeling like VHRecords put her the shelf to rot. She was pleased that Big Tank and the attorneys had worked the lawsuit between Black Beast Records vs. Vicious Heat Records.

THE URBAN RETROPOLITIAN MOVEMENT
"Understand Me"
THE URBAN RETROPOLITIAN MOVEMENT

Can Big Tank hear Kandice, can he feel her? She is looking for the kind of man that can understand and handle her. It's not rocket science or mechanics. It's just simple understanding her with sweetness and kindness, some sensitivity is all she need. Proceed with cautions because her love is deeper than any ocean.

No trigonology or calculus or all that tricky stuff. Kandice just needed Big Tank to under her. Looking at the time and trying to calm down before Big Tank arrived. She was upset and he was well aware. After thinking about how bad she wanted and needed the new recording contract, she would have to find forgiveness for Big Tank's actions.

On to bigger and of course better places like Hollywood California, Miami Beach, and Las Vegas the sin city scene. Kandice thought the recording contract would secure her future, but like most artist that wanted a record deal, she didn't understand the numerous amount of single-spaced pages of the recording contract.

Yet, Kandice had no other choice but to trust Big Tank and signed the recording contract that would also be a legal binding agreement between them. As a Major Label artist Big Tank assured Kandice that she would live the bling – bling life.

TOUCH AND GO "Tango In Harlem" I FIND YOU VERY ATTRACTIVE

Trying to assure Kandice, Big Tank told her not to worry about STARR writing her a #1 song. Business is business and at the end of the business deal STARR came out the winner in Kandice's eyes. She is the one with the new CD and now the tabloids are saying she had Rofiki's baby.

Unbelievable, Kandice knew for a fact that the tabloids and gossip columns were full of lies, but the video camera didn't lie. Kandice's belly rumbled trying to persuade her to eat. But, she knew she had to fight past the hunger pains and hold on to the $5 in her pocket. Just as she thought of getting up a very attractive shabby, but chic looking eccentric guy walked in the coffee shop carrying a worn black guitar case. She watched the man looking disheveled and confused.

MAXWELL "Til The Cops Come Knockin'" MAXWELL'S URBAN HANG SUITE

At first Kandice thought it was Neo Soul, R & B singer 'Maxwell' she was about to get up and run towards him for an autograph, but it wasn't. She couldn't help but find him interesting and thinking of the time they were fucking in the hotel until the cops came knocking with a warrant for his arrest for questions about another Hip - Hop artist murdered.

The mystery man was strongly attracting Kandice and she was now starring right at him and he looked straight through her as if she was transparent. It made Kandice check and make sure, she was looking as good as she thought, not to mention layers of makeup that ran even deeper than her cleavage.

Scrutinizing the eccentric dude with the guitar looking at his Timex watch and wondered who he was waiting for. Looking at the time herself, she knew it was time to go, but the waiter was now at her table with a coffee pot. Before the waiter could ask Kandice picked up the menu and scanned for the low price items.

SWEET COFFEE "Tango Noche" FLYING YOUR WAY

The scent of the coffee was welcoming and the caffeine was just what Kandice's body was screaming for as her gusty wild voice barked, *"Yes, coffee!."* Feeling a wave of panic, she wondered if she was at the right place. Until, she noticed Big Tank getting out the black limousine. Her nerves hit her so bad she almost peed on herself.

Still noticing the dude with the smooth skin, and wild hair, and smile that could charm her panties off (but she had none on). She was on him, but had to keep her kitty in check. Kandice was becoming strangely attractive to the dude with the cut up jeans, wearing a peace sign on his black T-shirt and both arms wore colorful African string beaded bracelets.

SWEET COFFEE "La Lumiére" MEMORY LANE

Yes, Kandice was checking out the fine guy with the guitar with the illuminated presence. She hadn't been able to make eye contact with him. She thought maybe, he would have noticed her from the television, the tabloids, or the sex-tape. But he looked at everything and everyone else as his eyes swept right past her. Making her feeling more insecure.

Viewing Big Tank getting out the limo with his cellphone to his ear, as usual, it made her feel humiliated. Remembering he liked coffee, she quickly told the waitress to bring her a cup of coffee with extra cream and sugar. Big Tank had a gangster - Hip - Hop cutting and scratching swag to his walk. Politicking sex in videos harder than Uncle Luke Campbell and an intelligent C.E.O. of his Fortune 500 and listed annually as one of the largest corporations in the US, based on the gross revenue, and how do you think he stay listed? Not bull-shitting, he reminded her, and anyone else that asked.

SHARIA "Question De Priorele" AUDIOPROD 2005

Walking into the coffee shop and stepping aside being a gentleman, Big Tank flashed his pearly white teeth holding the door for a woman with a baby carriage. As soon as he walked in the doors, the dude with the guitar stepped outside. No words need to be said, the King has enter the building looking swaggerific and impeccably dressed.

The tabloids often called Big Tank's 'Metro-sexual' due to his attire, manicures and pedicures and occasional facials. Setting off his outfit with a stunning pair of Black Prada sunglasses. He had never been seen or photographed publicly without his trademark dark shades, because of his one blind eye. Until the leaked sex tape that showed Big Tank without sunglasses, but also butt naked and his excuse for the shrinkage was the cold water shower scene to cool things off. They now knew Rofiki was the culprit setting up surveillance cameras and now nowhere to be found.

SABRINA MALHEIROS "Equilibria (Instrumental)" VIBRASONS

Regardless, Big Tank was now known for his sexy eel looking left eye, but was so – so – so – so damn fashionable fly. Everyone in the dimly lit coffee café surveyed him walking towards her. A New York fashionista some have labeled him Metro – Sexual. Big Tank was always ready for the camera and new fans. Counting every footstep as he walked strolled towards all cool to the beat of the music in her thoughts. From head to toe he was sharp.

1 – 2 – Big Tank was stepping in with his cellphone glued to his ear in conversation dressed in a designer double breasted suit, snake skin shoes, silk shirt. 3 – 4 Kandi's eyes traveled to all the platinum and diamonds all over his wrist and fingers. Not missing a beat 5 – 6 - she watched him seductively opened his chinchilla mink jacket exposing all the diamonds and gold around his neck. 7 – 8 – His sexy bald head was cleanly shaved and shinning 9 – 10 and he was in her face smelling good as shit.

SABRINA MALHEIROS "Passes" VIBRASONS

"Para papa para papa papa"

Night passes, Kandice see Big Tank in the air. As life passes by, she try to conquer him. But he don't come to find her. She want to have someone to love her. *"Lalalalalalala."* Stepping over all her bags and standing up to greet him. As expected he grab her ass in the quick embrace. Kandice tried catching a tear before it slid from her eye, wondering if her life would have been different if she was the woman with the baby carriage. A baby is what she thought every man wanted, until Big Tank told her, he had no intentions on creating life with any trick-ass-bitches.

Stomach grumbled, Kandice's noticed Big Tank inspecting a beautiful woman in a chic white business suit. Jealous maybe, Kandice couldn't help but wonder noticing a woman that was dressed in corporate attire who was probably on her coffee break and now eyeing Big Tank. What if she was the woman with the corporate career securing a different future?

Taking a second glance, Kandice had to look twice to make sure it wasn't the actress Halle Berry, but it wasn't. She noticed Big Tank chuckling when the woman finally got up prance her big ass past their table. Knowing, Big Tank wanted to get up and go with the woman that looked like one of his favorite actress. Then Big Tank noticed, Kandice checking him out and sitting there patiently waiting for him to finish his phone conversation.

SABRINA MALHEIROS "Passa (Venom)" VIBRASONS
(Portuguese)

"A noite passa eu vejo você no ar
E a vida passa eu tento te conquistar,
Mas você não vem me encontrar
Quero ter alguém pra me amar"

Never intimidated by other women. Shit, Kandice had the #1 Booty when the reality television shows. Awaiting '#1 Video Vixen' to be televised to prove. T'werking in a sexually provocative manner shaking what her momma gave her. Now she sat noticing a female cop drinking coffee café and wondering if she was a cop would she feel safer. Yes, she would have a license to carry and use. Kandice was still waiting for Big Tank to get off the phone. Most of the conversation, he was just agree or disagreeing.

TEENA MARIE "Butucada Suite" EMERALD CITY

Kandice was into new things and got a brand new bag superficial living was making her life a drag. The world stereotypes her, as she coins the phrase, 'Living for the hot wax and the printed pages.' She no longer wants to boss the bull around contrary to popular belief all she wanted to do is get inside Big Tank's head and play the funcky rhythms of the street, **"Batucada Suite - rhythms of the street."**

It was a mystery and still Kandice was trying to figure out whom Big Tank was talking to on the phone. She caught glimpse of happiness and something was pleasing him. She could tell in his stride that he was sleeping well.

Not like Kandice at the 'Butuc -Roach - Motel ' with bed bugs, because they were safe to get high, smoke, get smutted, get choked and slammed up against the wall with no complaints. Everything was starting to gross her out, but she played along. Now her faint smile held a touch of sadness looking at Big Tank's grin, his laugh, and his strange eel looking blind left eye hidden by the designer sunglasses.

YAMAM'NYM *"Love Don't"* DUE TIME

Wanting to purr like a kitty that just smelled catnip, sitting next to Big Tank the man that she thought would make the difference in her life. The only thing that seemed familiar was the scent of his expensive cologne. Hanging up the cellphone and never removing his sunglasses they made eye contact, and Big Tank's smile vanished. Trying to read his blank expression, Kandice waited for him to break out into laughter telling her, he had a new apartment for her and new studio sessions. Instead he said nothing observing his surroundings.

It was just like Big Tank to always check out and size- up every man in the place, to be sure no one was gritting on him, or hating, or ready to step up and rob him. Though most of the time he tried playing the discreet role, he was one of the most recognizable because of fame and fortunes. Everyone knew exactly who he was from all the MTV, BET awards and all those other music award shows. Big Tank seemed a bit uptight making his observations. Kandice picked up the cup of the tea and made loud sips to break the silence. Finally she couldn't take it any longer.

Though Kandice was pleased on how, she was handling Big Tank. Because repeatedly, every day she recited a prepared speech cursing him the fuck out! Nauseas and wanting to vomit, her head hanging feeling woozy with throbbing temples, emotionally all together messed up. She was blaming it on her nerves and paying attention to every word, every action, every remark and every pose as the pitch of Big Tank's voice alarmed her.

ZACHARY BREAUX *"Café Regio"* BEST OF SMOOTH JAZZ GUITAR (ISAAC HAYES)

Big Tank rubbing his head trying to figure out where to start. Then he just told her like it was in his 'Barry White' voice with his hardcore Brooklyn swag, *"Yo shorty listen up, take notes. In dis' music business shit happen overnight. Your job is to sell records and shake that ass. But, you have to go further and deeper than any other Video Vixen, and I have a cameo appearance lined up for one of Uncle Luke's videos. You need to go straight porn and master that industry with your talents. I have set you up with lingerie shoots and lubricant ads, and a Fellatio instructional DVD teaching women how to give good oral stimulation of the penis, cause you da best!"*

Listening to every word Kandice questioned, Big Tank's integrity and what he was trying to do with her career. She thought luckily for the out of court settlement her career would be able to continue with VHRecords. Now, Kandice sat with her mouth closed unable to agree and knew she had no choice but to consider, maybe soft porn in her video's, but she wasn't going to put herself through the humiliations of another sex tape.

TREMENDO MENDA "Intro" VIDALOGIA

Paying attention to the conversation, Kandice heard a heavy dose of sarcasm in his voice telling her, *"The music industry doesn't care if you can carry the powerful vocal range of many octaves. Those chicks ain't making the money, the big booty shakers like you – you will make the money."* Kandice was once told her, she sang with the power of a big woman and that power must come from her big ass, she took that as a compliment. Irritated and egotistical Big Tank was now also suggested that she go on a strict diet so she could be ready for the cameras and maybe dye her hair blond with colored hair streaks for flare. Bewildered she thought, *"Does he remember the day he told me that he loved my long dark Spanish wavy hair."*

MARIECHANN "Live My Life" MARIECHANN

Living her life, Kandice spent days looking at her empty bank accounts, she just wanted to live her life like, like she want to. The deep pitch in Big Tank's voice alarmed her because it was a bit rougher than normal. Something was bothering him other than their problems and she listened to him preaching to her. *"Kandice, you brought this bullshit on yourself. Now live with it and continue making me platinum hits and you'll be a household name internationally."* Kandice placed her elbows on the table to hold the mug study.

Head throbbing from the nonsense. When Kandice thought Big Tank was finished, she placed the mug on the table, wanting to scream. She pressed both hands over her eyes as they burned with weariness, shit was getting crazy. Removing her hands from her eyes wondering how? How did she let herself get this messed up?

The waitress appeared with a fresh cup of coffee for Kandice, but when she went to pour Big Tank another cup of coffee he objected and ordered a cup to go. Kandice really wanted to order a salad, but didn't get a chance, Big Tank handed the menus ready to go.

SANDY COSSET "Knock Down" AU BONHEUR

Growing uneasy by how Big Tank was looking and talking, Kandice heard all the under tones in his voice. She was just about to object until, he mentioned plans to set up studio time for her @ Vicious Heat Records. Before she could ask questions, his cellphone rang and Kandice looked outside and noticed that the limousine was outside and waiting.

Intuitions were telling Kandice to get up and run, but to where? Sulking because she didn't want to star as a vixen-porn-singer. She wasn't about to let any man know her down and pimp her, he must really be crazy to think the slick can out slick the slick, not this bitch. Though still uneasy under Big Tanks scrutiny. Everything he said made her feel uglier, despite all the cat-calls and compliments, she received. The waitress returned with the check and Big Tanks coffee in a tall Styrofoam cup.

For Big Tank business was business, he had to let things smooth out after the leaked sex tape, but he knew Kandice was a money maker and about making money too. Bringing the conversation to a softer tempo he said what she had been waiting to hear, *"I got a deal worked out. That is what I was on the phone about. We'll talk later when I get back."*

Exasperating with crossed arms Kandice mumbled, *"What am I supposed to do until later? I checked out the motel?"* Big Tank was ready and quick with his response, *"Go to another hotel or motel. I'm on my way to Miami to take care of some shit with A & R peep for your next video."* Kandice felt a ping of hope and then instantly it began to feel backwards and that was the bullshit, he did to her. She didn't feel like she had any other choice except but to do it his way. But doing it his way was causing her to be stressed and depressed.

CHUCK BROWN "Chuck Baby" WE'RE ABOUT THE BUSINESS
(Featuring K.K.)

The slick trying to oust slick the slick, Kandice knew this game and thinking, *"Hey watch out Big Tank because I'm coming for you. Baby girl Kandice is telling you what to do."* Listening to Big Tank trying to give her the run down. Challenging her with a smile that set her teeth on edge, thinking back to the day, Big Tank said he first seen her in the studio, a sexy lady with booty jiggling, and a banging body and a pretty face. So to see your pretty face at his birthday party, she was the present he wanted to unwrap.

"Big Tank don't give a what? (and she said)
"Big Tank don't give a fuck! (and he said)..."

"Big Tank don't give a fuck!" And no stranger to danger, Kandi Gyal knew Big Tank had been around the world from London to New York, but he ain't never met a girl like her. She took a look into his eyes knowing he was a crazy guy, the hit and run the Georgie Porgy type, he liked to kiss the girls and make them cry. He told her don't believe the hype cause he was cool. Enough about him, he wanted to talk about her. *"Big Tank don't give a fuck (owww)."* So, Kandice shoot a couple of jokes. She couldn't really protest. But it wasn't just about the recording contract, the meetings, the morning sickness, she asked him thickly, *"What's up with us? My period is still late."*

SUNLIGHTSQUARE "Three Degrees of Separation" URBAN LATIN SOUL

Three Degrees of Separation in a normal situations they would be lovers, forever. Three Degrees of Separation it's a simple celebration for Kandice's love for Big Tank, yes she do...

Big Tank rose to his feet as if propelled by an explosive force. He avoided her questions reaching in his pocket and pushing a pre-paid visa credit card with his face on the card, towards her. He was now in the business of pre-paid banking and planned to track every dime he gave her. In rhythmic arrogance he spat, *"Well, you better figure out what to do and how much it will cost to fix the problem."*

363

Ready to split Big Tank paid the check leaving a bigger tip than Kandice had in her pockets. He was up on his feet, straightening out his sunglasses holding the Styrofoam coffee cup snarling in her ear, *"I'm not with that baby shit!"* She began to gather her things to leave with him, but he stopped her explaining, *"I have some business to take care of. I just wanted to stop by and make sure you were cool. I'll catch up with you later."*

Baffled, because Kandice didn't expect Big Tank to take the news like a grain of salt and behave selfishly. She thought she would be living in his mansion in New Jersey since she won the #1 Video Vixen reality television show that offered the glamorous life of the "Bling – Bling" most of the people in the music industry wanted. He would always day dream talking to her about living in a 15 bedroom mansion in California with a pool, hot tubs and tennis courts, maids and a personal limousine driver and no kids and no pets.

KIM HILL *"Right Now"* RIGHT NOW (PRESTO Remix)

Kandice wanted her shit, right now... The bells of the coffee shop door were jingling loud and wildly against the door from the slam of Big Tank's exit. Kandice thought she noticed a women in the backseat of the limousine putting the window down. She grabbed her things and was out the door chasing behind him. And yes, there was another women in the car, in fact it was Lil' Pam, his ex and #1 female rap artist on the charts. Just before Kandice could bend down to pick up a rock the limo, it drove off.

The limousine was gone and the strings of a guitar were softly being plucked as an Alto voice sung out, *""Whenever Wherever Whatever..."* She was too humiliated to turn around as fatigue settled in pockets under her eyes, as she remembered how many nights she had already waited and waited for Big Tank's return. The pressure was so deep in her muscles, she could feel her body cramping up. She had to relax, breathe, understand, and regroup. Not lying, she was pregnant and if she was going to have anyone's baby it would be Big Tank's. It was obvious he didn't give a damn about the pregnancy.

MAXWELL "Whenever Wherever Whatever"
MAXWELL'S URBAN HANG SUITE

*"Whenever wherever whatever, baby
Whenever wherever whatever"*

The strings of a guitar were softly being plucked as the alto voice sung out again, *"Whenever Wherever Whatever..."* She wanted to scream shout and but what good would it do, Big Tank couldn't hear or see her, he was gone with the next chick. Emotionally lost, she needed peace and wanted to go home. *"Damn where is home?"* Arms crossed and cheeks sucked in and teeth biting down hard on the inside of her jaws. She looked like an angry fish gazing at cars zooming by. She prayed, *"GOD please grant me the strength, I need to continue."*

Spinning and spinning Kandice's head wouldn't stop. Feeling utterly miserable she quickly began realizing she was standing on the sidewalk outside of the coffee shop with her luggage. Just as a tear slide down her cheek the strings of a guitar was being plucked a remix from Maxwell into Jill Scott's song, still singing to Kandice.

JILL SCOTT "What Ever" BEAUTIFULLY HUMAN: WORDS AND SOUNDS VOL. 2

*"Whatever, whatever, whatever
Whatever, whatever, whatever
Whatever, whatever, whatever
Whatever, whatever, you want me to do"*

Turning around following the beautiful sounds of the voice. There was the good looking shabby dude sitting against the building with his guitar playing and showing off his multiple string talents on acoustic guitar. The guitar case was wide open and folks were dropping different denominations of dollar bills inside as they passed.

A small gasp escaped and quickly closing her mouth realizing, he was singing to her. Swallowing the sob that rose in her throat, Kandice walked towards him being pulled in by the rhythm of the sensual strumming pattern of his fingers plucking out an osinato groove on his acoustic guitar.

GROOVERIA "When Doves Cry" GROOVERIA
(PRINCE)

"When doves cry"

"Don't cry. Darling don't cry, don't cry, don't cry, don't, don't cry." Then he looked at Kandice and stopped playing his guitar. All she could do was wipe her tears and say, *"Wow that was beautiful."* Instantly she heard his accent that went unheard in his singing voice shocking her, he replied, *"Cha, bukekayo! No you're the beautiful one."*

The two of them where out on the side walk in chorus singing together. It was if magic dust was sprinkled and by the end of the song the guitar case was filling up with tens, twenties and many $ bills. In just one song over $100 was put into the guitar case followed by a sidewalk crowed clapping for the dynamic dual.

CARMEN RODGERS "Rain Dance" FREE

As bright as the rain on a warm summer day... The rain began to fall so fast and hard they had no choice but to go back inside the coffee shop. Now both of them inside from the rain and sitting at the same table. She wanted to object, but it was the only table available. Watching him quickly gathering up the money in the guitar case before putting it under the table. Then he counted out the money and handing her $50 saying, *"We must thank GOD for answering these prayers, because I was hungry."* Gladly Kandice accepted the money, nodding her head. Still there had not been but a few words, just a song exchanged between them.

Pushing a small 'Black Book' on the table towards Kandice, like it belonged to her. She assumed it was a Bible, as she watched and wondered if, he was trying to save her? She was eyeing the black book not wanting to ask if it was a Bible. But, wasn't she just praying for GOD's help? She assumed, he could be some kind of religious fanatic? But could he have felt the sadness that owned her? Because he sure seen the emptiness in her pockets.

GOAPELE "Change It All" CHANGE IT ALL

Oh, basically there are people left out from living comfortably can Kandice figure it out. She's been waiting restlessly for the words to a song. That could change it all. Now observing the café the way Big Tank had been scoping it out. The same waitress returned with two salads and Kandice was taken aback when he insisted on praying before they ate. After praying she looked at the black book on the table she asked, *"So Mr. Guitar player are you also some kind of preacher?"* He choked on his salad laughing at her.

GOAPELE "Strong As Glass" STRONG AS GLASS

Feeling strong than glass and happy to be sitting with Kandice, she took his breath away the moment he seen her. Assuming, she had to be waiting for someone other than him to come along. Now knowing there purpose was to meet he said, *"Actually, I'm just a man seeking salvation from the pains of this world and I feel you need comforting also."* Again she looked at the black book, but she didn't reach for it. Barely remembering a Bible verse.

MATAHARI "Mas Allá (Bolero Soul)" NO PARES!

Extended his hand across the table he introduced, *"Please apologize for my rudeness, I should have introduce myself sooner, you can't call me ZULU or X as in Xolani it means peace in Zulu, I am South African traveling the states studying music abroad."* After exhaling a long sigh of contentment Kandice said, *"Nice to meet you X my name is Kandice."* His reply was, *"I imagined you would have such a sweet name."* Letting go of the embrace of his very intimate hand shake, she wondered what his story was.

ANGÉLIQUE KIDJO "Black Ivory Soul" BLACK IVORY SOUL

"Wherever you live you'll find no one can take away
Whatever you feel inside your black ivory soul"

It was if a world of tamed soft winds rushed through to rescue his black and her ivory soul. Kandice couldn't believe that laughter was in

367

her voice, when just minutes ago, she was at the verge of exploding in tears running to the top of a bridge, ready to jump. He saved her and now sitting across from him and enjoying the company, she wasn't ready to be left alone and it didn't look like he was ready to go.

Thankful with sincerity, Kandice looked at him, as if she had nothing to lose. *"Look I don't know what can be gained from all this? But I have so much shit going on in my life and I guess it is that obvious that I'm in need of some kind of spiritual guidance or therapy."* Hearing the sorrow in her own voice alarmed Kandice. They were interrupted by the waitress announcing that the coffee shop would be closing soon. Her shoulders tensed noticing the time and nowhere to go.

ZAP MAMA "Yelling Away" ANCESTRY IN PROGRESS (Featuring TALIB KWELI, COMMON, and ?UESTLOVE)

"Yelling, yelling, yelling away
Going, going, going away
And fly away"

Never did Kandice see her day ending this way. She had thought that she would be with Big Tank chilling over in the mansion, but with him long gone in the winds of the sky on his way to Miami. She would have to take the subway to the Amtrak station, as much as she hated public transportation. Her face showed a sign of panic. She stood up apologizing, "I'm sorry but, I have to go.

"Yelling, yelling, yelling away
Going, going, going away
And fly away"

Rising out of his seat to stand with Kandice, Xolani stood up asking, *"If you need a place to stay I can help you."* He pushed the black book towards her. Putting the book in one of her many bags, she followed him a complete stranger carrying her bags.

"Yelling, yelling, yelling away
Going, going, going away
And fly away."

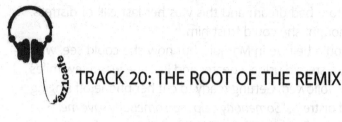

TRACK 20: THE ROOT OF THE REMIX

MARVA KING "Baby This Love" SOUL SISTAH
(MINNIE RIPERTON)

The things, Angelica say and do may not come clear through. Her words may not convey just what she's feeling. But she, hoped Mr. MLB recognizes what's right before his eyes. Oh, his heart should realize from where she's dealing. But it didn't and she just finished putting the last of her belongings in her car. Marquis L. Brown could keep the condo and all the materialistic things, he thought would keep her living in a pretty glass box. She paid the girl at the front desk to look out in case, he showed up unexpected. A woman would always have another woman's back, she assumed for two reasons. One, they like your man, and two, they don't like your man

VIVIAN GREEN "Save Me" BEAUTIFUL

*"Somebody save me 'cause I keep waking
somebody help me 'cause I can't get out"*

When they first met Angelica thought, Marquis would never yell or raise his voice. He's was so gentle in how he handled her. He loved her so different. It was amazing how he loved her. He was her prince charming riding on a white horse rescuing her, leading her on a steady course. Now it was feeling like a bad dream that she was living daily. It was like she was caught up in a whirlwind of tears and crying out from the nightmares after the sweetest dreams.

LIVE TROPICAL FISH "Believe" THE DAY IS TOO SHORT TO BE SELFISH
(Featuring DEBORAH JORDAN)

"It's hard to just let go..." Believing everything Marquis told Angelica that she was top priority, he even said he'd give his life for her. Every day

Angelica woke up to a bad dream and this was her last call of distress, leaving him. She thought she could trust him.

Yes, Angelica could believe in Marquis, but now she could see, who he really had been, a steroid using, cheater and liar. She was a few miles away and not being followed. Getting ready to cut her phone off singing out her last lyrics of distress, *"Somebody help me, somebody save me."* She thought of Rofiki and called his number. He immediately picked.

ANGELICA: *It's me Angelica. I'm about to leave the city. Just wanted to give you a holla' before I rolled out.*

ROFIKI: *Babe meh need to see ya – Meh got something for ya*

ANGELICA: *I'm coming for you*

ROFIKI: *Come fa meh babe*

KYMANI MARLEY "The Conversation" RADIO

Rofiki sounded out of breath, but Angelica understood him. She picked him up at Mickey D's on N. Broad Street. He hoped in the car looking disheveled with a hospital band still on his arm. He lied explaining, he was in an accident and wrecked his Hummer, checking out the black Mercedes, he knew she was a winner.

Teasing and flirting with Rofiki's dreadlocks Angelica said, *"Come run away with me and let me whisper sweet kisses in your ear."* He giggled, *"Jah, know meh won't hesitate. Meh gamed and will put it on you right here."* She smiled seriously, *"I want you safe in my arms safe from all the shots and the alarms come lay yourself down with me, be down with me."* He was a city boy and she already knew what Rofiki was about and fucking with him could be dangerous.

Fastening his seat belt Rofiki quickly asked if Angelica had any dough. Then had her go through the drive through and ordered 2 fish fillet sandwiches with pickles, stressing extra pickles, super-size fries and coke. Sticking to the vegetarian choices and added a strawberry Sunday, raising his voice to be sure they didn't forget the pickles.

DAMIAN "Juniour Gong" MARLEY, STEPHEN MARLEY, and YAMI BOLO
"Still Searching (Remix)"
RED STAR SOUNDS, VOL.1 SOUL SEARCHING

Still searching for a peace of mind, Rofiki grubbed on his Mickey D's the first thing most folks in his hood get when they get out of jail or the hospital. He directed Angelica to Montego Bay storage, so he could get his shit. The crazy thing about being kidnapped and hit on the head, most people would lose their memory.

It was just the opposite it made Rofiki remember everything. Things he didn't want to remember, but the most important memories were back. Maybe it was the couple of days in a coma and his mind weed free had him remembering the combination to the safe. He didn't need his black book, he remembered everything.

DIONNE FARISS "Stop To Think" WILD SEED – WILD FLOWER

Negro history, Angelica was already down with the program and knew she had to stop and think before she blow it, because it could lead down a path to the end of her career, her life. The words of Marquis echoed through Angelica's thoughts, *"See - I told you that life would get much harder. You thought you were smarter, but I'm always in control."* Her thoughts of Marquis ended when Rofiki asked, *"Yo ma where u been?"*

Angelica briefly explaining she had been out of town, but never forgot about Rofiki and was still rocking the LV sunglasses and would always remember him, saving her from walking to Philadelphia from New York. Mentioning that walk, Rofiki felt the pit of his stomach turn thinking about driving by her the first time. He said nothing listening to her talking as he grubbed on the fast food, fast. When finished eating, he and pulled off his hospital bracelet and putting it in the bag with the trash.

Feeling revived and ready for new moves, he continued telling her to turn left or right and rapping his sweet talk telling her when she called, he put everything off for her, and anytime she called, he promised to be right there.

JAH CURE "From My Heart" HEART & SOUL

Honest and straight from Rofiki's heart, hoping Angelica believed him. Until death do them apart. This love will never end coming straight from his heart Rofiki told Angelica, *"Gyal, meh running from the law and need to lay low, let's go."* But now that had him wondering what was Angelica running from.

Addicted to the streets, Rofiki was always ducking from the cops, living his life on the edge any minute it could be on, and babe she had been warned. Shocking him without saying a word, she reached in the back seat still driving and pulled out a black suite case so big it almost hit him in the head. She flopped a suit case on his lap at a red traffic light.

ESTELLE "Come Over" SHINE

Speeding through the combination and opening the case filled of gold and diamond jewelry and a lot of envelopes. She opened up explaining that she was on the way to Tampa, Florida. To get as far away to get her head together, and he was welcomed to join. She pulled out an envelope and closed the suitcase making sure it was locked, before putting it back.

The first time Rofiki saw Angelica, he knew was the gyal with the remedy. She flopped an envelope on his lap, and smiled trembled over Rofiki's lips smelling it instantly when she opened the suite case. She explained that she don't drink or smoke or do steroids or take any illegal drugs, though she occasionally drank wine if celebrating champagne.

Licking her lips pleased with pleasing Rofiki, Angelica explained, *"My name Angelica is the herbs of the angels. A biennial and one of the largest garden herbs. Considered a vegetable in some countries where people butter up and eat the raw stem. Angelica stems may be candied and added to cooking as well. The dried leaves are often worked into potpourri to act as a fixture for the scent. In magic the leaves of Angelika may be dried and then scattered around the outside of a home to enforce magical protection. Or added to ritual bath waters to aid in healing or help break hexes, curses and bad luck."*

ESTELLE "So Much Out The Way" SHINE

They got so many things to say right now and if a girl down. Once again Rofiki was amused with Angelica flipping script and breaking down her name. Now, he was also understanding where the stash and the jewelry came from, Rofiki was satisfied. Felling like no other girl could love him, ride for him and spoil him like she was doing. He saw, himself in her, and he would ride with her. She would be his Bonnie and he would be her Clyde. She let him know, she had his back through thick and thin, amused he agreed, *"Until we die."* That was a little too deep for her, she knew it was all talk and she liked hearing his sexy patwa and accent.

GURU "The Lifesaver" JAZZMATAZZ THE REMIXES

*"So many misconceptions, so many evil deceptions
I've come to give direction for I am the lifesaver"*

The streets are not safe and having Rofiki could be bullet proof and Angelica needed protection. So many times she wondered, is this really the end? Now thinking is this a new beginning? A new reality with so many misconceptions, so many evil deceptions have he come to give directions, is he the lifesaver?

NTJAM ROSIE "In Need" ELLE

*"I'm in need of open arms, no need to rush
Let's taking it slow"*

The more Angelica focus on something, the more powerful it becomes. The laws of attraction a beautiful phenomenon. Isn't it? The things they are attracted towards, tell a lot about them, after all they are about their attractions.

REEL PEOPLE "Alibi" SEVEN WAYS TO WONDER

Be Angelica's alibi, she crossed the line and will pay the fine. She'll sacrifice, her time if love's a crime. If they come looking for her, she'll be with Rofiki, baby. So Angelica guess they were on the run. They arrived just in time before the 'Montego Bay' storage area closed and Rofiki jumped out the ride and dashed inside. No questions and waiting and looking out for whatever, she thought looked suspicious. She had to watch her back too. *"Be my, be my alibi!"*

SY SMITH "Runnin' (Jah Child)" THE SYBERSPACE SOCIAL

Running, running, running, now! Rofiki came out running full speed like somebody was chasing him, but Angelica didn't see anyone, and she noticed he had changed his clothes and was carrying an old duffle bag and army jacket. She already had the car running and quickly unlocked the doors and reached over the passenger seat and swung the door open for him. But for him it wasn't fun and she was ready to have some fun, because she knew the best was yet to come as they spend all their days trying to outrun the sun.

Out of breath Rofiki hopped in the car and Angelica drove off in a smooth speedy glide through the streets watching Rofiki's frantic look and looking through the rear view mirrors. His mind was swirling in confusion and anger thinking, Oh Jah the safe was empty and the black book was laying inside, who was playing with his mind and their life? The safe was empty and his mind was twirling with who could have had his black book.

THE JT PROJECT "Messed With Me"
LOVE PASSION CORRESPONDENCE VOL. 3
(Featuring MAVIS SWAN POOLE)

Should have never messed with STARR, Rofiki should have thought twice before he cheated. She busted up his 32 inch rims, poured bleached all over his new Timberlands, and had his 'Black Book.' Bro you know, Rofiki should have never messed with STARR. She emptied the safe of countless amounts of cash and a package wrapped in black paper and left only the 'Black Book.'

SOULSHINE SESSIONS Exclusive Interview

AVERY SUNSHINE "Sunshine (Interlude)" AVERY SUNSHINE
(Featuring ROY AYERS)

Welcome to JAZZ1CAFÉ and I hope you've enjoyed Vol. 1: THE NEOSOUL STARR. The listening party is 24/7 and 365 days a year with SoulShine Sessions. I'm here now with the beautiful and naturally gifted *"Star of the story,"* STARR to talk about her new solo CD 'Soul Blue Illusions.' She's a songbird with an octave range that allows the ability to sing in the whistle register. Along with BearLove's beats that have no boundaries, clearly witnessed upon his production talents for a remix to the latest single off STARR'S new album.

Exhilarating, exciting, and electrifying are just a few of the many words that define STARR'S power performance. She received no vocal training, but phenomenon talent witnessed as the lead singer for the music group 'THE NEOSOUL STARR.' She is a superb vocalist and writes her own music. But more than just an artist, STARR is a busy woman currently working on projects for other artists.

Yes, she is a star! You've heard STARR'S voice all over the radio and witnessed in concert, and scene her face all over the entertainment news channels, newsstands, magazines, the tabloids, and in this book. Her business is now everyone's business, and a large out of court ca$h settlement that has her songs #1 and being sung internationally. With the sweetest taboo voice 'THE NEOSOUL STARRS' very own STARR is here to tell why, *"Bull-Shit Ain't Nothing But Chewed Up Grass."* Please welcome STARR!"

(Hands clapping sound effects)

STARR (bubbly): *Greetings and Love to all! I thank you, SoulShine for allowing me to talk uncensored – unedited, because the truth is, "Bull Shit ain't nothing but chewed up grass."*

SOULSHINE (smiling): *Greetings and It is good to see you again and thank you for giving me the exclusive interview. I'm just as excited as the listeners and readers to have you here. So let's get right to it and clear up some rumors. I've seen the pictures that have accused you of running around acting like MICHAEL JACKSON covering up your baby's face with blankets stretched over the entire body. I can understand not wanting to expose your baby's photo for strangers to judge, but not exposing the sex of your child and always dressing the baby in white. So, tell us did you have a boy or a girl?*

STARR: *My personal life is very private. My evolution is still a work in progress, but I'm now enjoying the roads on which I travel. "I am changing. I am evolving, I am growing and my music and family keeps me blooming.*

SOULSHINE: So what happened to Rofiki?

STARR: *When you mix in gossip, paparazzi, newspapers, etc., and the person that got me twisted up in all this bull shit that ain't nothing but chewed up grass, I raise my middle finger high and tell him to talk to the hand, he's not in my future or plans. I would rather spend this time talking about you how much I love JAZZ1CAFE. I'm a V.I.P. Member. I love the music and thank you for supporting THE NEOSOUL STARR.*

SOULSHINE: *"I Love You Too Boo! Thank you for tuning into the station. So how is the baby?"*

STARR: *"3 Months ago I was blessed with a healthy baby B. J. the spitting image of the father. (Changing the subject) Hey I want to give a shout out to THE NEOSOUL STARR!" BearLove, Joe Daddy, Ronny G, and DJ Jazzy X- I can't wait to get on your next mixology. I Love you guys like the flowers loves water."*

SOULSHINE (Jumping in on a rumor): *Could B. J. stand for BearLove Junior? I'm getting emails with the same question asking, "What is up with BearLove and STARR?"*

STARR: *THE NEO SOUL STARS is a compilation of musical artist and the drummer BearLove AND STARR are only musical friends. But don't get it twisted that is my homey and I thank him for putting me down - I want to thank everyone near and far for their support."*

SOULSHINE: *"Okay STARR I see you like to keep us guessing, lets rap about Neo – Soul."*

Many artists do not like the term: Neo Soul. Some think it stereo types them to a certain style. Some think the fans expect them to come on stage in jeans and t-shirts. Sistah's with their hair all over their heads, in need of a perm or a hot comb. But not everyone is trying to grow locks to stay in the game.

STARR: *"Neo - Soul, Nu - Soul, what is this music genre? There is nothing new about the music except for them adding N- E – O in front of Soul and the introductions of a new Artist. This for me stands for New - Energy - Of – Soul? It still has the same funky voyage of the 70's soul era with a splash of chill that makes you groove to its poetry in motion and there is definitely jazz influenced with the essential vibes of Hip-Hop!" It is about individuality – Free to be what you want to be. Everyone is free styling and doing what they want to do. Is that a crime?"*

SOULSHINE: *"So you don't mind being called a Neo - Soul artist?"*

STARR: *"For Real – For Real not at all. Neo-Soul, I except with a compliment."*

SOULSHINE: *"Is there any other genre you would like to be considered?"*

STARR: (states candidly) *"You could put me in all genres and I'm still going to do my thing. However you hear it, you hear it. There is a natural quality, connection beyond whatever I expected when I started making this CD. More than anything, this album is honest. It's about my life. I've been fighting for my independence and my struggle for freedom. Luckily I have the support of the audience who constantly let me know, they got my back."*

SOULSHINE: (Cracking up laughing) *"STARR, I know you're trying to keep your personal life out of the spotlight with all the rumors and gossip about your family. And, still no word on your mother $hantey Money?"*

STARR: *"Please keep me in your prayers, maybe in JAZZ1 CAFÉ Vol. 2 JAZZIBEL REMIXED there could be a blessing, though that story is about JAZZIBEL a jazz singer.*

SOULSHINE: *"Anything you want to share about your relationship with the #1 Video Vixen A.K.A Kandi-Gyal, Kandice Perez?"*

STARR: *Well, if your still reading up to this point, you know I have been going through a lot of trials and tribulations, but I never knew her, she knew me.*

SOULSHINE: *So what was up with the lawsuits?*

STARR: *"Our attorneys sat down and figured it out - straightened it out, and realized that management misrepresented us and perpetrated a big fraud and we never need to mention names, thank you.*

SOULSHINE: *"Girl, I'm so glad that you're a talker. Giving it to us straight! So tell it because I'm now getting tweets with the same questions asking, Do B. J. stand for Bluesy Junior? Folks want to know if you had a boy or a girl."*

STARR (smiling happy she had kept everyone on their toes guessing)

"Who's my baby Daddy is what everyone wants to know? But if I tell you, would that solve the problems in the music industry, change the price of tea in china, or bring world peace?"

SOULSHINE: *"Girl."*

STARR (laughing)**:** *"No, I can't tell it would spoil the ending. But I will give a clue there is a hidden track and more in the editorial review."*

SOULSHINE (Laughing too) *"I'm not here to be all up in your face or spread more rumors around. I'm here as a writer, radio hostess, music connoisseur, friend and certainly a fan that supports you and all the artist played @ JAZZ1CAFÉ.*

STARR: *"Yes, thank you for listening, reading, singing along and supporting the artist playing on the station and in the book 'JAZZ1CAFE." With all the* *illegal downloads, we appreciate you buying the book and music of the artists that put a lot of work in to their music. I'm talking hours and hours trying to make it all come together. So, thank you again for supporting and appreciate us by buying the music and not downloading it from unofficial sites." SoulShine Sessions, I too support your music movement and thank you for holding us all down and breaking it down along the journey. This is your show SoulShine, so I'll let you do what you do best, peace & love everyone!"*

SOULSHINE: *"Thank you STARR especially! Peace and love to everyone please don't forget to check out the website www.jazz1café.com and stay in contact and let me know your favorite music artist and song, so I can share with the world. Again thank you, thank you, thank you, thank you, Peace!"*

Just A Few Clicks Away from JAZZ1CAFÉ...

1. Download 'LIVE365 RADIO APP
2. Launch the LIVE365 RADIO APP
3. Type: JAZZ1CAFE (Click GO!)

BECOME A V.I.P. MEMBER!!! FREE 5 Day Trial Membership and No Credit Card Required!

Please become a V.I.P. Member and help support JAZZ1CAFÉ Internet Radio Station and the music artist. Portions of you subscription go towards the royalties for the songs played.

Enjoy zero commercial interruptions, no banners or ads, just you and the music. Listen on multiple devices, tablets & desktops. Go anywhere with the LIVE365 Mobile APP for. Listen in the comfort of your home on devices such as Sonos, Roko, WDTV, Grace digital wireless radio, Tangent, TIVO and more.

"There are two kinds of Stars. Those that are famous for what they're
And those that are famous for what they do!
I want to shine for what I do."

– Theresa Vernell

BLUZETTE: *Hidden Track*

STARR *"Bluzette"* SOUL BLUE ILLUSIONS

ROBERT GLASPER (music) "No Worries" DOUBLED BOOKED

BLUZETTE

In the sugariness of your sweet innocence
Your smile is always a touch of sunlight
Can't wait until you can get up and run around
So we can go to the playground
I'll always be around keeping you safe and sound
I will sing to my face turns blue telling the world how I love you

I've multiply - You and I - Wonder how
You and I – could be – me and my baby
When you're around nothing that can get me down
As sweet as Blueberry pie and you have your daddy's blue eyes
I will sing to my face turns blue telling everyone I love you

Bluzette
I Love you like the flowers love rain
Bluzette
I love you like the ocean loves the sand
Bluzette
I Love you like mommy is suppose too
Bluzette
(Sweet Laughter and Baby giggles)
Bluzette
Mommy's sweet baby girl
Bluzette
I love you true blue

Skin of Mahogany like mommies
We chill with ease in the soft summer's breeze
Your love I need my new little company
Love is all we need me and my baby

Peace and blessings you're my spiritual present
I've prayed for you and prayers do come true
My heart beats to your patter
When holding you nothing matters

Bluzette
Bluzette
Bluzette
Bluzette

GOD knows I have no regrets, I'm in love with you
Beautiful little pink you - Pretty baby girl
My whole world revolves around you
Truly blue and glued to you Bluzette

"Put tour hands together for Mr. Robert Glasper -Piano Solo"

In the sugariness of your sweet innocence
Your smile is always a touch of sunlight
Can't wait until you can get up and run around
So we can go to the playground and spin around
I'll always be around
I'll always be around
Bluzette
I Love you
Bluzette
I love you
Bluzette
I Love you
Bluzette
Bluzette

THE NEOSOUL STARR: EDITORIAL REVIEWS

The Philadelphia singer and songwriter STARR sends out lyrical tendrils that attach themselves to the listener so an exchange of emotions can take place. She will take you to romantic and warm, as well as lyrically chilling and stark. As always, her "sound" is wholly her own - a distinctly hushed and warm tones. STARR possesses an unusual kind of vocal power that carries a great deal of intensity and passion. She is a singer whose clear, crystalline voice is an instrument of impeccable beauty.

STARR spectacular debut "Bullshit ain't nothing but chewed up grass" featured on 'THE NEOSOUL STARR.' Now the long awaited solo album 'Soul Blue Illusions' by Neo-Soul artist STARR is again #1 on the charts. She really blows us away singing with the clarity of a fine diamond and the simplicity of a performer confident in her style and interpretation to carry the message without the clutter of over-styling. This album has the singer not only deepening her sound, but also very rich and mellow, hitting classic vibes with a hip-hop sensibility. The tracks on this debut set are wonderfully produced, blending together jazzy instrumentation and heavy beats with warm arrangements that are both totally fresh, yet also infused with a classic approach to the music. The music is a treasure and will be one of the best new Neo-Soul albums of the past.

STARR has grown to become one of Philadelphia's favorite female vocalist with her rich, lustrous voice heard on the song, 'Bluzette.' STARR'S cool contralto, which is heard throughout this album is a spicy stew cooked with ample helpings of soul, jazz, R&B, and inspirational. This CD, self-produced, features mostly mid-tempo renditions of a jazz-fusion ditty, all original compositions. STARR'S vocal weight and fluent delivery echoes the talents of many great soul artist played on the internet radio station JAZZ1CAFÉ.

The album is dedicated STARR'S daughter 'Bluzette' and husband Belvender which means 'Beautiful.'

STARR has the type of voice that can effortlessly be described. Her angelic range is as impressive. STARR'S husband, Belvender 'Bluesy' Francesca is the inspiration in the album title 'Soul Blue Illusions.' The love that inspired STARR'S to feel the emotions beautifully-written narratives about living life and loving to the fullest. STARR doesn't leave a dry eye, as she sings out hoping to touch the spirit of her mother $hantey Money in a inspire song called "Come Back!" Through her experiences STARR brings her poetry to motion and extols the greatness of "GOD" and her man "Bluesy," who are both her driven purpose for heaven

-Jazz1Café, T. V.

SPECIAL THANKS

To My sweet loving mother, Barbara Jo... Mom thanks for introducing me to many of my favorite musical artist. I remember the day you brought home 'Minnie Ripperton's' album 'Back Down Memory Lane.' Then 2 weeks later after reading in Jet Magazine, we read she passed away and we cried together... Thank you for taking me to musical plays and many historical restaurants... From Philadelphia to New York. The old Kelly's Seafood Restaurant @ the old 'Reading Terminal' in Philadelphia to Sylvia's Restaurant in Harlem, New York. Our first play in New York was "Momma I Wanna Sing" Staring Desiree Coleman... And many years after that we traveled back to New York to see 'The Color Purple' Staring 'Fantasia,' and of course we dined at Sylvia's (Soul Food) Restaurant.

Remembering my 12th Birthday when I wanted a tape recorder so-so-so bad. My mother had to work, so I took the train into the city of Philadelphia to 'The Sound of Market Street.' Safely back home with blank cassette tapes and placing next to the radio to record every song.

Remembering Philadelphia's 1st Hip-Hop concert in 1982 @ The Spectrum and sure we were front row! Thank you mom for the music and the countless years of 'Essence Magazine' subscriptions that I too collect.

For my 16th birthday she took me to see my favorite gospel artist 'Tremaine Hawkins.' We were second row and... So many experiences you've given me and the knowledge gained from each and everything... And every birthday my mother still sends me a card. There are so many memories we have shared through adulthood, womanhood, motherhood. I thank God you are my mother!!!"

Always thanking GOD for my family! The Williams, The Quarles, and Kanty Roberts, Mr. Herbert B. & Mrs. Barbara Smith thank you for the continuous prayers. Chris Keeys (R.I.P. 02/26/11), Andrew Keeys, Lauren Keeys, Ashlyn Keeys and Tierra Keeys, Caprice Roberts and Ethan Roberts, Marsades Watson and Marissa Beck. Thank you for truly loving me unconditional. And to Lady T's grandbabies, Milan Keeys, Armani Keeys, Lauren-Vera Keeys and Gianni Keeys, only heaven knows how much you mean. My kisses are yours forever, I love you all endlessly!

-Theresa Vernell

SONG DIRECTORY
(ARTIST "Song" ALBUM)

DEDICATION:

ANGELA JOHNSON "Hurts Like Hell" IT'S PERSONAL
LISA CHAVOUS & THE PHILADELPHIA BLUES MESSENGERS "Knocking On Heaven's Door" BLUES ADDICTION
ERYKAH BADU "Telephone" NEW AMERYKAH PART ONE (4TH WORLD WAR)

INTERLUDE

RACHELLE FERRELL "Peace on Earth" RACHELLE FERRELL
DJ CAM "He is Gone" SOULSHINE (Featuring CHINA) (Remix KID LOCO)
AVERY SUNSHINE "Blessin' Me" AVERY SUNSHINE
LEJUENE THOMPSON "This Too Will Pass" METAMOPHOSIS
THE ROOTS 'A Peace of Light" HOW I GOT OVER (Featuring AMBER COFFMAN, ANGEL DERADOORIAN, HALEY DEKLE)
S.O.U.L. "Praying Spirit" SOUL SEARCHING
SOUL TEMPO "Trust In God" TRUST IN GOD

WELCOME TO SOULSHINE SESSIONS

DJ CAM "Welcome to SoulShine" SOULSHINE (Featuring INLOVE)
MONDO GROSSO "Star Suite I – New Star" MG4
CHOKLATE "Thank You" CHOKLATE

TRACK 1: WHAT'S IN YOUR HEADPHONES?

MINNIE RIPPERTON "Baby This Love" ADVENTURES IN PARADISE
JILL SCOTT "Do You Remember" WHO IS JILL SCOTT?
WILL DOWNING "I TRY" A DREAM FULFILLLED (ANGELA BOFIL)
KINDRED THE FAMILY SOUL "Stars" SURRENDER TO LOVE

SADE "Never As Good As The First Time" PROMISE
LIZZ FIELDS "When I See Love" BY DAY BY NIGHT
ATJAZZ "All That" LABFUNK
THE FLOACIST "What R U Looking 4?" FLOETIC SOUL
KYMANI MARLEY "I'm Back" RADIO
LIZ WRIGHT "Speak Your Heart" THE ORCHARD
N'Dambi "Broke My Heart" LITTLE LOST GIRLS BLUES
MAYSA "What about Our love" MAYSA
INCOGNITO "Where Do We Go From Here" POSITIVITY
SY SMITH "Broke My Heart" PSYKOLSOUL
INCOGNITO "Don't Be A Fool" WHO NEEDS LOVE
NUSPIRIT HELSINKI "Trying" SAINT GERMAIN DES PR É S CAFÉ III
VIVIAN GREEN "Caught Up" BEAUTIFUL
4HERO 'Star Chasers" TWO PAGES
CONYA DOSS "Coffee" POEM ABOUT MS. DOSS
LES NUBIANS "One Step Forward" ONE STEP FORWARD
FIVE POINT PLAN "Sign Your Name" RARE
JULIE DEXTER & KHARI SIMMONS "Fooled By A Smile" MOON BOSSA
SWEET BACK "You Will Rise" SWEETBACK (Featuring AMEL LARRIEUX)
AYO "Down On My Knees" JOYFUL
KIM HILL "Right Now" RIGHT NOW
2000 BLACK "Dealt A Bad Hand" A NEXT SET OF ROCKERS
N'DAMBI "I Can Hardly Wait" PINK ELEPHANT
RHONDA THOMAS "Breathe New Life" BREATHE NEW LIFE
AYAH "He Don't Want It" 4:15
DEBORAH BOND "Don't Waste Your Time" DAY AFTER
GOAPELE "Salvation" EVEN CLOSER
CAROL RIDDICK "Brown Eye Girl" MOMENTS LIKE THIS
AMEL LARRIEUX "Your Eyes" BRAVE BIRD
LAURYN HILL "Lost One" MISEDUCATION OF LAURYN HILL
ADRIANNA EVANS "Calling Me" EL CAMINO

TRACK 2: JAZZ1CAFÉ

MONDAY MIRCHIRU "Philosophy Road" ROUTES
ROBERT GLASPER EXPERIMENT "Let It Ride" BLACK RADIO 2 (Featuring NORAH JONES)

INDIA ARIE "Thank You" SONGVERSATION
SLEEP WALKER "Wind" NEUJAZZ (Various Artist) (Featuring Yukimi Nagano)
PHUTURISTIX "Give It A Miss Lads" FEEL IT OUT
2000 BLACK "So Right" A NEXT SET OF ROCKERS
BLUE SIX "Music and Wine" BEAUTIFUL TOMORROW
ERYKAH BADU "4 Leaf Clover" BADUIZM (ATLANTIC STARR)
NICCI GILBERT "Rhythm And Blues" GROWN FOLKS MUSIC
4HERO "Holding It Down" Featuring LADY ALMA
AQUANOTE "One Wish" THE PEARL
ERIC DARIUS "What's Her Name" RETRO FORWARD (Featuring ERIC DAWKINS)
FLOETRY "Now You're Gone" FLOETIC
JOHN LEDGEND "Tonight" THINK LIKE A MAN (Soundtrack)(Featuring LUDICRIS)
DJ CAM "SoulShine" SOULSHINE (Starring INLOVE)
ROBERT GLASPER EXPERIMENT "Baby Tonight" BLACK RADIO2
YAHZARAH "Strike Up The Band" THE BALLADS OF PURPLE ST. JAMES
JILL SCOTT "Let It Be" THE REAL THING WORDS AND SOUNDS VOL. 3
DJ JAZZY JEFF & AYAH "Tables Turn" BACK FOR MORE
AMEL LARRIEUX "For Real" BRAVEBIRD
ERYKAH BADU "Orange Moon" MAMA'S GUN
FLOETRY "Say Yes" FLOETIC
THE ROOTS "You Got Me" THINGS FALL APART (Featuring ERYKAH BADU)
ZHANÉ "This Song Is For You" SATURDAY NIGHT
ALISON CROCKETT "Love Is Stronger Than Pride" BARE (SADE)
LIZZ FIELDS "Simply put" BY DAY BY NIGHT
JILL SCOTT "Running Away" HIDDEN BEACH PRESENTS THE VAULT VOL. 1
MIKE PHILLIPS "Heart Beat of The City" UNCOMMON DENOMINATOR
TRIBALJAZZ "Blues For Bali" TRIBALJAZZ
ME'SHELL N' DEGEOCELLO "Outside Your Door (Talk To Me)" PLANTATION LULLABIES
MICHAEL FRANKS "Mr. Blue" THE ART OF TEA
GEORG LEVIN "Can't Hold Back" CAN'T HOLD BACK
SNARKY PUPPY "Free Your Dreams" FAMILY DINNER Vol. 1 (Featuring CHANTAE CANN)
SNARKY PUPPY "Something" FAMILY DINNER Vol. 1 (Featuring LALAH HATHAWAY)
YAMAMA'NYM "Mr. Incredible" 2:00 AM
RUFUS "Fool's Paradise" RUFUS FEATURING CHAKA KHAN

BONEY JAMES "Dedication" SHINE
ALISON CROCKET "How Deep is your Love" BARE
JULIE DEXTER "Ketch A Vibe" DEXTOROUS
IMPROP2 "Is it cool?" DEFINITION OF LOVE
KEM "Love Calls" KEMISTRY
DAVE MCMURRAY "Love Calls" I KNOW ABOUT LOVE
URSULA RUCKER "Black Erotica" MA AT MAMA
ZO! "Make Love To Me" SUNSTORM (Featuring MONICA BLAIRE)
LINA "Morning Star (Interlude)" MORNING STAR
DJ KHAMIN BROWN "Funkopolitan – Full Attention"
DIRECTIONS IN GROOVE VOL. 2 UNTIED FLOW
NAJEE "Dis N Dat" THE SMOOTH SIDE OF SOUL
JAZZANOVA "Another New Day" IN BETWEEN
J. SPENCER "Till I Found you" CHIMERA

TRACK 3: Co-Starring

ZAP MAMA "RAFIKI" ZAP MAMA (Featuring THE ROOTS)
MESHELL N'DEGEOCELLO "Forget My Name" COMET, COME TO ME
NAS & DAMIAN MARLEY "Patience" DISTANT RELATIVES
ZIGGY MARLEY "True To Myself" DRAGONFLY
SIZZLA "Smoke Marijuana" THE OVERSTANDING
ALICIA KEYS "101" GIRL ON FIRE
FREEWAY "Flipside" PHIALDELPHIA FREEWAY (Featuring PEEDI CRAKK)
REEL PEOPLE "Can't Stop" SECOND GUESS
RAHEEM DEVAUGHN "Love Drug" LOVE BEHIND THE MELODY
KELIS "Ah Shit" KELIS WAS HERE
TREMENDO "Intro" VIDALOGIA
SUNLIGHTSQUARE "As The Beat Goes On" URBAN LATIN SOUL
MINT CONDITION "Bossalude" 7...
COMMON "Come Close" ELECTRIC CIRCUS (Featuring MARY J. BLIGE)
DWELE "Wants" W.ANTS W.ORLD W.OMEN (W.W.W.)
STEVE SPACEK "Dollar" DILLANTHOLOGY 1 AMY WINEHOUSE "Just Friends"
BACK TO BLACK
BREAK REFORM "And I" REFOMATION
THE AVILA BROTHERS "Mix It" THE MOOD: SOUNDSATIONAL
SUNLIGHTSQUARE "Faya" URBAN LATIN SOUL

LES NUBIANS "War In Babylone" ECHOS (Featuring QUEEN GODIS)
KYMANI MARLEY "Fell In Love" THE JOURNEY
SLAKAH THE BEATCHILD "Ain't Nothing Like Hip Hop" SOUL MOVEMENT VOL. 1
SUNLIGHTSQUARE "Gengere" URBAN LATIN SOUL
XANTONÉ BLACQ "Samba De Lagos" THE HEAVENS AND BEYOND
KELIS "Circus" KELIS WAS HERE
FUNKILINIUM "Like I Never Left You" FUNKILINIUM
RADIO CITIZENS "The Night Part 1" BERLIN SERENGETI
NOTORIOUS B.I.G. "Party and Bullshit" NOTORIOUS SOUNDTRACK
BEYONCÉ "Freakum Dress"
BUBBA SPARXX "Ms. New Booty" THE CHARM,(Featuring YING YANG TWINS)
USHER "She Came To give It To You" SHE CAME TO GIVE IT TO YOU
(Featuring NICKI MINAJ & PHARELL WILLAMS)
RHIANNA "Birthday Cake" TALK THAT TALK
BLACK STAR "K.O.S. (Determination)" MOS DEF and TALIB KWELI are BLACK
STAR (Featuring VINIA MOJICA)
VISIONEERS "Apache (Battle Dub)" HIPOLOGY
JSOUL "Frequency (Remix)" BLACK SINATRA
JAY-Z & KANYE WEST "Nig*as In Paris" WATCH THE THRONE
TANK "Dance With Me" STRONGER
BIGGIE SMALLS "Juicy" BEST OF BIGGIE SMALLS
CONYA DOSS "So Fly" POEM ABOUT MS. DOSS
RICK ROSS "Magnificent" DEEPER THAN RAP (Featuring JOHN LEGEND)
ELLA VARNER "Refill" PERFECTLY IMPERFECT
SNOOP DOGG "Beautiful" PAID THA COST TO BE DA BO$$ (Featuring FERRELL)
GROOVE THEORY "10 Minute High" GROOVE THEORY
2 CHAINZ "Birthday Song" BASED ON A T.R.U. STORY (Featuring KANYE WEST)
THE BRAND NEW HEAVIES "We Won't Stop" THE BRAND NEW HEAVIES
REMIXES
LIL' KIM "Lighters Up" THE NAKED TRUTH
MARY J. BLIGE "I Can Love You" SHARE MY WORLD (Featuring LIL KIM)
FAITH EVANS "Just Burnin' (Burning up Remix) FAITHFULLY (Featuring P.
DIDDY AND FREEWAY)
CHINGY "Pulling Me Back" HOODSTAR (Featuring TYRESE)

TRACK 4: THE CITY OF SISTERLY LOVE (Double Play)

ZHANÉ "My Word is Bond" SATURDAY NIGHT
ZHANÉ "Love Me Today" PROUNOUNCED JAH – NAY
MUSIQ SOULCHILD "Ms. Philadelphia" LUVANMUSIQ
AMEL LAURRIEUX "Get Up" INFINITE POSSIBILITIES
AMEL LAURRIEUX "For Real" BRAVE BIRD
FLOETRY "Butterflies" FLOACISM LIVE (Michael Jackson)
FLOETRY "Say Yes" FLO'OLOGY
JAGUAR WRIGHT "Self Love" DENIALS, DELUSIONS & DECISIONS
JAGUAR WRIGHT "Same Sh*t Different Day (part 1)" DENIALS, DELUSIONS & DECISIONS
VIVIAN GREEN "Emotional Roller Coaster" A LOVE STORY
VIVIAN GREEN "Free As A Bird" GREEN ROOM
LIZZ FIELDS "What We're Left With" PLEASUREVILLE
LIZZ FIELDS "I Gotta Go" BY DAY BY NIGHT
URSULA RUCKERS Release" SILVER AND LEAD
URSULA RUCKERS "I Million Ways To Burn" SUPA SISTA
RES "For Who You Are" BLACK GIRLS ROCK
RES "Golden Boys" HOW I DO
JAZZYFATNASTEES "All Up In My face" TORTOISE AND THE HARE
JAZZYFATNASTEES "Breakthrough" ONCE & FUTURE
JAZMINE SULLIVAN "Lions, Tigers and Bears" FEARLESS
JAZMINE SULLIVAN "Excuse Me" LOVE ME BACK
PATTI LABELLE "If Only You Knew" I'M IN LOVE AGAIN
PATTI LABELLE "You Are My Friend" PATTI LABELLE
PHYLISS HYMAN "You Just Don't Know" LIVING ALL ALONE
PHYLISS HYMAN "Living In Confusion" PRIME OF MY LIFE
JILL SCOTT "Slowly Surely" WHO IS JILL SCOTT?
JILL SCOTT "So Gone" THE LIGHT OF THE SUN
DJ JAZZY JEFF & AYAH "Forgive me Love" BACK FOR MORE
AYAH "Slow It Down" 4:15
THE FLOACIST PRESENTS "Just Breathe" FLOETIC SOUL
THE FLOACIST "Speechless" PRESENTS FLOETRY RE: BIRTH
MARSHA AMBROSIUS "Cupid (Shot Me Straight Through My Heart)" FRIENDS & LOVERS
MARSHA AMBROSIUS "Your Hands" LATE NIGHTS & EARLY MORNINGS

JOSEPHINE SINCERE "Shame" WILDFLOWER (EVELYN CHAMPAGE KING)
JOSEPHINE SINCERE "Still Feels Good" WILDFLOWER
EVELYN CHAMPAGNE KING "Love Come Down" GET LOOSE
EVELYN CHAMPAGNE KING "Don't Know If It's Right" SMOOTH TALK
BAHAMADIA "Spontaneity" KOLLAGE
BAHAMADIA "Confess" (Non-Album Release) (THE ROOTS Remix)
CAROL RIDDICK "You Better Not Hurt Me" MOMENTS LIKE THIS
CAROL RIDDICK "Fairytale" LOVE PHASES

SOULSHINE SESSIONS: NEO – SOUL 101

INCOGNITO "Everybody Loves The Sunshine" BEES+THINGS+FLOWERS
MONDO GROSSO "Star Suite II – Fading Star" MG4
ERYKAH BADU "Certainly (Flipped It)" BADUIZUM

TRACK 5: TURNTABLES OF OUR SOULS

DEZZIE "Let It Rain" DYING DAILY… A JOURNEY THROUGH SPIRITUAL GROWTH
OLI SILK "Ahead of the weather" ALL WE WANT
INCOGNITO "Heavy Rain Sometime" TALE FROM THE BEACH
JAMIROQUAI "Virtual Insanity" TRAVELING WITHOUT MOVING
VISIONEERS "Run For Cover" DIRTY OLD HIP HOP
PROPHET BENJAMIN "Throw Wine" THROW WINE
DREADLOCK TALES "She Has A Soul Of Fire" SYNCHRONICITY
BREAK REFORM "Fractures" FRACTURES
JAZZTRONIK "Spur" ZOOLOGY
ROY HARDGROVE "Interlude" THE RH FACTOR HARDGROVE
ALI SHAHEED MUHAMMAD "Lord Can I have This Mercy" SHAHEEDULLAH
AND STEREOTYPES
THE ROOTS (Black's Reconstruction) "75 Bars" RISING DOWN
THE REBIRTH "Everybody Say Yeah" THIS JOURNEY IN
THE ROOTS "The Pow Wow" RISING DOWN
URSULA RUCKER "Untitled Flow" SILVER AND LEAD (Featuring KING BRITT)
FRANK MCCOMB "More Than Friends" The Truth Vol. 2
ERYKAH BADU "Telephone" NEW AMERYKAH PT. ONE WORLD WAR
QUESTLOVE "Good Bye Isaac" QUESTLOVE
ANGELA JOHNSON "Hurts Like Hell" IT'S PERSONAL
REAL PEOPLE "High" SEVEN WAYS TO WONDER

REEL PEOPLE "Can't Stop" SECOND GUESS
JILL SCOTT "Dear Mr. & Mrs. Record Industry" THE VAULT VOL. 1
STATELESS "Falling into" ART OF NO STATE
QUESTLOVE "The Lesson Part 1" (INSTRUMENTAL)
ERIC ROBERSON "Obstacles" THE VAULT VOL 1.5
DEBORAH BOND "Nothing Matters" MADAM PALINDROME
AALIYAH "If Your Girl Only Knew" ONE IN A MILLION
PHONTE "Not Here Anymore" CHARITY STARTS AT HOME
KEM "A Mother's Love" INTAMCY: ALBUM III
GROOVE THEORY "Good 2 Me" GROOVE THEORY
GEORGIA ANNE MUDROW "Break You Down" EARLY
LAFAYETTE AFRO ROCK BAND "Darkest Light' MALIK
JOHN LEGEND "She Don't Have to Know" GET LIFTED
JOHN STEPHENS "Sun Comes Up" JOHN STEPHENS (JOHN LEGEND)
PHYLISS HYMAN "Living All Alone" LIVING ALL ALONE
PHYLISS HYMAN "Prime Of My Life" PRIME OF MY LIFE
TALIB KWELI "I Try" THE BEAUITFUL STRUGGLE (Featuring MARY J. BLIGE)
LADY B "To The Beat Y'all"
QUESTLOVE "Represent" INSTRUMENTAL
J. DILLA (JAY DEE) "Bullshit" (Instrumental)
QUESTLOVE, HERBIE HANCOK, LIONEL LOUEKE and PINO PALLADINO
"Power Refinement" BONNAROO
THE ROOTS "Good Music" ORGANIX
ROY HARGROVE "Bullshit" THE RH FACTOR- HARD GROOVE (Featuring
D'ANGELO)
THE FOREIGN EXCHANGE "All The Kisses" DEAR FRIENDS: AN EVENING
WITH THE FOREIGN EXCHANGE
RICH MEDINA "Music" CONNECTING THE DOTS
NORMAN BROWN "Rain" CELEBRATION
TEENA MARIE "Black Rain" LA DONA
DJ JAZZY JEFF & AYAH "Hold On" BACK FOR MORE
STATELESS "Falling Into" THE ART OF NO STATE (SWELL SESSION BOY
WONDER Remix)
DEBORAH BOND "Sweet Lullabies" DAY AFTER
THE FUNKYLOWE LIVES "Float Through The Stars" CHILL OUT IN PARIS 5
(Introduces Kings Of Lounge)

TRACK 6: SPEAKERS BOOMING DA FUNK

CHAKA KHAN "Jamaica Funk" (TOM BROWN)
URBAN MYSTIC "Where Were You" GHETTO REVELATIONS
ZIGGY MARLEY "True To Myself" DRAGONFLY
LES NUBIANS "El Son Reggae" ONE STEP FORWARD
STEPHEN MARLEY (Acoustic) "Fed Up" MIND CONTROL
CHERINE ANDERSON "Angel" ONE LOVE – DANCE HALL QUEEN
MESHELL N'DEGEOCELLO "Friends" COMET, COME TO ME
BORN JAMERICAN "Gotta Get Mine" YARDCORE
DJ CAM "Only Your Friends" FILLET OF SOUL
BEAT PHARMACY "Slow Down" CONSTANT PRESSURE
CHERINE ANDERSON "Kingston State Of Mind" THE INTRODUCTION
KYMANI MARLEY "Dear Dad" THE JOURNEY
SKALP "Funkin' For Jamaica" FROM MY HEAD TO YOUR FEET (Featuring SISTA PAT)
DREADLOCK TALES" She Has A Heart Of Fire" SYNCHRONCITY
BOB MARLEY "One Love" THE VERY BEST OF BOB MARLEY & THE WAILERS
JULIAN MARLEY "All I Know" AWAKE
FOREIGN EXCHANGE "Leave It All Behind" LEAVE IT ALL BEHIND (Instrumental)
ERYKAH BADU "On & On" BADUIZM
BOB MARLEY "Rastaman Chant" A REBEL'S DREAM (Featuring Busta Rhymes)
RADIO CITIZENS "Everything" BERLIN SERENGETI
BUJU BANTON "Not An Easy Road" TIL' SHILOH
SOULSTICE "Illusion" ILLUSION
JAMIROQUAI "Too Young To Die" EMERGENCY OF PLANT EARTH
ZIGGY MARLEY "Personal Revolution"
PEEDI CRAKK "Rum-Pum" P. CRAKK FOR PREZ (Host Big Mike)
BEANIE SIGEL "Hustlas, Haze And Highways" THE SOLUTION
SLAKAH THE BEAT CHILD "Delete" BEAT TAPE VOL 4
DREADLOCK TALES "Follow The Sun" SYNCHRONICITY
ANDRE LOUIS "Sadness" A STATE OF MIND
TRIBALJAZZ "Riders On The Storm" TRIBALJAZZ,(Featuring Jim)
THE PHARCYDE "Runnin'" LABCABINCALIFORNIA
VISIONEERS "Runnin'" DIRTY OLD HIP HOP
THE ROOTS "Streets of Philly" THE BEST OF THE ROOTS (Featuring J. PERIOD & BLACK THOUGHT)

ZIGGY MARLEY "Shalom Salaam" DRAGONFLY
STEPHAN MARLEY "Jah Army" (Featuring DAMIAN MARLEY & BUJU BANTON)
REACH "Jamaica Funk (Funkin Fo Jamaica)" (TOM BROWNE)
JAH CURE "Run Come Love Me" GHETTO LIFE (Featuring Jah Mason)
JAY Z "Public Service Announcement (Interlude)" THE BLACK ALBUM
TOM BROWNE "Funkin' For Jamaica" (WALTER JUNE Remix)
METHOD MAN "Let's Ride" 4:21... THE DAY AFTER (Featuring GINUWINE)
LUPE FIASCO 'I Gotcha" FOOD & LIQUOR
TOM BROWNE - new Jamaica funk (Newfunkswing Remix)
OUTKAST "Prototype" SPEAKERBOXXX / THE LOVE BELOW
VIVIAN GREEN "Keep Going" A LOVE STORY
JAGUAR WRIGHT "Free" DIVORCING NEO 2 MARRY SOUL
TOWA TEI "Funkin' For Jamaica" (SHINICHI OSAWA Remix)
LYFE JENNINGS "Statistics" I STILL BELIEVE
MARAR HRUBY "Is This Love" FROM HER EYES (BOB MARLEY)
MARA HRUBY "The Panties" FROM HER EYES
RAHEEM DEVAUGHN "Black & Blue" THE LOVE AND WAR MASTERPEACE
J. SPENCER "If It Feels Good" BLUE MOON
LIZZ FIELDS "Ride On" PLEASUREVILLE

TRACK 7: #1 VIDEO VIXEN

BEYONCÉ "Partition" BEYONCÉ
WHITNEY HOUSTON "Million Dollar Bill" I LOOK TO YOU
SADE "Punch Drunk" PROMISE
SPACESTAR "Cosmic Odissey (Remix)" NU: JAZZ ITALIA
ALEX BUGNON "Around 12:15 AM" SOUL PURPOSE
LAURYN HILL "Social Drugs" UNPLUGGED
ALICIA KEYS "If I Ain't Got You" UNPLUGGED
ALICIA KEYS "You Don't Know My Name" UNPLUGGED
J-KWON "Tipsy" STILL TIPSY
JAZMINE SULLIVAN "Round Midnight" OLD SOUL
ROMINA JOHNSON "Boogie" SOUL RIVER (House Remix)
ALICIA KEYS "Love It Or Leave It Alone / Welcome To Jamrock" UNPLUGGED
(Featuring MOS DEF, COMMON, DAMIEN MARLEY, and FRIENDS
KEISHA COLES "A Different Me (Intro)" A DIFFERENT ME
COOLY'S HOT BOX "Let Me Get Some" TAKE IT

DRAKE "The Real Her" TAKE CARE (Featuring LIL WAYNE & ANDRE 3000)
AMERIE "Can't Let Go" ALL I HAVE
KEYSHA COLE "Make Me Over" A DIFFERENT ME
JILL SCOTT "One Is The Magic Number" WHO IS JILL SCOTT?
AALIYAH "One In A Million" I CARE 4 U

TRACK 8: THE STARR OF A STORY

GRENIQUE "The Star of a Story" BLACK BUTTERFLY
MARVA KING "Sistah" SOUL SISTAH
CONYA DOSS "You Are My Starship" POEM ABOUT MS. DOSS
PSYCHE OF SOUND "Burning Up" PSYCHE OF SOUND
KAZZER "Pedal To The Metal" GO FOR BROKE
RUBEN STUDDARD "If Only For One Night" THE RETURN
THE INTERNET "You Don't Even Know" FEEL GOOD (Featuring TAY WALKER)
FRANK SANATRA "The Coffee Song" MAGIC OF OLD BLUE EYES
CARMEN RODGERS "Love" FREE
KENYA SOULSINGER "Lovetopia" THE LOVE YOU TO LIFE ALBUM
FARNELL NEWTON "The Bluest eyes Revisited" CLASS IS IN SESSION
V "Born Again" THE REVELATION IS NOW TELEVISED (Featuring JILL SCOTT)
EUGEE GROOVE "Café Del Soul" BORN TO GROVE
MARCUS JOHNSON "Potomac Ridge" THE PHOENIX
WYNTON MARSALIS "I Guess I'll Hang My Tears Out To Dry" STANDARD BALLADS
TORTURED SOUL "Fall In Love" INTRODUCING TORTURED SOUL
ERYKAH BADU "Annie" BADUIZUM
ERYKAH BADU "Certainly" BADUIZUM
J. DILLA (Jay Dee) "Bullshit" (Instrumental)
SALT -N- PEPA "Push It" HOT, COOL & VICIOUS
UTFO "The Real Roxanne" UTFO
ROXANNE SHANTE "Bite this"
QUEEN LATIFAH "U.N.I.T.Y." BLACK REIGN
JEAN GRAE "My Story" JEANIUS
URSULA RUCKERS "Philadelphia Child" SUPA SISTA
DIANNE REEVES "Better Days" DIANNE REEVES
ALEX GOPHER "The Child" NU-JAZZ DIVAS VOL. 2
ZOÉ "City of Love (Philadelphia)" LET'S FLY

JILL SCOTT "GOD Bless The Child" JILL SCOTT COLLABORATIONS (Featuring AL JARREAU & GEORGE BENSON)
MARY MARY "Yesterday" MARY MARY
TRIN-I-TEE 5:7 "Won't Turn Back" TRIN-I-TEE 5:7
WILMINGTON CHESTER MASS CHOIR "Stand Still" STAND STILL
SMOKEY NORFOLK "I Need You Now" I NEED YOU NOW
KIRK FRANKLIN AND THE FAMILY "Real Love" KIRK FRANKLIN
HEZEKIAH WALKER "I'll Make It" LOVE FELLOWSHIP CHOIR
CHERYL PEPSI RILEY "Stephanie" ALL THAT
KIM BURRELL "I Come To You More Than I Give" EVERLASTING LIFE
YOLANDA ADAMS "I'll Always Remember" SAVE THE WORLD
LISA MCCLENDON" Grace Grace Grace" SOUL MUSIC
LEJUENE THOMPSON "This Too Will Pass" METAMORPHOSIS
LEJUENE THOMPSON "Like A Butterfly" METAMORPHOSIS
DEBRA KILLINGS "Without HIM" SURRENDER
PAUL OWENS & APC "He Reigns" COMFORT ME
YOLANDA ADAMS 'The Battle Is Not Yours" YOLANDA LIVE IN WASHINGTON
NATALIE WILSON & THE S.O.P. CHORAL "When you need a friend" THE GOOD LIFE
TAKE 6 "If We Ever Needed the Lord Before (We Sure Do Need Him Now)" TAKE 6
KIERRA SHEARD "This Is ME" KIERRA "KIKI" SHEARD
DEITRICK HADDON "Love Him Like I Do" LOVE HIM LIKE I DO (Featuring RUBEN STUDDARD and MARY MARY)
DEZZIE "You'll Never Hurt Me" HERE I AM
URSULA RUCKERS "Church Party" MA'AT MAMA
AMANA MELOME "Searching For Myself" INDEGO RED
AMEL LAURRIUEX "Searchin' For My Soul" INFINITE POSSIBILITIES
MARY J. BLIGE "My Life" MY LIFE
LEDISI "Lost & Found" LOST AND FOUND
KEZIAH JONES "Hello Heavenly" LIQUID SUNSHINE
JIMMY ABENY "Star of The Story" RETURN TO FOREVER
MARY J. BLIGE "Be With You" MY LIFE
MARY J. BLIGE "I'm The Only Woman" MY LIFE

INTERMISSION: JAZZY SMOOTH LOVE SESSIONS

D' ANGELO "Really Love" YODA THE MONARCH OF NEO-SOUL
DEBORAH BOND "Love's Been Waiting" DAYAFTER
WILL DOWNING "Run Away Fall In Love" CHOCOLATE DROP
BEVERLY KNIGHT Send Me, Move Me, Love Me" PRODIGAL SISTA
ERIC ROBERSON "Punch Drunk Love" THE BOX
KEM "Nobody" PROMISE TO LOVE
PHIL PERRY "Ready For Love" READY FOR LOVE
EMERALD JADE "I Found Love" A NEW CLASSIC
MARK BAXTER "Love Is True" MARK BAXTER THE LADIES MAN
BRIAN MCKIGHT "Don't Take Your Love Away" TEN
IMPOMP2 "The Definition Of Love" THE DEFINITION OF LOVE
BILAL "Love Poems" 1st Born Second
DA TRUTH 'New Found Love' MOMENTS OF TRUTH

TRACK 9: "BULL SHIT AIN'T NOTHING BUT CHEWED UP GRASS"

THE ROOTS "Act Won" THINGS FALL APART
THE ROOTS "Dillatude The Flight of Titus" HOW I GOT OVER
THE ROOTS "The Next Movement" THINGS FALL APART
THE ROOTS "A Peace of Light" HOW I GOT OVER (Featuring Amber Coffman
and Angel Debadoorian and Haley Dekle)
DJ CAM "Afu Ra (Interlude)" SOULSHINE
QUESTLOVE "Mind Diving" (www.youtube.com)
J SOUL "Intro" URBAN RETROSPECTIVE
ROBERT GLASPER EXPERIMENT "Lift Off / Mic Check" BLACK RADIO
(Featuring SHAFIQ HUSAYN)
J. DILLA (Jay Dee) "Bullshittin" (Remix Instrumental)

TRACK 10: PREVIOUS CHICKS

MUSIQ SOULCHILD "Previous Cats" JUSLISEN
STEPHEN SIMMONDS "Killing & Religion" THIS MUST BE GROUND
ASOTO UNION "Make It Funky" (We've Got Funky Jazz) ASOTO UNION
MOONCHILD "Misinterpretations" BE FREE
CONYA DOSS "Friends" BLU TRANSITIONS
KYLE JASON "Cat-O-Tonic" REVOLUTION OF THE COOL

CLARA HILL "Morning Star" RESTLESS TIME (Featuring: THIEF)
SLAKAH THE BEATCHILD "Living For The Rush" SOMETHINGFOREVER
QUINTESSENCE "Sticks & Stones" TALK LESS LISTEN MORE
MUSIQ "Halfcrazy" JUSLISEN
ALEX BUGNON "Giant Steps" SOUL PURPOSE
JILL SCOTT "Gettin' In The Way" WHO IS JILL SCOTT?
LIVE TROPICAL FISH "Breathe Again" THE DAY IS TOO SHORT TO SELFISH (Featuring: LAURNEA)
ANGELA HAGENBACH "You Keep Calling Me" POETRY OF LOVE
EUGENE IV "Voices" STARVING ARTIST
LAURNEA "Trash" I REMEMBER
THE SAXPACK "Falling For You" THE SOUND OF FM RADIO
JAZZYFATNASTEES "The Lie" THE ONCE AND FUTURE
FLOETRY "In Your Eyes" FLO'OLOGY
LYNN FIDDMONT "Lover Man" LADY LYNN FIDDMONT
THE RURALS "Save It" RURAL SOUL
ATJAZZ "Before" FULL CIRCLE (Featuring CLARA HILL)
THE RURALS "Relax Your Soul" RURAL SOUL
ESTELLE "So Much Out The Way" SHINE
ERRO WROTE THIS "Previous Cats" ERRO WROTE THIS
FRANK MCCOMB "Actions" THE TRUTH
MUTLU "Damage" MUTLU
JEFF BRADSHAW "Lookin'" BONE DEEP
THE MANHATTAN TRANSFER "The Zoo Blues" BRASIL
JARRROD LAWSON "Think About Why" JARRROD LAWSON
THE MANHATTAN TRANSFER "So You Say" BRASIL

TRACK 11: THE B-SIDE

CHOKLATE "Suns Out" TO WHOM IT MAY CONCERN
QUEEN AAMINAH "Keepin' It Real" LOVE REIGNS
ERYKAH BADU "Rim Shot" BADUIZM
URSULA RUCKERS "1 Million Ways To Burn" SUPA SISTA
VISIONEERS "Smoker" VISIONEERS
KIM HILL "Taxi Cab" SUGAHILL
QUESTLOVE, HERBIE HANCOCK, LIONEL LOUEKE, AND PINO PALLADINO "Culture Freedom" BONNAROO

SMOOTH JAZZ ALL STARS "A Long Walk" A TRIBUTE TO JILL SCOTT LIZZ WRIGHT "Walk with Me Lord" SALT
D'NELL "This Thing" 1st MAGIC
ZHANÉ "Crush" SATURDAY NIGHT
BOYZ II MEN "It's So Hard To Say Goodbye To Yesterday" LEGACY GREATEST HITS

THE EXTEND BEATS...

ZAMA JOBE "Taxi Ride" NDAWO YAMI
TAFE FIVE "Permanent Midnight" NU-JAZZ DIVAS VOL. 2 (Featuring YULIET TOPAZ)
A TRIBE CALLED QUEST "Find A Way" THE LOVE MOVEMENT
DAVID ANTHONY "Smoke One" THE RED CLAY CHRONICLES (Featuring EARL KLUGH)
FERTILE GROUND "Take Me Higher" SEASONS CHANGE
JILL SCOTT "Crown Royal" THE REAL THING WORDS AND SOUNDS VOL. 3
JAZMINE SULLIVAN "Braid Your Hair" GILLES PETERSON THE BBC SESSIONS VOL. 1
FOREIGN EXCHANGE "Sweeter Than You" LEAVE IT ALL BEHIND
FOREIGN EXCHANGE "Valediction" LEAVE IT ALL BEHIND
ESTELLE "Dance Bitch" THE 18TH DAY
LEDISI "Trippin'" TURN ME LOOSE
AQUANOTE 'Waiting" THE PEARL
EUGEE GROOVE "Café De Soul" BORN TO GROOVE
ABNIQUE "Reminisce" THE WAY HOME
CHRIS GODBER "Ain't No Stoppin" MY OFFERING
DON E "You Got a Friend" THE COLORED SECTION
ERIC BENET "News For You" THE ONE
GWEN BUNN "A Baby" THE VERDICT
AMARIE "Outro" ALL I HAVE

TRACK 12: BEAUTIFUL SOULS

MARY J. BLIGE "A Beautiful Day" NO MORE DRAMA
ALISON CROCKETT "Everything Is Beautiful" BARE
ALISON CROCKETT "Nappy" ON BECOMING A WOMAN
BAHAMADIA "Beautiful Things" BB QUEEN (Featuring DWELE)

AYANNA GREGORY "Intro" BEAUTIFUL FLOWER
DJ KAWASAKI "Intro" BEAUTIFUL
JOY JONES "Beautiful" GODCHILD
CAROL RIDDICK "Beautiful" LOVE PHASES
RA-RE VALVERDE "RV Intermission" A BEAUTIFUL MESS
RHONDA THOMAS "Peaceful Blessings" BREATHE NEW LIFE
RA-RE VALVERDE "Complicated" A BEAUTIFUL MESS
DJ KAWASAKI "Shooting Star" BEAUTIFUL
BRENT JONES AND T. P. MOBB "Beautiful" WOW GOSPEL 2003
BLUESIX "A Beautiful Tomorrow" A BEAUTIFUL TOMORROW
PHUTURISTIX "Beautiful" FEEL IT OUT (Featuring Jenna G)
PRINCE "The Most Beautiful Girl In The World" THE GOLD EXPERIENCE
JEFF BRADSHAW "Beautiful Day" BONE DEEP (Featuring FLOETRY)
DAVE MCMURRAY "Beautiful You" I KNOW ABOUT LOVE
ANITA BAKER "Perfect Love Affair" COMPOSITIONS
QUEEN LATFAH "Simply Beautiful" THE DANA OWENS ALBUM
YAMAM'NYM "Beautiful" DUE TIME
PHONTE "Gonna Be A Beautiful Night" CHARITY STARTS AT HOME
BRIAN OWENS "Beautiful Love" MOODS & MESSAGES
JILL SCOTT "Epiphany" BEAUTIFULLY HUMAN

SOULSHINE SESSIONS: INDIE IS THE NEW MAINSTREAM

ADRIANNA EVANS "Walking In The Sun" NORMADIC
MONDO GROSSO "Star Suite III – North Star" MG4
BUTTERFLY BROWN "Painted In Blue" 5 ON THE BLACK HAND SIDE
PHUTURISTIX "Sunshine Lover" FEEL IT OUT (Featuring AMMA)
DIONNE "Move (DUB Mix)" HELIUM

TRACK 13: PLAYING MY SONG

TIORAH "Got It Going On" NOONDAY CAFÉ
DAVE MC MURRY "Radio Days" I KNOW ABOUT LOVE
ESPERENZA SPALDING "Radio Song" RADIO MUSIC SOCIETY
RADIO CITIZEN "Density" BERLIN SERENGETI
ROBERT GLASPER "Calls" BLACK RADIO 2 (Featuring JILL SCOTT)
LYFE JENNINGS "Radio" THE PHOENIX
CHRISETTE MICHELE "Mr. Radio" I AM

ANGELA JOHNSON "On The Radio" IT'S PERSONAL
ESPERENZA SPALDING "Vague Suspicions" RADIO MUSIC SOCIETY
KYMANI MARLEY "One Time" RADIO
RADIO CITIZEN "Test Me" HOPE AND DESPAIR (Featuring URSULA RUCKERS)
LUPE FIASCO "State Run Radio" LASER (Featuring MATT MAHAFFEY)
ROBERT GLASPER EXPERIMENT "Black Radio" BLACK RADIO (Featuring MOS DEF and YASIIN BEY)
THE ROOTS "Radio Daze" HOW I GOT OVER (Featuring BLU, P.O.R.N., DICE RAW)
ROBERT GLASPER "Trust" BLACK RADIO 2 (Featuring MARSHA AMBROSIUS)

TRACK 14: "'CAUSE YOU SHOWED YOUR ASS"

N'DEA DAVENPORT "Bullshittin'" N'DEA DAVENPORT
VISIONEERS "Hip Know Cypher" DIRTY OLD HIP HOP
KYMANI MARLEY "The March" RADIO
DAMIAN MARLEY "Pimpa's Paradise" WELCOME TO JAMROCK (Featuring STEPHAN MARLEY and BLACK THOUGHT)
FREEWAY "What We Do..." PHILADELPHIA FREEWAY
ADRIANA EVANS "7 Days" NOMADIC
RHIANNA 'Rehab' GOOD GIRL GONE BAD
DRAKE "Cameras / Good Ones Go Interlude)" TAKE CARE
CIARA "Body Party" CIARA
TREY SONGZ "Sex For Yo Stereo" TREY DAY
MIGUEL "Vixen" ALL I WANT IS YOU
JHENE AIKO "Hoe" SAILING SOUL(S)(Featuring MIGUEL)
KELLY ROWLAND "Kisses Down Low" TALK A GOOD GAME
NEYO "Mirror" IN MY OWN WORDS

TRACK 15: MOVE INTO MY GROOVE

ALICIA KEYS "Listen To Your Heart" GIRL ON FIRE
ERYKAH BADU "Fall In Love (Your Funeral)" NEW AMERYKAH PART 2: RETURN OF THE ANKH
ANGIE STONE "U Lit My Fire" RICH GIRL
GERD "Fire In My Soul" PERSPECTIVE (Featuring MARILYN DAVID)
MARILYN SCOTT "You Don't Know What Love Is" HANDPICKED
ZO! "Black Cow" JUST VISTING THREE (Featuring PHONTE and SY SMITH)

MICHAEL FRANKS "I don't Know Why I'm So Happy I'm Sad" THE ART OF TEA
AMY WINEHOUSE "Tears Dry On Their Own" BACK TO BLACK
INCOGNITO "Blue (I'm Still Here With You)" WHO NEEDS LOVE
ANANDA PROJECT "Many Starred Sky" FIRE FLOWER
MARSHA AMBROSIUS "I Hope She Cheat On You (With A Basketball Player)" LATE NIGHTS & EARLY MORNINGS
EDDY MEETS YANNAH "Take A Little Trip" FICTION JAR
WALTER BEASLEY "Barrack's Groove" FREE YOUR MIND
BEBEL GILBERTO "Baby" BEBEL GILBERTO
GREGG KARUKAS "Soul Kisses" GK
MOET "Jr. Butterfly" MOET MEETS BLUEY
LIZZ WRIGHT "Fire" SALT
BILL LAURANCE "Swag Time" FLINT
KYOTO JAZZ MASSIVE "ME Outroduction" SPIRIT OF THE SUN
MAYSA "Feel The Fire" FEEL THE FIRE
GREGG KARUKAS "Believe In Me" GK
KENNY LATTIMORE "Never Too Busy" KENNY LATTIMORE
YAHZARAH "Fire Fly" HEAR ME
MAYSA "I Can't Help It" FEEL THE FIRE
LIZZ WRIGHT "Wake Up Little Sparrow" DREAMING WIDE AWAKE
SADE "War Of The Hearts" PROMISE
THE ROOTS "The Fire" HOW I GOT OVER (Featuring JOHN LEGEND)
CHAKA KHAN "Through The Fire" I FEEL FOR YOU
TEENA MARIE "Marry Me" CONGO SQUARE
IMPROMP 2 "I Wanna Marry U" It Is What It Is (Featuring JUDITH HILL)

TRACK 16: DON'T DISTURB THE GROOVE

THE SYSTEM "Don't Disturb This Groove" DON'T DISTURB THIS GROOVE
KIM HILL "Sunny Blue" SUGAHILL
URSULA RUCKERS "L.O.V.E." MA'AT MAMA
THE BAYLOR PROJECT "More in Love" THE BAYLOR PROJECT
JANITA "I Only Want You" SEASONS OF LIFE
BEADY BELLE "Tranquil Flight" BELVEDERE
ZERO 7 "In the Waiting Line" SIMPLE THINGS
N'DAMBI "Imitator" PINK ELEPHANT
TRIBALJAZZ "La Tormenta" TRIBALJAZZ

ROLAND KOVAC ORCHESTRA "Northern Lights" SOUND OF THE CITY BERLIN
THE CINEMATIC ORCHESTRA "Familiar Grounds" CITY LOUNGE VOL. 4 DISC 3
THE TAO GROOVE "Cha Cha Cha 57" FRESH GOOD
TOURTURED SOULS "We Like Tequila" DO YOU MISS ME
ADINA HOWARD "Butt Naked" THE SECOND COMING
XSCAPE "My Little Secret" TRACES OF MY LIPSTICK
KENYA WEST "Gold Digger" LATE REGISTRATION
MISSY ELLIOT "Get Ur Freak On" MISS E... SO ADDICTIVE
JAMMIE FOXX "Blame It" INTUITIONS
RASHAAN PATTERSON "Water" WINE & SPIRIT
JAGUAR WRIGHT "One More Drink" DIVORCING NEO TO MARRY SOUL
NUSPIRIT HELSINKI "Seis Por Ocho" NUSPIRIT HELSINKI
SOUL'N SODA "Tomorrow" BARLOUNGE CLASSICS / LATIN ADDITION
SLAKAH THE BEATCHILD "The Cure" SOMETHING FOREVER
KIKI SHEARD "Faith" THIS IS ME
CARLEEN ANDERSON "The Preacher's Prayer" SOUL PROVIDENCE
RACHELLE FERELL "Prayer Dance" SOMETHIN' ELSE
LEELA JAMES "Prayer" A CHANGE IS GONNA COME
TRIBALJAZZ "Blues For Bali" TRIBALJAZZ

SOULSHINE SOUL SESSIONS: INTERNATIONAL UNDERGROUND RHYTHMS

INCOGNITO "Everybody Loves The Sunshine" BEES + THINGS + FLOWERS
BRAND NEW HEAVIES "Music" GET USED TO IT
JAMIROQUAI "Cosmic Girl" TRAVELING WITHOUT MOVING
US 3 "Make Tracks" HAND ON THE TORCH
A TRIBE CALLED QUEST "Jazz (We've Got) Buggin' Out" THE LOW END THEORY
BUCKSHOT LEFONQUE "Music Evolution" MUSIC EVOLUTION
DIGITAL PLANETS "Rebirth Of Slick (Cool Like Dat)" REACHIN' (A NEW REFUTATION OF TIME AND SPACE)

TRACK 17: JAZZ1CAFÉ THE REMIX

ANGELA JOHNSON "Be Myself" REVISITED, EDITED & FLIPPED (KERMIT & JALON Remix)
JILL SCOTT "Breathe" THE REAL THING: WORDS AND SOUNDS VOL. 3

GURU 'Respect The Architect" THE REMIXES by HILLSIDE (Featuring RAMSEY LEWIS, BAHAMADIA, BUCKWILD - Remix)

THE ROOTS "The Coming" ...AND THEN YOU SHOT YOUR COUSIN (Featuring MERCEDES MARTINEZ)

CITY LOUNGE "Still In Time" CITY LOUNGE (Featuring MICATONE)

JAMES PERRI "The Power" NUDE DIMENSIONS Vol. 2 (ATJAZZ REMIX)

LIV WARFARE "Groove DJ" EMBRACE ME

ZHANE "Hey Mr. DJ" SATURDAY NIGHT (Remix)

DJ CAM "The Show" SOULSHNE

THE ROOTS "Proceed 2" HOME GROWN THE BEGGINER'S GUIDE TO UNDERSTANDING THE ROOTS, VOL. 1

KINDRED THE FAMILY SOUL "Meant To Be" SURRENDER TO LOVE (KING BRITT Remix)

SUPER-PHONICS "P.A.R.T.Y" INTERSTELLAR

LIZ FIELDS "It's Ok T Love Me RE-PRODUCED (HOT COCO Remix)

ERYKAH BADU "Next Lifetime" HEARTACHE & MORE (LINSLEE Remix)

FLOETRY "Say Yes" FLOACISM (Remix)

J. DILLA (Jay Dee) "Bullshittin" (Remix Instrumental)

BAHAMADIA "Philadelphia" BB QUEEN (Featuring DWELE)

LAURYN HILL "The Sweetest Thing" MS HILL (Remix)

THE ROOTS "Waok (Ay) Rollcall" PHRENOLOGY

YAHZARAH "Black Star" BLACKSTAR (Remix)

THE ROOTS "Don't Say Nuthin" BEST OF THE ROOTS: J. PERIOD PRESENTS (Remix)

TRACK 18: PEACE AND BLESSINGS (Outerlude)

RACHELLE FERRELL "Peace on Earth" RACHELLE FERRELL

DJ CAM "He is Gone " SOULSHINE (Featuring CHINA)

AVERY SUNSHINE "Blessin' Me" AVERY SUNSHINE

LEJUENE THOMPSON "This Too Will Pass" METAMOPHOSIS

THE ROOTS 'A Peace of Light" HOW I GOT OVER (Featuring AMBER COFFMAN, ANGEL DERADOORIAN, HALEY DEKLE)

S.O.U.L. "Praying Spirit" SOUL SEARCHING

SOUL TEMPO "Trust In God" TRUST IN GOD

LISA MCLENDON "Go" SOUL MUSIC

CECE WINANS "Everlasting Love" EVERLASTING LOVE

SAUNDRA WILLIAMS "Hidden" BLESS THE DAY
SUE NEIL "My First Love" THROUGH THE FIRE
SHEREE BROWN "A Lil' Mo' 2 Go" FIRST FRUIT
CYNTHIA JONES "No Apology" SOULOLOGY

TRACK 19: REWIND, PLAY IT AGAIN

AARIES "Baby This Love" ALWAYS REMEMBER (MINNIE RIPPERTON)
ERYKAH BADU "Bag Lady" MAMA'S GUN
MAJAHBA "Womanizer" SOUL UNSIGNED VOLUME 1
SLOW TRAIN SOUL "Sexing The Cherry" SANTIMANITAY
SHAUN ESCOFFERY "Break Away" SAINT GERMAIN DES PRES CAFÉ IV
(KOOP Remix)
YAMAM'NYM "My Life" DUE TIME (MARY J. BLIGE)
THE URBAN RETROPOLITIAN MOVEMENT "Understand Me" THE URBAN
RETROPOLITIAN MOVEMENT
TOUCH AND GO "Tango In Harlem" I FIND YOU VERY ATTRACTIVE
MAXWELL "Til The Cops Come Knockin'" MAXWELL'S URBAN HANG SUITE
SWEET COFFEE "Tango Noche" FLYING YOUR WAY
SWEET COFFEE "La Lumiére" MEMORY LANE
SHARIA "Question De Priorele" AUDIOPROD 2005
SABRINA MALHEIROS "Equilibria (Instrumental)" VIBRASONS
SABRINA MALHEIROS "Passes" VIBRASONS
SABRINA MALHEIROS "Passa (Venom)" VIBRASONS (Portuguese)
TEENA MARIE "Butucada Suite" EMERALD CITY
YAMAM'NYM "Love Don't" DUE TIME
ZACHARY BREAUX "Café Regio" BEST OF SMOOTH JAZZ GUITAR
TREMENDO MENDA "Intro" VIDALOGIA
MARIECHANN "Live My Life" MARIECHANN
SANDY COSSET "Knock Down" AU BONHEUR
CHUCK BROWN "Chuck Baby" WE'RE ABOUT THE BUSINESS (Featuring K.K.)
SUNLIGHTSQUARE "Three Degrees of Separation" URBAN LATIN SOUL
KIM HILL "Right Now" RIGHT NOW (PRESTO Remix)
MAXWELL "Whenever Wherever Whatever" MAXWELL'S URBAN HANG SUITE
JILL SCOTT "What Ever" BEAUTIFULLY HUMAN: WORDS AND SOUNDS VOL. 2
GROOVERIA "When Doves Cry" GROOVERIA
CARMEN RODGERS "Rain Dance" FREE

GOAPELE "Change It All" CHANGE IT ALL
GOAPELE "Strong As Glass" STRONG AS GLASS
MATAHARI "Mas Allá (Bolero Soul)" NO PARES!
ANGÉLIQUE KIDJO "Black Ivory Soul" BLACK IVORY SOUL
ZAP MAMA "Yelling Away" ANCESTRY IN PROGRESS (Featuring TALIB KWELI, COMMON, and ?UESTLOVE)

TRACK 20: THE ROOT OF THE REMIX

MARVA KING "Baby This Love" SOUL SISTAH (MINNIE RIPERTON)
VIVIAN GREEN "Save Me" BEAUTIFUL
LIVE TROPICAL FISH "Believe" THE DAY IS TOO SHORT TO BE SELFISH (Featuring DEBORAH JORDAN)
KYMANI MARLEY "The Conversation" RADIO
DAMIAN "Juniour Gong" MARLEY, STEPHEN MARLEY, and YAMI BOLO "Still Searching (Remix) "RED STAR SOUNDS, VOL.1 SOUL SEARCHING
DIONNE FARISS "Stop To Think" WILD SEED – WILD FLOWER
JAH CURE "From My Heart" HEART & SOUL
ESTELLE "Come Over" SHINE
ESTELLE "So Much Out The Way" SHINE
GURU "The Lifesaver" JAZZMATAZZ THE REMIXES
NTJAM ROSIE "In Need" ELLE
REEL PEOPLE "Alibi" SEVEN WAYS TO WONDER
SY SMITH "Runnin' (Jah Child)" THE SYBERSPACE SOCIAL
THE JT PROJECT "Messed With Me" LOVE PASSION CORRESPONDENCE VOL. 3 (Featuring MAVIS SWAN POOLE)

SOULSHINE SESSIONS: Exclusive Interview and Editorial Reviews

AVERY SUNSHINE "Sunshine (Interlude)" AVERY SUNSHINE (Featuring ROY AYERS)

BLUZETTE: Hidden Track

ROBERT GLASPER (music) "No Worries" DOUBLED BOOKED

COMING SOON

JAZZ1CAFÉ

VOLUME 2: JAZZIBEL REMIXED

CONTACT: JAZZ1CAFÉ RADIO

Be a part of the growing JAZZ1CAFÉ Radio artist and have your music featured on JAZZ1CAFÉ Radio. Live365 is an officially licensed ASCAP, BMI and SESAC site. Live365 pays music royalties to labels, artists, songwriters, and publishers through established royalty collection organizations including ASCAP, BMI, SESAC, and SoundExchange.

JAZZ1CAFÉ is always open to help support the music and introducing listeners to a new song and lyrics. Welcoming music artists, especially from the Jazz, Soul, Neo-Soul, R&B, Jazzy-Hip-Hop genres, to submit your music for possible inclusions on JAZZ1CAFÉ Radio.

JAZZ1CAFÉ deeply respects the artists for their work. Our goal is to put together a collection of music that will be most pleasing to listeners. In submitting your material for consideration, the more professional your package is, the better chances (mail hard copy of CD and promotional items, I Love them autographed).

SOULSHINE SESSIONS is the real deal as in 'Sugar Hill' and if you feel your music genre flows right into the program, I would love to play it. Please submit music or learning more about Jazz1Café? Get in touch via the website or mail your music and I'll get back to you as soon as possible.

JAZZ1CAFÉ, LLC
P.O. BOX 48455
Tampa Florida 33646
Email: Jazz1café@Jazz1café.com

www.Jazz1Café.com

Printed in the United States
By Bookmasters